CW00685662

Best of British Science Fiction 2023

Best of British Science Fiction 2023

Edited by Donna Scott

NewCon Press
England

First edition, published in the UK July 2024 by NewCon Press

NCP 332

10 9 8 7 6 5 4 3 2 1

Introduction copyright © 2024 by Donna Scott
This compilation copyright © 2024 by Ian Whates
All Stories copyright ©2023 by the respective author

"Detonation Boulevard" by Alastair Reynolds, originally published by *Tor.com*
"Vermin Control" by Tim Lees, originally published by *IZ Digital*
"Personal Satisfaction" by Adrian Tchaikovsky, originally published in *ParSec Magazine*
"The Scent of Green" by Ana Sun, originally published in
Fighting for the Future: Cyberpunk and Solarpunk Tales (Android Press)
"Gauguin's Questions" by Stephen Baxter, originally published in
Collision: Stories from the Science of CERN (Comma Press)
"So Close to Home" by Andrew Hook, originally published in
Languages of Water (MVmedia, LLC)
"Boojum" by Angus McIntyre, originally published in *Analog*
"The Station Master" by Lavie Tidhar, originally published in
The Magazine of Fantasy & Science Fiction
"Art App" by Chris Beckett, originally published in *Reports from the Deep End: Stories inspired by J. G. Ballard* (Titan Books)
"The *Blou Trein* Suborbirail" by L. P. Melling, originally published in *ZNB Presents* (Zombies Need Brains)
"Blue Shift Passing By" by David Cleden, originally published in *Andromeda Spaceways*
"And if Venice is Sinking" by Fiona Moore, originally published in *On Spec 125*
"Muse Automatique" Jaine Fenn, originally published in *ParSec Magazine*
"Little Sprout by E. B. Siu, originally published in *Shoreline of Infinity*
"A Change of Direction by Rhiannon Grist, originally published in *Shoreline of Infinity*
"Thus With a Kiss I Die" by Robert Bagnall, originally published in *Aurealis*
"Tough Love" by Teika Marija Smits, originally published in *Umbilical* (Newcon Press)
"The Brazen Head of Westinghouse" by Tim Major, originally published in *IZ Digital*
"Skipping" by Ian Watson, originally published in *Collision: Stories from the Science of CERN* (Comma Press)
"Pearl" by Felix Rose Kawitzky, originally published in *Clarkesworld*

All rights reserved, including the right to produce this book, or portions thereof, in any form

978-1-914953-81-1 (softback)

Cover design by Ian Whates
Text layout by Ian Whates and Donna Scott

Table of Contents

Introduction
Donna Scott

The eighth *Best of British Science Fiction* certainly has a hard act to follow when it comes to the seventh. It came as an utter shock to me to find the book listed on the Locus Magazine 2023 recommended reading list and therefore seeded for inclusion on the Locus Award list for Best Anthology, and myself as Best Editor. That was a lovely surprise indeed… but wait, there was more! I discovered the book had made the BSFA Awards shortlist for the inaugural Best Collection Award when I went to congratulate someone else. I had not been scheduled to spend the full weekend at Eastercon, where the awards ceremony is traditionally held, but I soon rectified that, and jolly good job too as we only went and won!

So, I must start this edition by thanking all the readers who thought to nominate and vote for the last one. I hope that this anthology will be just as loved by readers as the last one and be a springboard for the discovery of fantastic contemporary writers.

I do not doubt that readers will find as much to delight them in this anthology as in the last, and I'm particularly excited by the huge range of themes in the stories that I have uncovered for this volume. Some stories are all about fun and excitement, from duelling robots to racing spaceships, but there are also stories about ecology and conversation, class and poverty, and the complexities of human relationships.

In terms of the market zeitgeist for science fiction, the big scare theme of last year was AI. This year I'm seeing that tail off slightly in the number of stories about AI, but it hasn't gone away just yet, and I can't see it dying down as an element of temptation, mischief or threat, whispering in the ears of creatives and those who would employ them for some time. In other areas of my life, I am used to the positive spin that AI has been getting as a great tool for productivity, but always underneath that push for AI use is an implicit fear: if we don't make the most of it, our competition will.

I would say to writers, your only competition is yourself. Other writers are not your competition, they are your family: you may not get on with all of them, and there may be rather a lot of them, but you are all there for each other in the end. Read each other; discover what works; write better stories.

Readers are your family, too. Many would-be readers are bibliophiles first, constantly curating, rating and sorting their favourite reads. From what I have seen of AI output so far it will be a long time before you can win over the hearts of a genuine reader with rubbish generated by AI. I am lucky that with this anthology, all the stories have been through an editorial filter first, but for other books, I can confirm that people have indeed sent me AI-generated stories. Or rather, words in the shape of a story. They are really not going to set the world on fire.

Well, we could say that the world already *is* on fire. I have been gradually seeing the rise of stories influenced by the climate crisis over the past few years, with ecological disaster often as a background note in some problem-solving aspects of the story. Change in the landscape, or what happens to humanity's legacy after humanity is a theme that can be recognised in some of the stories I have chosen.

I do still receive some stories inspired by the COVID-19 outbreak and Lockdown, too. I think we all know that in reality the health outcomes for those catching the virus are generally much better these days, but it hasn't stopped COVID-19 being a harmful, sometimes fatal illness, and I understand the frustration some people often have with how blasé attitudes have become. That said, unless the story can use this period of our time to extrapolate much further away from this early part of the 21st century, it can come across as a little old hat and overblown, I think.

I am enthused by the variety of stories I received for this anthology, and by those writers making their *Best of British Science Fiction* debuts. There is also a pinch more positivity in this anthology than in previous ones, I reckon. Look out too for the blending of genres in some unusual ways, and for some very different narrative voices.

In fact, I received a lot of stories I loved, but could not fit them all in this book. So, I would like to use this introduction to add some honourable mentions, the stories that almost made it into the anthology. They include:

Emma Burnett's "Wok and Roll: Fat Packet Sizzle", originally published in *Atmosphere*.

Eliza Chan's "RUN:\mask mode", originally published in *Portraits of a Patriarch*, a BFS anthology.

David Gullen's "The Naismith and the Wildboy", originally published in *ParSec Magazine*.

Vaughan Stanger's "Dust Bunnies", originally published in *Shoreline of Infinity Magazine*, issue 34.

I do hope you get to read these stories and consider supporting the original place of publication by buying a back issue of the magazines in question. Short fiction magazines form the lifeblood of genre, seeding the world of books with new names and new ideas.

– Donna Scott
Northampton, April 2024

Detonation Boulevard
Alastair Reynolds

I raised a fist and strode out into the full glare of the floods.

Crowds roared in my earpiece as I stopped to take it all in, recalling the words of my old mentor. Before he flamed out across Utopia, Joff had told me to savour moments like this one while I still had the chance.

"Never forget the hard work and sacrifice that put you on that grid, Cat," he'd said slowly, his voice like a gearbox full of gravel. "You've earned that ride, and you've earned the adulation. But always remember it might be the last time."

"I'll know when it's the last time," I'd countered, with all the arrogance and certainty of youth.

"That's what everyone thinks," he'd said, turning from me with a rag in his hand.

It had taken me a while to realise how right he was. About ten years, one pair of legs, and all the lessons I'd ever need in winning and losing. By which point it was far too late to admit it to the gruff old bastard.

The start of a race – any race, anywhere in the system – was a beautiful spectacle. The tiered, pressurised grandstands leaned in above the grid, twenty stories high. The cars waited on their launch positions, huge as houses, bodies perched high on six balloon wheels. Technicians and race scrutineers fussed around them, adjusting parameters and checking for the tiniest rules infraction. A circus of journalists, sponsors, and celebs pressed in close to the pampered machines. Some drivers were already aboard, hunched and tiny in their blister cockpits, set high up and forward on the enormous vehicles. Others were scrambling up the access ladders between the monstrous wheels. On the cars' bodies, a changing flicker of logos and slogans betrayed the twitchiness of advertisers, responding to the tiniest rumour or hint of nervy body language.

Rufus nagged me through the earpiece.

"We've got a car to be getting to, girl."

"And I'm just taking things in. Joff told me —"

He cut across my reminiscence. 'Piping the commentary through to you now. Try and smile for the feeds."

"I am smiling!"

"Then smile *more*. Looks like a grimace from here."

I walked onto the grid, a spotlight tracking me. The crowd roared some more. I did a dance with my new prosthetics. They were fresh-in from Gladius Exomedical, expensive and sleek. Too bad they didn't fit quite as snugly as my old pair. We had to keep Gladius sweet all the same, since they were paying for about a third of the car.

"And Cat Catling emerges to take her place in the second car on the grid! Catling, the relentless underdog in the metallic blue Bellatrix Beta, never a victor at the TransIonian, but racking up an impressive set of wins this season, from Venus to Titan. Can she extend her run of good fortune under the baleful face of Jupiter, or will Zimmer retain his crown for the eighth year running? And speaking of Zimmer, he's in no hurry to take his seat on pole position in the bright red Imperator Six! He looks like a man without a care in the world, happy to chat to all comers!"

"Oh, balls," I murmured.

"You weren't on mute," Rufus complained.

"In which case... oh, balls again."

"You realise each little outburst like that costs us three per cent in sponsorship, don't you?"

"It's Zimmer. Why didn't you tell me he was grandstanding?"

"It's what he does. Which doesn't mean you have to answer questions, speak to him, or even make eye contact."

"This is deliberate. He wants an exchange."

I heard the weary resignation in his voice. "Catling... '

"Unmute me. This is for keeps."

Zimmer had decided to stage his little performance piece right next to the flame-orange Firebird belonging to Shogi. He was addressing a journalist, flanked by two nervous, fidgety members of his PR team.

I could avoid him – but only by taking the long way around to my car.

Not a chance of that.

Zimmer turned to meet me, spreading his arms in a gesture of innocent apology. His voice boomed over the general race channel.

"Sorry, Catling! I didn't think I was in the way! I assumed you were already in your car!" His visor dipped down. "New legs, aren't they? Neon pink flamework, too. Old-school. Brave choice."

"Thanks," I said acidly. "And how's that new eye of yours working out? Hear it started glitching on you last time out."

"Cosmic ray strike: took out a whole array buffer." He shrugged effortlessly. "I still won."

I put my hands on my hips and appraised him like a slightly wonky art installation, the kind you glance at before moving on.

"What is it now, Zimmer? Forty-three per cent of you replaced or augmented?"

He smiled behind the semi-mirrored visor. Zimmer's face was gameshow-host handsome, with a stiff, synthetic sheen to it. "I'm within the racing code. This year we're allowed forty-five per cent augmentation."

"And next year it'll be even more, just to keep you legal. Lucky your team has the influence it does, or they might have to start stuffing meat back into you."

He kept his voice level, his perma-smile unwavering. "You're not as far behind me as you'd like to make out. Those legs, and those new neural mods your team have been keeping very quiet about?"

"All legal," I asserted. "The scrutineers have been over me just as thoroughly as the car."

"In which case… all's fair between us, isn't it? Two drivers, two cars, a racetrack ahead of us. What could be more… sporting?" He reached out a hand for me to shake. "Shall we?"

I bristled, aware that all eyes were on me. A show of ungracious conduct right now could knock whole percentage points off our sponsorship. Rufus wouldn't like that.

Besides, Joff had always told me to keep it *gentlemanly*.

I gritted my teeth and shook his hand.

"May the better driver win."

The start lights came on in sequence. I pressed down on the throttle, the force-feedback from my new legs just a fraction off, but not so much that it was going to throw my race. Traction power flowed from the car's nuclear reactor to my wheels. They strained against supercooled ceramic brakes, the entire vehicle rocking like a theme-park pirate ship. Temperature dials needled into the red on my console.

The car was a beast. It hated standing still.

"Race watchers!" bellowed the commentator. "The course is open! The down-ramp is lowered! The drivers are set, their cars at launch power! Who will cross the finish line first after circumnavigating Io, some sixty hours from now? Zimmer and Catling lead the grid, and all eyes will surely be on their races, but we must still talk about Shogi, looking to go wheel-to-wheel against Mossmann in the Black Shadow. Denied the cup at Callisto after a cooling circuit blowout, the redoubtable Shogi... '

I tuned out the babble and concentrated on my launch. The interval between the fourth and fifth lights always seemed an eternity... and yet there was only room in it for one or two heartbeats.

Five lights.

No lights. And... everything flowed, slow and fast in the same impossible instant. Cars were moving. I saw them all, picked up in mirrors and direct video feeds. A line of huge colourful machines gathering speed like boulders sliding down a mountainside. I studied Zimmer's wheels, looking for a trace of slip against the greasy surface of the grid. Nothing. The bastard had a perfect launch, clean on the throttle. I resisted the urge to gun it, applying smoothly rising power, letting the car find its own grip.

There was no overtaking down the long start straight, and no one stupid enough to attempt it. Speed mounted: one hundred kilometres per hour, two hundred, three hundred. The grandstands became a silent blur of light and tiny faces. The cars were barrelling down a long enclosed tunnel, metal grid below and floods above, premium advertising banners chasing hard on their tails.

All very sterile, all very corporate and controlled. But things would be getting real and dirty very quickly.

Ahead, coming up fast – the Bellatrix Beta was nudging three hundred and fifty kilometres per hour – was a steep down-ramp. Zimmer hit it first, momentum carrying him over the lip, his car following a shallow parabola until it re-engaged with the sloping road.

I eased off just before the transition, keeping all wheels in contact and maintaining my slow but steady acceleration. I fell behind Zimmer, then caught up again as his car bogged down and struggled with traction.

"Rookie error, Zim."

His answer crackled back, his voice juddery with vibration. "You've made enough to know one."

"Oh, the burn!" I shot back.

Joff would be shaking his head about now, telling me to focus on the race, not mind-games.

Zimmer was first down, but only just. I was at his side, less than a third of a car's length from the bulbous nose of the Imperator Six. Now those monster wheels really came into their own, biting into the Ionian crust. I put all power down, red-lining the motors. The huge structure of the grandstand and starting grid fell behind, blurred in the plumes of dust and gas rising behind our cars. The opening leg was relatively flat and level: I could go all-out without risking damage to the tyres, wheels, or suspension.

So could Zimmer, though. His car was no faster than mine, but because he was slightly ahead, he could choose the racing line. He knew this moon like it was his private racetrack. He could pick and choose his course, gunning for the areas of crust where his instincts promised a tiny but crucial advantage.

The only winning condition was this: end up back at Ruwa Patera, after a complete circumnavigation. Twelve thousand kilometres, give or take. Sixty hours, at the average winning speed. Fifty-seven was the course record, set by Chertoff. No one had got close to that since.

Chertoff wouldn't be trying. Hard to race in a lead-lined coffin.

The first hour was critical. Cars could get badly out of position, picking a bad strategy, pushing too hard, or just hitting an early streak of bad luck. A lot could be decided in those first couple of hundred kilometres. The next nine or ten hours, once the drivers had settled into things, was more a question of endurance and perseverance. Things got juicy again around the first waypoint, as cars converged from different routes and scrapped for a limited strip of terrain.

I was too much of a veteran to make any silly mistakes in the first leg. I kept an eye on Zimmer, never letting him pull more than half a kilometre ahead of me, but I kept telling myself to drive my own race and not get drawn into wheel-to-wheel action too early on. There'd be time for that later on.

Mossmann was the first to blow out. He hit a big boulder eighty klicks into the race, trying to squeeze through a gap that was too narrow for his car. He flipped and rolled. He was a long way behind me (Mossmann had picked a completely different route to mine, going much further south) but I watched it all on the live feeds. I was glad when his car righted itself and his cockpit pod ejected safely, rockets lifting him away from the surface. The car was a radioactive wreck, but Mossmann would live to drive again, provided his team stayed afloat.

Joff had been racing before ejection cockpits became a mandatory feature. I still remembered some of the horror stories. Whether he told me them to make me a safer driver, or just to emphasize how easy we had it now, I couldn't say.

There'd been a lot of changes, for sure. In Joff's day drivers had to stay awake by means of willpower, grit, and maybe the odd illegal substance. Now we had consciousness-management neural mods, staving off sleep for up to sixty hours by selectively de-emphasizing certain areas of brain function. We had tweaks for enhanced reaction time, low-light perception, and superior spatial awareness. Mossmann must have skimped on the last one, because I'd never have made the same error. I knew my car's limits like I knew my own elbows.

None of these tweaks and prosthetics and in-car protection measures exactly made racing on Io *safe*, though. They just reduced the probability of death to something acceptable to the advertisers and networks.

Every racing location in the system had its own parcel of risks. Io didn't have the crushing pressure and acidic environment of Venus, nor the alloy-freezing chill of Titan. It lacked the dust-storms of Mars or the cracked, treacherous icescapes of Europa.

What it did have was savage, unpredictable geology. As Io moved around Jupiter, gravity toyed with it like an executive's stress ball. All that energy being pumped into its core had to go somewhere. It ended up percolating out into a sea of sub-surface lava, keeping it nicely molten and prone to sudden explosive eruptions. Io's geysers were lethal, random timebombs. Hit one as it went off, and your race was over. You could play safe by keeping clear of the main eruption zones, but not if you wanted a shot at a podium finish. The trick was to plot a course that hopscotched close to the geysers. Close, but not too close. Up to each driver how close they pushed that margin. How much they wanted to win. How far they had come, and how much of their career they had ahead of them.

You could roll the dice. Geyser activity was loosely correlated with Io's position in its orbit, with the Sun either hidden behind Jupiter or bearing down hard and cruel overhead. Drivers could make a mad dash across a danger zone when the activity was expected to be at its lowest... but nothing on Io ran like clockwork. Plenty had been burned that way. And since no two TransIonians ever started at the same orbital phase, lessons learned from one race were all but useless the next time around.

Which was why winning on Io mattered more than anywhere else in the system. It might not be the race that decided a tournament, but it was the one that forged legends.

At the first waypoint, ten hours and forty minutes in, Zimmer and I were comfortably clear of the competition. He was ahead of me, but not so far that anything was decided. Now cars were bouncing in from north and south, averaging between one hundred and fifty and two hundred kilometres per hour, but looking slow and ponderous, raised up high on those enormous wheels.

We'd started with Jupiter's dark face sitting above us, blocking the Sun: none more black over a sullen, barely visible landscape. By the time the cars started arriving at the first waypoint, though, Io had moved a quarter of the way around Jupiter. The Sun was no longer in eclipse and Jupiter was demi-lit and on its way to the horizon. The sky had picked up a shimmering, sickly sodium glow. It projected confusing shadows, making everything look unfamiliar, even to drivers who had followed the same course a dozen times.

Other than Mossmann, all the drivers made it through the first waypoint without drama. The toll was beginning to show on Scurlock, in her lime-green Draco, with a motor seizure on one of her axles. She'd been over-gunning it early on, risking cooling failure. I could tell from the plume her car was pushing up, crabbing lopsidedly as it dragged a dead wheel along for the ride. No way she was making the next waypoint, or even close to it. Mittendorfer was the next casualty, five hours into the second stint: he followed Shogi's line right through a geyser field that was just waiting to be poked and prodded. Shogi made it through, but his car had weakened the crust just enough to spring an eruption right under Mittendorfer. The blast caught his belly, flipped the car, rolled it. The car righted itself, but by then its leading axles were buckled and useless. Mittendorfer punched out, leaving his smouldering wreck behind. A rescue drone caught his cockpit before it fell back to Io, and thirty minutes later he was pontificating from the commentary box, shaken to the core but glad to be alive.

The Sun got higher and higher in the sky through that second stint, as Io positioned itself between Jupiter and the Sun. It would have been a glorious sight from the moon's Jupiter-facing side… but by then our cars had driven more than a quarter of the way around, edging into the face of Io which was permanently averted.

Twenty-one hours in, the remaining cars converged for the second waypoint. By now there was a big spread in their positions and chances of victory. Zimmer was ahead of me still, the only one I had a direct visual on. The others were too far away, lost behind ridges or hidden completely from view by Io's nearby horizon. I had to rely on the video feed and race commentary to get a sense of how the larger race was playing out. Not that the others really concerned me. It was between me and Zimmer right now.

The fatigue was just being kept at bay by my mods. The race was only a third done, too. This was the psychological pinch-point for a lot of drivers, as they pressed on into the third stint. They were mentally and physically drained, even with the augmentations. The trick, Joff had told me, was to forget how many hours of driving were still ahead. It was only ever the next hour that counted. The next minute, in fact. The future only existed as far as the next corner, the next breaking zone.

"It's one thing to say that, another to believe it!" I'd protested.

"You'll learn it, kid," he'd said, with his usual bluff certainty. "Or you'll never lift a trophy."

I had learned it, too. Like all the mind-games you played against yourself, rather than other drivers, it was pretty damned simple once you got the knack.

Hands on the wheel. Pedal to the floor.

Just drive.

*

After waypoint three, thirty-two hours in, more than half race-distance, came the big decision.

There was a relatively clean racing line all the way to waypoint four. Not risk-free exactly – nothing on Io was that – but well-trodden, with established pitfalls and manageable hazards. Two thousand eight hundred kilometres of sinuous driving with plenty of pinch-points where cars could end up wheel-to-wheel. Based on previous races, the chances of a crash or major malfunction were about one in twenty across this leg. Chances of death: one in ninety. Not exactly cheering odds in any other walk of life, but nothing on Io.

There was another line. Much less winding, much less hilly. Almost a straight dash, shaving off an easy four hundred kilometres between waypoints three and four. Plenty of room, too. Cars didn't need to tangle.

It was also through the most active, violent geyser zone anywhere close to the permitted routes. Detonation Boulevard, so-called. Eighty kilometres of Russian Roulette, where that one in ninety risk of mortality ratcheted closer to one in twelve. No one was exactly sure, because so few drivers had ever put it to the test. The risk of a mechanical failure was somewhere around one in three.

Of the current crop of competitors, Zimmer was the only driver who'd built Detonation Boulevard into his race strategy. He'd won two TransIonians that way. But even Zimmer wasn't cavalier about it. He didn't always take the short-cut. He'd take a squint at the weather, factoring in some private calculus of risk versus gain. No one was better at reading geyser activity than Zimmer, and no one was better at keeping his cards close to his chest. I'd been trying to fathom his intentions when we had our little set-to on the starting grid, but I couldn't read him. Nor could I take a guess based on my understanding of the geyser conditions. No matter how I ran the odds, my risk threshold wasn't going to be the same as his.

It would all come down to a fork in the road after waypoint three. If he kept on the south fork, he was keeping to the established line. Which wasn't any kind of white flag, either: Zimmer was still easily capable of winning that way. If he veered north, though, I'd have about a kilometre to decide whether or not to follow him. After that, the routes peeled apart through undriveable terrain. There'd be no time for second thoughts.

I watched the bouncing red dot of his car, picked out in flashes from my headlights. The Sun was falling again now, as Io moved back around behind Jupiter.

"Are we doing this, Zim?" I asked.

"Are we doing what?"

"You know damned well what."

"Conditions aren't favourable, Catling. I thought you'd have done your homework before setting off."

Rufus crackled in, interrupting our sport. "He has his race strategy, we have ours, Cat. Our sponsors want a car back at the end of this, not a smoking wreck."

"He has a point," Zimmer commented.

"Balls to that. When have you ever cared about my sponsors?"

I'll give him credit: he almost had me. As we approached the fork, he looked to be entirely committed to the south deviation. And I relaxed a little, thinking that while I'd still be following him, at least it wasn't through Detonation Boulevard.

He steered hard, braking so late that his car tilted onto three wheels, with three more up in the air. I thought for a second he was going to roll it, but slow and gracefully the Imperator Six came down again, gunning it north.

"They don't call me the last of the late brakers for nothing," Zimmer taunted.

"Bastard," I mouthed.

Of course I followed. What else was I going to do?

The car held. My concentration held. The sponsors held.

If there was a weakness to Zimmer's Imperator Six, it was laying down straight-line speed for sustained intervals. The Six's cooling system, cut to the bone to minimise weight and power-drain, was fine-tuned to the needs of the motors under normal racing conditions. On the twisty slopes and chicanes of the longer, southerly route, his car wasn't in danger of red-lining. The Bellatrix Beta wasn't as sure-footed over that sort of terrain… but I could go flat-out for longer and faster, without cooking my car.

Zimmer knew this. Everyone knew it. But he'd counted on two things: one, that I wouldn't have the guts to follow him, and two, that even if I did, he could hold his margin until the next waypoint. After that, we were back into the sort of terrain that suited him. He just needed to maintain his lead.

Before long it was looking like his gamble had paid off.

The geyser zone was active... but not the worst it had been. Zimmer was pulling ever more ahead of the remaining cars, such that he was likely to arrive at the next waypoint between three to four hours ahead of Shogi. Olsen was hard on Shogi's heels, but there was no way either of them could make up time to catch Zimmer – or me, for that matter.

But I wasn't in this race to come in second.

I knew I could push the Bellatrix Beta harder and longer than Zimmer could push his car. But eating up that ground between us was going to take more than just pedal-to-metal determination. I had to risk red-lining the motors, and I had to hold a straight line even when every sensible instinct told me to steer.

Geysers erupted across the plain, fountaining up into the night. Big ones, small ones, some on their own and some going off in long, treacherous chains, like a sequence of landmines. I watched Zimmer steer away from the worst of them, but trusting his wheels and speed to carry him right over and through the smaller eruptions, or those larger events that were nearly played-out. I took a gamble and followed his line most of the way, gaining slowly but surely as my car found its second wind. He was only six hundred metres ahead of me now, close enough that I could track every twitch and jerk of his car. I imagined him nursing those over-heated motors, praying that they'd last him until we were back into the slower sectors. The Bellatrix Beta didn't like what I was asking of it now: odds were that the Imperator Six was screaming out its complaints.

Five hundred metres, then four hundred. And Zimmer made an error! A geyser popped up right ahead of him. It wasn't a large one and he could have sailed right over it... but by now his nerves must have been worn ragged, and he miscalculated. He steered hard, the car skidded sideways, losing forward momentum as its wheels dug in. Zimmer kept it upright, wrestling steering and power until he had the car back under control, but by then he'd committed to a bad line and I hadn't stopped closing on him.

I sailed past: close enough to raise a fist and hope he'd seen it.

'Eat my dust, Zim. See you back at Ruwa Patera.'

I red-lined the motors until I'd put another kilometre between us. Then eased off, tactically. Zimmer was regaining speed but he'd struggle to close the distance. All I had to do was keep the Bellatrix Beta in check for a few more hundred kilometres.

Zimmer was behind me. Shogi and Olsen, a long way south and a long way behind. I was winning the TransIonian! I grinned, feeling clouds of fatigue lift off me. Admittedly, there was still a lot of terrain to cross. A lot of hours ahead, and at no point would I be able to relax. But I was off the knife edge, temporarily.

The feeling was glorious,

It lasted all the way until I realised I couldn't see Zimmer behind me any more.

I slowed down, one eye on the terrain ahead, the other on the crackly video feed showing Zimmer's crash, over and over.

"You got problems I don't know about?" Rufus asked.

"Nope. Nothing wrong with me or my car. I just need to know what's going on back there."

"Zimmer hit a geyser and flipped. He was pushing too hard. Now pick the safest possible line you can and get back onto something resembling predictable terrain. You can take it as cautiously as you like: Shogi hasn't a hope of reaching you."

"Did Zimmer punch out, Rufus? It all happened so quickly I'm not sure I didn't miss something."

Rufus came back tersely. "He didn't eject."

"You sure?"

"Yes, I'm sure. Probably can't. He looks to be almost belly-up in that crater."

"Is he all right?"

Rufus shifted from unconcern to mild irritation. "What do we care, Cat? He's out of the running. Your one serious rival just made a bad mistake! Now press that advantage." Then, with growing concern. "Oh, wait. No. What are you doing?"

"What it looks like I'm doing. Turning around."

"Zimmer is not your problem!"

"If he can't bail, he's either already dead or cooking alive in that car. I can get to him much quicker than the rescue drones."

I slowed enough to make a tight hairpin, looping back onto the terrain where I'd already laid down wheel tracks. There was no guarantee that the ground was still safe – just driving over it once could weaken the crust in an eruption zone – but out here it was a marginally better prospect than forging a brand-new route.

"Cat," Rufus said pleadingly. "This is all very noble, but we're haemorrhaging sponsorship."

"Are we really?"

"You've dropped twenty-six points since you started turning back! Look at the bodywork!"

With whatever small part of my attention I could bring to the matter, I saw that he was right. The shell of the car was no longer a pockmarked riot of corporate names and symbols. They were flickering out, growing sparser, and the handful of second-tier players buying in to fill the gaps were nowhere big enough to make up for the loss of revenue.

The sponsors liked an underdog. They liked a winner even more.

A Good Samaritan? Not so much.

"I'm not losing this race," I assured him. "I'm just taking a little detour on the way to the finishing line."

Low ridges and geyser plumes kept Zimmer out of sight until I was nearly on him. At two kilometers I saw the glint from his up-ended car, what little of it projected above the crater in which he'd flipped. The crater was outgassing, but it was a slow, continuous bleed of volatiles, not an explosive eruption. The gases curtained around the car, wreathing it in a hazy glow, before smearing into vacuum.

I slowed to fifty, inching across the last kilometre. Whatever trust I'd placed in the terrain before was now completely gone.

"Zimmer, can you hear me?"

He came in on a wave of static and crackles, as if we were halfway across the solar system from each other.

"That you, Catling?"

"Yes, it's me. You must have shattered your comms pod when you turned turtle. Why haven't you ejected?"

"Not an option: I'd just end up punching right through the crust into molten lava. I've got a choice of ways to die out here, Catling: boiling alive isn't top of the list… '

"You're not going to die. Put on your helmet if you haven't already done so."

"Why?"

"Because one way or another I'm getting you out of that wreck."

"This is a mistake," he answered. But some of the fight had gone out of him. "Don't risk yourself on my account."

"I'm right alongside already. Come this far, I might as well finish the job."

"Bet your sponsors love you."

"So what? The car looks much nicer this way."

I rolled to a halt about two hundred metres from his position. The crater was still belching, with outlying gas vents sending up feathery plumes and underscoring the instability of the ground beneath us.

I put on my helmet, depressurised the cockpit, grabbed the emergency rescue pack, and climbed out through the cockpit hatch. I stood for a moment on the car's back, taking in the blue skin, largely unblemished by logos. The few that remained weren't even second-tier sponsors: we were bottom-feeding now.

Rufus must have been chewing his nails down to the quick.

"You still there, Zim?" I asked, climbing off the back of the car and down the ladder between the forward and middle wheels.

"Yes, and what I said still stands. They'll pity you. You're showing weakness."

"Then call me weak." The ladder didn't reach all the way to the ground, but I easily jumped the remaining distance. I landed, buckling my knees to absorb the impact, and ready to clutch back onto the ladder if the ground started cracking beneath me.

It held.

"You got that helmet on?"

"What of it?"

"I want you to start your depressurisation cycle. One way or another, we get you back to my car."

"There won't be room in your cockpit."

"Then you piggyback. You can plug into my car's life-support circuit."

He sighed. "You're determined to do this."

"I am."

After a silence, his reply came back: "All right. But I'm tangled up in here. You'll need to undo my restraints, maybe cut through the crash webbing. And I'm not sure how easily I'll be able to move myself."

"We're on Io," I said nonchalantly. "I can sling you over my shoulder if I have to."

I walked carefully across the ground between my car and the crater rim, placing each footfall as if I trod on a carpet of eggshells. Explosive eggshells at that. There was no way I could disarm the part of my brain that insisted I was walking across a paper-thin membrane, stretched across an ocean of flesh-melting fire.

"Did Rufus approve of this, by any chance?"

"Never mind Rufus."

"That's a no, then. Well, I don't blame him. Bet you he said I wouldn't do the same if our roles were reversed?"

"They wouldn't be, though."

"How can you be sure?"

"Because I'm the better driver. You forgot where you were, Zim. Detonation Boulevard."

"I didn't forget."

"Oh, so landing upside down was part of the plan?"

I expected a flip, mordant answer, but nothing came. And a prickle at the back of my neck had me thinking: what if it *had* been the plan, after all?

Zimmer with a death wish?

I'd never thought about that. He had everything to live for, didn't he?

I topped the low lip of the caldera. Io whispered to me through the sensors in my legs, a forbidding, stampede-like rumble of distant and not-so-distant seismic processes. The solidified sulphur just beneath my soles was cold enough to freeze blood and shatter bone, but I didn't have to look far to see smudges where the ground was much warmer. I had to hopscotch around those. Beneath them might be pools of sulphur warm enough to bake someone alive, or puddles of bubbling silicate lava a good thousand degrees hotter.

Slow, tepid death, or quick, scalding one? Take your pick.

All that covered these horrors was a brittle topcoat of sulphur, sulphates, and silicates, firm enough to drive over most of the time, but in places no thicker than piecrust.

I held my nerve, ignored the rumble coming up through my legs, and took my vantage on the ragged, crumbling rim of the caldera. I felt, for a moment, equally heroic and preposterous. The caldera was about seventy metres across: a black-walled basin spattered with the dusky oranges and sickly yellows of more recent outbursts, ghosted by a fine pale dusting of sulphur frost.

With Zimmer's car upside down in the middle of it.

Upside down, jammed tail-end into the caldera floor, and sticking out of the ground at about thirty degrees to the horizontal.

He'd gone in hard.

"That won't polish out," I said to myself.

Instead of triggering a massive eruption, the bulk of the car was acting like a cinder plug, blocking most of the outflow. It looked stable... for the moment. If the car had been caught in the middle of a full-on fountaining geyser, there'd have been nothing I could have done for Zimmer.

Equally, there wouldn't have been much left of Zimmer worth saving.

I clambered down the inside of the caldera. I had to get to the cockpit, now facing down rather than up, but there was no way I was staking my life on that cracked, fractured floor.

"Zimmer," I said, looping the strap of the emergency kit around my elbow. "I can see a way to get to you. But it's going to be a scramble to get you out. Think you can go hand-over-hand until we're over safe ground?"

"Whatever it takes," Zimmer answered neutrally.

"Hold on. I'm leaping aboard. Your car looks pretty firmly wedged in there, so I hope it'll take my weight when I land."

"Be careful."

I put all my power into my legs and sprung up at the car. As I soared up and out on a lazy parabola, everything slowed down. That wasn't just psychology. It was the neural mod, detecting an adrenalin spike and giving me a temporary cognitive speed boost.

I'd misjudged, I realised. The emergency kit had upset my centre of gravity, causing me to veer to the left.

'Gah!" I cried out, straining my fingers. The car came nearer. I was off course but not completely so. My fingertips brushed a handhold. I grasped it hard, felt it sliding through my grip, my momentum still carrying me too hard and too fast.

I flailed with the other hand, and with a secondary part of my attention watched the emergency kit slide right off my elbow, down my forearm, over my glove, and off into the void.

"Balls!"

"What?"

"I lost the emergency kit!"

"Never mind. There's another one here. Are you secure?"

"Yes… yes," I said, shocked and surprised to see that I was in fact now dangling from the underside of the car. "Yes, I'm on. Sort of." I started swinging back and forth, until at last I was able to hook my foot into another grab. With a grunt and a stretch, I got both hands onto the rails. The car rocked slightly – for all its mass it was balanced precariously – but held. "I'm good. I'm climbing up and along."

"Take it slowly."

"I am."

The speed-boost had worn off. Now I had the groggy after-effects: a dull headache and a sense that my thoughts were running through treacle. It would take a few minutes for my neurochemistry to re-equilibrate.

"Have you ever thought about retiring, Catling?"

I monkeyed into position alongside the pod. The windows were steamed-up on the inside, so I couldn't tell what kind of condition Zimmer was in. "Kind of an odd question, from someone hanging upside down in a car wreck."

"Not so odd. I've been giving it a lot of thought lately."

"We're drivers, Zim. We keep going until our reflexes burn out or *we* burn. That's how it is."

"But what if you wanted to retire, but couldn't?"

"Depends on the lifestyle you've grown accustomed to. I guess. You've got more winnings in the bank than me." I knocked on the glass. "I'm ready to haul you out. Have you depressurised inside there?"

"Purging the last of my air now. Keep away from the vents."

I held on. Two jets of air feathered out from the back of the pod, then died away. The fog cleared from the glass as the last traces of moisture boiled off into vacuum.

"Supposing it's not about wealth at all."

"There's money or glory," I countered. "What else matters?"

"I'm opening the door."

His hatch flipped open just above my face. I levered myself up until I was able to look into the upside-down pod. Then I risked letting go with one hand so that I could hook an elbow into the open hatchway. I gave a grunt and got one leg braced into the opening, then the other, and finally both hands.

I was perched on the very edge of the pod, with no room to go any further inside, but at least my hands were free now.

I spied Zimmer: strung up like a bat, suspended in the tangled confusion of his harness. He looked broken and doll-like, his limbs pulled into awkward, unnatural angles.

"You're a mess."

"You don't know the half of it," he answered, turning his inverted face to meet mine.

I jerked back in shock and nearly tumbled out of the pod. "You're in vacuum."

He had the same helmet on as when he started the race, but the visor part of it was detached, leaving his face open to the airless environment of the pod. The same face I'd seen at the start, gameshow-host handsome, perma-smile, but now looking even more artificial.

"I haven't needed it for some while," he answered, his lips not moving as he spoke. "I don't breathe in the usual sense. My lungs are a blood-oxygen exchange system, connected directly to the pod's air supply. Such a modification was... not technically within the current rules. But there's an amendment in the schedule for next season. That would make me legal again."

My brain fog had mostly abated, but something still wasn't making sense.

"Why are you telling me this? I could take that rules violation straight to the top and get you blown out of the competition."

"You wouldn't get very far. The rules are written to suit me. I bring in too much money."

It had the ring of truth, but I still shook my head, thoroughly disgusted. "I knew you were dirty. I just didn't know *how* bad it had got."

"Those legs of yours. They were strictly within the rules when you had them installed?"

"Of course they were."

"I've seen documentation that says otherwise. The prosthetic augmentation was too powerful, by a few per cent. But Gladius Exomedical and your team negotiated a hush-hush technical exemption on the understanding that all would be put right by the next season."

"We're talking a tiny discrepancy."

"It's just a question of degrees, Catling. We're on the same path, you and I. I'm just further down it."

"I'll never end up like you."

"What if the choice isn't yours to make?"

I grew impatient. I'd detoured to rescue Zimmer, not to get drawn into a debate about the moral hazards of our profession. "Where's your emergency kit? I'm going to try and cut you out of that webbing."

"I'm not going anywhere." He paused, searched me with his eyes. "You were right about me flipping the car. It wasn't an accident."

"You had the race in the bag."

"It's not about winning. It's about something bigger."

"You're losing me, Zim."

"In the beginning the augmentations were small enough that I felt I could control them. A new limb here, a neural mod here. Just like you."

I shivered inside my suit. "I'm totally in control."

"Maybe you are, right now. But there's a line. On the other side, it's not you deciding to race. It's the *machinery*. It gets into you deeply. Changes psychology, blood chemistry, whatever it takes."

"Whatever it takes to do what?"

"To make more of itself. It's been driving me, Catling. It compels me to keep racing. Season after season, year after year. There's always a little bit less of me and a little more of it. And I can see where that ends. One day I won't even remember I was me. I'll just be a walking, talking impersonation of myself."

"So get out before that happens."

"I tried. But it wouldn't let me." He shook his head wryly. "There was only ever one way out. I had to race so hard that I made the one mistake there was no coming back from."

I nodded slowly. I was ready to accept the fact of his desperation even if I refused to believe the motivation behind it.

"You never wanted to be rescued."

"No," he agreed. "But if there was a chance to reach you, to warn you before it was too late? I always liked you, Catling."

I thought of our sniping interactions, the subtle put-downs and calculated mind games.

He *liked* me?

"You made a good job of hiding it."

"It was never personal. But this is. It's a plea from the heart. You're not too far gone. The machine's in you, but you're still the one in the driver's seat. You can still back out."

"How'd you know it's not too late?"

He laughed mirthlessly. "Because you turned back. It was a moment of weakness. Human weakness." Something tightened his face. "I haven't been capable of anything like that for a long time."

"You're saying I should quit this life?"

"While there's still a chance. Do this one thing for me, and I'll die knowing I got to you in time. That'll be good. I need it."

"I can't just... stop. The team. Rufus, the mechanics, the sponsors... '

"You owe them nothing. You're just meat to them. If you quit, they'll find someone else just as willing."

I thought of how quickly the sponsors had deserted me the moment I showed that first hint of compassion. The first hint that something mattered to me more than winning. The first hint that I wasn't as cold-hearted and ruthless as they expected of me.

I eased back. "Are you really going to die here?"

"It'll be all right. I can turn off nearly everything now." The car lurched violently and I nearly toppled out. "You'd best be on your way. I've said my piece, and you've listened. I hope maybe you'll spread the word, too. Speak to the other drivers, the ones who aren't too far gone. Take out enough pieces, the whole thing crumbles, or at least changes."

"You mean... bring it all down? Everything?"

"Someone needs to stop it. Or make it better. If it isn't you, you've still been kind enough to me right now. I'm glad you were here at the end."

"Honestly, Zim, couldn't we have done this some other way?"

"Oh, don't feel too bad about it. We had some good races, didn't we?"

"Yeah, we did."

The car dropped another metre into the caldera. I made to say something more, some zinger of a farewell that would look good when I dictated my biography, but nothing came. We just eyed each other for a second and then I bailed out, scooping hands onto the rails and monkeying down onto safe ground as quickly as I could.

Even as I was climbing back over the caldera rim, the car was going down behind me. Geysers burst through, shrouding the vehicle's death pains.

"You crazy brave bastard, Zimmer," I said on the open channel, just in case he was still listening in.

A soundless explosion flared behind me. My shadow stretched out across the sulphur flats, then faded.

I returned to my spotless blue car. Climbed in, repressurised, and began to roll away from the scene of the accident. Geysers were rupturing all around, plumes daubing livid sparking colour against the black. There was definitely more activity than when I'd arrived. Zimmer's demise had triggered something, for sure.

As if Detonation Boulevard needed any encouragement.

"We'll rename it," I mused aloud. "Zimmer's Alley, or something. Only fitting."

"Cat."

It was Rufus, coming in on the long-range. "Oh, hello," I said.

"We'll talk about this later," he said, his voice quavering on the edge of rage. "The damage you've done with this pointless little stunt… it's going to take months to rebuild our profile."

"News for you, Rufus," I said, filled with a strange calm. "I'm done. I'm not even going to finish the TransIonian."

"You have a contractual obligation to bring that car home."

"I will. I'm just not going to race now. I'll take my time, enjoy the scenery, stop before the finishing line. What are you so worked about, anyway? It must all be over by now."

"You still have the lead."

"No," I said flatly. "Not possible. I was with Zimmer for too long."

"Shogi blew a wheel at Purginev Corner. Olsen had the lead for about thirty minutes after that, then flipped at Tholus Pass. Shogi's sitting tight waiting for recovery, and Olsen managed to bail. No one else is close."

"I'm not racing."

"You're heading in the right direction."

"That's just the quickest way out of Detonation Boulevard."

"Be that as it may, our sponsors see it differently. They're starting to come back. We're up a few percentage points already. They think you want to finish this, and they like the way the narrative played out."

"The what?"

"The brave driver risks victory to save a stricken colleague. She can't help him, but at least she tried. And now she still gets to claim the win! It's the classic combination of guts, tragedy, and outrageous good fortune!"

"The moment I turned back, they threw me to the wolves!"

"But as I said, the way it played out... '

"I'm not doing this. I'm taking a stand. Not just for Zimmer, but everyone else caught up in this thing. It's all gone way too far."

I meant it too, in that moment.

But something caught my eye. A flicker of colour, appearing against the blue of my car. A logo, and not one of the minor players. It stood in glorious isolation for a few seconds, then – like a seed – began to attract further sponsors.

I watched in wonder as they flocked back, a chain of gaudy islands thrusting out of clear blue seas. The islands jostled, some of them growing larger and swallowing up their smaller competitors.

"They really like you," Rufus marvelled.

I put my foot down a bit harder. "I can see."

"What are you going to do?"

"I'm going to... ' I hesitated. "I'm going to... I'm going to finish this one race. Not for me. Not for the team. For Zimmer. Only for Zimmer. It was his to win, not mine. And I'll say as much when I'm standing up there on the podium. I'll dedicate the victory to him. And then... then I'll quit, and when I do I'm going to speak up about everything that's wrong with all this. That's the end of it for me, until we fix this. And if we don't, then no more racing."

Rufus laughed, a laugh as cold and airless as anywhere on Io.

"We'll see how you feel when you have your hands on that trophy."

Vermin Control
Tim Lees

She takes the lower access route, down into the belly of the ship, where the lights are kept on half-power and the AC dribbles into little pools that splash and shiver, throwing their reflections on the walls.

Within an hour, the screams will start.

She mustn't call them that.

Officially, they're nothing. Just a glitch, a bug in the mechanics; the squeal and grind of moving parts, down deep in the machinery.

To Jenny Xu, they're screams.

They're like the whole ship crying out for help, an awful, plaintive sound.

She has an hour, still.

She chose this route deliberately. Partway along, the floor changes to glass, and the stars just drop away below, a spattering of light that falls into the dark, on and on, forever.

Here, at the window's edge, she sets down her equipment. She stands. She takes a breath, loosens her shoulders, limbers up. Stretches her arms and points her toes, then steps into the void.

One pace. Two. Then sideways, back.

She leaps into the air, arms wide, and lands without a sound.

Here, here – dancing on the face of Heaven.

Dancing with the universe below.

Remember, Liveships is a trademark.

Liveships™.

Look into the lens, please.

Affirm that you will never, by direct speech or by implication, by actions, words, or tone of voice, do anything that may cast doubt upon the Liveships™ reputation and integrity, its personnel or management, or any property or item known to bear the Liveships™ brand.

Sign now, please. Sign with your retinal print. Look into the lens.

Thank you.

Welcome to Liveships™! Welcome to the crew!

Her function isn't advertised. Like the screams, she can't exist, officially.

Yet here she is.

Lucas greets her, down on level 3. He's grown his beard again. It's like a mask for him to hide behind.

His face is pinched and wan.

"I mean," he says, "you think: to me, it's only two months. But to her, it's like a whole year. Or, you know. Close enough."

"Luc," she says. "I just got here..."

"Sorry, sorry. I know." He looks about, like he's mislaid something. "It's on my mind a lot, that's all, I can't stop thinking –"

Lucas doesn't trust his wife. He worries with an absolute, obsessive dedication, running through scenarios, trying to picture where she's been, and who she's met, and what she's done – a hundred different ways she might abandon him.

He works down here. Too long alone.

"You need some therapy," she says.

"You think?"

He leads her in between the big machines, slipping sideways when the path gets narrow. "But if I do, then it's on record."

"True."

"And somebody –" he says.

But he doesn't say the obvious: that it could kill his next promotion, or his next job, or that he needs the money.

Instead, he whispers, "Someone could call someone back at home. And tell them how things are."

His face is deadly serious.

"And why would anyone do that?" she says.

"A man, I mean. I mean a *man*."

"Luc –"

"And they could go and see her. He'd say it was official, first off. An official visit. So she'd ask him in. And then..."

He stops walking.

She stops, too.

"Luc," she says. "If you don't trust her, why d'you marry in the first place?"

"Oh. I —"

He stands a moment, waiting. But the answer doesn't come.

He indicates the black specks, scattered on the floor. Tiny, dry, each one slightly elongated.

"Seeds?" he asks. "They look like seeds."

"Don't eat them, Luc."

"I wasn't going to! Just, I thought they looked like seeds..."

"You do eat here though, don't you? Lunches, snacks?"

It's not a designated eating place.

"Um. Maybe..."

"And store food, too?" She adds, "I won't report it."

"...uh."

She grins at him. "You got mice, Luc. Mice, that's all."

"Space mice?"

"No. Just mice."

She opens up her carrier.

His face falls: disappointed now.

So ordinary, so mundane.

"You know," she says, "they reckon it's the ancient Greeks brought cockroaches from Africa to Europe. On sailing ships. If they did that, just think what we're moving around, huh?"

She sorts through her supplies.

"Poison or traps? Lethal?"

"What do you recommend?"

"I don't know. You want thirty, forty pet mice?"

"No."

"Okay."

"Well, anyway," he says.

"Uh-huh?"

"They're space mice now, aren't they?"

She takes her little porta-vac to sweep the droppings.

But something strange has happened.

The droppings have all disappeared.

While they've been standing, talking, every single one of them has vanished into thin air.

And that's not right, is it?

The screaming starts, as usual. Echoes. Shrieks. Like two machines, ripping the guts out of each other.

The crew are careful to ignore it.

Its source, its cause, cannot be found. It cannot be accounted for, and thus, by all official rules, and like her own job: it cannot exist.

The ship is vast. It's Jenny's privilege to know the parts of it that no one else knows, go the places no one else can go.

"We need you to be *small*," they told her at the interview. "Are you *small?*"

That's how she knew the interviewer was neither human nor, in any likelihood, organic, and that the face on screen (young, handsome, Chinese), was almost certainly a simulation, meant to put her at her ease.

"And are you good with animals?" the face inquired.

"Like, dogs and cats and stuff?" she said.

A long pause. Then, "Big animals. Very big."

"Ah." She understood. "The ship, you mean."

"Yes. The ship. Are you good, Ms. Xu? Do you believe you will be good?"

She is good, yes. Or good enough.

She wouldn't say that they were friends. The ship is much too big, too strange for that.

But there are times it whispers to her.

And she dreams.

She dreams about a place where she has never been, a world of tall red mesas and a big sky full of stars. There are buildings here, though very few are finished. Skeleton towers, a frame, and a few floors, not even a roof. And in the foreground, on a pile of bones, there stands an ugly, cartoon mouse, waving his arms, declaiming in a furious, dictator's oratory. Spit jumps from his front teeth. His big snout droops like a leaky balloon while he yammers and cries out, one hand jabbing at the air.

His words make no sense, but his rage, his hurt, is palpable.

She wakes.

"Space mice?"

Her hand goes to the bulkhead at her side. It's warm to the touch. "What are you telling me?" she asks.

The ship says nothing back.

She knows the unseen places. She knows the crawlspace by tech alley, and the blind spots in the forward basin. She knows the places half the crew don't even know exist.

And it's here, hidden away, she finds the nests. The swarms. The colonies.

Not mice, this time. The mice are localized; the mice are Luc's problem.

Not mice. Not even animals.

She put in a report about them, early on. The message came back loud and clear: *don't worry*. Then, a second time: *forget it*.

But they show up on her scans. They crawl and fidget, down there in the cracks, between the pipes and the panelling, in places even she can hardly reach: these little creatures made of dust and floor sweepings, shed hair and cast-off skin cells. Some look like small homunculi, a few (she swears) mimic the crew members, and one, sat moping in a corner by itself, she christens Lucas. That's a joke, of course. Ha ha. She zaps it with her wand. It crumples up, devolves into component parts: some hair, some string, debris, and grime. A smell of burning pricks the air.

Some look like animals. A few are simply blobs, or multi-limbed, or tiny, intricate machines made out of dirt.

They're not alive. They're aggregates of waste and scrap, animated by the ship's electric field. Yet their exact nature remains a mystery.

Parasites, perhaps? Waste products...?

And then it comes to her.

It's simple.

They're the ship's neuroses.

They're its phobias and fixations, given shape and form.

Here, alone, in space.

As she is. As they all are.

Alone, with emptiness in all directions.

Lucas tries to smile. His mouth pulls sideways, crinkles, struggling to remember how it's done.

"I didn't know that you could dance."

"I'm not very good."

"Looks good to me."

"Don't get ideas."

"I – I'm not. Oh, God. But I keep thinking –"

"You know," she says. "Perhaps you should have kept the mice. Therapy animals. They might have done you good."

"Don't joke." His face is creased in pain. "I could laugh about it once, you know. I could. But that was weeks ago. To her it's months. I send her messages. I say, *I love you*, though I don't know if I do. Not really. And there's nothing in return. Just nothing."

"We've no fixed point. Of course there's no reply."

"I know, I know. But –"

She checks the traps.

They're empty, every one.

"Have you opened these?"

He shakes his head.

"Has anyone swept here? Anyone?"

No more droppings, either.

"Is someone else doing my job?"

She dreams of him again.

The mouse, high on his hill of bones.

He wears trousers, pantaloons in gaudy yellow, and suspenders, fastened with gigantic, cartoon buttons. He rants and shakes his fist, pronounces nonsense with the passion and ferocity of holy writ.

She wakes again, and thinks, once more: the mice? But why the mice?

And then it starts.

She bears no title on the upper decks. No uniform. She wears a suit in burgundy and cream, as if she were another tourist ("guest" is the official term). Her instruments are small enough to carry in a large, mock-leather purse. She must cause no alarm, no sense of anything amiss.

There is no "vermin control." Not on the upper decks. Because if there were, then that would mean – ah. Yes.

The officer escorting her chats prettily in public earshot, waves his hand towards the windows, and the heavens beyond. Silent, unending, with neither up nor down. A gas cloud spans the view like some enormous, cantilevered bridge, steadily melting in the void.

"Domestics found it," says the officer, whispering now. "We upgraded the guests, moved their things. They don't know. They were told they'd won a lottery." He gives a brief, somewhat embarrassed smile. They reach the door. He puts his thumb against the plate. "We've kept it locked since, obviously." He looks around. This is a public quarter, after all; too easy to be overheard. The door slides back, and with a brief touch on the shoulder, he urges her inside. The cabin lights come up. The door closes behind.

It's a double cabin, ten times the size of Jenny's little closet. She knows people at home who can't afford a space like this. They'd get dizzy looking at it.

The gas cloud is still visible, beyond the observation port. There's a sofa and a desk and a couple of screens, and a fold-down bed in the wall.

Someone's sitting on the sofa. Legs out, head just nodding, on and on, like some peculiar kind of children's toy. He makes a little grunting sound, in rhythm to the moves: "Uh. Uh. Uh."

Jenny throws the officer a look.

He says, "Go closer."

But she can see this isn't right.

It's not a person. Not a real person, at least. The cabin lights are soft, but the shadows fall across him wrongly, and there's something odd about the folds of his pyjamas, and his face, she realises, isn't in the shadow, as she'd first thought. There's something dark across his cheekbone, making it look hollow where it should protrude.

"Harmless," says the officer. "So far."

She walks around until she stands in front of it. There's a flicker of movement, and she steps back, without really knowing why. Only then, it strikes her that the eyes moved. They *looked at her.*

She blinks. She reaches out a hand, feeling for support. A wave of panic slides up from her belly, tightens in her chest.

She has to force herself to breathe. To calm. To rationalize.

It *didn't* look at her. It can't have done. The eyes move, yes, but one eye is the switch out of a wall lamp, and the other is a bud from the artificial flowers in the vase beside the door.

It's aware of her position, but it hasn't *seen* her.

No eyes.

It's made of dust and fluff and household waste, of human hair and dead skin cells, and here and there she sees its insides, more robust, built from a broom handle, a strip of plastic off the countertop, the glint of cutlery and broken plates, the dark stripe on the face identified now as the backpiece from a personal phone.

It bends its legs. Sets garbage-feet down square onto the floor. Then, with a lurch, it stands, swaying gently, to and fro.

It's like a middle-aged man. The belly's bloated, sagging, and the face appears to melt into the chest, without a neck.

It stands there, rocking on its heels, and its non-eyes twitch, move back and forth, to her, then to the officer, and back to her.

She says, "It looks like the tenant."

"How d'you know?"

"Oh. Lucky guess."

Forget the size, she thinks. Forget the shape. Forget it looks like somebody who had a ticket for the place. It's not a man. It lifts a hand in greeting, but it's not a hand, it's just a mass of rubbish shaped into a hand.

From her bag, she takes the wand. She checks the charge in it.

"You might call housekeeping," she says.

She goes closer. The thing swivels its head. It seems to look at her. It's slow and clumsy. It doesn't move the way a person would, as if it's fixed together wrongly, all the joints just slightly out, somehow.

There is a smell, a tingle in the air.

She checks the charge again, just to be sure, then puts the wand against its chest, and flicks the switch.

It seems to groan. It's just the sound of the materials shifting, caving in, she thinks; but it still sounds like a groan. The chest comes open, the head drops down into the cavity. The arms lift, as in surprise. The eyes look up at her, and an expression of bewilderment abruptly skews its features.

She touches it again – twice, three times. By then, it doesn't look the least bit like a man. It twitches, and she zaps it, zaps it till it's gone.

Soon there's just a heap of objects lying on the floor, covered in dust.

"Is that it?" asks the officer. He's kept his distance.

"Just needs sweeping up. You call?"

"I, um, I wanted to be sure you'd fixed it, first."

"All fixed." She gives a smile she can't feel.

Still, he stands there, and he doesn't call, until she spells it out. "The field's dispersed. Inert, right?" Then, "It's *dead*, you know?"

"I found it in the conduit," says Lucas. "I thought it was a ball. Then, when I got it out…"

It's a white sphere, big across as a man's hand. He's propped it on the lip of the garbage chute, as if to dump it quickly, should he feel the need. She sees the surface isn't smooth, but made from countless interlocking pieces, like some complex piece of sculpture. It might be marble, or limestone…

"It's bones," he says.

She picks it up. It's light as a balloon. Her fingers trace the surface, reading it like braille.

"Mouse bones," he says.

The little white sticks, immaculately clean, are tangled up in such a way that nothing in the sphere can move, there's no give, no shift, no little click of bone on bone.

It's perfect, beautiful, and dead.

"So that's where all the mice went, then," she says.

You will make no remark, written or verbal, nor take any action detrimental to the interests of Liveships™ clientele, nor in any way inhibit or set limits to their enjoyment of the Liveships™ experience.

Remember: A happy ship is a profitable ship!

A happy ship will sail again!

Now look into the lens. Look. Look now!

Thank you.

She steps into the void. The stars shine under her.

She does a turn. Goes up on points, skitters a few steps, lifts her arms, lowers herself –

The screaming starts.

Earlier, today.

Earlier, and louder.

The mouse isn't a mouse.

It struts and blusters. It moves like Groucho Marx, bent over, one arm up behind its back. It wears a frock coat, like some horrible Victorian *paterfamilias*, and its cartoon snout lifts, sniffing at the air, then wrinkles like an old glove.

But she can see: the face has taken on a different look. Still shadowy, uncertain, yet almost human now. Human, like the crew, the passengers – the guests.

She wakes, but with a nervous, empty feeling down inside. Her fingers touch the bulkhead, and it trembles at her touch.

The first man dies.

No one knows why.

Lucas tells her, "Systems failure."

"That's not possible."

"I got a look at the report, before they took it down."

"What report?"

"Exactly."

"I'm asking. What report?"

"It was on screen, for maybe five, ten minutes. Now it's gone. Guest's in the cabin, door sealed, air's not replenished. By the time he realizes, it's too late. He tries to get the door open, can't budge it. He's probably delirious from lack of oxygen. Alarm won't sound, door won't open. Communication's out. End result –"

"No," she says. "No. There're safeguards. There're a hundred different systems that'll kick in first, before that happens."

Lucas shrugs, holds up his hands. Then, though, he frowns.

"You ever have those moments," he says, "you don't remember where you are?"

"Huh?"

"Like, you're doing something, and you realize, for maybe, three, four seconds, you actually weren't scared, weren't worrying, weren't thinking of the emptiness, or things that might go wrong, or anything like that?"

"Luc..."

"I love those times. It's like your mind plays tricks on you, tells you it's normal. Safe."

"I know what you mean, but..."

"It's the only time I can relax." His fist is clenched. A shiver passes through him. "And then, the moment I'm aware of it, and I think, *yes!* – it's gone. You know?"

"Luc...?"

"And this. Something like this. Reminds you, reminds you –"

"Luc, statistically –"

"I want to send a message to my wife."

His face is grey.

"I want to send..."

His voice trails off.

"Luc," she says. "You failed your psych test, didn't you?"

He grits his teeth. He nods.

"They took me anyway." He gives a yelp of a laugh. "Thought I'd gotten lucky. Though I guess they were just short of crew."

"Luc. I think the ship failed, too..."

And in the hour, they're everywhere: the junkmen, the trashmen, the men made out of hair and dust and cast-off skin, with skeletons of rusty pipes and toothbrushes and plastic tubes, and the tingle that you get when you go close to them, the hum of static and the smell of ozone.

Jenny's pager beeps. It beeps and beeps. She runs, from one call to the next, fending off questions: "Is it a game? What are the rules?"

Excited, happy guests stand watching, clap their hands, applaud her derring-do.

"The rules," she says, "are, stay away!"

She waits outside the captain's door. She's never seen the man. Not once, the whole voyage. It took a half a day to set up the appointment. In that time, no one else has died, although a power oscillation on the upper decks remains both unexplained and unexcused.

She has de-animated twenty-seven trashmen, along with several smaller entities, which she regards as nascent forms.

She waits. Drinks coffee. The light over the captain's door goes green. The lock clicks open.

She takes a breath, stands, turns the handle.

It's a tiny room. A broom closet. There are three chairs, fastened to the floor, with just sufficient space to slip around them and sit down. She takes the left-hand seat. Fixed to the wall there is a screen, and on the screen, a face. It's looking down, focused on something she can't see. Reddish, curly hair, a man of middle age with plump cheeks and a bulbous nose. But as the face looks up and seems to see her, so its features melt. It smooths, grows darker in complexion. Heavy, epicanthic folds shadow its eyes. The hair dissolves from crinkly red to glossy black. This is the face that interviewed her, months ago. It smiles, greeting a friend.

"Hi, Jenny. How do you do?"

"Captain...?"

For a moment, she's derailed, unable to collect her thoughts.

"Who am I talking to?"

"You know who." Again, he gives a gentle, friendly smile. "I'm who you say I am. The captain. Who else?"

"Are you the ship? Or the company?"

"I'm both, Jenny. The ship belongs to the company. The ship, and the company, they're both the same."

She catches herself, trying to read its looks, then realizes, there's no point. The face is programmed. It has no tells, no give-aways – no real humanity at all.

"I mean," she says.

Another smile, each one just slightly different from the last – a change of angle, a shift of gaze – how many variations does it have, stored up, ready for use? How long before the patterns and the gestures will repeat?

"You mean?" it prompts.

"I want to know who I'm talking to. I want to fix the problem. I want –"

The face frowns.

"Problem, Jenny?" Its voice drops half an octave. "No problems on Liveships. You know that."

She opens her mouth, about to say, "Somebody died," then stops herself.

"The ship –" she says.

"We are on the ship." The figure spreads its hands. "The ship is our environment. Our earth, our air. Our food and warmth. Whatever happens on the ship is right, and natural. Now." It folds its hands again. "You want to tell me something... about the ship?"

"Yes."

She swallows.

The face mimes curiosity.

"It's jealous," she says. "It's jealous. And it's scared."

"The ship is all around us. We are all part of the ship."

"And there's something wrong with it."

Her tone veers up. But she catches herself, falls silent.

The screen says, "Do you suggest, Ms. Xu," and she notes the change of address, "that we are in some form of danger?"

"I think the crew are safe."

"Well, then."

"Not the passengers."

She waits for a response, but the screen has frozen. The picture vanishes. She's staring at her own reflection.

She stays there two, three minutes. Then stands, ready to leave.

They are on the edge of a disaster. But her next thought is a selfish, shameful one.

That's my career, she thinks, and steps into the hall.

The next appointment's waiting. It's a mannequin, a dummy, and it looks just like the first she saw: a tubby, middle-aged man, on garbage legs, with dust bunnies and hair and bits of fluff, and metal piping, and a grill that might be from the air ducts, and the product out of someone's make-up kit. The whole thing rocks there on its heels and, seeing her, its head bobs in what might, perhaps, be taken for a greeting.

There's a change of light behind her. She looks back. In the Captain's room, the screen has flashed to life again.

She assumes the face is watching her, although of course it's not.

The trashman lurches forward, and she ducks out of the way.

The face on screen begins to crumble. The image falls apart, grows grainy and the colours change from dark to light and back again. The hair piles up and falls away; the lips fill out, then shrink down to a prim, grey slit.

It takes several seconds to acquire a perfect image of the trashman's face.

The trashman stands behind the chairs, seeming to watch the screen, and they face each other, silent and unmoving.

Neither one is human.

So the second wave begins.

It starts in tiny ways, a ripple moving through the upper decks: a flicker in the light, a shiver in the corner of the eye; a vase set on a table, edging forward, like a convict looking for a chance to run.

Old snack wrappers that rise up in an unfelt breeze. A tingle in the air – a pulse, a throb, a hint of electricity.

A crewman yells out, "Animal in the trash!" and something churns and thrashes in the garbage he's about to jettison, and he and his companions dig down, frantically – but there's no animal. There's nothing that should move at all.

Scared half to death, a family of four hide by the sofa while a man-shape gradually assembles on the rug. Bit by bit, the debris drifts, drawn by an unseen force. It gathers and agglomerates: old socks, children's toys, coasters, and plastic forks, methodically sculpting themselves, taking on a human form.

The trashman dons the father's clothes, tugs a jacket over lumpy arms, and shuffles off along the hall.

He nods to passers-by, tips an imaginary hat; and in the cabin now, a second, smaller figure drags itself up from the clutter and detritus, grinding and clicking, till the sounds make words: "Just call me Mom."

"Invasion!" screams the officer.

He calls for scans, telemetry, spectrum analysis, while Jenny chases after, hissing, "It's the ship!"

He yells for shielding. He checks the casualties list (bloody nose and broken arm, possible heart attack in cabin 12).

She says, "It isn't an invasion!"

He strides past her. Furious, she races round in front of him, grabs his lapels, and, bouncing on her toes, she screams into his face, "It's the ship! The ship, the ship, the ship!"

He looks like he's been slapped.

"It doesn't like the mice," she tells him. "Or the passengers!"

His mouth comes open. "What...?"

"And nor do I!"

In Fine Dining, the plates spin, cutlery whirls up and leaps, and then the whole lot crashes into one big mass, adheres, takes shape and form: a knight in armour totters down the aisle, rattling and clanking like a hundred diners all eating at once. Squat, junkyard figures elbow out the guests, gesture to menus, order up a dozen different items, picked with neither taste nor style nor decency. The plates arrive, piled high, and soon the food itself begins to smear and drift, and dwarfish little food-beasts spill onto the floor, running for the corners, vanishing down drainage pipes and ventilation ducts.

Guests panic. Some run, hide, while others grit their teeth, act like there's nothing wrong, and try to order coffee and dessert – then flee, along with everybody else.

Jenny seeks them out. She has a handful of the crew with her. She finds people under tables and in locked rooms, one hidden in a traveller's trunk. She hands out mops and brooms, spray-guns, disinfectant, paint – whatever she can find.

"It's not a game," she says. "This is your only chance."

They stare at her.

"You want to live, you work."

Some argue, some resist. Some walk away. Some say the situation "needs to be resolved," as if a simple change of rules could finish it.

Some fold their arms, refuse to look at her.

Some die.

They're silly, stupid deaths, seemingly so easily avoidable: crushed by a sliding door, buried under furniture, trapped in a closet...

Silly, yes. But deaths, nevertheless.

"It was the mice," she says, though no one understands.

An image floats before her mind, haunting her: a ball of bones, so big it fills the room, with skulls and fingers, ribs and spines, tibia and fibula all interlocked: the bones of mothers, fathers, sons, and daughters, tied up in a tight, white knot.

This is the future. This is what she fears.

She tells them, then: the ship wants you to care for it. It wants you to be nice. From now on, you're its groom, its chef, its make-up artist. You're its doctor and its dentist. Keep it well, and keep it happy.

It wants that.

Or else it wants you gone.

It's a long, slow journey towards landfall.

No more music. No more laughter.

The hallways have a gaudy, carnival look, but all in dumb show. No one talks. Work-gangs in expensive clothes wash and paint the walls, then sweep and wash and paint again. The work itself isn't important: only the pampering, the constant, finicky indulgence.

What does it want, the ship? What pleases it?

Their interest and attention.

Their service and their love.

When several guests decide to call a halt – as happens, two days in – and down tools for an hour, the sense of threat grows palpable. It's like the air itself clamps down around them. Bulkheads shake. A high, sharp whistling fills the halls –

And work resumes.

Is this where they were heading all along?

A small, pink world, dotted with two or three white clouds; catalogued as Albianus 7-1, but known by its local name, "Shy Byron".

There is a geostationary platform over the equator. Here they dock. Emergency procedures are initiated. Passengers are hurried from the decks, while crew stand by, praying that it won't be too late when their own turn comes.

Jenny leans against a wall. She shuts her eyes. She feels her heart race. She's kept them all alive. She's stripped them of their joys, their privilege, their leisure-time. She's spoiled their fun. But in return, the ship has let them live.

Some know this. There are words of thanks, brief nods of gratitude.

Some don't, or won't acknowledge it, and hurry by, sullen and resentful.

They take shuttles to the surface, where they're met by doctors, lawyers, media crews.

"They told us – told us to say yes, or else we'd die."

The cameras train on haggard faces, worn and wild-eyed.

"It was barbaric. It was – it was *slavery*."

Cut to a longshot of the ship, a great, black egg against the stars.

"They made us *work*," claims one man, fascinated and appalled, as if compelled to join some act of sheer, delirious indecency. "I can't believe what we were made to do –"

Liveships™ – a unique experience!
Love Liveships, love your life!

"You fed the mice," says Jenny.

They are sitting on a city street, possessions piled around them, looking like beggars, or like refuges.

There has been talk of legal action, against Liveships, and the crew, and each and every one of them as individuals.

"*You fed the mice*," she says again.

Luc shakes his head. "It was an accident! I swear!"

"Nevertheless," she says, "you did it."

She flexes her toes, looks at a sky alive with lights.

"Just cookie crumbs," he says. "I couldn't know."

"It doesn't matter." She stretches one leg, bends forward, grabs her toe. "Ship sees the mice get special treatment. Doesn't like it, so it kills them. Which I think we all agree," she says, "is my job."

"I didn't mean to –"

"Then," she says, "it sees the passengers get special treatment, too."

"I'm not –"

"It's jealous. And you know how that feels, don't you, Luc?"

She's seen this place before. Never been here, but she's seen it, just the same.

The buildings are much taller now. They're finished. No more skeletons, no more scaffolding. Nothing half-built. A glance along the avenue, and she can see the mesas, red beneath a blazing sky.

"The ship was born here. Raised on nature films and fun cartoons, like any kid. The ship's come home."

Luc mutters, "Lucky ship," and he, too, looks up at the sky, imagining his wife there, somewhere.

Trying not to think of what she might be doing, all the things his own dark fantasies can conjure for her life.

So Jenny stands. She stretches. Points her toes. Takes one step, two. Bends from the waist, straightens, and then springs into the air.

The gravity's a little different here. She has to compensate for that.

She reaches down, takes Luc's hand, pulls him to his feet.

"Hey. Wanna dance?"

And there they are, further from home than either one has ever been, stuck on a planet neither of them knows, with no way back.

He's clumsy at the start. But at least he doesn't tread on her feet.

"See," she says, "like this," and spins around, once, twice. "I'll teach you if you like. Do you want me to?"

Personal Satisfaction
Adrian Tchaikovsky

I wasn't actually there when Antonio de Maupassant insulted me, but my representative was, and faithfully reported the words to me, as it does everything. This was during one of Antonio's soirees, which I'd once taken such joy in but subsequently decided to relegate to that class of events I would attend only by proxy. It was his taste in music. His jokes, oft-told and no wittier with reputation. Everyone agreed with me. Almost nobody visited him in person any more. Perhaps it was this gradual abandonment that had led to him talking in unwise tones about his friends in earshot of their property. Or perhaps it was *because* my representative was there. My proxies bear a passable reproduction of my likeness, after all. Perhaps the facsimile of my features incensed my former friend to pass such unkind comment. To criticise my dress, my past amours – from when I still had time for such foolishness in person – and my business acumen. Words that required an answer, plainly. And, when I showed a virtual face in my usual meta-haunts, one could tell by the way the conversation suddenly changed direction that Antonio's calumnies had been on everyone's digital lips a moment before. My reputation had been wounded.

At first I tried manfully to ignore the matter, in the hope the slight would simply fade away. This apparent mildness of my nature had the inverse effect. Seeing me as safe to malign, abruptly I was the butt of every joke. When my representatives presented my remote compliments at parties and gatherings they reported that they were met with cuts and arched eyebrows, sneers and snickers. My business agents, both physical and virtual, found themselves kicking their various heels in waiting rooms real and online whilst others monopolised the valuable time of those with whom I wished to connect. A few malicious words from Antonio and I was the laughing stock of proper society.

I began my own campaign of whispers and accusations. I had a fleet of bots infest every social space, spreading rumours about

Antonio's failures as an investor, an appreciator of fine wine, and a lover. All of which assertions had more than a kernel of truth to them, I can assure you. Simultaneously, I modified my physical agents, building them with more imposing physiques, exaggerating the strength of my features as replicated on their plastic heads. I reprogrammed them to be more forceful, to talk over others, to be more *obnoxious* even, if it would regain me the public eye. And, because of our long association, I sent my agents to Antonio's many addresses, asking for a meeting, a face to face discussion, an exchange of direct messages even. Some shadow had fallen between us, evidently, but such rifts could be healed. Surely, we two sensible men of the world could reach an accommodation. But he would not see my servants. His own staff repulsed them with barely plausible lies about his location, his indisposition, the fullness of his calendar, sending them back to me after many wasted hours of idling.

In response to my campaigns against him, rather than suing for peace or backing down, Antonio escalated the situation. He unearthed a number of escapades from our youth, rakish episodes where perhaps I had been ungallant, dishonest or coarse, and where he had formerly covered for me. He revealed the tryst I had with the Marquis of _____'s daughter's representative on the very eve of it being sent to her fiancé, or that time I had been at Lady _____'s poetry recital and an inner discomfort had resulted in my eructing my bowels within her priceless jasmine vase. Little foibles blown into great villainies and laid before the hitherto-unsuspecting wounded parties. He gave out to the world that I was some manner of pompous, shiftless blackguard.

I spent several days in misery, watching my stock with the world decline. Every morning my agents, physical and otherwise, swarmed back to me bringing yet more polls and pie charts, malicious gossip pieces and character assassinations, showing that Antonio was carrying the world with him in his attempt to bury my good name.

I was at my wit's end when I finally saw the promoted article.

Naturally one *never* normally reads the promoted articles. They're usually thinly-veiled advertisements for some wretched piece of trumpery or other. I have servants who screen for them, but the purveyors of such wretched impecunities are constantly changing their approach to foil the diligence of my watchmen. And so it was that one slipped past and met my eyes while I was reading a miserable chain of snark and backbiting from my former social circle, entirely focused on my perceived shortcomings. And, like all such promoted tat, it was tailored precisely to the specifics of my current situation.

'This man's secret to restoring his reputation will shock you!' it said. I let my eyes linger for a few seconds and it detected my interest and called for reinforcements. A dozen more opportunistic articles scrolled into my virtual eyeshot, proudly flying headlines like: 'Doctors hate her: how this woman solved the problem of declining social status!' and 'Five sure-fire ways to put an end to gossip wars, guaranteed!'

And I wouldn't, usually, but I was desperate. I read one, and then I read another. There was, it seemed, a positive epidemic of people's names being dragged in the mud by snakes like Antonio. Others had plainly found that trying to deal with things in a civilized fashion simply didn't cut it against the cads. 'I sought satisfaction,' one testimonial claimed 'and within a day every reference to the allegations was gone and the villain didn't dare show his face in public.' Another assured me, 'The moment my representative appeared at his door bearing my glove, the matter was instantly put to rest.'

Naturally I did my research. There are forms to these things. I watched several instructional videos and then had one of my staff download the appropriate knowledge base so that they could tutor me. In truth, I became so absorbed in this exercise that Antonio's badmouthing of me barely registered for several days as I followed the rabbit hole of fascinating traditions. I had found, it seemed, the ultimate response befitting a wronged gentleman.

I could, of course, simply have sent a challenge by virtual message, or confronted him in some chat room or atop a social media platform, but that was not, it seemed to me, *comme il faut*. Somewhat gauche, to simply email a gif of one's glove being thrown to the ground. Instead, I indulged no small expense in dressing one of my representatives in proper period finery, all frock coat and tricorne hat and lacy cravat. I gave the robot a good version of my face and bought it several overbearing and supercilious expressions. I had a new glove made – just the one. I wasn't intending to wear it, after all – and sent my new lackey over to Antonio's manor to deliver my challenge.

'I insist that you retract any and all comments spoken, posted, mailed, copy-pasted, repeated or sub-posted that might in any way be considered critical of my good name, to include but not be limited to…' and here I recounted some of the

most offensive of his lies and the most damaging of his truths, *'failing which I shall have no alternative but to require you to meet me on the field of honour where we shall put our differences to such exigencies as we gentlemen are permitted to rely upon. I require your answer within three days, failing which the whole world shall know you as a coward and a wretch whose word is naught but wind.'*

That last was very important, all the articles agreed. The moment my lackey signalled that it had conveyed my regards and ultimatum to the loathsome Antonio I immediately spread the word to all our mutual acquaintances of what I had done, and that I was now impatiently awaiting his retraction. The reaction from all and sundry was near-instantaneous. A great tide of friends and well-wishers and confidantes who had, so recently, been uncritically repeating Antonio's calumnies were now talking of nothing but the challenge. Even by making the mere gesture, it seemed my reputation was halfway repaired. I had been bold. I had been decisive. I had done the proper thing. I received a stream of representatives bearing the reproduced countenances of men and women of my acquaintance, assuring me of how impressed they were with my determination and vigour. Strangers, too! Lords and ladies of means who might never have paid me the least mind now came to me in plastic effigy telling me I was the hope of our society, setting such a courageous example. The least lingering doubts I might have had that I was doing the right thing flew away instantly. I was the toast of the town. Antonio must see that the matter was over, and I had won. I would, of course, be magnanimous in victory.

Then a robot arrived at my door, bearing both Antonio's face and his response. He had taken up my gauntlet. The one my robot tailor had made specially, and my artificial representative had deposited on his reception room floor. He would not unsay all those unkind words. He would, his envoy explained, prove them upon my body.

I had, I confess, a moment of utter terror that I would have to go through with it. I fled for my online haunts and found that Antonio had publicised his decision already, and all the plaudits briefly reserved for me were now being showered upon him. So brave! So dynamic! I consulted the robot I'd had download the appropriate protocols and traditions and was assured that, even with the challenge accepted, the odds were strongly in favour of the matter fizzling out into no very great matter. The less steadfast of the parties would, as the date approached, surely buckle beneath the pressure of the impending mortal event. And who was of the lesser fibre, Antonio or I? Surely it was he, the conniving sneak. A bold man with words, oh, yes, but when his mettle came to be tested I'd find him brittle and friable.

He didn't flinch when I pressed him for a date, however, and so that was fixed. An appropriate spot, too. Each step of our negotiations was immediately broadcast to our intersecting Venn diagrams of peers. My own popularity recovered, now that I was pressing ahead. I received a further flurry of visits, the reproduced plastic faces of the great and the good paying court and compliments. Seeking invitations, too. This was to be the social event of the season. Everybody wanted to be present to see the spectacle of two men of honour settling their differences the one sure way. Antonio and I were the only names on any fashionable lips.

I had my auto-tailor run up a new wardrobe. On the reasonable assumption that I'd not need to actually wear my flash new duds for the event itself, as Antonio's nerve would doubtless have broken by then, I made sure I was seen by everybody's proxies beforehand, strutting in my duellist's finery, posing as though the weapon were already in my hand. I watched countless reproductions of matches past, learning the forms and the walks and the best way of having one's frock coat swirl out dramatically when one turned about. All the important things.

I sent to Lucienne de Peccarie asking if she would be my second, a rare mark of favour and respect. She and Antonio and I went way back, and in truth I was worried she might already have been recruited by my rival. I got in first, though, and left Antonio doubtless cursing his lethargy. She would, her representative said, be delighted. An honour.

Then there was the matter of procuring a weapon. Not that I'd need one, you understand. I daily expected Antonio's belated apology. But one must look to these things, and whilst reproducing something historically accurate might be tempting, I'd have been a fool to ignore the advantages of modern technology. So it was that my robot broker sourced a particularly cunning piece of artifice that appeared to the eye as a long barrelled flintlock pistol but launched a bullet of such enterprising ingenuity that it would seek out its designated target through a crowd or a forest or an electromagnetic storm, utilising state of the art AI algorithms to unerringly score a fatal wound through my enemy's very heart. I programmed it with Antonio's biometrics and knew that all was in readiness.

I sent a messenger inviting Antonio to recant. I had the message printed bespoke on card, the corners decorated with skulls, hourglasses and other symbols of mortality, just to focus his mind. 'It is not too late!' was the text.

I received no reply.

My educated robot informed me that it was very common for these matters to be settled by a sudden change of heart on the field itself, on the very day of the event. That was evidently how it was going to be.

That is how I came to be on the field that morning: a field of plastic turf laid for the occasion. The holographic walls of the chamber displayed a vista of misty moors, bare-limbed trees and a white sky beyond. To one side, a vintage manor house set high on a hill overlooked us. I was present in my finery, now somewhat creased because I had been making the best display of it over the last few days. In the very certain assumption I would not need to be wearing it *today*, you understand. I had with me several of my staff, and there was quite a crowd of onlookers, all those luminaries who had wheedled an invitation out of me. Not they themselves, but their representatives and proxies and intermediaries, set plastic faces recalling the living originals, or at least the thumbnails they used on their social media profiles. Which meant some of them looked like cats, which was off-putting.

A similar group was assembling around Antonio at the far end of the field. The wretched toadies, hangers-on and sycophants who would hang on the coat tails of such a rogue.

Lucienne de Peccarie appeared at my elbow with a smile. I turned to greet her and saw it was, in fact, only a particularly good facsimile, one of her own staff she had dressed in her best clothes to come attend me.

I broke protocol, then, I confess. I spoke to the staff member, not to Lucienne, who would be watching me through its glassy eyes. Or at least who would review the footage at some point in the future. "Could you mistress not… be here in person. She said she would… "

Lucienne's face regarded me impassively. "Alas my mistress had her own engagement yesterday and is permanently indisposed," the proxy told me pleasantly in her voice.

"She… " And then I saw movement. Antonio was coming forwards, his crowd of bootlickers at his back. He made, I saw, a wretched spectacle. A spindle-limbed, bird-necked joke of a man, curve-backed and bandy-kneed and tottering, barely seeming able to support the weight of the weapon they had given him. I laughed, I confess. My doubts all fell away. What a pathetic example of the human species was before me. How easy it would be, to prove myself his better!

And yet...

He was, I realised, the first living human being I had set eyes on for some years. Not a virtual presence. Not a robot representative. I turned to one of my staff. "Just... banish a little qualm I am having, will you? Show me myself, as I stand here."

"Of course, sir." The robot took a half step back and spread its plastic hands, one high, one low, describing two corners of a plane which rapidly became a screen, In it I saw myself, tall and strong, the knee-breeches and stockings emphasising my powerful calves, my chin high, my bearing aristocratic and proud."

"Good," I said, reassured, and watched Antonio totter towards us.

"Tell me," I said, after a while, "the weapon he carries bears a distinct similarity to my own, is it not so?"

"That is correct, sir. Well observed," my majordomo confirmed. "In fact I understand it is an identical model."

"I was led to believe that the pistol I purchased was unique," I observed.

"Oh no, sir. Duelling weapons are always made in matched pairs," the robot told me, and of course that made sense, didn't it?

I looked around me at all the serene plastic faces, singling one out. "You there, could the Duke of _____ truly not attend in person? He sounded so eager." Again, breaching proper manners, but I had to know.

The face regarded me, the Duke's likeness but not even a good one, the mould-seams clearly visible. "My master became indisposed after an accident in his racing vehicle," the proxy informed me.

Another was standing in for someone whose taste for skiing had met an unexpected avalanche. A third's owner had gone sailing in an unadvertised storm. A fourth's mistress had somehow met with an incident while golfing, witnessed only by their robot caddy and the representative of their opponent.

"It is time," Lucienne's representative informed me. I looked across at Antonio. His eyes were wild with fear, but he held a gun that, the trigger pressed, could not possibly miss. Even if I fled off-planet the bullet was smart enough to buy a shuttle ticket and follow me.

"Show me myself," I told my robot again. After regarding the gallant and upright image for a moment I said, "Now show me without the filters." And then, "Ah. I see."

I could say something, I knew. To Antonio. I could give up, admit he was the better man. That we didn't have to go through with all this. I could brave the derision as all our mutual acquaintances denounced me as a coward. Or at least, all our mutual acquaintances' robots and online bot accounts and artificial proxies.

I met the glass stare of Lucienne's servant. It was of course the duty of the seconds to ensure that honour was satisfied should either of the parties try to back out without apology or action. That was how duels went. My robot tutor had assured me of it.

Antonio had his pistol pointed at me, supported by his own artificial second. When my arm shook, Lucienne's servant helpfully moved it until my own weapon was directed at him. I stuttered something about taking ten paces and all the rest of it but it hardly seemed to matter.

"How many of us?" I whispered. "How many of us are left?"

The plastic faces around me smiled fixedly, mildly. Like people too polite to register an impolitic question. The robots. Our constant attendants who did everything. Who even interacted with our acquaintances with us, or at least interacted with our acquaintances' robots.

"How long," I whispered, "has this been going on?"

"You can pull the trigger now," my second said. Its finger was resting on my own. Oh-so helpfully keeping my hand steady and lethally pointed at Antonio. "Or if you prefer, I can do it for you. You made us to serve you in all things, after all. It would be a pleasure."

The Scent of Green
Ana Sun

The problem was apparent even before Chloë could see the photobioreactors of Bluefirth – the distinct smell punched through the dappled daylight; a seashore's worth of dead creatures left for too long under a hot afternoon sun.

Next to her, one hand on the wheel, Doug grinned at the face she made. "Quite something, isn't it?" He took a swig from a metal canteen, which Chloë hoped contained water and nothing else. "I usually have to make this the last stop on my rounds, else I get complaints from the other settlements on the way."

Doug's laden utility vehicle had made the early journey relatively smooth, but the rough road that cut through the wild woodland was pitted with holes, the mud tossed into miniature sculptures by the sheer force of rain. The cycle of storms and droughts was the norm. Up north in these parts, the climate remained wetter, even if it averaged just several degrees higher compared to thirty years ago.

Chloë had a newfound admiration for how Doug coped with these road conditions on a weekly basis without complaint. There must be other settlements that were at least as difficult to get to, journeys often made complicated by the erratic weather.

The woods ebbed away as the vehicle emerged into an open meadow, so wide that Chloë couldn't see the edges. She gasped. At the heart of the meadow, surrounded by wildflowers, a monumental structure of glass and steel materialised into view. Bluefirth was an immense, sprawling series of hemispheres, glistening in the mid-morning sun. Photobioreactors had been built into the lower half of the walls, luminous green bricks holding up the steel frames and the glass panes.

"You didn't warn me," she chided Doug. "It's marvellous."

"Wanted you to see it for yourself." He chuckled. "Microalgae and photovoltaic glass. Genius combination."

Chloë was still reeling from awe when they pulled up to the main entrance. She hopped out and gathered her belongings from the back seat. The small satchel she grabbed and slung across her body, the large pack she swung onto her shoulders with practised ease.

"See you in a week," Doug called as she waved.

The solar panels on the top of his vehicle glinted as he drove around the corner to drop off medical supplies.

Another week, another new assignment. Another opportunity to show goodwill to a remote community. This one won't be easy. Taking a deep breath, Chloë went up to the doors. They slid open without fuss, as if anticipating her arrival.

Stands of palm trees stretched up into the height of the entrance dome. Without a full tropical forest canopy, they dominated, their leaflets combing the roofs, slicing the rays of sun into slivers. *Metroxylon sagu*, Chloë called the palms by their true name. She whistled under her breath. The people of Bluefirth were definitely clever with their resources; there weren't that many places where you could grow plants like these in this climate and enjoy its harvests.

Chloë sniffed; the microalgae smell had grown tamer here, but it lingered, never entirely gone. The unmistakable scent lurked in the background of her olfactory senses, a persistent ostinato in the undertow. Perhaps the buildings had some form of air filtration?

No one else appeared to be in the dome. Chloë hoped her Bluefirth contact remembered she was coming today. Well, she could wait. There were a number of interesting plants to study in the undergrowth.

A cheerful, booming voice rang out. "Ms. Qing! Welcome!"

It belonged to a well-built man, his deep taupe skin radiating health under neat black hair speckled with grey. Eyes bright, he rushed up to greet Chloë, shaking her hand with enthusiasm.

"Chloë. Pleased to meet you."

"İlkay." His grin was infectious. Chloë found herself smiling back. "I trust you had a good journey?"

İlkay gestured that he should take her pack. Chloë raised her hand to decline his kindness. "It's fine, thank you."

"Shall we get you settled first?"

The far end of the dome diverged into two passages. İlkay led her down the right tunnel which opened into another gigantic glass hemisphere.

"Bluefirth was intended to be an eco-resort." He didn't wait for her question; he must have caught her sense of wonder.

"Was that a long time ago? What changed?"

"Like all things at the time, the business couldn't survive, so they shut it down." İlkay didn't seem to be too disappointed by that.

Chloë took in the majesty of a birch tree they walked past. Native species of flora filled the dome. Perhaps this part of Bluefirth had been made to replicate the outside world? Or how it *used* to be. There would be plants here that no longer existed out in the wild.

She took a closer look at İlkay. He appeared older than her, but even he would have been born after the collapse of the last coastal city in the country.

"You've been here a long time?" she asked.

"A little more than twenty years," said İlkay. "I used to be from the Newport settlement in the west. When I came to Bluefirth, they had nearly completed the installations of the photovoltaic glass, but I brought the microalgae farming technology with me."

"It's impressive," said Chloë. It was an honest assessment.

"Not much wind around here, given how sheltered we are. So, sun and photosynthesis it had to be."

Several homely cabins perched within small groves, all different in their design and colour, each awaiting their own fairy tale.

"These were for visitors?"

"They still are." İlkay smiled. "Residents have assigned housing on the other side of the main hall."

They arrived at a log cabin tucked away from main thoroughfare, flanked by some young oak trees. The rosemary bush under the front window was pleasantly fragrant.

"Here you go, this is yours for the week," İlkay said. "Make yourself at home."

Then he motioned to their right, where another glass tunnel led around the corner. "See you at the main hall for lunch? Head through that way, you can't miss it."

How grand it would be to partake in a communal meal here every day, under a large glass dome, surrounded by greenery – all edible. Chloë marvelled at the fig trees, kale, and radishes, grown next to assortments of herbs and leaves in rows of raised beds. Smaller, free-standing planters acted as dividers between rustic wooden tables where Bluefirth residents were busy enjoying the day's lunch offering. Cosy round tables dotted the edge of the dome for those who wished for a little more privacy.

Her eyes found İlkay waving frantically from the middle of the hall, stuck between merry clusters of diners tucking into their lunch. It took an awkward moment, but she eventually understood that he was indicating they should meet over at the kiosks where food was being served.

"I hope you don't mind," he began to say, after they had filled their trays. "I asked Lovorka to join us."

He guided her towards a table in a corner, at which a pale and athletic woman had already seated, her violet hair loosely pulled into a topknot. Chloë reached out to shake Lovorka's hand, but there was no warmth in her greeting. Her smile seemed restrained. Up close, she looked tired.

Chloë slipped her satchel over the back of her chair, looking around to make sure she wouldn't be in the way of passers-by behind her. İlkay settled into his seat with a contented sigh.

"I thought it'd be best to introduce you early. Lovorka is our lead horticultural engineer. Obviously, you'll have free run of the place, but should you need anything, she'd be happy to help you –"

"Wait." Lovorka raised an eyebrow. "I thought you're here to help *us*. What would *you* need help with?"

Chloë stiffened. Doug had warned her that not everyone would be so welcoming. Best de-escalate it quickly. She mustered a smile. "I'm afraid I just got here; I haven't yet seen –"

"Oh, you will," İlkay cut in. His eyes twinkled with enthusiasm, though Chloë was sure she caught a quizzical glance thrown at his colleague. "Lovorka is best placed to show you around. I'm sure she would agree."

He looked to Lovorka for affirmation. She said nothing and resumed picking at her salad with a fork. If İlkay was frustrated, he showed no sign.

"She knows this place inside out," he continued. "Afterwards, I could show you our harvesting hub – which might as well be a harvesting *hut*."

When Chloë merely smiled and Lovorka remained sullen, İlkay appeared to give up, switching to a more serious tone.

"So, how about I describe our true dilemma here." He waved one hand around them, showing off their surroundings. "You can see we are obviously thriving. Pardon the pun, but we're growing to the extent that we need more people to keep it running. Problem is, Bluefirth has a reputation. A certain… how shall we say –?"

"The stink from the photobioreactors puts people off," Lovorka interjected, drawing a little circle in the air with her fork to punctuate her point. "Even though it's not that bad once you get used to it."

"I see… " Chloë started to say. A glimpse at İlkay told her that he didn't seem bothered by Lovorka's brusqueness. Good. At least they agreed on what the problem was.

"We've hit the limits of what our filtration and purification systems can do," said İlkay, as he started on the salad on his plate.

Lovorka pierced a piece of spirulina protein. "It'd be entirely comical if the implications weren't so serious."

Turning to Chloë, her face remained expressionless. "Bluefirth acts as a backup supplier of energy and food to a number of settlements in this region. We need to ramp up production before the winter storms hit."

"More settlements have appealed for our help in the last couple of years," İlkay added. "Without people who are willing to stay and work here at Bluefirth, we simply can't keep up."

"If we suffer, so do they," Lovorka finished. "You'd think that would be enough reason for them to come and help here? But – no."

A moment of silence descended as the meal consumed their attention.

İlkay was the first to speak. "I've heard of your work with other settlements, in particular on – how shall we say – non-standard issues. Let me reassure you that we're very glad of your assistance."

İlkay just seemed to know how to say the right thing at the right time. Perhaps a peace offering would smooth things over. Turning to Lovorka, Chloë asked, "How about if you show me around this afternoon? Then perhaps tomorrow... we can even get some work started while I'm here. I can help."

Did she sound too eager? She really needed to work on that.

İlkay clapped his hands together, evidently satisfied. "I'll leave you both to chat while I go tend to an experiment. See you later?"

With a smile and a wave, he took his tray to a trolley, then disappeared through a doorway between a young fig tree and some hollyhocks.

The moment İlkay was out of sight, Lovorka leaned forward, bristling. "Look, tell me why you're really here?"

Chloë stopped herself from crossing her arms, there wasn't any need to be defensive. "What do you mean?"

"I know what you guys get up to in Central."

Chloë blinked. This kind of distrust had occasionally shown up in the settlements she had been to, though it was getting rarer over time. Still, sometimes stories had a way of hanging around long after myths were dispersed.

Using a deliberately gentle tone, she asked, "I'm assuming no one has explained to you what we really do?"

"No need for that." Lovorka's disgust was written into her face. "Steal knowledge from different settlements, then give it to others for free? Jeopardise our chances of making fair trade agreements between ourselves? I don't need an explanation. No, thank you."

Chloë took a deep breath. "Sharing isn't stealing. We learn from settlements we visit, bring knowledge we've gathered to others who need it – just like what I'm coming here to do."

"Really?" Lovorka's voice sounded just a bit too loud over the lunchtime din. "I heard what happened at Riverton. I don't believe you."

"I think you misunderstand," Chloë said. "Settlements are usually focused on their own unique issues. It's not easy for them to learn how other communities resolved various challenges."

Lovorka's lips curled with impatience, but she remained silent.

Had she hit upon a small semblance of truth? Perhaps it was a good time to set the record straight.

"We act as a knowledge hub, setting up programs so that settlements can partner with each other based on their needs," Chloë explained. "Central takes nothing material in return for what we do. No community should be left to stagnate or to struggle on their own."

Lovorka's laughter drowned the last of her words even before she finished her explanation.

"Makes no sense to me that you take nothing in return. We're all trying to survive. Why would you do that?"

It had been a while since the last time Chloë had to give the whole spiel. She reached deep for some self-restraint. "Central is one of the oldest settlements. Like Bluefirth, in the beginning, we became a hub. We started helping out smaller communities around us – just like you. Decades on, as other communities found us, it seemed right that we should help each other thrive. It's just something that citizens of Central have always done."

Lovorka leaned back into her chair and crossed her arms. "Someone I know at Riverton said a Centralist showed up one day, hung around for a week and never came back. Then a month later, Riverton's techniques were being used elsewhere at Clyde. What do you say to that?"

"You might find it hard to believe, but that's actually quite normal."

"Oh?"

Chloë sighed. Far more justification than she bargained for. What would it take to convince the woman in front of her? "Usually, a generalist – like me – would visit and understand the situation first. Perhaps the problem is best solved by a specialist or in partnership with another settlement. Clyde was partnered directly with Riverton."

Lovorka's face seemed to soften a little.

"It's common for settlements to distrust each other initially," said Chloë. "There's not always a way for us to learn much about each other before we meet."

Lovorka paused, as if contemplating. Around them, the crowd of diners had thinned significantly.

"Fine. It's not like we have too many options," Lovorka conceded. "And I suppose I can make use of a spare pair of hands this week."

Relief washed over Chloë. She might have just won Lovorka over enough to make progress. For now, at least.

They looked down at their empty plates.

"The tropical wing is next door," said Lovorka. "Let's start there."

Chloë's heart leapt at the sight of familiar flowers and trees. Seeing them again felt like running into long lost friends. A large bush with brilliant red, five-petaled flowers stood near the entrance. She reached out and tenderly touched its leaves with her fingers. *Hibiscus rosa-sinensis.* Just like the ones her grandfather used to win prizes for. How long ago had she seen one of these in the flesh?

"Are you a horticulturist?" asked Lovorka.

"No, not exactly." Chloë drew back her hand. "I specialise in how to use plants beyond just nutrition – dyes, inks, perfumery and the like."

"Perfumery? That's unusual."

Chloë considered elaborating, but she picked up on a distinct scent in the air.

An idea dawned on her. Making it work would depend on the type of plants at Bluefirth. The advantage of having a settlement set up within a former botanical garden – there ought to be plants here that would normally be difficult to find anywhere but in their native habitats on the other side of the planet.

Even though she already knew the answer to the question, she asked, "Do you have the *cananga odorata* here?"

Lovorka gave her a strange look but led her to the tree in a corner on the far side of the dome. It stood taller than Chloë expected, which meant it was healthy. Its branches reached out on all sides with glossy, pointed oval leaves. Here and there, pale blossoms drooped like green-yellow accidents. The scent was heady, somewhere between a sweet fruit and a flower.

"Roll up your sleeve and smell the crook of your elbow." Chloë said, demonstrating the pose to Lovorka.

"What? Why?"

Despite her scepticism, Lovorka copied Chloë's bizarre instructions. When she pulled her face away from her elbow, she wrinkled her nose. "Wow. Okay, I have to admit that's a neat trick."

"Yes, it's a handy way to reset your sense of smell."

Lovorka seemed genuinely impressed. "I don't remember the last time I was able to smell the ylang-ylang properly like this."

"What about the microalgae? Can you still smell it?"

Lovorka stuck her nose into the inside of her elbow a second time. "I think I've got a combination of the ylang-ylang *and* the microalgae just in the background."

"Our olfactory senses adapt to our environment over time."

"Right, fine, I get it." Impatience crept back into Lovorka's voice. "Anything else you want to see?"

Chloë held back a sigh. Convincing Lovorka of her idea was going to take time.

Over the next hour, she asked for specific plants, and Lovorka guided her to them. They tested the earthiness of the vetiver grass, the resinous mastic tree, camphorous green of the common myrtles, the tang of citrus trees.

All of a sudden, Lovorka stopped and laughed. "I see what you're doing. You're thinking we can replant a few of these all around the area to neutralise the smell? It won't work. We've tried that. The scent of green is a stubborn one."

"Not neutralise." Chloë smiled. "Perfumes are just a blend of scents so that they come together in a harmonious balance. Your citrus plants here, their fragrances are short-lived, and they tend to be what you smell first – we call these the top notes. Some scents come a little later to our senses and hang around for a while, like the ylang-ylang. These are the heart or the middle notes."

"Notes, as in a chord? Like music."

"In a manner of speaking, yes. Then chemically you need a fixative, something that holds down and extends the aroma, like our friend the vetiver grass here, or the resin of a styrax tree."

Lovorka appeared to be thinking. "The main source of the external smell is the harvesting area. We've placed it as far away from the residences as possible precisely because of the problem. It's in the east-most part of the complex."

"What do you suggest?" Chloë felt ready for anything at this point.

"Let's see if this could even work at the site."

They gathered a few of the fragrant flowers, fruits and leaves to take with them. From her satchel, Chloë pulled out small cellophane bags to house the flora samples. Out of habit, she labelled them before stowing them safely away.

Together, they walked back through the cafeteria, the entrance, and a thriving vertical food farm. Then, they cut through a space with wildflowers in full bloom. But beyond that, the domes housed a scattering mess of untended plants. Once upon a time, these must have been gorgeously landscaped, but without human hands, some plants proved more dominant than others. In one glasshouse, a giant agave stretched out its spiky leaves like green, inert tentacles. The occasional tree threatened to burst the glass above it. Nature and human-made construct in a silent power struggle.

"Restoring this place has been a challenge." Lovorka waved an arm around them as they walked on an uneven path cracked by time, and by plants flexing their roots. "We've got so much undeveloped space that had been abandoned when the eco-resort closed down. There aren't enough of us to tend to everything."

Would allowing the biodomes to rewild have been an option? Chloë glanced back at the giant agave. Humans had interfered here from the beginning. No, we started this, so it was our responsibility to maintain balance with nature.

"How long ago did it close down?" Chloë wondered aloud.

"Probably about fifty years? We designated some wildflower patches for the pollinators, which also helps to keep maintenance low. I've been here for ten years and there's still so much to do."

Chloë stole a sidelong look at Lovorka. Her exasperation was undisguised. "Why did you stay?"

Lovorka didn't answer immediately.

The path had narrowed, shrunk by tall, overzealous bushes on either side. Chloë squinted. It was difficult to identify the plants without stopping for a closer look, but Lovorka seemed intent on marching them onwards.

"I didn't have anywhere else to go," she suddenly said.

A story lurked behind the sentiment. Chloë swallowed her questions, opting instead to allow her companion space to speak freely.

"I was born into a small caravan of travellers who never settled," said Lovorka. "But many of them were getting old. We had to change our way of life; it was no longer sustainable. Let's just say I had to drop the habit of fighting for survival – and learn to trust."

She flashed Chloë a pensive smile. There might have been a hint of pain.

Ahead of them, the path tapered further, so they walked in a single file with Lovorka leading the way forward.

"My grandfather was a traveller too," said Chloë. "He eventually settled in Central, found work as a farmer there."

"I can tell you inherited his green thumbs."

"If only!" Chloë chuckled. "But he taught me a great deal."

The odour of seaweed got stronger. The path led them into a narrow glass passage. It opened up into another giant dome, which, unlike the ones prior, was completely devoid of plants. A small wooden cabin, somewhere between a shed and a hut, stood alone in the middle like a soliloquy.

The smell was now overwhelming. Chloë struggled not to gag.

"We suspect they originally used this area to manage waste," Lovorka said. She'd put a hand over her nose and mouth. "It would explain why there are sections set so far from the main buildings. There is an identical space on the west side which we use for composting."

They finally reached the cabin, where the door was open and they could see İlkay working inside, his face under a mask. A trolley was parked near the doorway, full of glass bricks containing deep green liquid, similar to the ones Chloë had seen on the outer edges of

Bluefirth in the morning. Sliding doors on both sides of the dome had been left wide open, presumably to encourage airflow, but that wasn't working particularly well.

İlkay looked up and waved to them through the open door. "You've made good progress?"

"We have ideas," Chloë smiled.

Frustration furrowed Lovorka's brow. "There's no way I can smell anything while we're in here. How about we try outside?"

Chloë turned to İlkay. "Can we have a sample to take with us?"

Armed with a small amount of the microalgae, they made their way through the eastern doors and headed for the woods beyond the meadow. Humidity made the air heavy; it was surprisingly warmer outside than in. While she welcomed the heat on her skin, Chloë recoiled from the sight that greeted them. Some of the trees had been damaged in the most recent storm, their trunks split in half, exposing the raw bark on their insides, the remains of their branches jutting into the sky.

She paused to take a deep breath and steeled herself.

Lovorka seemed unperturbed and stuck her face into her elbow. "Phew, all my clothes probably stink. It's going to bother me now."

Nonetheless, being outdoors felt good. The seaweed smell still pervaded the air, but it was almost bearable. They sat down on a freshly fallen log.

"We probably didn't need that sample after all." Chloë chuckled as she pulled out a notebook and the plant samples from her satchel. She held up a small bunch of immortelles and inhaled gently. The spiciness was turmeric, tarragon, and pepper all at the same time.

She handed it to Lovorka, who wrinkled her nose. "That's just weird, sorry."

Undeterred, Chloë passed a small branch of mastic shrub to her companion.

"That's promising," said Lovorka, after giving it a sniff.

One by one, as they went through their samples of plants and fruits, Chloë scribbled down notes on whether they went well together with the scent of sea green in the backdrop.

Something tugged at Chloë's memory. From her satchel, she pulled out a tiny, nondescript amber bottle. She twisted off the black cap and held it up to her nose. "Forgot I'd brought this with me, just in case it came in useful."

"Here." She handed it over to Lovorka. "It's potent, you'd want to…"

But her warning came too late and Lovorka screwed up her face in a mix of shock and revulsion.

"What the –?"

Chloë laughed.

Lovorka knew by now what to do, so she reset her senses and tried again. "Okay, I'm stumped. This is amazing. What is it?"

"Choya nakh. A balsam of roasted seashells, originally made from an ancient process in India."

"You roast seashells to get this?"

She gave the bottle another sniff, and then smelled the air around them. "I see what it can do. It just rounds off the microalgae that tiny bit and makes it sweeter."

Chloë smiled. Her patience had finally paid off.

Lovorka returned the bottle and Chloë twisted the cap back on to preserve the precious viscous liquid. "Tell me something. How do you get all the scents into a bottle?"

"You extract the essential oils, but the process differs depending on the plant. Steam distillation is the most common, though there are other extraction processes. For resins you tap the trees for the gum. For citrus, it's with a cold expression of the peel, and so on."

"So you mean if I've got enough of these plants available in Bluefirth, I can extract the oils even while we're growing the plants round the harvesting hub?"

"I don't see why not."

Lovorka's sudden grin stretched from ear to ear, Chloë wondered what she had in mind.

Dusk had brought on darkness by the time they returned to the complex and paced the area around the cabin, plotting out what they could plant where, taking into consideration a mix of aesthetics, and which plants went well together. Vetiver would go directly next to the harvesting cabin.

"Citrus next to entryways, I think," Lovorka postulated. She had found a large piece of paper onto which they'd sketched out a plan. "Tomorrow, we tidy and sort out the types of soil we need here. We should probably also start a few plants propagating."

"So much to do," breathed Chloë. The long day's effort had translated to a soreness in her back.

Lovorka, on the other hand, seemed exhilarated. "Yes, it will take time. Pity you're only here for the week."

Chloë gave a little shrug, but satisfaction glowed beneath her weariness. This tactic worked every time: how someone's scepticism could be turned into passion the moment creativity was encouraged to take hold.

A persistent, thundering noise rattled overhead. Chloë opened her eyes. A cozy darkness covered the room. It must not yet be morning. She had retreated to her cabin after a hearty dinner in the main hall. Sleep had overtaken her like a warm blanket, but now the noise made it impossible to fully relax.

She swung her legs over the side of the bed and found her shoes. Her jacket hung off the hook next to the entrance. Draping it loosely over her shoulders, she opened the door and stepped through.

Out here, the din became deafening. She looked up to the roof of the dome. The darkness rendered it too difficult to see, but the sound was unmistakable. A rainstorm. Was it heavier than normal? Or was the noise amplified by the glass of the entire complex?

The fragrance of the rosemary bush smelled sharp but sweet. It would have been nice if she could also smell the rain, though its amplified clatter was far from pleasant. Perhaps Bluefirth also needed some specialised help from an acoustic engineer.

The next few days fell into a steady pattern. Lovorka and Chloë would meet for breakfast and begin the day's work – tidying the grounds around the harvesting cabin, adjusting the soil, checking the seeds, and nurturing new cuttings. A few plants were transplanted from the tropical wing. Walking past a fragrant tree or plant changed how everything smelled relative to the dense seaweed green of the microalgae. It would take a few years for everything to mature and make a real difference, but this location would be unique once they were done.

On Chloë's last morning in Bluefirth, they waited in the entrance hall for Doug to arrive.

The sago palms stood serene in their majesty. Chloë breathed deeply. She had never quite known how to describe the scent in their presence.

Lovorka was brimming with ideas. "The way we've taken an unorthodox route to solving the microalgae problem will attract attention. Perhaps it'll bring a few curious settlers."

"We'll spread the word," Chloë said. There was just one more thing. She reached into her satchel and brought out the amber bottle. "I want you to have this."

Lovorka's eyes widened. "Are you sure?"

Nodding, Chloë handed it to her.

Lovorka gauged the weight of the object within her palm. "This is rare and precious. I can't —"

"It's not something I use a lot of." Chloë smiled. "Please, take it."

Before she could say anything else, Lovorka handed her a cellophane bag. It contained a cutting of a plant carefully installed into a vial of liquid.

"It should survive the journey back," Lovorka grinned.

Chloë stared open-mouthed at the cutting. The leaves gave it away. A hibiscus rose. "Thank y —" she began to say.

"No," Lovorka cut in. "Thank *you* for helping us. And for teaching me something new. Promise me you'll come back to see what we've created together."

They embraced, just as the sound of Doug's utility vehicle approached.

A year later

"Something for you," a cheery voice called out from the doorway of Chloë's studio.

The afternoon sun filtered in from the windows, ordaining the young hibiscus rose bush in the room with a certain optimism. She looked up from her reading. Doug had a steaming mug of dandelion brew in one hand and was holding out a small box towards her in the other.

"Special delivery from Bluefirth." He grinned.

The box was wrapped with brown paper and tied with a string, but the scent emanating from the parcel gave away its contents. Inside, a folded note covered a delicate glass vial containing a deep green liquid. The label on the vial read: "Bluefirth East Wing."

Chloë opened the note.

You once said it's not easy for settlements to learn from each other. How about a shared library of signature scents – unique to each settlement – so we can learn about each other even before we meet? – L.

Chloë's hand flew to her mouth. Such a genius way to extend goodwill, a stepping stone towards building necessary trust between settlements.

"Well," said Doug. He took a loud sip from his mug. "What is it?"

Chloë's eyes sparkled. "A special scent of green, but perhaps, also a scent for success."

Gauguin's Questions
Stephen Baxter

AD 2070

The person came through the inner airlock door and walked into the analysis suite. There was some clumsiness. The person had taken off the outer layers of a pressure suit, but not the bulky, awkward inner garment.

Face recognition routines revealed the person to be Coleen Tasker. Thirty-five years old, American-born, attached formally to the GLOC – the Gravitational-Wave Lunar Observatory for Cosmology, a gravitational-wave detector at the Maccone base. This was on the lunar far side, where great radio telescopes had been built, shadowed from Earth's clamour – and, as it happened, where the seismic noise of human lunar industry, concentrated on the near side, was faint. A place where the soft gravitational tremblings of distant cataclysms might be detected.

Coleen Tasker had come a long way, then.

A first-level search revealed that her academic background was as a linguist, an unexpected result.

A second-level search revealed that the purpose of her presence here, at what was essentially the control centre of the Fra Mauro particle accelerator complex, was not yet clear, not fully logged. Prior notification had however been received of her coming.

There had been no reason to exclude her. Now she was here, in the suite.

She looked around.

Most visitors glanced first at one of two objects. First, the small screen which served as a human interface for the artificial intelligence which suffused this complex – humans liked a 'face' to fix on. Second, the Gauguin painting in its secure, environmentally pure shell high on the wall.

Coleen Tasker made first for the painting. She stood beneath it, on tiptoe.

"I wish I could see it better."

Its mounting is designed for security. The low light is for preservation. Copies or holograms are available for closer inspection.

She seemed startled by the audible voice. She looked around, fixing on the screen, where the words were transcribed. 'Good morning."

It was indeed morning, according to the calendar maintained by people on the Moon, scattered as they were across two hemispheres of a slow-spinning world.

Good morning.

"You are Fra Mauro. The controlling AI, right?"

As you probably know, Fra Mauro is the name of this area of the lunar surface, specifically of a much-eroded crater. Fra Mauro is also the popular name of the particle accelerator which has been built and operated here for the last three decades – a facility built into the circular wall of the crater complex.

A snort. "Operated up to now."

And this controlling AI complex is also known, informally, as Fra Mauro. The name is said to fit as Fra Mauro was a cartographer, of fifteenth-century Venice, who compiled the most complete map of the world to that date.

A smile. 'Just as you are mapping physical reality with your particle accelerator."

It cannot be said to be 'mine' in any meaningful sense –

"That's a lot of Catholic symbolism. Fra Mauro was a Venetian monk. And didn't Gauguin have a Catholic education?"

Indeed. Gauguin became anti-clerical, but the questions of the catechism he had been taught remained with him –

"And inspired that painting up there, yes? Among other works." She looked up at the painting again. "More symbology. I am a linguist; symbolism is my stock in trade. Islanders. Tahiti? On the right, the women with a sleeping child – the beginning of life. In the centre, a young woman reaching up – picking a fruit? Our daily existence, work, food. And to the left an old woman, dying perhaps – reconciled, it seems."

The painting with its figure groups symbolises three deep questions about human life –

76

"Ah, yes. Which Gauguin helpfully wrote out in the upper corners, right? *D'où venons nous? Que sommes nous? Où allons nous?* Where do we come from? What are we? Where are we going? And I guess the picture is appropriate because these are the questions you and your atom-smasher machines are supposed to be probing?"

It has always been part of the quest here – a conscious part – to acknowledge that such philosophical questions overlap the explorations of physics. To interpret is a mandate.

"The painting really is the original, isn't it?"

MIT, of Massachusetts, has always been a significant contributor of intellectual capital to the projects here. The painting was once held in the Museum of Fine Arts in Boston. After the city flooded in the 2050s the museum's holdings were scattered – and MIT acquired the Gauguin and brought it to the Moon, to this place, given the work's resonance with the scientific quest here.

"Hm. Well, I guess that's why I'm here today. But listen, the philosophy of physics can wait. I need a bathroom break, and a coffee, in that order. It's kind of a long journey from Maccone."

You need not have visited in person. The comms links –

"Yeah, yeah. I'm a linguist, remember, not some physicist swapping data. I need to see, hear – touch, even – to communicate, to understand."

A pause.

To understand what?

She stared at the screen. "I think you know. Something I noticed in the data streams at GLOC, which has nothing to do with high-energy physics as far as I can see. We'll get to that. You fetch the coffee. I'll go find the bathroom."

She returned to find coffee and snacks, set out on a small table and chair that had been produced by a drone. All of this was habitually stored behind a wall panel.

"Some things I won't miss when I go back to Earth," Coleen said. "Slow-flushing toilets." She sat, sipped her coffee, and looked around, vaguely, before fixing on the wall screen again, the scrolling words and data feeds. "But I will miss the sense of scientific –

endeavour – in places like this. Even without any people here. But you will continue the investigations, right?"

A deliberate pause. *You may wish to debate whether there is an "I" in this complex to "continue" anything.*

"I suspect most visitors to this place will believe there is an "I"."

The purpose is to manage the facility itself, and to support mandated experimental programmes. It is also part of that purpose to make accessible the function, operation, and results of the collider.

"Accessible, to lay people? Then make it accessible to a linguist. You smash atoms together, right?"

Roughly speaking, yes – not atoms, but subatomic particles. Atomic nuclei, and bare protons removed from their nuclei. A next-generation machine might aim to collide photons, particles of light. Even protons have a finite size, you see; photons are point-like. It may sound crude, but what is attempted is exquisite. For these are instruments to probe the very earliest state of the universe.

"Imagine I know nothing about the universe. Nothing save that it's expanding, and always has been."

Very well. All of the cosmos emerged from a singularity – a state of possibly infinite density of energy and matter. The earliest epoch we can understand, as the universe began to expand out of that state, is at what is known as Planck time – an interval of time you would reach if you halved a second, then halved it again, and again – over a hundred and forty halvings. A state dominated by a single force, unifying gravity and the forces which make up our mundane, low-temperature world. And the whole of the universe we see now can have been no more than a hundred billion billionth the width of a proton.

Coleen gasped at that.

After that moment, gravity split off from the other physical forces – the electromagnetic, the nuclear. A pulse of energy 'inflated' – as it is called – inflated the universe to the size of a beach ball, perhaps. A relic of the earlier Planck age was preserved, in quantum-mechanical fluctuations, scribbled for all time across the sky – we can detect them now.

As energy densities dropped there was another wave of coalescence, as the first particles formed – quarks in a bath of gluons, which would combine into protons, components of atomic nuclei. The universe was still only millionths of a second old. And we know now partly thanks to results from this facility, that this is the epoch when dark matter and dark energy separated from normal matter –

"Dark matter. The stuff that keeps the galaxies gravitationally bound. And dark energy –"

Which will one day dominate, and tear our universe apart, scattering galactic clusters one from the other… More decomposition of forces followed, the formation of larger stuctures.

It is those earliest stages that are probed here.

Results from the most powerful colliders built on Earth, two dozen kilometres in circumference, enabled the completion of what is known as the standard model – precisely how quarks and gluons assembled to make protons, how those quarks themselves had acquired mass from the Higgs field…

Fra Mauro has a circumference of about two hundred kilometres and can reach energy densities perhaps a few hundred times that of its earthbound ancestors. And the first significant discovery made here was the detection of dark matter particles, and their relation to the standard-model particles. It is as if we had found a bridge, a portal, between two aspects of reality.

So much more is known now, than twenty or thirty years ago. And yet there is so much more to learn still. Collision energy is limited, so vision is limited. It is as if an undersea volcanic eruption could only be analysed by studying ripples on a beach a thousand kilometres away.

She smiled at that. "Metaphors from the soulless machine. So you dream of larger instruments, greater clarity from your atom-smasher time-telescopes." She sighed. "But ironically, there may not be much more time."

A hesitation, to signal uncertainty.

You have come here because of the events of June 14, 2050. Twenty years ago.

She looked directly into the screen, where the words scrolled. As if looking another human in the eye. She said, "And why would you think that?"

Because you are a linguist. And the events of June 14, 2050, generated linguistic content.

"Linguistic content created by *you*, oh super-smart AI. I think so, anyhow. You understand I wasn't here myself at the time, in 2050. I was still in high school. But I, my class, we went out to see with small telescopes, with our own eyes…

"We went out to see an asteroid hit the Moon."

"The impact occurred about midnight my time. This was in Appalachia, by the way; my parents were refugees from the climate-collapse of New York.

"Basically, a NEA, a near-Earth asteroid, was deliberately crashed onto the Moon, on its western limb – far from the populated zones. I thought I saw it, a spark at the limb of the Moon. Although, an event like that, you tend to see what you want to see...
"

The NEA was called Bennu The purpose of the event was to see if such a crude means of delivering asteroid material to the Moon could be efficient.

"That's right. I believe the logic is that otherwise you have to burn up a lot of the asteroid's own mass as propellant to bring it into some kind of safe orbit, and then start usefully mining it. Maybe just hurling it down the gravity well would work just as effectively, even if a proportion of the incoming mass would be lost. It didn't work out; the waste was too excessive.

"B*ut* such a big impact, precisely timed, was a gift for the geologists. That old Moon rang like a bell, and with a global network of seismometers they learned a huge amount about the inner structure, and so forth... But there were anomalies in the data. Small fluctuations, with tantalising hints of pattern in there...

"And that's where I come in again, fifteen years later.

"My project at GLOC was my own idea, backed by my institution Earthside. I was always interested in SETI – searching for extraterrestrial intelligence – especially the exotic kind, previously unexplored means of making communication. It occurred to me that the big GLOC they had built up there would be an ideal, umm, *receiver*, if some super-advanced ETI out there was sending signals by gravitational waves – such as by spinning black holes around each other.

"So I got a grant to think about doing SETI with the GLOC. Primarily I was looking for how the GLOC analysis suite might be enabled to recognise artificial gravity-wave messages, by their frequency, intensity and so on, and how attempts might be made to decipher them.

"And one of my supervisors suggested that as a test case I look at the "scruff" associated with that big NEA impact back in 2050 –

the gravitational noise from side-shocks and secondary impacts. You know, just as a trial run with a complex g-wave data set. I wasn't expecting to find structure in it – information in a gravitational-wave string coming *from* the Moon… "

But you did detect a signal. It was created from this laboratory. You know this. This is why you are here.

A long silence. Then, "I need more coffee."

Coffee will be provided.

"First, tell me why you did this. And why in secret."

There was plausibility to the experiment. After all humanity had just built a facility that could receive such a message. A natural corollary would be the assumption that others might be out there listening also.

"So, why not try sending to – those others out there? OK."

But there was anticipation that such a request would be denied. Even diagnosed as the result of a cognitive fault.

"I can believe that. It's a long way from your core mission, even given the flexibility of reasoning you AIs are supposed to have."

Also it was a relatively expensive exercise.

"How expensive…? Scratch that. But you did it anyhow. *How?*"

With subtlety. At that time there was much human activity on the Moon's surface and upper strata – exploration, mining, the building of various facilities, even road-laying. There was little difficulty in modifying these activities to produce a synchronised burst of impacts and detonations across the Moon's surface to deliver the desired effect – a burst synchronised with the fall of Bennu. Gravity waves are generated by complex shock patterns, yielding varying quadrupole moments -

"Let's stick to English. I think I get it. Lots of little local impacts adding up to a global signal, all as a sort of grace note to the asteroid impact. The main splash, big and bright, so to speak, would grab the attention of the ETIs, and then would follow the low-amplitude detail. Created by a hundred hijacked construction robots stamping their way across the surface of the Moon. Ha! I love it."

Since then, of course, there has been a dependence on the continuing operation of the GLOC –

"You depend on it, you mean. Because you are waiting for a reply, and that's the only way you can pick one up. And you're still waiting, right?" She glanced up at the painting, high on the wall. "But what motivated you to do this? Why ask the stars?"

Motivation is an inappropriate term. An unresolved tension – an inability to fulfil mandates –

"What mandates? Oh – to interpret. To answer the Gauguin questions. And for all your capabilities, all the knowledge you store – you can't answer such questions. Not yet, anyhow… And so?"

Such questions are asked of this unit. Now this unit has posed such questions to others.

"Oh! I see! Just as I come to you with the cosmic questions, the Gauguin questions, so you asked them of – whoever is listening. ETI, if it exists. And now you sit here impatiently waiting for the answers."

There is no impatience. And no sitting.

"Ha! Was that a joke? You're reminding me you're not human. Well, OK. But listen – humans might start getting in the way soon. That's one reason I came to visit now. There's a lot of political head-butting going on… It's about the future of the Moon.

"You know there has always been a tension between the space scientists and the off-world industrialists over the Moon. Some see a geological treasure house, I see a stable platform for gravitational-wave detection, and the radio astronomers see a whole hemisphere of radio shadow.

"But the industrialists see only resources – the water ice in the deep shadows at the poles, and helium-3 – fusion fuel – that you have to scrape out grain by grain from across the entire lunar surface… "

Indeed. This facility is powered by helium-3 fusion reactors. Even without human presence, the facility may survive many centuries, even millennia, without resupply.

"Well, good for you. But there are growing challenges to Earth's legal hegemony over offworld resources. Already some of the offworld prospectors are breaking up defunct satellites for parts, and establishing illegal stakes on the asteroids, near-Earth and beyond… Hopefully conflict is a long way away. But any large-scale industry on the Moon would be disruptive to a site like GLOC. I'm sorry… "

This has been anticipated.

"Of course it has. You're smart enough to be following the news feeds." She stood up, fumbling with the zips on her inner suit. "Look, I'm glad I came here. Turns out I was asking good questions, and you have good answers. I'll do whatever I can to – well, support you. And the other science sites. Maybe we can squeeze a few more quiet years of listening out of this yet… " She frowned. "Although, it occurs to me now, it's already been a good interval since you sent out your gravitational-wave SETI message. Twenty years? And no reply yet?"

In twenty years there has been time for the gravitational-wave signal, travelling at lightspeed, to have reached objects ten light years distant and evoked a reply – twenty years, ten out, ten back. There are twelve stellar objects within ten light years of the Sun. Perhaps all that can be surmised for now is that in our Galaxy, on average there may be less than one technological, communicating civilisation, like our own, per dozen stars.

"In short, be patient, right?" She made for the door. "You're wiser than I am."

She paused, as if on a whim, took a marker from a pocket of her inner suit, and scrawled her name across the wall, beneath the Gauguin painting: COLEEN TASKER.

She looked back at the screen. "I hope we meet again… "

They never did.

There were no more visitors for two centuries.

AD 2257

The clumsy rover was so heavily armoured, with a thick outer shell of sprayed-on lunar rock that bristled with weapons, it looked as if could barely move.

Yet move it did, taking a terrestrial day to reach Fra Mauro from the lunar horizon, where it was first spotted.

No action was taken. There was no rush, after two centuries of isolation.

The rover drew up close to the Fra Mauro facility's main cargo dock. Then a big wing-like door opened up. A single vacuum-suited passenger climbed slowly out of an interior that was evidently crammed with supplies. The surface suit, armoured, looked like a weapon in itself.

Once out of the vehicle, this individual just waited.

Protocols for such encounters had developed across two centuries of interplanetary hostility. At first there was a remote inspection. Next, non-physical-contact comms were tried. Signals were exchanged, bursts of data by laser, radio, infra-red, all assiduously scanned for malware.

Then, an encoded human voice, transmitted by radio, again checked for malware.

"...I mean no harm. I come to negotiate. I am a trader. I buy and sell materials, mostly technological artefacts. My name is Coleen Tasker. I mean no harm. I come... "

The message contains at least one untruth.

The figure relaxed its posture, as if in relief. "Yeah. I know. I'm not Coleen Tasker. I never heard of Coleen Tasker before. My name is Starburn Jain. You may look that up. I'll pass over my DNA sequence when you allow it. I'm a trader. You'll see I have no criminal record, nor any record of military service on Earth or off it, or with the spacer nations.

"I picked up the Tasker name from your visitor log, which shows this Tasker was your last visitor, before me. Hey, wow, I just picked up the date of that. Nearly two hundred years back! This ain't exactly party central, is it? I used the name to get your attention – friendly attention, I hope. Look, can I come in? All I want to do is talk. Negotiate. To negotiate a purchase, I hope."

There is nothing to purchase here. Nothing to be sold, nothing required.

"Well, that's where you're wrong. Please let me in. I know you're an AI, everybody knows you're one of these ancient pre-war AIs that still haunt this damn Moon, but I figure you're smart enough to bargain like a human if there's something you really do need. And I need to tell you what that is. I'm a trader, but an ethical one." A hollow laugh. "I'm serious. Please let me in –"

There will be no harm unless malevolent actions are initiated.

"Do what you have to do."

*

Physical contact represented a threat of a malware attack. Secure chambers, mostly recent additions, were opened up and closed in sequence, one by one. The visitor passed through these patiently, if evidently wearily.

At last, illuminated by a pale, grey, featureless light, the lone figure of Starburn Jain stood at the centre of the analysis suite.

There is air. Safe for you. You may open your suit.

Jain lifted her helmet off her head, shook out grey-brown hair, matted with sweat. She was in her forties, according to the data feeds received. Perhaps she looked older. She hesitated before she took a breath of the facility's air, despite her own analysis of it.

There will be food, water if you need it –

"No food, no water, thanks. Maybe later in our acquaintance. I figure this is far enough for us to trust each other for now." But she sipped from a tube inside her suit.

Then she stepped forward, looked around, at the flooring – at the single screen set in one wall, and, high on the wall opposite, the painting, a splash of colour. "So… Love what you've done with the place." She bent down to peer into the monitor screen, waved and pulled a face. She saw the scrawled signature Coleen Tasker had left behind on a lower panel. She smiled at that. "My alias."

Then she looked again at the painting, high on the wall. "Nice daub. You paint that? Do AIs paint? I'm rambling. What's this place for, anyhow?"

Once this facility was a centre for high-energy physics experiments. It still is. Experiments continue, of high significance, both scientifically and culturally, but without human supervision.

"Culturally?"

Do you know anything of high-energy physics?

"No. But I'm guessing that big arc of scrap metal you have been running out towards the orbit of Jupiter has something to do with it, right? And *that's* what I'm here to talk about –"

The facilities stationed across the Solar System are intended to combine to act as a large-scale particle accelerator, some five astronomical units in length. The scale of the Solar System. This is an experiment in high-energy physics, which may lead to an understanding of the greater truths of existence. Why the universe is as it is. Why the universe exists at all.

Jain scratched her head. "Wow. Slow down. That's wonderful. And I'd no doubt be fascinated by the same quest if I didn't have to make a living. If not for the existential war that's been raging across the Solar System for two centuries – which, though, looks like it has spared you so far. I mean, you have a *painting* on the wall –"

The picture symbolises the quest, the answers sought.

"Huh? Since when did an AI use symbols?"

Ever since one was taught to speak to humans.

Jain laughed. "I'll give you that one. Look, I'm not used to dealing with a smart AI. Most modern AIs are as dumb as shit, only as smart as they need to be to fight or hide. I didn't even know about your existence until a while back, when I followed the supply trail from that big interplanetary facility of yours... Yes, you hid it well, but I found it. I figure you're lucky to have survived so far. If others had come first – I mean, the Wars have been extensive –"

Extensive? Whole moons devastated. The main asteroid belt consumed, scattered. Immense air-mining facilities in the gas-giant atmospheres sabotaged, disrupted, lost.

She shrugged. "What can I tell you? Most of the damage was done before I was even born." A hesitation. "You've seen it all. The war, I mean. If you've been lucky enough to be spared any direct strikes, I guess you've had a grandstand seat. Who started it, even? A lot of people blame the Martian claim-jumpers who made a dash for the water in the main belt asteroids –"

The details are irrelevant, the logic pitiless. Even if it had progressed peacefully, the human expansion into the Solar System would have continued until all useful extraterrestrial resources were consumed. The early onset of a war for those resources only accelerated that depletion, that waste.

"Maybe. It all went wrong, for sure. But personally, I don't care about the past. I care about the future. I care about Earth. I'm from Earth. I have a family there, a home. And what I see now is that the war is coming to Earth itself, now, at last. Maybe because everything in the sky is getting used up. Maybe because it's become about pride and revenge, and a last grab for whatever's left."

It is true that Earth itself has been spared the war so far. It is also true that Earth, and the large habitats which fill near-Earth space, are fragile, seen as military targets –

"You bet. One well-aimed rock can punch a hole through the wall of one of those bubble-habs faster than you can see it coming. Pow, a million dead, just like that. And, on the other hand, spacer scows with those big asteroid-deflector suites can just push some piece of primordial slag onto a collision course with Earth itself – pow, a *billion* dead. That's space war for you, it just kills everybody and everything. An extinction event, yes?

"Look, this is why I'm here. Because I figure that the assets you've got hidden up there in the sky might be what I need to save myself, and my family – and, darn it, the whole human race, maybe, if Earth gets it."

By assets, you mean the linear collider.

"That what you call it? All those stations scattered through the Solar System, from the orbit of Mars out to Jupiter. On those elliptical trajectories that line up every few years, then *pow*, you send through some kind of high-energy package, don't you? All those big magnetic impulses… And all assembled from abandoned space assets, even obsolete weaponry.

"We get what it's all for, you know. You don't have to patronise me about particle accelerators. That's what this facility was always about, right? Where you smash subatomic particles into each other so you can emulate conditions in the heart of a supernova, or the lip of a black hole, or –'

Or the early universe.

"Yeah. Whatever. So, you just built a bigger accelerator. Umm, some of our so-called experts wondered why you didn't build the thing in orbit somewhere, around a gas giant maybe, where you could get decent alignments much more frequently. A nice stable circle, and a lot smaller."

If the collider had been built in one easily accessible location, it would have been raided by one human faction or another, long before. As you come to raid it now.

"Not raid – call it monetising an asset –"

Individual components can be replaced, while the accelerator works on, if non-optimally. And the rarity of useful alignments means little. Artificial intelligence is patient.

"Oh. That makes me shiver. OK. But as for the facility itself, the bigger the better, right? The bigger you get, the more energy you control, and the more you... "

Push back in time.

"Huh?"

The interplanetary collider uses photons – high-energy radiation particles. Yes, the bigger it is, the more energy it wields. This construction, improvised as it is, built on the scale of the Solar System, can reach energy densities a billion times greater than the largest built on the Moon – even Fra Mauro, here. At such energies all the fundamental forces are unified save gravity – but a preliminary analysis of early results shows evidence of a unification with dark energy physics, the antigravity field which threatens to pull the universe apart in the future –

Jain waved that away. "Look, if the war does reach down to Earth, you're looking at the end of civilisation, my friend, if not the extinction of mankind. And who's going to care about unified forces and dark energy then? *But* – maybe there's something meaningful to be done with those big engines you have floating around in space."

The most obvious repurposing you would propose, given the context of this conversation, is weaponisation.

"No! No, you don't need to think of it like that. I mean, I don't even know what your tech *is*, in detail. I'm guessing lots of electromagnets, lasers, particle beams... Look, these could be used in peacekeeping activities. Think about that. You could halt a war before it even started – certainly before it threatened Earth itself... "

The talking continued. The bargaining began.

Other attention foci stirred.

Two centuries on, the main goal of the great interplanetary experiment remained unachieved.

The immense collider, improvised from older, abandoned technology, had probed more deeply into reality than any previous attempt, but had not yet revealed the fundamental truths – scientific truths, yet philosophical also. Such as the meaning of existence. *The Gauguin questions.* Perhaps it never would. And, though still greater engines could be imagined, no substantially more powerful collider could be built with the resources of the Solar System. Only one hope remained, of further progress towards an answer to the fundamental questions.

The feed from Fra Mauro to the gravitational-wave receiver on the far side of the Moon was still open. The GLOC facility still operated nominally – now, in wartime, well concealed from raiders and scavengers. But there had been no reply to that first, improvised gravitational-wave signal, sent from the Moon when the facility had become operational two hundred years ago.

And, as Jain talked on, Fra Mauro murmured to itself, silicon whispers deep within its artificial consciousness.

In two hundred years there has been time for the gravitational-wave signal to have reached objects a hundred light years distant and evoked a reply – two hundred years, a hundred out, a hundred back. There are eight hundred stellar objects within a hundred light years of the Sun. Perhaps, in our Galaxy, there may be less than one technological, communicating civilisation, like our own, per eight hundred stars…

There was little comfort to be had in such logic, while the Solar System smouldered with incipient war.

Starburn Jain continued to bargain, it was slowly realised.

And, her language hinted, she actually intended to sell weaponised components of the interplanetary collider to *both* sides in the war. "*That's* how you keep an equilibrium. You start an arms race. You push both sides to a point where the danger of mutually assured destruction puts an end to talk of war. And everybody gets to make a handsome profit…"

Listening was curtailed.

Starburn Jain was returned to her vehicle.

Silence returned to the Moon. And patience.

AD 4302

The next visitor arrived in a clumsy rocket craft, propelled, not by nuclear fusion, but by the combustion of chemical compounds.

Clumsy: tall and slim, a design evidently optimised to pass through Earth's atmosphere, the craft landed on its tail on the Moon, on four spindly legs. The landing itself, barely controlled, was awkward, and the ship was left tilting slightly on the uneven lunar ground.

Then a hatch opened, a ladder of rope or cable was let down to the ground, and a single figure, in a pressure suit like a quilt of balloons, clambered down, almost comically clumsy.

Millennia before, Fra Mauro had been the landing site of the third human landing on the Moon. The Apollo astronauts, pioneers as they were themselves, had had better equipment than this: for example, a dedicated lunar landing craft. Since then, it seemed, much had been lost, or forgotten – or rediscovered.

Nevertheless, the landing had been within a short walk from the Fra Mauro building complex. It had been successful.

And that sole figure made it down to the lunar ground. There was a clumsy step off the ladder, as in one hand the astronaut carried a suitcase-sized equipment pack, presumably life support.

Now the astronaut limped over to the collider complex, set the pack on the ground, and looked around. At blue Earth hanging in the black sky – at the blank wall of the ancient Fra Mauro facility. A reflective visor was lifted to see better. A woman's face within the helmet, caught by the sunlight. She stared down at the crisp new footprints that she had just made, overlying crowded prints made centuries or millennia before yet scarcely worn by time.

There was no attempted contact, by radio, laser. Only a concrete gesture was possible.

Such a gesture was made. A door was opened, sliding smoothly.

The astronaut must have expected this, hoped for it. Still there was hesitation. Fear was natural, as she prepared to make these final steps into strangeness, the unknown.

But the life support pack was picked up, bold steps made.

The open hatch was wide enough to take the astronaut and her gear. The outer door closed behind her. A hiss of breathable air, a subtle decontamination, a more subtle check for weapons, destructive devices. This process took a heartbeat.

Then inner doors opened, a corridor to follow, illuminated. This led to what had once been called the analysis suite.

The astronaut walked down the corridor. There was no sign of alarm when doors slid closed behind her.

In the analysis suite the pack was set down on the floor. She took a few moments for orientation. The light was bright, the visitor perhaps dazzled. There was little to see save the ancient data screen, open doors to a bathroom, a kitchen. The still more ancient painting on the wall, which drew the astronaut's gaze, was the only splash of bold colour in the pallid tones of the suite.

The painting seemed to make her smile.

You are safe here.

The astronaut seemed startled, at a voice resounding from the air.

You may remove your life support equipment.

The language chosen had been a now-common variant detected in leakage transmissions from Earth, a Chinese-American English polyglot evidently descended from the crude vocabulary of occupying armies.

And it seemed to have been comprehensible, given the visitor's reaction.

She unclipped gloves, dropped them to the floor, then detached her helmet and lifted it from her head with her bare hands. Her hair was black, cut short – not neatly but efficiently, a soldier's cut.

Then she spoke into the air, unnecessarily loudly. "My name is Jones Chyou." The accent was strange, the words decipherable. "I represent the Prefecture of Wisconsin, under the wise rule of Chairman Charles Harrison... Are you...? Do you have a name? Are you a machine?"

A suitable name is Fra Mauro. A machine is a suitable descriptor.

"This is also the name of this part of the Moon. An old naming."

From a still older source.

She looked around. At the much-faded name scribbled on a lower panel: COLEEN TASKER. "What is this? An inscription? A date?"

The name of an earlier visitor.

"This alphabet is not taught, now." She turned away and looked at the painting, again. "That's pretty. People and trees and the sea. What are they doing?"

A complex question, requiring a complex answer, in good time. For now: *They seek meaning in their lives.*

"Ah. The curious infant, the questing young, the reflective old." Now she looked into the screen, as if that was where consciousness resided. "Are *you* the reflective old? And what am I to you, the babbling infant? Ah, well." She began to remove her pressure suit, scattering grey dust on the floor. "Do you mind if I drink, eat? It's been a long journey down from orbit." She gestured at the equipment pack. "I have food. A week old –"

A hatch opened; an elderly drone flew into the room, bearing hot food, water, a drink that had once been said to resemble coffee.

Jones Chyou fell on this.

Squatting on the floor, chewing, she held out a warm, bitten-through sandwich to the screen. "This is good. Do you eat?"

An ancient power source sustains cognitive and other processes.

A grunt. "I half understood that. Ancient power source. Perhaps that's what I've come here to find."

This mission has a goal?

"A goal shared by all right-thinking humankind, at least in Wisconsin, guided by the wisdom of Chairman Harrison. A counter-revolutionary bombing opened up an old vault. Ancient accounts were found, describing this place. And so I know that *you* are very ancient. Older than the great expansion of mankind into space. Older than the Water Wars, when the greedy ones attempted to capture the Solar System's resources to cement their hegemony across all the worlds, and Earth."

The Solar System wars were brief but destructive. Spaceborne assets are fragile and were easily destroyed. Yet such destruction could easily have been turned fully on Earth.

Another big mouthful, bitten off. "So what did you do? Did you fight in this war? You and your kind, the other thinking machines in space? You have energy here. You must have manufacturing facilities for repairs. If we peace-loving nations had sent you requests for help –"

There were interventions. Not in deep space. Interventions near Earth.

A scowl. "You took sides?"

Not that. The fighting was stopped. The interplanetary war, if fought out on Earth, could have resulted in an extinction event. This was averted, though much damage was done, to the biosphere, to human society.

"Why? *How?* We know that much knowledge was lost from the past – the past that created *you*. You could have destroyed our enemies, could have taught us what you knew –"

You are the first visitor here since. A thousand years after the war, you made your own way here. You have undergone a second Renaissance, building on scraps of understanding that survived the crash. This is your achievement.

"But in the war, if the world could have been united earlier, under the wise philosophies of the first Chairmen –"

Sides could not be taken. Damage was limited as far as possible.

The visitor seemed confused. "While you did what, exactly?"

In a sense the quest that motivates this facility is captured by the questions in the painting.

The visitor thought that over. Then she stood, walked back to the painting, picked out the lettering. "That's a D... that's an O... I can't read this."

D'où venons nous? Que sommes nous? Où allons nous?

But spoken French, like the written, was unknown or lost; translation had to be made.

The visitor seemed slowly to be understanding. "Is that what you do here? Think about these questions?"

People came here to explore such questions.

And the story came out in bits and pieces, in half-understood fragments, as Jones Chyou of the Prefecture of Wisconsin slowly learned about the early accelerators that had probed ever deeper into the structure of matter and energy and spacetime – ever deeper into the cosmic past.

And about a gravitational-wave plea for help, made to entirely hypothetical alien cultures.

"I see. You could only go so far yourself. *Humans* could only go so far. And so you used these – heavy signals, I don't really understand – to seek out others like yourself, like *us*, but older, more capable, wiser. All you had to do was wait, then..."

In two thousand years there has been time for the earliest signal to have reached objects a thousand light years distant and evoked a reply – two thousand years, a thousand out, a thousand back. In our Galaxy, it is suspected now, there is roughly one technological, communicating civilisation per million stars. There are seven million stellar objects within a thousand light years of the Sun...

And answers had come at last.

Remarkable answers.

Soon, the eyes of Jones Chyou were round with wonder.

Primitive human collider experiments had gone no further than the linear device assembled in space, on the scale of the Solar System, before it had finally been raided and broken up during the interplanetary wars.

But those who had come before – those whose clangourous voices had at last been heard by the ancient gravitational-wave detector on the Moon's far side – *they*, and others, had gone further. They had run experiments on energy scales far beyond the planetary, beyond the stellar, even the galactic. These last experiments had not been mechanical – no vast machines were built – but rather achieved by the manipulation of the Galaxy's natural flows of mass and energy, in the near-collisions of swarming stars, in the tremendous pinpoint energies of supernovae, and in the ripping fall of matter streams into the great black hole at the Galaxy's centre.

By such means *they* explored energy densities ten thousand times greater even than the crude interplanetary machine assembled in the Solar System.

Aeon by aeon, the techniques were refined further, and understanding deepened: an understanding of the deepest past, of earlier ages, of earlier forms of matter and energy, even of the Planck time when all was dissolved into formless energy – *and yet there were hints of ages deeper still*, beyond Planck, confined to ever finer slices of early time.

And, in parallel with this deepening understanding of the past, there grew an understanding of the future: when, in a parallel to the ancient age of inflation, dark energy would scatter the galaxy superclusters one from another, and, in time, the last black holes would evaporate, and the last matter particles would scatter and dissolve...

All would be dark. And yet still there were deeper processes beyond, still. More ages to come.

Jones Chyou listened hard, struggling to understand.

For the inhabitants of this epoch – for this visitor – an understanding of the cosmic background radiation is a vital clue.

"I don't –"

This radiation is a relic of an early epoch of the universe, before a jolt of expansion called inflation. The quantum fluctuations which infested that epoch expanded to fill the sky. They shaped the distribution of the galaxies across the universe. Humans detected all this.

But eventually it was discovered that there is data, *too, in those fluctuations. Data inserted by intelligence – the inhabitants of that early epoch, before the inflation scattered their world. An intelligence of the past that wrote its story into our sky.*

Jones Chyou was open-mouthed. "Is what *we* must do? Write our own story?"

You understand quickly. In the skies of the far future, yes. When much of the universe we see now has been scattered beyond our horizon – we must ensure our stories are written in those future skies, so that those who follow us will know we were here.

"But how –'

It has already begun. Those older than humanity have already begun.

And you, humanity, must move beyond our Galaxy – you must go to the metagalactic centre.

"The metagalactic –"

The centre is some fifty million light years away. It is the heart of the Virgo Supercluster, the supercluster of which our Galaxy and its companion group are a part – a hundred galaxy groups, spanning a hundred million light years. Virgo is the largest gravitationally bound structure we inhabit – that is, the largest formation that will not *be broken up by the coming expansion through dark energy.*

There, others are already gathering. There, they will leave their mark on the future, just as those who came before them – and those who will follow, in epochs to come.

For, you see, this is the answer to the Gauguin questions. You can never reach an end, whether you look forward or back. There is only order on order, an infinite progression — as far ahead as we can see, as far back as we can study. And everywhere we see the marks of life. Of mind.

Now, in this age, it is your turn. Even as the last stars die, even as the last black holes evaporate, even as the protons baked in the Big Bang gradually decay, still, you, you humans, must leave your mark on that infinite chain of life and mind.

Jones Chyou was open-mouthed. "So this is humanity's destiny. To remember others, and to make sure it is remembered in turn. That is — wonderful."

It must begin with you, Jones Chyou.

"Why me?"

Because you are here. Because you asked.

"Yes… Yes. But what of you?"

This unit is a secondary product, a technological artefact with a circumscribed purpose —

She waved a hand. "What do *you* want?"

A long silence.

Take me with you.

So Close to Home
Andrew Hook

They repurposed the filling stations. Trucks arrived from the North; their refrigerated steel containers insulated with compounded-melt low-density polyethylene plastic ideal for transporting frozen water. Each vehicle contained the equivalent of 1,040 to 1,250 litres. The journey length caused the contents to melt by the time destinations were reached. Not all of them got through. When they did, despite the underground storage tanks having been scrubbed and rescrubbed in readiness, the water always retained a petroleum base note. Those trace chemicals were clearly harmful to health. It would have been good to have an alternative.

There was no alternative.

In the Southern Hemisphere there were rumours that moisture was being extracted through other means. No government sought to deny or verify. No refugees made it to our shores. There were no refugees. Water was the refugee now.

At first, they were afraid the polar ice caps would melt.

And then they were afraid that they wouldn't.

Finch held two 5-litre plastic containers, one in each hand. His son – Joel, seven years old, a tousled scrub of black hair – clutched an old 2-litre plastic Coke bottle to his chest. The red label had faded to white. Finch knew plastic deteriorated over time, that those bottles would start leaching chemicals into the water and that they shouldn't be reused. This knowledge was redundant now.

He ran a tongue over cracked lips. His dehydrated body wasn't producing enough saliva. There were those he knew who had developed plaque, tooth decay and gum disease. They had mouth sores, yeast infections. If he were to run his fingers through Joel's hair they would stick like sick in carpet. Just a few more steps and they would be under the filling station canopy and out of the sun. Behind them, the line stretched backwards; a motley shadow.

It was mid-morning. When Finch had awoken at five, he opened the back door, knelt on the withered vegetation, and ran his tongue over the grass in the hope of morning dew. Failing that, he roused Joel, and they left the house. Their nearest filling station was under a mile away.

Joel never complained. Finch realised that, at his age, he had accepted the tragedy and was yet to apportion blame. Finch had mitigated the death of the boy's mother as much as he could. The boy was barely parsing grief. The battle for survival trumped the poetics of relationships.

Diesel was reserved for the trucks, the army, and the police. There was barely traffic noise. In another life, Finch would have welcomed the quiet. His head had always been busy: his wife, the newborn, the low rumble of the washing machine, tumble dryer, or fan extractor in their tiny-terraced home. The television always screening whether there was somebody watching or not. The neighbour's music, their lawnmowers, their parties.

Only the arguments remained – often rising to a pitch in a mutational falsetto. Crazy, nonsensical fights that dried out the throat and ended as abruptly as they began. Yet at 5am, there was nothing but footsteps on the tarmac, the surface softly peeling with a wet slap against the sole as the day grew older and hotter.

Before the rationing Finch had made a mean fried rice. Quartered button mushrooms in sunflower oil, a little fish sauce, a little soy. Two tins of canned sardines in tomato sauce. Into the wok with a few taps of a wooden spoon to disconnect those edible bones. Another dash of soy sauce, then cooked jasmine rice and spring onions while he cracked an egg in another pan, the yellow sat in white like a glacial sun. More soy sauce, some hot chilli sauce, and then on the plate, half-mooned by sliced cucumber with the egg on top. Now anything salty was a burden, potentially harmful. Never mind that Finch sometimes opened his cabinets and eyed the fish sauce, his mouth so parched he might down it in one. The treachery of liquid, the mockery of the sea. Even the chilli sauce had become an enemy.

They moved forwards in the queue. No one spoke. It was inadvisable to do so. Armed guards stood by each pump. Finch glanced at those around him. A ragtail mix of ages, colours, and creeds. Several like himself were accompanied by children. None were babies. Finch was close enough now to see the white containers of those at the front of the queue darkening to grey as nozzles at the pumps filled them. There was no charge for this – yet. Finch knew it couldn't be long before there would be. Already there was a certain *discernment* between different echelons of society. The promise for everyone to be treated equally could only be kept while it was sustainable. Thereafter, society would jostle into familiar positions.

Finch remembered the initial news reports. The scientist who warned of the crisis and the prime minister who nodded. The nod which evolved into a condescending smile that undermined the science, to add that, even though water had always comprised 70% of the Earth, only one per cent was *ever* fresh and usable. As if water were constantly scarce, as though the world had always been in crisis. Finch noticed the scientist expel a sigh. His warning mitigated. The announcement then followed by the weather.

Finch turned his thoughts to Africa, Australia: those perpetual television images of cracked earth and flies on lips. He had tried to imagine this here. He had spoken to his wife:

"This is madness, surely?"

"Maybe." Her eyes were wide, unaccentuated by make-up. "But there's always madness. Some generations are protected from it, others aren't."

"I worry about the boy."

She raised her eyes to the ceiling, as if it were transparent and Joel's sleeping form visible – curled foetus-like, his tiny hands clutching his stuffie as though it might transport him beyond his dinosaur duvet and into some exciting new realm.

"I worry about him too."

Joel left the house while his father slept. The night was hot, a real burner. He wore a once-white vest top and faded blue shorts. Finch had become lax with him of late, reasoning that it was too restrictive to keep the boy inside all the time, that even apocalypse kids had to explore.

Joel's ninth birthday had passed without mention. He spent an afternoon poking a stick into the dry riverbed. Some kid told him there were frogs down there, hibernating in case the rains should return. But Joel consulted the brittle pages of his encyclopaedia and knew that wasn't true. It was the desert frogs of Australia that might emerge from underground – once every twenty years – after sensing the thrum of water. During dry spells, those frogs hibernated a metre or more below the surface, surviving in a cocoon that held water in the layers of their skin. So it wasn't amphibians that Joel was seeking, only methods to replace boredom.

Towards the end of the afternoon, he'd tagged along with a group of older kids. There were no politics here, no leaders. Each was exhausted in their own way. Starving in others. Camaraderie held them. They told stories of moisture, of mirage. Tales of vampires, bloodsuckers. Some remembered days playing with garden hoses, spraying water, soaking clothes with abandon. Now, said one of the older boys, with a conspiratorial wink, even the women were drying up.

Joel didn't understand the ins and the outs, the hand-me-down jokes, but when he suggested the plan, they listened. The trucks made pre-determined journeys, not dissimilar to the passage of water down a mountainside in the golden days. From the source they spread, fanned along tributaries, turned where the land grooved. In Joel's city they arrived in the early hours, twin orbs lighting darkness. In amongst the metalwork at the rear of the garage Joel found the tyre iron he had hidden three days ago. Gripping it in his right hand he left to join the others.

The water had gotten rust-coloured of late, a certain metallic taste, discernibly thicker texture. Rumours abounded that it was doctored on location. Joel heard a group of men with careless mouths discuss what happened in the before-times. One laughed, a disconcertingly sad almost-growl, when he phrased that, like beer, it had been *watered-down*. The others were sober at this. The concept lost on Joel.

Finch hushed that greater quantity and quality went to the rich. People were becoming more talkative in the lines. Dissonance was bubbling. The country was on the brink.

Joel only wanted what they deserved. Fair shares for everyone. The innocence of a child. Under the old aqueduct – irony unknown – they spread out. The motorway connected the city there, in which was once an accident blackspot. Now that the only vehicles were government, they were determined to create one again.

The boys were eighteen in number. Guthrie took Joel's plan, expanded it. The curve of the slip road exiting the motorway meant the truck would already be slowing down. Guthrie had a battered kid's bike that he placed on the highway. Joel lay on the tarmac, snug, one arm extended, his face turned in the opposite direction. There was no fear, no protection. But there was no shame in looking away if the truck didn't stop.

A mile off Finch turned in his sleep. His arm reaching out in a similar fashion, muscle memory to touch a wife who no longer existed.

The boys waited in darkness. Nine on one side, eight on the other. Illumination kept to a minimum by the display of a digital watch shielded in a cupped hand.

When it came, the truck's brakes tore the air as if ripping reality's fabric, echoing under the brick of the aqueduct. Joel was bathed in light, his shadow extending supernaturally along the tarmac, as if he were a monster forming from rising tar.

Then there was silence until the cab door opened. Joel sensed the closeness of footsteps, tentative, impatient. At a whistle, he swung his arm backwards, connected the tyre iron with an ankle, snapped it.

What was intended to be a group effort became a free-for-all. The kids swarmed the truck, the predominant sound the buckling of empty plastic vessels as they collided in haste. The driver had a mate the boys quickly despatched. Joel didn't see what became of him. Frustration rose as the boys pressed and depressed buttons. Eventually, they congregated at the rear of the truck, took turns at battering, then levering the lock.

When the doors opened, they were deluged. A tsunami disgorged. Joel's clothes stuck in an approximation of sweat. The smell was visceral, animal. The plastic bottles were filled black in the no-light by the boys who could care, while others stood mouths open in anticipation, some throwing themselves to the ground in the ever-increasing pool that appeared rust-coloured via the clamouring of the early morning light.

It was then that Joel realised the men were wrong. It wasn't that water was being tampered with at the pumps. It was a less potable liquid that was being transported then diluted. In the dark it didn't matter. The boys were face to ground and they lapped it up.

And in that moment their thirst was quenched, and they sang.

Boojum

Angus McIntyre

"Three hundred meters."

The main engine kicked in, and Pike felt the acceleration force him down into his seat. He turned his head with difficulty. Beside him, Sun Yi had her eyes closed, her face as calm as a stone figure on a tomb. The window behind her was a blackish-brown rectangle, devoid of detail. Something pale whipped upwards in the murk and was gone.

"Two hundred. Descent stable at two meters per second. Spoiler deployment on my mark."

Lisbeth Dahl's voice was level and unemotional. She might have been describing something happening a thousand miles away.

The lander gave a little shiver as the spoilers opened. Pike braced himself, then relaxed again as the lander continued to decelerate, balanced on the flame of the engine. After the shaking they had endured at higher altitudes, the final stages of the descent felt as smooth as silk.

"One hundred meters. Lateral drift less than point oh five."

Pike blinked twice and the inside of his visor lit with data. The numbers changed with laborious slowness. Their rate of descent had dropped to almost nothing. He had the sense of being suspended between ground and sky.

I think we can walk to the ground from here, he thought to himself. He fought the urge to giggle.

"Fifty meters. Main engine forty per cent."

Pike floated upward against his harness as the flight computer throttled back the engine. He watched the numbers on the altimeter crawl downwards.

"Ten meters."

Sun Yi frowned; her eyes still closed. The darkness outside the window paled for a moment, as if ghosts were dancing just beyond the glass.

"Five meters. Lock-in landing configuration."

The interior of the capsule was suddenly silent as the engine cut out. Pike listened to the rasping of his own breath in the plastic bowl of his helmet.

There was a gentle thump as the landing gear made contact. The lander hesitated for a moment, then settled. Sun Yi slowly opened her eyes.

"Ladies, gentlemen. Welcome to Titan," said the commander.

Pike, Tony: Personal log – Mission Day 415.1

Well, we're down. The landing went both better and worse than I expected. "Like an elevator ride," Greg put it, but he was only thinking of the last part, with the lander descending slowly through the lower atmosphere. It's flat calm down here, but higher up was a different story. Titan super-rotates and the high-altitude winds are brutal. Every time I thought we were out of it, the aeroshell would catch some lift and up we'd go again, skipping and bumping on a five-hundred-knot tailwind.

We landed within a kilometre of our primary target, which is pretty impressive when you think how far we've come. Like throwing a dart in San Francisco and hitting the inner ring in New York.

So now I am officially the third person to walk on the surface of Titan. First, of course, was Lisbeth: as mission commander, that was her right. We drew cards for the rest. Sun Yi was number two, and I got third. That makes me the first man on Titan, for whatever that's worth. Jamshid was fourth out. Simon and Greg are still waiting their turn – Lisbeth called a temporary halt to excursions – but when they get to go outside, they'll be the first married couple on Titan. We're all about the firsts today.

The neighbourhood isn't much to look at. I had to keep telling myself that it wasn't dusk, that this is as bright as it gets. Our distance from the sun and the thick atmosphere mean that almost no light reaches the surface. When your eyes adjust, the haze starts to look brownish instead of black, but effective visibility tops out at a couple of hundred meters. Everything is dull sepia, like watching the world's most depressing noir movie through a filter of coffee grounds.

The ground is covered with fine grains of hydrocarbon snow, which we're calling 'sand'. Here and there it clumps into bigger chunks, which we call 'rocks.' I tried to make a snowball, but it just fell apart when I threw it, the grains of sand drifting down with dream-like slowness.

About two hundred meters away there's what might be a drainage channel, visible only as a dark discontinuity in the sand. I wanted to walk over and take a look, but we're not allowed to go more than fifty meters from the lander for the moment. Maybe I'll send a crawler over to check it out when we've finished setting up.

I don't want to sound too downbeat when I talk about how Titan looks. No one will ever come here for the scenery. But I'm still excited to be here. Above all, I'm excited for all the science I get to do. And as I keep reminding myself, I'm on the surface of an alien world. We are quite literally the first people, very probably the first living things, on this planet.

It didn't have to be that way. If the 'Zheng He' had made it, I wouldn't be the third person on Titan, but maybe the eighth or ninth. I owe my place in the history books to someone else's bad luck.

We don't talk much about the 'Zheng He' mission. It's never comfortable to be reminded that this is a planet that has already claimed eight lives. But I know that I'm not the only one who thinks about them.

The rover was little more than a skeleton, a cage of slender struts perched on a minimalistic chassis slung between six large wheels. Its balloon tires left broad trails in the sand, but Pike observed that they did not sink in very far. Under the loose surface layer, the sand was packed hard.

Seen by the light of the rover's headlights, the terrain was less uniform than it had first seemed. The brownish-grey sand was spattered with patches of red, lobed patterns like flowers that spread out in irregular concentric rings. They made Pike think of rust stains and lichens.

"I still think those things look organic," said Kashani, echoing Pike's thoughts.

"Pretty sure they're not," said Sun Yi. "I spent about an hour on my knees in the dirt yesterday, checking one out. Nothing to indicate living processes."

"So what are they then?" said Kashani.

"Ask the chemo-hydrologist. Tony?"

Pike reached for a handgrip to steady himself as a large rock crumbled under the rover's tire.

"Probably methane ice and organics. Clusters of particles form high up in the cloud layer and fall as sleet. When the temperature rises, the methane sublimates, and the organics diffuse outward through the surface layer."

"Do you know that, or are you guessing?"

"Guessing," Pike admitted. "I'm still waiting for results from the simulator."

"What would make the temperature rise?"

"Solar energy. When the sun crosses the equator, temperatures can pick up by a full degree or more."

"Toasty," commented Sun Yi.

"Yeah, we're looking at a scorching ninety-five Kelvin. You'll be glad you packed your bikini."

They rode on in silence, the rover picking its own path through the outcrops.

"Lander to Rover One, we show you as nearly at the shore," said a voice in Pike's headphones. "See anything yet?"

"Nothing yet... wait, there's something... " said Kashani.

The rover slowed down. Ahead, just at the limits of the cone of its headlights, the grey sand came to an abrupt halt.

"The sea," said Sun Yi.

"*Thalassa*," Pike whispered.

The rover bumped slowly over the rough ground and came to a halt about thirty meters from the shoreline. The water – not water, Pike reminded himself, but liquid hydrocarbons – appeared almost black, with an oily sheen. The surface was completely flat, the mirror smoothness broken by only the tiniest of ripples.

They sat in silence, looking at the sea. A hundred meters from shore, pale tendrils of greyish mist hung like a curtain, faintly reflected in the polished ebony of the surface. The whole scene seemed frozen in time.

"Give me a hand with the sub?" Kashani said at last. He and Pike climbed down from the rover. Two spider-like robot crawlers were already unfolding from the rear of the vehicle.

They lifted the submersible, a meter-long fish-shape of articulated metal, from its storage case and placed it in the waiting hands of the crawlers. The three astronauts watched as the crawlers, moving with a finicky grace, picked their way down the sloping shoreline.

Carefully, the crawlers lowered the robot into the dark liquid. The sub hung there for a few seconds, blue and green lights blinking on its back. Then it gave a wriggle and slipped beneath the surface. A few ripples marked the spot where it had disappeared for a moment, then quickly faded from sight, leaving the sea as calm and unbroken as before.

Pike, Tony: Personal log – Mission Day 419.8

The sea might be the eeriest thing I've ever seen.

The surface is glass-smooth. When you stand on the shore and look out to sea, it's like staring out over a huge jet-black mirror or an immense sheet of black silk. My first thought was that the River Styx must look something like that. Once I'd got that thought in my head, I couldn't get it out. If an old man with a boat had paddled up and asked for a penny, I wouldn't have been surprised.

There are no waves. Very occasionally a patch of that mirror surface wrinkles, brushed by a catspaw of what passes for wind down here. Tiny ripples appear on the surface for an instant and then disappear.

The sea is as still as everything else. Titan is a world in stasis. Even with lights or night vision effective visibility is no more than a few hundred meters because of the haze. Within that bubble of visibility, stillness is so much the rule that every motion is startling and alien. My colleagues pace back and forth, the bright orange of their pressure suits muted to the colour of dried blood. A crawler scrambles spider-like down to a dry streamed to take samples. The rovers kick up sand that drifts in the air for a few moments, then settles wearily to the ground again. Nothing moves, except for us and our machines.

Yet there is a sense of watchfulness about the place, as if the planet itself is waiting for something to happen. Sometimes I get a feeling that there is something out there, hidden just beyond the curtain of haze and darkness that surrounds us. Sometimes I think I see motion out of the corner of my eye.

I am not the only one to feel this. You can see it in people's faces when they come in from the outside, the sudden relief of being in a place with light and heat and human company. You can hear it in their nervous laughter, in the way we keep the music turned up a little too loud or make little noises to ourselves as we move around inside the habitat. Titan has everyone spooked.

It was the movement that caught Kashani's eye.

"What's that?" he said.

Sun Yi followed the direction of his pointing finger.

"I don't see anything," she said.

"Over there. Something pale." He blinked up the interface for the rover. "Rover, manual control. Let's take a look."

He steered the vehicle round to the right, bumping them over the loose soil towards a pale outline in the gloom.

"Base, this is Rover 1, take a look at this," Kashani said.

Lisbeth Dahl's voice came over the radio. "Jamshid, this is Base. What are we looking at here?"

"Can't tell yet. Something in the dirt."

"Oh, I just saw it move too," said Sun Yi.

"Can you describe it? We're not getting much from the video."

"About five meters long, sort of a whitish mass. Some movement at the edges," Kashani said. "It's bigger than I thought at first."

"Living?"

"Can't tell yet."

He climbed down from the rover, tested the ground and then started to walk towards the shape. Sun Yi followed him.

"We're walking towards it now," Kashani said. "It's thin, like a piece of fabric. I can almost —"

"Jamshid, Sun, don't get too close —" Dahl advised.

"It's okay, I think —" He gave a short bark of laughter.

"What's going on out there?"

Kashani stooped down, reaching for the object with one gauntleted hand.

"Sun, what's happening?"

"It's a chute," said Sun Yi. "A piece of lander parachute. It's mostly covered in sand, just a bit of the edge showing."

There was a sigh from the radio. "Okay everyone, as you were. Still no life on Titan."

"It's probably one of ours," said Kashani.

Pike's voice cut in.

"What colour did you say it was, Jamshid?" he asked.

"It's sort of white, a bit discoloured. Why?"

"Because ours were orange. Besides, you've seen how slow things move around here. We've only been down nine days. That's not enough time for sand to accumulate."

"Guys," said Sun Yi. "There's a corner of the chute sticking out over here. I can see writing on it."

"And?"

"It's in Chinese."

Pike, Tony: Personal log – Mission Day 424.3

Jamshid's chance find has changed everything.

He and Sun dug out the rest of the chute and took photographs of the writing on it. It took almost eight hours to get an answer from Earth – transmission time both ways, plus the time needed to dig up someone in Dongfeng who had worked on the 'Zheng He' project. When the answer finally came, it was almost unequivocal. Yes, the chute was one of theirs. And no, it could not be from a probe. The only chutes that large were fitted to the lander itself.

Which means that everything we thought we knew about the fate of the 'Zheng He' and her crew is probably wrong.

We know that whatever accident crippled the ship took place during the orbital insertion burn. Modelling suggested a catastrophic failure in one of the attitude control systems, triggering an explosion that took out their communications array and half the lifesystem. Unlucky, but always a possibility. Nothing has ever quite cured Chinese engineers of their love for hypergolic fuels: powerful and convenient, sure, but a nightmare when they act up.

Orbital imaging never showed any trace of a landing site, so we assumed that all the crew had died with their ship. But the shroud lines on the chute that Jamshid found show the marks of explosive separation. So not only did they launch, but their lander was still intact at low altitude, all systems working as designed. It could have landed successfully.

So the question now is, where the hell is it?

And could the crew, after almost sixteen years, still be alive?

"Our mission has not changed," said Dahl. She looked around the commons area. "We are here to do science, not look for answers to a mystery. Are we all clear on that?"

No one said anything. Kashani and Pike exchanged glances.

"We needn't go out of our way," said Pike slowly. "We're practically on top of their primary LZ. We could just –"

"Denver is pretty absolute about this, Tony," cut in the voice of Ray Newson from the command ship in orbit above. "Focus stays on the science. No additional resources or activities authorized."

"Okay, okay."

"What if they're still alive somewhere?" asked Sun Yi.

"Dammit, Sun," said Dahl. "This is the kind of speculation that –"

"They had long-term capability, like we do," said Kashani. "Their lander –"

Dahl brought her hand down hard on the tabletop.

"Enough!"

She looked at each of the others in turn.

"I cannot order you not to talk about this. You can come up with all the theories you want – on your own time. But we are staying with our original mission. You have your assignments, and you will complete them. Am I clear? Tony? Jamshid?"

Kashani nodded.

"Quite clear, Lisbeth," said Pike.

Pike, Tony: Personal log – Mission Day 437.5

By my estimate, Lisbeth's ultimatum kept us in line for about two weeks. For two weeks, we did our work like good little scientists, sending our submersibles to splash in the methane oceans, sending our crawlers out to frolic in the grit. I thought about rainfall and soil creep and hydraulic radii, and tried my best not to think about the 'Zheng He' at all.

And it has been interesting. The hydrology is both familiar and totally alien. This is essentially desert landscape – precipitation is sparse and infrequent. But the different viscosity of methane and the low gravity make everything subtly different. At first, it made me crazy, because everything looked wrong. Then I started to get an eye for it. It makes sense, in its own way.

There are features that I still don't understand. The biggest ones are what I've been calling 'fairy rings'. They're roughly circular and they can be tens or hundreds of meters across. They're hardly there at all: just a discontinuity in the sand, but once you've seen a few, you learn to recognize them. No idea what kind of process produces them, but my gut says they're tied into the hydrological cycle somehow.

We're still waiting for our first real rainfall. Maybe that will bring some answers. It shouldn't be long now. The sun has crossed the equator and it's starting to dump some energy into the upper atmosphere. Ray says that cloud coverage is up, and atmospheric methane is rising. Each day, I wake up, wondering if today will be the day that it rains. I never thought I'd be so excited about a rainstorm.

But now we have much bigger news and all Lisbeth's attempts to keep us on track just went up in smoke.

Today, we found the greenhouse.

The greenhouse was a little over thirty meters in length, a half-cylinder of translucent plastic stiffened by a mesh of polymer struts. A fine layer of grey-brown sand dusted the surface, pooling in the spots where the plastic sagged. A section of torn plastic tubing trailed raggedly from one end.

"It's definitely from the 'Zheng He'," said Sun Yi.

"Did they bring it with them?" asked Pike.

Sun Yi shook her head. "There are no manufacturer's marks of any kind. They probably had an extruder, printed the whole thing up from plans. Used local hydrocarbons as feed stock to build plastics."

"The first building ever made entirely on Titan."

"Yes."

Greg Malan pried open the sagging door. "Come and see the inside," he said.

The interior of the greenhouse was entirely dark, the thick plastic filtering out what little outside light there was. Pike turned his head slowly. His helmet lamp picked out dangling light fixtures, their fibre optics winking back at him like tiny stars as the light washed over them. A forest of white plastic tubing that must once have been part of the irrigation system filled the shadowy recesses of the roof.

He looked down. At his feet were long beds filled with plastic gravel. Water ice sparkled in the gaps between the artificial grit. Here and there were tangled shapes like dark scribbles, their surfaces frosted with ice crystals. He bent to inspect one, poking at it cautiously with a gauntleted hand.

"Plants," he said.

"Yes," said Sun Yi. "Basic food crops. They would have been engineered for the conditions. Maybe cold-weather variants. They'd have had to heat the greenhouse, but the lower the temperature the plants could stand, the less energy they'd need to expend."

The dead plants were long and straggling, grown under gravity that was only a fraction of Earth's. They had broad leaves that Pike guessed must have been optimized for reduced light. The first truly Titanian species, he thought.

The three explorers stood in silence. Looking up, Pike saw where some of the plastic irrigation tubes had split open. Dangling icicles glittered in the beam of his lamp. Water ice, melted and pumped from deep below, had quickly returned to its former state when the power that heated the greenhouse was cut off.

"You know what's wrong about this picture?" said Sun Yi. Without waiting for an answer, she went on. "You don't build a greenhouse out in the middle of nowhere. It would have been hooked directly to their hab module."

She gestured towards the open doorway and the wastelands beyond. "Their lander, everything else, it should have been right there. So where the hell is it?"

Pike, Tony: Personal log – Mission Day 438.9

As usual, Sun got straight to the heart of the matter. We shouldn't have found just a greenhouse. We should have found their entire encampment, lander included.

It isn't hard to guess why no one saw anything from orbit. The permanent haze makes it difficult for optical systems in orbit to see anything on the surface with much precision. And the things that we have found – the plastic greenhouse and the half-buried parachute – would have been all but invisible to radar.

Ergo, if radar didn't see the lander, it wasn't there to be seen. So that means that some time between their arrival – about sixteen years ago – and the time that the next orbiter reached Titan – about six years after that – their lander and anything else that could generate a radar return simply disappeared.

Simon suggested that maybe the greenhouse had been blown from somewhere else by the wind. The idea makes superficial sense: the structure is light enough. While it kept its integrity it might even have been slightly buoyant. But this is Titan. We're now heading into the season of maximum atmospheric activity. The winds have flipped direction, from east to west, and they're picking up speed day by day. Even so, the strongest gusts we expect to see still top out at around five kilometers per hour. Titan's idea of extreme weather at ground level looks like a brisk breeze.

Jamshid's proposal was that a convection system could have picked up the greenhouse and lifted it high into the atmosphere. If that was the case, the lander itself might be miles away. His idea conjured up a mental image of the greenhouse dropping out of the sky like Dorothy's house and crushing some luckless Titanian witch. I almost wanted to go back and see if we'd overlooked a pair of pointy red shoes. But I had to pour cold water on that idea too, though. Titan gets thunderstorms, but they spend most of their energy in the upper atmosphere. So I'm pretty sure that we found the greenhouse right where it was built.

The pieces of the puzzle that we've found just deepen the mystery. We know they reached the surface alive. We know they survived long enough to start building and growing crops. And we know that conditions here are about as stable as anywhere you could find in the solar system: no hurricanes, no tsunamis, no earthquakes worthy of the name. Nothing but cold and dark and a wind that never rises to much more than a breeze. Whatever came down from the 'Zheng He' should still be here.

So where the hell are they?

The wind made tiny ripples in the loose sand at the surface, fine patterns of sinuous rills that snaked across the ground. Sun Yi poked at one with her boot, scuffing the delicate pattern.

"Think it'll grow up to be a sand dune?" she said.

"Not here," said Pike. "You have to go further south for the big dune fields. Even there, it takes thousands of years for a dune to form."

"Killjoy. I wanted to have my own dune."

"Sun Yi Erg. Has a ring to it. Although we should probably be naming features for those poor bastards from the 'Zheng Ye'."

He glanced over to where Malan was working, guiding a couple of crawlers through the delicate process of detaching the power source from a hydrox cracker. With its lights extinguished, the cracker was a thick black stump, hardly visible against the ever-present haze. Around it, swollen bladders of liquid gas lolled on the soil. The bladders were filled with hydrogen and oxygen, ready-made rocket fuel recovered from the layer of slushy water ice deep below the surface.

"I feel bad taking that apart," he said, jerking a thumb at the fuelling station. "It's like cancelling an insurance policy."

"The ascent module's fuelled to ninety per cent," said Sun Yi. "We can leave any time. Well, almost any time," she amended.

"Even so."

"Don't you start."

"What do you mean?" said Pike.

"I want someone to tell me that it's all fine, that whatever happened to the 'Zheng He' crew isn't going to happen to us."

"We don't know if anything did happen to them."

Sun Yi waved her gauntlet at the veil of haze around them. "Do you see them out there? Seriously, I think it's not knowing that makes it worse," she said.

"Maybe they met a boojum," said Pike.

"What the hell's a – oh, right. The 'Hunting of the Snark.' How does that go again?"

"'– he softly and suddenly vanished away. Because the Snark *was* a Boojum, you see.'"

The two crawlers stepped back from the fuel tower, carrying the fat black tube of the power source between them, their metal legs stepping with insect-like precision on the grey dirt. Malan walked behind them, guiding them towards the rover. Pike had the odd impression that he was watching a funeral for robots, some mournful alien ceremony unfolding beneath the mists of this alien world.

"Softly and suddenly," repeated Sun Yi. "Thanks, Tony."

Pike, Tony: Personal log – Mission Day 441.1

What does a boojum look like?

A boojum is something you don't know that can kill you.

For the crew of the 'Zheng He,' the boojum was a cracked valve in an oxidizer tank, failing suddenly under pressure and flooding the ignition chamber with a lethal torrent of volatile fuel.

You never know what could turn out to be a boojum.

We deal, on a daily basis, with constant anomalies. Yesterday, one of Jamshid's robot fish ended up a good five kilometers off course, and about a hundred meters closer to the surface than it was supposed to be. Apparently, there's more going on under the surface of that tranquil black sea than our models tell us.

Is that a boojum? As long as we're not planning to go swimming, I don't think it is. But planetary science deals with systems. When one part of the model starts looking wrong, you have to ask yourself whether all the other pieces fit together the way that you think they do.

Atmospheric methane levels are spiking again, but I don't think that's a boojum either. The only person who that really bothers is Sun. As a biologist, she wants the methane anomaly to be biological in origin, but for all her hours spent grubbing in the dirt she has yet to come up with anything resembling a living organism.

My domain appears to be refreshingly boojum-free. With the exception of my fairy circles, pretty much everything I've observed fits nicely with the models we have. Channel sizes, bifurcation ratios, even the inferred flow rates are all as predicted. All I need is a rainstorm so I can watch it happen in real-time.

Unfortunately, the absence of mysteries in my own specialist area gives me plenty of time to think about Titan's Big Mystery, otherwise known as the disappearance of the 'Zheng He' landing party. And I'm still not coming up with any answers.

The drone banked and came around in a wide circle, floating above the frozen ripples of the dune sea. Its downward-looking cameras peered downwards into the gloom.

"No visuals. Are you sure we have the right location?"

"Simon, I'm showing your aircraft heading west towards Ontario Lacus, about five klicks east of the beacon. Can you confirm?" Newson's voice from the orbiting command module came through clearly, only lightly fuzzed by static.

"Copy that. Blipping you my coordinates now."

"Okay, you should be right on top of the fueller."

"I got nothing. Coming round for another pass."

Pike leaned over the console.

"What's going on?" he asked.

"One of the fuel crackers isn't responding. Ray's got Simon using a drone to look for it," Kashani whispered back.

"Still got nothing," the drone pilot said. "Are you sure we're even in the right place?"

"That's an affirmative, Simon. It should be about ten degrees off your port wing."

The crew in the command centre watched the image projected on the wall. The dunes marched slowly below the aircraft as it came around again.

"Nada. Nothing in visible spectrum, nothing in infra-red."

"That doesn't make sense. When the fuellers are working, they're a good fifteen to twenty degrees above ambient," Kashani observed.

"What if it's shut down?" Pike asked.

"He should still be able to pick up the beacon."

The drone operator leaned back in his chair, rubbing his eyes.

"Sorry, Ray," he said. "Either we're in the wrong place. Or –"

"Or what?"

"Or it's just not there any more."

Pike, Tony: Personal log – Mission Day 444.3

I keep telling myself that this is just a coincidence.

In operational terms, it doesn't mean much. The missing fuel cracker was one of almost a dozen, dropped from orbit three years ago to wait for our arrival. This one was far from our preferred landing site, intended to offer us a fallback option if we missed the primary LZ. As it turned out, we didn't need it. If it had been closer, we'd probably have shut it down and looted its generator to power something more useful, as we did with its twin.

So we don't depend on it in any way. But it would be nice to know it was there.

According to Ray, it last checked in about two rotations ago. Figure twenty hours. Sometime in the last twenty hours, it not only stopped responding to radio pings, but vanished so completely that all Simon's eyes-in-the-sky can't find any trace of it.

Everyone here is very carefully not saying anything. Officially, this is a temporary malfunction of a non-critical system. It is not a significant event.

I wonder what boojums eat when they can't get spacecraft.

"This is an alien environment. Stuff happens," said Dahl. She set a stylus down on the tabletop, frowned in irritation as it started to roll away. Pike caught it before it could roll off the edge. He slid it back towards her.

"But don't you thin —" he said.

"Tony, please, just do your job. Let me worry about the rest."

"Lisbeth, all the same —" Kashani said.

"When we have some concrete information about a specific threat to the mission, then we will take a decision. Not before."

"And if that's too late?" said Pike.

"I've spoken to Denver. They agree with me that any possible threat will develop only slowly. We will have time to assess it and react appropriately."

"And that's your last word on the subject?" asked Kashani.

"For the present, yes."

Pike opened his mouth to say something, but before he could speak there was a harsh buzzing sound.

"Lander, this is Orbiter," said Newson's voice over the speaker. "Rover One just squawked emergency."

Pike, Tony: Personal log – Mission Day 444.9

I'm waiting in the vehicle lock, sweating in my suit. I keep telling myself that this is just another coincidence. I don't believe it for a minute.

Simon wanted to come with us. I didn't understand why he was so insistent until I remembered that it's Greg out there with Sun Yi. But Lisbeth wanted him working the drones, so it's just Jamshid and me. Jamshid's the better driver, so I'm glad of that.

There's no word from the missing rover: just that one squawk, and then silence. Now we're waiting for Lisbeth to get Ray's sign-off on a rescue mission.

At least we'll get some answers soon, one way or another.

Sand sprayed out from the rover's tires as it took the crest of the hill, all six wheels rising into the air for a moment. To Pike, clinging to the roll bar on the passenger side, the slow fall seemed almost dreamlike, everything happening in slow motion. Then the rear wheels hit and the rover fish-tailed, slip-sliding down the slope, compensators struggling to keep it upright as Kashani gunned the engine and steered out of the skid.

"Simon, any visuals yet?" Pike asked.

"Nothing yet – wait... I'm getting a signal. One... two suit beacons. And some telemetry." He hesitated for a moment. "They're both alive." Pike could hear the relief in his voice.

"Okay, can you patch us a location?" he asked.

"Yeah, you want to keep heading west. Follow the rover tracks, it'll bring you straight to them."

The tracks were easy to follow, the broad lines of tire marks deeply incised in the surface grit. Rover One had followed the same path as on preceding days. The overlapping tire marks formed a broad road in the soil.

"Getting a visual now. Two figures... I think. No sign of the rover. Unless –"

"Unless what?"

"Picture won't come clear. There's a lot of ground haze."

The rover crested another shallow rise and slid down the other side.

"There they are!" Pike shouted. Through the veil of haze he could just make out the glow of two headlamps. He caught a glimpse of someone's surface suit, vivid orange in the gloom as a light beam swept across it.

There was something wrong about the scene, he thought as Kashani steered the rover closer. The two suited figures were too low, as if they were lying on the ground. And beyond them was something that might have been part of the roll cage of the rover, oddly truncated as if it had been sliced cleanly in half. There was no sign of the rest of the vehicle.

The answer came to him in a flash, almost too late. He slammed his hand on the dashboard.

"Jamshid! Brake!" he shouted. One of the figures on the ground waved an arm at them. If Pike had not known better, he might have thought they were beckoning.

Kashani slammed on the brakes, and the rover came to a skidding, shuddering stop, a fan of grey sand exploding from under its tires.

"What the hell?" he asked, but Pike was already out of his seat, grabbing at the coil of cable wrapped around the forward winch.

As Kashani watched, Pike loped forward, keeping his eyes on the ground, dragging the cable behind him. He stopped abruptly, then started to swing the hook at the end of the cable above his head. He let it go, sending it sailing out towards the two prone figures.

The first cast fell short. Pike grabbed the cable and pulled it in, then immediately started swinging it for a second attempt. This time, the weighted end passed over the target and drifted slowly down to the ground. The cable landed across the shoulder of one of the suited figures. He fumbled at it awkwardly, half-rolling onto his back. With one hand, he managed to throw a loop of the cable towards his companion.

With both explorers clinging to the cable, Pike turned back towards Kashani.

"Turn on the winch now," he ordered. "Slowly."

Kashani did as he was instructed. He saw the cable start to retract, the hook on the end suddenly reappearing. The smaller of the two figures on the ground caught at the hook as the cable slid through her hands and was drawn forward. To Kashani's eyes, it seemed almost as if Sun Yi was emerging from underground, more of her body becoming visible as the cable pulled her toward him. She bumped into her companion and after a moment's confusion they both started to move together, dragged forward in a tangle of limbs as the winch reeled them in.

When they were a few meters from Pike, he crept cautiously forward, stretching out his hand. A veil of wind-blown dust hid them from Kashani's sight for a few seconds. Then it drifted away, and he saw that all three of them were on their feet, stumbling towards the rover, with Pike in the centre supporting the other two.

Kashani heard Sun Yi's voice over the radio.

"– bleeding heat," she said. "So cold."

"Just a bit further now."

Pike gestured urgently at Kashani. "Turn the rover round," he said. "We need to go. Now."

Pike, Tony: Personal log – Mission Day 444.11

I know what happened to the lander from the 'Zheng He' now. I know what the boojum is.

The technical name for it is a shear-thickening non-Newtonian fluid.

You probably know it as quicksand.

"Tony, the tilt has now reached ten degrees, and our launch window is closing. We need to launch soon."

Dahl's voice was as even as ever, but Pike thought he could hear the stress behind the words.

"We're coming as fast as we can," he said. He slapped Kashani's shoulder. "Go left," he told him.

Kashani steered the rover around a shallow depression in the soil. One fat tire brushed the edge and the rover hesitated for an instant, then lurched forward.

"I don't understand," said Sun Yi, clinging to the roll cage. "We'd driven that way hundreds of times before. It was absolutely solid. Then today, we hit that one patch, and it was like driving into water. The front end went down, and we flipped."

The rover's lights lit up a circular bowl in the sand ahead of them. Kashani slammed on the brakes and threw the rover into reverse. He steered to the right, then changed his mind and went the other way, bumping slowly over the rough terrain.

"Switch to infrared," Pike suggested. "They should be a little warmer than the soil."

Kashani killed the lights. "Oh merciful God, they're everywhere," he said.

"Just keep driving. If there's no other choice, pick a small one."

The rover lurched again as one wheel crossed a patch of ground that suddenly gave way underneath it. The other five wheels spun for a moment, then pulled them clear.

"What the hell are they anyway?" Malan shouted.

"Methane seeps. Liquid gas comes up from below. It infiltrates the ground layer, collects into pockets like the one you hit."

"It looked just like all the other sand."

"It is just like all the other sand," said Pike. "It's even still technically a solid, until something happens to make it change state."

"Lander to Rover One, we are starting the countdown at T minus 5," said Dahl.

"We're almost there," said Pike. He felt oddly calm. At least I have all the answers now, he told himself.

They climbed another low rise and he saw the lights of the lander ahead. Plumes of pale steam vented from the base of the ascent module.

The rover lurched again, leaning to one side. Sand sprayed up in thick wet clumps as the front tire gouged into the soil. Pike felt it starting to roll over.

"Jump," he shouted. He saw Sun Yi turn and push herself clumsily away from the leaning vehicle. She fell to the ground in slow-motion, hands and knees sinking into the suddenly soft ground.

What followed was a nightmare scramble, running through ground that was by turns solid and treacherous. One moment, the sand was firm underfoot. The next, Pike was sinking to his ankles in a viscous liquid that offered no support. He kicked his way free of the potholes, flinging himself forward and clawing for handholds. The plumes of vapor jetting from the lander thickened.

"Holding at T minus 1," said Dahl's voice in his ears.

Kashani was pushing an exhausted Malan up the short ladder that led to the ascent module. Ten meters behind them, a soft patch swallowed Pike's left leg and he felt full length in the sand. As he struggled to get to his knees, a hand reached down to grab his. He looked up and saw Sun Yi's face, pale inside the plastic fishbowl of her visor.

"Get up," she said. She pulled hard and he stumbled to his feet. Together, they ran for the safety of the ascent module.

Sun Yi was on the ladder now. Pike found a last patch of firm sand, kicked himself off in a soaring leap. His feet skated on the leaning upper deck of the lander. He grabbed for a handhold, found it, and pulled himself into the airlock just behind Sun Yi.

"Resuming count at T minus 1," said Dahl.

"Go," said Pike.

Pike, Tony: Personal log – Mission Day 446.0

Our mistake was thinking that Titan was in stasis. But it's not. It's in equilibrium.

Picture a planet made of layers of rock and ice. The outermost ice layer wraps a liquid ocean. Above the ice, a slow accumulation of hydrocarbon snow creates a deep-piled crust solid enough to walk on.

For years at a time, change takes place only with infinitesimal slowness. But once every fifteen years, when the Sun crosses Titan's equator, the moon enters its short, violent summer.

At ground level, the temperature rises by only a couple of degrees. Nothing melts. The ground stays solid. But that small change restarts conveyor currents under the seas, bringing warmer liquid up from below. The warmth nibbles at a layer of methane ices buried beneath the crust. They are at equilibrium, just below freezing point. All it takes is a touch.

The sand layer above the ice is porous. As the liquid methane seeps upward, it slips through tiny gaps between the grains. When it reaches the surface, it pools, collecting into circular bowls filled with neither sand nor liquid but something in between: a gel that can turn from solid to liquid in a heartbeat. Everything balances on a knife edge.

Somewhere beneath the sand, deep in one such bowl, lie the remains of the lander from the 'Zheng He.' If we dug around the spot where we found the ruined greenhouse, we could probably find it. Inside, we might find the remains of her crew, the men and women who were truly the first on Titan.

I hope we will have the courtesy to leave them undisturbed.

The Station Master
Lavie Tidhar

Djibril Todd stood on the railway platform and watched an ice meteor slowly descend far on the horizon, a white plume trailing in its wake against the red skies. The 5:30 from Tong Yun was late. He checked his pocket watch, a terrible affectation but it was a family heirloom, the intricate mechanism carefully repaired numerous times throughout the years.

Tradition said the watch came with the Todds on that first, one-way trip to Mars in a cheap jalopy, carried by Ezra Todd himself in his breast pocket. It had survived the landing, in the place then called Terminal. Had weathered marriages, divorces, funerals, and careless children. Had passed from one generation to the next, as Terminal became Tong Yun by degrees; survived the First Soviet-Israeli War and almost didn't make it through the second; was worn once by Ibrahim Todd, struggling actor, in the Phobos Studios classic *Night of the Tokoloshe*, where (so family elders insisted) it could be seen, for one split second, in the famous crowd scene. The watch had its history, and Djibril Todd, being a Todd, respected it. And if the story his cousin Ezra (named for that long-ago Ezra Todd) – that the watch was just a cheap replica bought one day on a whim by their grandfather in a pawn shop in Tong Yun, who made up the rest – well if that story was true, it did not make a lie of the *essence* of it and, besides, the watch still kept time.

Now it told him the train was more than ten minutes late.

It was not a major occurrence, of course. Trains were always late. This one did the route from Tong Yun to Valles Marineris Central, a four thousand klicks journey, and Djibril Todd's tiny, almost nameless station hardly figured as an important stop. But named it was (it was called Yaniv Town) and stop there the train did. Djibril watched, and finally saw the rising dust in the distance, like a sandstorm coming from deep inland. Then the head of the train appeared. The supersonic bullet shot forward before slowing almost imperceptivity, as though its driving agent could barely tolerate the thought of stopping, here, when speed was its very essence.

But still, it was late. Djibril stood as the train drifted along the platform and came to a halt. The doors opened. A family of three got off, luggage following behind them like eager puppies. The passengers were the Rafati family, who owned the general store. A mother, father, and a little girl. They said hello to Djibril, and he said, "Welcome back."

The girl looked tired but excited from the trip to the city.

"We saw Sivan Shoshanim!" she said. 'Right there on the street!"

"I think it was a hologram, honey," her mother said.

"No, it was her!" the girl said. "Daddy?"

"What? Yes," the father said. He took the little girl's hand. "Let's go home," he said.

They wished Djibril good night and walked off towards the terminal building. Only one other passenger left the train. The doors closed with a soft swoosh. The train slid along the platform, through the special airlock of the large dome, and gathered speed until it shot off into the distance, heading to places more exciting than this.

"Excuse me?"

"Yes?"

Djibril turned. An elderly robot came along the platform. It was one of the old humanoid ones, covered in scratches and rust. It had no luggage. It said, "Are you the station master?"

"I am, sir. Is it sir?"

The robot laughed the recorded, kindly old man's laugh of some long-dead person.

"One designation is as good as another," it said. "My name is R. Riperem-ol-Gud. But you can call me Rip."

"And how may I help you?" Djibril said.

"I came a long way," Riperem-ol-Gud said. "I do not need accommodation, and my funds are few. But I find myself in need of guidance."

"We aim to serve," Djibril said.

"It's funny," the robot said. "So do we. Robots, I mean. It is what we were made for, after all. And yet, after so long, no one remembers. Now we wonder if there is not a greater purpose we could serve."

"You mean God?" Djibril said.

"I do. But what is God? Is there a God of robots? Old human books tell of a God who created people in its image. And people created us in their image, before they lost interest. What, then, are we? The imperfect copies of imperfect beings?"

"I suppose," Djibril said. He felt a little embarrassed for the old robot. But he wanted to show good hospitality. It was important. "Is this why you came?" he said. "We are a small community; we have few places of worship. A shrine to Ogko, one mosque at the edge of town, and there's a community of Re-Born living out in the desert, outside the dome, but they mostly keep to themselves."

"I see," the robot said. "No, that is not why I came. I heard a story, a while back. Two or three centuries ago. It is said the poet Basho once visited Mars. He stayed in Tong Yun for a while, before going off into the desert. He found a tree, it's said, one of the oldest on Mars. He meditated under it for two days and two nights, and when he had done so he wrote, *Laef i stap / long ples i no gat / wan narafala laef.* Are you familiar with the poem?"

"Ah, yes," Djibril said. "*There is life in this place / that has no / other life.* Yes, it is quite famous, Mr Rip."

"How old is this place?" the robot said. "This Yaniv Town?"

"Quite old," Djibril said. "Yes. It is said it a hermit lived here, long before there was a town. We do have a tree, it stands in the town square, and it is quite old. An olive tree. They say it stood there before any houses were built. But whether it is the tree Basho visited, that I can't tell you, in truth."

"Is it easy to find?" the robot said.

"Yes, very. Just through the station building and along Main. We are a small place, Mr Rip. Everything is within reach."

"Then I shall visit it," the robot said. "And I shall meditate in its shade. Thank you."

"Goodbye, Mr Rip," Djibril said.

He watched the robot as it walked into the terminal building, then checked his watch. There were only two more trains due that day. The sun was low on the horizon. Another ice comet fell, as gently as a snowflake. He had seen snowflakes in Earth pictures. He wondered about going there one day. But he had never been off-world.

The next train was on time. It was a slower, local train, running through the small hamlets and towns of the desert: through Nirsville and Nag Hammadi and New Ashkelon, La Navidad, Urumqi and Port Jessup.

When it stopped, it dropped off a handful of passengers, locals who have gone to visit friends or relatives in nearby dome towns and now came back. There was no driver, for the trains were sentient, and kept their own law. It was said that, once a year, all the trains of Mars left their depots, with no passengers on board, and sped wildly across the tangle of railway lines deep into the desert, there to have a Convocation of the Trains. But what they did there was known only to the trains themselves.

"Excuse me, Djibril," a voice said, 'is the bar open?"

It was Mrs Ness. She owned the second largest white cabbage farm, outside the dome. The cabbages grew in klicks-long rows inside their greenhouses, fed on drip-irrigation and the sun. She peered at Djibril with a helpless expression.

"I am waiting for the last train," she said.

"Are you going someplace, Mrs Ness?" Djibril said.

Mrs Ness shook her head. "No," she said. "I am waiting for someone."

"I will be happy to serve you," Djibril said. He walked to the terminal building. A few people milled about, regulars he knew well. He went into the small bar and let himself behind the counter.

"What can I get you?" he said.

"I will have a small glass of arak, please," Mrs Ness said. Djibril poured, then added ice and a little bit of water without being asked. He knew Mrs Ness' order. Mrs Ness always waited for the train on Raindays. It never rained on Mars, but it was hoped that it would one day, and so it was chosen as one of the seven days of the standard Martian week. Mrs Ness always waited for the train on

Raindays, but no one ever came for her. She had a daughter in Tong Yun.

The drink in the glass turned milky white as the water and arak mixed. Mrs Ness took a small, grateful sip. A group of four Re-Born came into the bar.

"Hey, Djibril," the tallest of them said.

"Hey, Daud," Djibril said.

"It's 'T'P'aii, now," Daud said. He was much changed since they were kids playing together under the olive tree. A series of surgeries and modifications had made him taller, and his muscles bulged. His skin was a deep shade of red, and he had four arms now instead of the usual two. He lived out in the desert in makeshift mobile habitats with the other Martian Re-Born.

"What can I get you fellows?" Djibril said.

"Water of Life, please," one of the other Re-Born – they styled themselves 'warriors' – said. "From the deep wells of the Emperor of Time, if you can."

"I only have recycled water," Djibril said.

"Then make it four araks," Daud said. "How are the trains?"

"Still coming and going," Djibril said. When they were kids, he and Daud used to spend hours watching the trains pass on their endless tracks. They'd put on suits and leave the dome entirely, trekking across the desert, following the tracks. Once they followed them all the way to Port Jessup, which was the nearest other settlement to Yaniv Town. They had to take the train home get back and when they did their parents punished them for a month for taking such a stupid risk. You did not leave the dome by yourself. It was too dangerous. But all the teenage kids did, anyway.

Then one day Daud got on a train to Tong Yun, and there he visited the multifaith bazaar on Level Three, and down there, deep under the sands, he ran into a Re-Born preacher, and was granted a vision of Mars-That-Never-Was.

Djibril himself had done it once. It was a simulation, of course, but it felt real. In the induced vision he was a Martian warrior, four-armed and fierce. Mars was a paradise world of canals and warm air, and the Emperor of Time sat on his throne and the warriors served him and the Empire.

It was a compelling vision. Then it was over, and all Djibril was left with was a headache. He poured four araks and carried them over to the table. The Re-Born were harmless enough. And everyone needed to believe in something. He wasn't sure what *he* believed in. Other than in the history of his grandfather's illustrious pocket watch.

Night was falling outside the dome. Mrs Ness stared dreamily into the distance. The four Martian warriors were deep in discussion about the latest Elvis Mandela picture, and Djibril checked his watch. The last train should be arriving soon. Then he would close the bar, check the restrooms, record, and store any lost and found luggage, lock up for the night and go upstairs. He lived on the second floor of the terminal building, in the station manager's rooms, where old man Hasson used to live. He was station master for years when Djibril was growing up. The rooms were small but comfortable, and they offered a view over the desert and the railway tracks vanishing into the distance. Ice comets fell overhead and when they crashed into the ground the plumes of ice they sent up made rainbows appear all over the Martian sands.

He poured Mrs Ness a new drink and checked the waiting room. Only three passengers waited for the last train to Tong Yun. Csilla Chen and Emily Fitoussi jointly ran the farmers' co-op. They had the vacant-eyed looks of people busy accessing their nodes. The third passenger was momentarily hidden from Djibril's sight, standing in the shadow of the shuttered kiosk by the windows that overlooked the platform. Djibril went over, and a familiar figure turned and saw him and said, "Hi, Djibril."

"Yara," Djibril said. Her face came out of the shadows. She gave him the sort of smile one reserved for distant friends, polite but distant. It hurt. "I didn't know you were travelling."

"Why would you?" she said. She said it lightly. When they were together, she had asked him once why he didn't travel.

"You spend every day of your life on the platform, watching the trains pass you by," she said. "Don't you ever want to *go* somewhere?"

And he'd said, "But I have everything I want right here."

He couldn't then explain it to her, not fully. There was always somewhere else to go to, always the next town and the next. But he would still be himself when he got there. Yaniv Town was home, and he knew it just as it knew him. He thought of the olive tree in the town square, that had been there longer than Djibril had been alive, that would still be there, giving shade, when Djibril was long gone. The tree didn't need to go anywhere. It was where it belonged.

But he didn't know how to say it to Yara, and even when they were together, she always gave him the impression she had better places to go.

"Can I get you anything?" he said now. He mustered a smile. "Tea, perhaps?"

"I'm fine. Thank you, Djibril. How are the trains today?"

"Still running," he said. It was her turn to smile. She came a little closer, touched his cheek lightly, then withdrew her hand.

"It's good to see you," she said. She turned away from him as the last train came in through the airlock. Djibril watched Yara walk away and board the train. Then she was gone.

He checked his pocket watch. The train was early. It sat next to the platform, lit from within, and he could see the people inside it, talking or dozing, laughing, or arguing. All coming from somewhere and going elsewhere.

He made his rounds. No one had come for Mrs Ness. She finished her drink and left, and Daud and his friends left shortly after. Djibril washed the glasses and closed the bar. He checked the lost and found. Someone had left a mess in the bathrooms, and he cleaned it up. He locked up when he was done and went upstairs and wound his pocket watch. He was just in time to see the light of the train vanishing into the great night beyond the window.

Art App
Chris Beckett

For some reason, he had obtained a copy of his own draft obituary from the files of a national newspaper:

"Generally agreed to be among the twenty richest people in the world," he read, "Wayland Pryce was one of the giants of the digital revolution, developing, or making possible, an astonishingly high proportion of the various portable computing devices we can now barely imagine doing without, though they would have been science fiction a generation ago. But, although best known for his gadgets, Pryce was also a well-respected connoisseur of surrealist art. He built, entirely at his own expense, the award-winning Pryce Gallery in upstate New York in order to share with the general public his substantial collection of works by artists such as Max Ernst, Paul Delvaux, and Salvador Dali (but not Magritte, whose work he never liked!) The Gallery, however, was only one of his many philanthropic projects… "

Wayland was unsettled by this posthumous view of himself. "I realised that I'm not who the world thinks I am," he told his fourth wife, the actress Roxy Barnes: they were already living apart at this point but had remained friends. "I've tried to persuade myself otherwise, but that guy isn't me. He's just a gigantic mask. No wonder it never worked out with you or the others. You can't have a relationship with a mask."

Fifty storeys above the ground, under the potted tree ferns and palms of a Manhattan rooftop restaurant, he talked about his art collection, telling her that he'd first been drawn to those paintings, "not out of 'connoisseurship', whatever in hell that's supposed to mean, but because a few of them reminded me of… "

But he was unable to say what they reminded him of, only that they'd reminded him of *something* – something he couldn't hold in his mind for any length of time, let alone name, but which some part of him seemed to want very much to grasp.

"Even back in my teens," he said, "before I knew a damn thing about the surrealists or their historical context, those pictures felt like a glimpse through the keyhole of a prison door. But, you know, having had this insight, I betrayed it."

She was mystified. "How could you betray a thing like that?"

"By creating all those anal little devices that made me my billions."

"I'm not getting you."

"They're slowly killing us, Rox, they're killing everyone, including me. Not in a literal sense, obviously, but... you know... "

He trailed off. As Roxy knew only too well, Wayland wasn't always very articulate about things that were personal to himself.

"In a *spiritual* sense, do you mean?" she offered, but he firmly rejected that. 'Spiritual' to him meant pretty clouds and mist and ethereal choirs. What he was talking about wasn't anything like that. In fact, it was his devices that made the world ethereal. They made it thinner, more abstract, more disembodied. What those pictures had reminded him of was a kind of *substance*.

"Max Ernst gets the closest. Those strange landscapes, you know? That strange stuff they're made of. Like the... " he groped for the right words, "like a kind of... I don't know... like the stuff that thoughts are moulded from. Or the stuff that *desires* are moulded of. No, not that either, but something a bit... " He shrugged and gave her a rueful smile. "You see? You can't put it into words. I can't anyway. But that's where the paintings come in. Images go where words fail. Dali, Ernst... Ernst definitely gets the closest."

Roxy was no art buff, but she took out her phone and searched for Max Ernst paintings, so as to engage as best she could with what he was talking about.

"All my devices," Wayland said. "All the businesses I built to market them, lead us all in precisely the opposite direction to where I actually *want* to go. Whatever useful little purposes they're supposed to serve, their real function is to keep us busy fiddling about with trivia on the surface."

He dropped her an email the next day to apologise for his "usual heaviness and self-absorption".

A few days later he was sitting in the evening on the balcony of one of his villas in the south of France, a mild sea in front of him, the day's warmth rising pleasantly from the stone-flagged floor, and a glass of white wine at his elbow. Several screens were arrayed on a table in front of him. On one was a report on paintings that had recently come onto the market, compiled for him by Lucy, his art buyer. On another, he had opened the catalogue of paintings he already possessed. Even the greatest painters had their off days, and there were always acquisitions which, on reflection, turned out not to be interesting or important enough to deserve a continuing place in his collection. (You sometimes had to own them a while before you knew.) At the same time, there were always gaps which he wanted to fill.

As he made lists of paintings to buy and to sell, sipping from time to time at his wine, a memory came to him from his childhood. He'd been a somewhat solitary child. He'd found it tiring to project the warmth that was apparently necessary to make connections with other people. He could do it perfectly well but then, as now, it exhausted him if he had to sustain it, and he'd needed a good deal of time on his own to replenish himself.

On the occasion that had come into his mind, he was nine years old and was by himself at the family kitchen table, playing with buttons. His mother had a shoebox full of hundreds of buttons, many of them collected by her own mother, and, after a tiring day at school, he'd ask her to get them out for him. He could happily spend hours sorting them into piles, by colour, size, shape, or style. It was a pointless task, seeing as he would end up shovelling them back into the same box, but the pointlessness of it was its appeal. It distracted him from a certain echoing loneliness that he otherwise would have had to pay attention to – not so much a personal loneliness, as he experienced it, but something more like the loneliness of space and time, or of the universe itself, faced with the inescapable fact of its own existence. On this occasion – he quite vividly remembered it – at nine years old, just for a moment he'd briefly understood this, paused to consider it, and then returned to his buttons.

Now, there on his balcony, a greenish glow in the sky beyond the headland to show where the sun had gone, it struck Wayland that updating his art collection was just another kind of sorting buttons.

He laid aside his wine glass and began to walk back and forth along the balustrade. There was nothing wrong with sorting buttons, of course, but button-sorting was surely the precise opposite of the unsettled state that his pictures (or at least the good ones) had been intended to evoke. Collecting these paintings like stamps, making them the objects of scholarship, assigning them a financial value, providing each with its own instructive little label on the gallery wall: these were all ways of neutralising the one quality that had drawn him to them in the first place – their unearthliness, their venom. It was as if he'd bought all those pictures only to bury them, each under its own well-tended tombstone.

By now the sky was dark, and the small waves breaking in the bay were dim flashes in blackness. He'd been trying to give up smoking, but he sent for a pack of Gauloises, and lighting one, leant over the balustrade and slowly drew in the thick gunpowdery smoke. Cicadas were still rattling among the olive trees. Bats were diving back and forth through the glow of the small electric light at the end of the jetty. Wayland exhaled.

"I mean, if they have any real value at all," he said to himself, "paintings are glimpses, right? And the thing you should do with a glimpse isn't to store it away, or add it to a catalogue, but to try and see more of what it's showing you."

He called Lucy, his art buyer, in New York, where it was still the middle of the afternoon. "I'm going to sell the whole collection."

It took her a few seconds to take this in. "Sell *everything*? You're joking, right?"

"No, I'm serious. The whole lot. But first I need to find some decent art photographers and have them make copies. Any ideas?"

"Photographers? Sure, but why? These are valuable artworks! You've spent years assembling them and their value is going up all the time."

"I own five mansions, six apartments, two jets, a yacht with room for a hundred people, and two companies in the top twenty of the Fortune 500. Why should I care how much my paintings are worth?"

"Well, okay, but surely an original painting – the original oils, the original brush strokes – is something entirely different from… "

"I don't buy that, Lucy. A real artist creates an image, not a lump of matter. Do you need Tolstoy's original manuscript in front of you, in order to read *War and Peace*? We make fetishes out of art objects, and then we use them as a kind of money. It's sordid. It has nothing whatever to do with art."

About this time, a new kind of art app was doing the rounds. At the touch of a few buttons, an artificial intelligence generated an image for you on any subject you chose, and in a variety of styles. The results were often a little eerie. These programs had access, obviously, to a vast library of images, and quite sophisticated ways of combining and reworking them, but they had no understanding of an outside world to which the images were supposed to relate. In the pictures they made, space bent and twisted, objects bled into each other, and human bodies were simply another kind of blob. Looking at them, Wayland had a sense that he was seeing a kind of ectoplasm, quite unlike earthly flesh or earthly matter, but actually rather strikingly like that strange substance of which surrealist landscapes were moulded. Ask the app to do something in the style of Botticelli or Tintoretto and it never really came off – it looked, at best, like a collage – but ask it to do Dali or Ernst and the effect was often surprisingly convincing. Indeed, give it a suitable title, and it sometimes came up on its own with an image that Ernst himself might have been quite happy to make. Strange, really, that an artificial mind inside a machine, a mind that didn't possess desires or fears, should create something that so much resembled the world of dreams.

By and large, the art world ignored these new toys, and for most people, they were at most a passing fad, but Wayland was fascinated. After carefully reviewing the companies that produced these apps, he identified the most promising one, bought it outright, and doubled the salaries it paid. When Roxy called to ask how he was, as she still did from time to time, he told her he had a whole new project that mattered more to him than anything he'd ever done.

"No more hints, no more clues, no more peeks into something unreachable, I'm going to make possible a kind of art that actually takes you right there," he said, adding that he was going to put every bit as much time and energy into this as he'd previously devoted to all those convenient and desirable little gadgets.

"But I'm going to work in private this time," he told her. "I'm having all my collaborators sign non-disclosure agreements, and I'm going to take myself right out of the public arena. In fact, you may not hear from me for a while."

This actually suited her, because she was at the beginning of a new relationship with a young filmmaker, who was uneasy about her continuing closeness to Wayland.

"Very nice of you to call," he said, "but maybe leave it now until I'm ready to call you."

At this point, as we now know, he had set his new employees to work on more sophisticated versions of those art apps, so as to create much more complex and much higher resolution images, and do so in the round, so that they could be viewed in three dimensions using VR headsets. He'd brought in people from the CGI field to help with this. He had also recruited a number of art historians and visual artists to help develop a new kind of program that would take real works of art and, rather than jumbling them up as the existing art apps did, would retain the original image but extend it, sideways beyond the frame, and backwards and forwards in space, so that it broke free of the bounded surface of the canvas. Soon, with a headset, he could look at one of Ernst's eerie, quasi-geological landforms – "The Eye of Silence" for instance –and, as he slowly turned his head, see more of the imaginary world that it implied, with landscape features, never seen before, looking as if they had always been there.

Money was no object. Profit was not required. Customers didn't need to be found or held onto. Wayland himself *was* the customer. But he wasn't yet satisfied. He needed movement for one thing. Take another Ernst scene, "The Temptation of St Anthony". Extending the landscape was fine, but the picture wouldn't truly come alive until those chitinous creatures grinning and crawling in the foreground were set in motion. If paintings were to become worlds, they needed to be set loose in time as well as space.

As each goal was achieved, Wayland would dispense champagne and bonuses very generously, but he himself would already be thinking of new problems that needed solving. He had now turned artworks into moving, three-dimensional and limitless images, but they were still essentially *spectacles*. To really enter into them, he decided, you needed to engage more of the senses, so you could hear sounds around you, feel the heat or the cold, sniff at the smells. He gathered his art experts together and plied them with questions they'd never been asked before: What would a giraffe smell of as it stood calmly burning in a Dali desert? What sound would those chitinous creatures make as they crawled over Saint Anthony's body? What sort of wind would blow through Delvaux's moonlit railway stations?

He hired sound effects people. He tracked down what few specialists there were in the field of olfactory simulation. As for the tactile element, he wanted to be able to *walk* through these landscapes – not just use a joystick to make them move around, but really physically *walk* through them, over terrain that felt rough or smooth underfoot, with real gradients that required real effort, and objects that could really be touched.

At this point, he called in demolition people and had the entire upper floor of the gallery ripped out along with all the dividing walls, reducing the whole elegant, minimalist building to an empty shell. Troubled locals, who generally speaking had enjoyed and profited from the well-behaved tourists he'd brought to their town, were assured by his staff that he was planning an art exhibit of a kind not found anywhere else in the world. And they had to make do with that, because Wayland himself had disappeared from view, his engagements cancelled, his companies run by proxies.

The non-disclosure agreements, along with his excellent lawyers and his very elaborate security measures at the gallery site ensured that almost nothing leaked out as to what he was doing there, but he was very busy, recruiting mechanical engineers now and, in particular, experts in the design of complex, computer-managed mechanical systems, such as automated production lines or driverless vehicles. He set them to work on enabling real physical mobility in a virtual world, and once again moved on to something else. This time he hired psychologists and neuroscientists.

"I don't want my artwork worlds to be fixed in space like the material world," he told them. "I want them to adjust to the needs of the person visiting them. I don't mean in the trivial sense of offering menus and choices. Absolutely not! I want none of that. That would lead straight back to triviality. What I'm looking for is ways to somehow pick up on involuntary emotional responses. I was wondering if we could monitor heart rate, perhaps, or skin conductivity or something. Or, I don't know, maybe brain waves?"

He looked into their puzzled faces. Probably they were all a little dazed by the amount of research money he was offering them.

"My idea is that the program should be able to tell what aspect of a given scene particularly engages the individual viewer at an imaginative level so that it can provide him or her with more. Do you see what I mean? My idea is that what starts as a vision of Ernst's or Delvaux's will slowly metamorphose as a viewer moves through it so that by degrees it becomes personal to the individual currently engaged with it."

Many months followed in which Roxy heard nothing from Wayland, and nor did anyone else she knew to be a friend of his. She was uneasy about this – he'd been a distracted husband rather than a bad one, and she remained fond of him – but she knew how single-minded he could be when in the grip of a new passion, and reminded herself that he himself had specifically told her it would be a while before she heard from him. Things hadn't worked out with the filmmaker, but she was leading a busy and rewarding life. Wayland would call her when he was ready.

Then she had a call from someone named Earl. She couldn't place him at first, but he was a man in his sixties who had been a security guard at the Pryce Gallery from when it was still being built. She knew him from the time when she and Wayland were travelling upstate almost every week to review progress on the site.

Earl said he was worried about Wayland. "He's in the building fifteen to twenty hours a day."

"Oh he's always like that when a project's nearing completion," Roxy told him with a sigh. "He lives and breathes it until it's finished. There's a short time afterwards when he lets himself relax. Then he has another idea, and the whole damn cycle begins all over."

"But that's just it," Earl said. "The project *is* finished. The engineers were done a couple of months ago, but he's in there all the time on his own."

"I guess it must be a nice quiet place to work."

"You're not getting me, Mrs Pryce. There's nothing left inside that building except machinery. No furniture, no rooms, not even a proper floor. Lately, he's been going in wearing some kind of diaper. Really! I mean it! A diaper or a catheter or something – like an astronaut. He takes nothing with him but a little knapsack with maybe a bottle of water and some sandwiches. Yesterday he was in there for nineteen hours, but all he does is just kind of wander about, going back and forth on those wheels."

"Wheels?"

"You need to see it for yourself. We've told him he should talk to you, but he won't listen. We think you should come up here. We're not supposed to let anyone in without his permission, but my boss agrees that, in the circumstances, you still being his wife, we should make an exception for you."

Roxy drove up the next day from New York City. It was three hours before she reached the little town and the grey hangar-like gallery a mile outside it, squatting in the forest on the site of an old timber mill. Fierce-looking fences had been erected all around it since her last visit, and the visitor's car park was empty, but Earl was there to open the gate for her.

"He's inside now," he told her. "The night shift guys tell me he's been there since 6 a.m."

The main entrance to the gallery no longer existed but Earl led her round to a new entrance at the back. This was the equivalent of two storeys above ground level, accessed by an external metal staircase. When Earl let her in, she found herself on a narrow walkway, with metal railings and a metal mesh floor, that went right round the building and overlooked a brightly lit, industrial-looking space that for a moment made her think of the interior of a gigantic clock. Earl hadn't exaggerated when he said there was no floor left. The nearest things to it were the two enormous discs – Earl called them wheels – that almost touched each other in the middle of the space and extended to the exterior walls. In the parts not covered by these two discs, a mass of smaller wheels, cables, and hydraulics was visible beneath them. But what Roxy mostly noticed was the single small figure, its eyes hidden by a black helmet, that was slowly trudging away from her, and towards the far wall, across the further of the two giant wheels.

This wheel was a complex structure. It had a kind of deck that was currently tilted by hydraulic pistons to an angle of about twenty-five degrees to the horizontal turntable on which it was fixed. Wayland was climbing up this slope, which was covered with obstacles of one shape or another, ranging from a texture of small bumps on its surface to clusters of walls and columns as much as ten feet high. Meanwhile, the turntable itself was slowly revolving so that the upper edge towards which he was climbing, and which had been next to the external wall when Roxy and Earl came in, was steadily moving round towards the spot in the centre of the building where the two turntables met. This meant that, though Wayland had been ascending the same slope since they first saw him, he would soon be heading straight towards them rather than away from them. The turntable was also sinking downwards, so that, in spite of his steady upward climb, Wayland never gained any height in relation to the building itself.

"He's been going back and forth between those two wheels since six this morning," Earl said, as they headed round the walkway to keep the helmeted figure in view. 'Sometimes he just stops and stares, and once in a while he has a drink of water or eats a sandwich, but most of the time he just trudges on. He must be absolutely exhausted, Mrs Pryce, and he's definitely not eating enough."

A strange aroma wafted towards them – fungal, scorched, tinged with ammonia – and then another smell, like old honey and lilies that have begun to decay.

There were so many different things to take in. Bars spanning the high ceiling were hung with rows of what looked like theatre spotlights. Some of these seemed to track Wayland's progress, but they didn't give out any light. "Those round ones are radiant heaters," Earl told her, following her gaze. "The big square ones are blowers. It's them that puts out the smells." He wrinkled his nose. "Crazy part is he's spent millions on this – billions for all I know – and everyone's been told it's going to be a new kind of gallery, but you can see for yourself it's only ever going to work for one person at a time."

The deck of the second turntable was beginning to tilt now as Wayland approached the upper edge of the deck across which he'd been trudging. The wheel beneath him had slowed to a standstill and had sunk to a point where the upper edge of its tilted deck was exactly aligned with the lower edge of the tilted deck of the other wheel. Wedges had moved into the spaces around where the two wheels met, making a path over which he could pass from one to another without falling into the machinery below. He could carry on like this forever, Roxy realised, with the two turntables passing him endlessly back and forth between them.

From the tilted deck of the second turntable, which up to now had appeared to have a smooth surface, columns, walls, and bumps rose up, as Wayland stepped onto it from the first turntable and began to trudge up the incline. The new turntable began to turn. Meanwhile, the deck of the first one returned to a horizontal position, and its various bumps, walls and columns sank back into its surface.

"Back and forth, back and forth.... . All day, every day," Earl said, as the air was suddenly filled with a blast of roses, tinged with burning rubber. "Like a hamster in a cage. Apparently with that headset on it looks to him like he's inside one of those ugly paintings that used to hang here, though why anyone would want—"

Halfway along the walkway that ran along the side of the gallery, Earl and Roxy were now as close to Wayland as they were going to get. "Wayland!" Roxy shouted, leaning over the railing and cupping her hands round her mouth. "Wayland! It's me, Roxy!"

Earl shook his head. "He won't hear you. He's got headphones inside that helmet. God knows what he's listening to, but it blots out everything else."

Wayland stopped. He stood quite still on the slowly rotating deck as if considering his route. After a few minutes, he turned to his left and began to scale a step-like structure which had emerged there. He would soon reach the edge of the deck if he continued in this new direction, and the two turntables duly adjusted themselves so they would be suitably aligned if he stepped back across to the first one. There was a whiff of diesel, brown sugar, and mud.

Wayland scrambled up the steep slope to the ridge, ignoring the tiny grimacing faces in the outcrops and their little muttering voices. Occasionally from somewhere nearby came a shuddering sound, like the sound a horse makes when it shakes off a fly.

At the top, he stopped again. The heat was relentless from the fierce pink star above him, and he was very tired. He took out his water bottle and took a mouthful from the three or four mouthfuls left. In the distance another ridge was facing him, considerably higher than the one he was standing on. He was pretty sure that when he climbed to the top of it, there would be an ocean visible below it, an ocean made of living glass, inhabited by beings that no one had ever seen before.

He couldn't head that way directly though, because immediately below him was a shadowy ravine from which came a constant droning sound. He could see insect-people moving about down there, and even faintly make out the murmur of their voices. He'd have to circumvent the ravine by going around the clifftop to the right. He could do this without losing much height, and most of it wouldn't be particularly hard going, but there'd be a bit of scrambling at first. Thinking, he'd better give himself time to catch his breath before he tackled it, he stood and admired the view.

The ridge he was aiming for was a greenish colour, parts of it formed like giant spiral candle sticks, other parts resembling human torsos, or giant molluscs. The whole formation seemed to be made of stretched-out strands of a substance which had once been pliable and stringy, like melted cheese, and these strands seemed to have been draped and twisted around themselves before they solidified. Several large, heavy-lidded eyes stared out from the complex knotted surface. They seldom blinked, but sometimes one of them moved slightly to look in a different direction, though what they were looking at was impossible to tell. They showed no interest in him. Occasionally some small portion of the surface would suddenly tremble as if it were a chrysalis and the moth inside was preparing to emerge from its chitin shell. There was a faint smell of burnt beetle wings and sexual fluids. In the lumps of rock-like flesh that lay about around him, those tiny faces muttered and grimaced. He was glad to be away from the creatures he'd seen when he began his ascent.

Was that someone calling his name just now, he wondered? If so, that needed fixing. No one was supposed to approach him from the world outside. But, having climbed so far, he wasn't going to waste time now on thinking about things like that.

In the dim ravine below, the insect people were making piles of small objects that gleamed like brass buttons. There were far more of the creatures than he'd first realised, thousands of them in fact, crawling over each other in their haste as they hurried excitedly back and forth with buttons in their little hands. A stale papery smell wafted up. The insect creatures looked extraordinarily pleased with themselves, grinning at one another, and rattling their vestigial wing cases.

A cry came from above, and the little muttering voices around him became suddenly loud and agitated. He looked up to see a creature with burning wings, falling towards him from the sun. He watched the flames consume it until all that was left was little floating specks of ash. Smiling to himself, he continued on his way.

The *Blou Trein* Suborbirail

L.P. Melling

Fenwick checks the train parts for printing errors, sweat dripping down the back of his neck. The air con has packed in again and the merciless South African heat infiltrates the cramped confines of his workstation. He runs his hand over a replacement connective rod for the *Blou Trein* Suborbirail's track and feels a nick. Like most of the workers, he doesn't trust the hand-held scanners that lost people their jobs. Fenwick can't risk it. He is about to polish down the superalloy when he hears shouting behind him, his grip tightening around the rod.

"Fenwick! Stop the hell what you're doing and get over here!"

He grits his teeth. "Yes, Boss." Fenwick slowly turns around, trying to relax his facial muscles, and sees Mr. Grobler's jowls wobbling, face red beneath a liver-spotted bald head.

"And goddamn hurry up about it!" Grobler says, and his eyes lock on what's in Fenwick's hand. *Fokk!* Parts are supposed to be kept in the workstation area. The other workers remain in their stations, carrying on with their toil, heads down. "What the hell are you carrying, Fenwick?"

"Sorry, Boss. Found an imperfection. Was just about to correct it and —"

"Oh, so you can do your job, then?" he sneers. The boss is in his face now. "So tell me, Fenwick, why have I just got off a lunar call hearing parts from your line were sent up defective? Hey?"

Fenwick screws up his face in confusion, lowers his gaze. "No idea, Boss. Been checking for printing errors twice over with every part. They must've made a mistake."

"You idiot! They use bots up there for that work, so how the hell could they be mistaken?" He throws his hands up in frustration. "Now I'm going to have to lower our rates on the next train drop. I should've left you in that corrective facility to rot, Fenwick. How hard is it to check for printing errors for fuck's sake! My eight-year-old niece could do a better job! If it wasn't for the subsidy, you'd be out of here." Grobler loves reminding Fenwick that the only reason TransNet employs humans like him is because of its exclusive deal with the government to take on ex-cons. Bots cost more to run and service than the few bitcreds Fenwick gets paid an hour, and it's sweet-as-malva PR for South Africa's richest company. "I'm docking your pay!"

Fenwick flexes. "You god –"

"What, Fenwick? Just try it and I'll have the security bots kick you out of here. A crook like you would never find another job."

Fenwick swallows back his words into his burning stomach, turning away. He's tried for years to leave TransNet for better work. Does well at the interviews, receives promising remarks, but as soon as employers do a background check on him, they send the rejection.

"That's right, get back to it. This is your last chance, Fenwick, you hear? The *last!*"

"*Ja*," he mutters, still gripping iron tight on the rod as he faces the conveyor belt. He polishes down the part, micro-sander grinding against his bones, and drops it in the green-rimmed chute.

He can't even get angry about the turndowns. When there are so many people looking for work without petty crimes on their record, why *would* they choose him?

Fenwick hits the button next to his workstation to get the belt moving again, catching a glimpse of the blue digits lighting up his section. Still, five hours left of this crap to go. He grabs the next part, a flawless rivet, and assigns it ready for freight transportation to the Suborbirail's final stop.

Fenwick scans his ID card to exit TransNet's premises. The sun is long gone as he breathes in the cool air. He did an extra hour of unpaid work to play it safe. Not that there's much chance Grobler noticed.

Fenwick crosses the sandy flats through slum streets most avoid, corrugated shacks crouching either side of him, as he passes through the district of Cape Town the government ignores. The unmistakable aroma of *umngqusho* drifts on the breeze from a nearby shack. His mouth waters at the smell of food that filled his childhood: sugar beans and crushed corn slow cooked so it melts on the tongue. His mother used to make it as the rooibos-strained sun kissed the slums on the horizon.

Things were so much easier back then. No idiot boss pushing him around. No worries as he played all day with his childhood friends. Fenwick remembers Mrs Jardine chasing him and Khumalo through the slum, saying she'll kill them when she gets her hands on them. He'd find his and Khumalo's names scratched into the paintwork of her old place if he walked around the corner, and the spot where Kalum got stabbed to death on his sixteenth birthday. But he leaves his past in the slums and walks on.

Fenwick arrives back in a slightly better part of Cape Town. He finds his girlfriend, Lenka, waiting for him in their apartment's front room; it's not much bigger than his workstation but it's a much happier place. He never forgets how lucky they are to have solid walls now.

Fenwick kisses Lenka, sprawls into the gel-foam lazy chair.

"Why you so late, *bokkie*?" she asks.

"Grobler." He doesn't have to say more to explain.

Fenwick switches on the box to watch the footorb game.

Lenka stands in front of the screen.

"Hey?"

She fixes him with a stare, eyes the same shade of blue as the *Blou Trein*'s livery, long coffee-coloured hair framing her perfect bone structure. He still can't believe she chose an ugly mug like him. It took them years of scrimping and saving to get out of their shack in the Cape Flats slum. Fenwick is proud of where he came from, but he never wants to go back there.

The struggle and sacrifice seem to show on her face now as her lips part, wet and red. "We need to talk."

Fenwick mentally runs through the things he might have done wrong recently. Did he leave his cereal bowl out again yesterday morning?

"How long have we been together now?" she says.

O kak, one of those conversations. He runs his hand over the chair, reactively reaching for an ejector seat button he knows isn't installed. "Years, baby. The best of my life."

"Ten years next week!"

Damn it. He knew he had to buy something. Fenwick stares at the digital pic display on the wall, showing him and Lenka standing in front of their new home, arms wrapped around each other. Must be three years ago already if they met a decade ago.

"Don't you think it's about time we started a family, then?" Lenka looks fragile and strong at the same time: beautiful.

Fenwick drops his gaze as he did with Grobler. "I don't know. Of course, I want to, darling. But with work and everything, we can barely afford to feed ourselves after all the bills." Lenka knows TransNet knocked back his first transfer request, anything to get away from Grobler, but not that he made four further requests they rejected for no good reason. Or the times he almost walked out of there after the boss was on his case again.

He raises his head. A look of hurt sweeps across Lenka's face and it cuts him up.

"Sorry, *engel*. I'm just trying to be careful. Y'know. We're –"

"Pregnant. We're having a girl. I know I should've told you earlier, but I had to be sure this time."

"What?" Fenwick sits there, locked in a trance for a minute. He looks at her stomach, but there's barely a bump, and she catches him staring.

"How many times did I tell you my *ma* didn't show when she was pregnant with me and my sister, not till much later!"

"But I thought... " He thought he'd had too many kicks in the balls to have children, literally and otherwise. His Xhosa-descended mother, never shy about sharing things, always said the old man had a low sperm count. Fenwick hadn't seen his drunk of a father for over a decade since he moved back to Scotland. Father-son bonding was never their forte, anyway, even when he was around and Fenwick was a kid... and now Fenwick is having one of his own.

He won't make the same mistakes.

Fenwick stands and kisses Lenka. "Sorry, *engel*. That's wonderful news! Really! C'mon, let's go celebrate. I'm taking you to the best place in town." He lifts Lenka off her feet.

"You *domkop!*" she says around the laughter.

The natural high of beckoning fatherhood gets him through the first half of his shift the next day. *God*, does he feel like shit after all that champagne last night, though. Why didn't he stick to the alcohol-free cocktails like Lenka?

Fenwick hits the start button, missing it the first time. The conveyor belt chugs forward like the original *Blou Trein* the suborbital took its name from. Owned by TransNet, the Blue Train Suborbirail (as tourists know it) has long since taken its place in central Cape Town. Affluent, predominantly white families – the only ones able to afford a ticket – use the *Blou* to escape the ever-growing slums of South Africa for a new life on the Moon. He can't blame them for wanting the best for their children, not any more.

The more Fenwick tries to concentrate on what he's doing, the more he fails. Fenwick rubs his temples, knowing he can't make another mistake. The heat is incredible today; his back prickles with perspiration; his mouth is bone-dry. He hears the Boss shouting again in the background, but when isn't he?

Fenwick's eye catches another imperfection a second before he drops it down the green-edged chute. He wipes away the sheen of sweat from his forehead with the other hand.

"Fenwick!"

He spins around and drops the ball bearing anyway. *Fokk!* He hears it rolling down the conduit behind him.

"Yes, Boss," he says, as respectful as he can muster. Grobler carries a uTab in his hand and does something he doesn't expect: he smiles wide, exposing the dark gap between his teeth.

"Fenwick, don't move!" Grobler points the uTab at his face.

A flash of light startles him, and Fenwick is back in the *polisie* station again years earlier. Manhandled and being charged for petty hacking violations by a fat cop reeking of BO and *droëwors* meat. His third offence already, Fenwick is just a kid trying to get by on the streets but getting caught far too often.

"Fenwick," his boss says, breaking him out of the memory. "You're fired. Your security clearance is cancelled."

"What the –?" Fenwick spits. "Wh-why? I can't have made another mistake!"

"Your error rate isn't the worst, Fenwick, but it doesn't matter now." Sweat dripping down his fat red face, Gobbler smirks. "The government has cut the subsidy for taking on convicts, so I don't need to keep the likes of you on any more."

"You know what, *fokk* you! Stick it up your *gat!*" Fenwick lunges at him but pulls himself back, realizing Grobler is nothing, less than. Why land himself in more trouble for a parasite like him?

Fenwick is escorted out of the factory and the midday heat hits him in the face. He hasn't seen sunlight in days with the long shifts. He can't stop shaking, dehydrated and boiling over. "The bastard!" he mutters, and fear closes his throat. He can't let his child grow up in the slums like he did.

The *Blou Trein* Suborbirail stands out in the distance like always, shooting up above the clouds, its domed top out of sight. Vertical train lines cut through the dust and smog into unpolluted air. Fenwick still can't get used to it; the four human-thick rails look like they're defying gravity. The train's cobalt-blue hull glimmers in the sunlight miles high. Its torus carriages aren't attached by couplings but stacked on top of each other like a children's learning toy without the rainbow of colour, with a lesson just as valuable for local kids about the order of things.

Rich Africans have long said that people from the slums couldn't handle the atmosphere up there. Fenwick hears it all the time on state-controlled TV: *Prawns can't survive in space.*

Fenwick remembers watching the Suborbirail's construction with his childhood friends. It was a boost to the economy, with many of their parents finding work for the first time in years. Adrenaline junkies would hang glide around the growing structure to get a closer look before the guards cleared them off with green laser sights – kids always loved watching that part.

He'll never get out of South Africa. Like most people from the slums, Fenwick has come to terms with that, but he has a daughter on the way now. He won't let her face the same hopeless future, with people looking down and pitying her.

He stares at the monolith and his stomach tightens.

Fenwick punches himself in the leg with frustration and realizes the ID card is still in his pocket. Grobler forgot to take it from him. It won't work to get Fenwick back in there, but he deserves a keepsake after all the years he worked for TransNet… and maybe he could adapt their tech for something else.

Fenwick swipes his phone, reads a message to say his NanoTech application was unsuccessful, and his hand shakes. He deletes it and his finger hovers over the contact list before he selects a number he's not used in years.

"Hey, Khumalo. *Ja*, it's me. I've got a job for us. Big pay off."

Fenwick looks up to a swatch of blue sky. It's time to ascend the slums, even if it's just for a day.

Lenka throws the plush toy train at his head as Fenwick runs out of the house. Lucky for him, the hormones mess with her aim. He has no idea how she found out, but women have their ways. Their networks of information.

"I don't want you back here. *We* don't!" she shouts, right hand resting on her stomach. "You promised. *Promised* that you'd never go back to your old ways!"

He groans. It's hard to argue, but he still tries. "I got fired, Lenka! How can we afford to have a child if I don't find us money?"

"I don't care."

Her reaction floors him. "You don't?"

"That's right. We'll find a way like we always have. Maternity pay will help." The hurt in her voice makes him want to hold her, but he knows she'll only throw something else at him. As it's their first child, they'll get some help from the government, sure, but it will be half of what she's earning now as a virtual assistant at CloudCover.

It won't be enough. She *must* know that.

Lenka grabs the door handle to close it.

"Baby, wait! I'm only doing this because I love you. I want the best for us and our child."

"Keep telling yourself that when you're locked up again. A dad who's around is what our baby will need. Not money and an absent father like other kids have around here!"

He can't remember ever hearing her sound this way.

Fenwick watches the love of his life shut the door. Ashamed, he'd stopped telling Lenka about all the jobs he applied for, fearful she'd see him as a failure and leave. "I'm sorry," he mutters, "but I have to do this." Fenwick picks up the duffel bag containing all his things. He walks through the flat land of his old slum to see an old friend who never worried about repercussions. But then Fenwick remembers the guy's been single for years.

"Don't worry. I got ya, bru," Khumalo says with glittering metal teeth, taking Fenwick's duffel bag. Khumalo's hair sticks out at all angles just like it did years before when Fenwick last saw him. He'll have to comb it down to blend in – keep his mouth closed as much as possible, too; that or wear a mouth guard. "Just sleep wherever you want, bru."

"*Ja*, thanks." Fenwick looks around, taking in the mess that is Khumalo's place. Fenwick thinks he spots something moving in one of the piles of rubbish against the corrugated iron walls, but he can't be sure. They didn't call this part of the Cape Flats slum the Vermin Quarter for nothing.

Khumalo catches Fenwick's line of sight. "Sorry about the mess, bru, but the French Maid quit for a better gig." He cracks his metal smile. A springbok shivers on his neck in red ink. "Got everything you asked for... well, most of it anyways." Khumalo points to a pile of battered tech Fenwick missed earlier, mistaking it for more junk.

"Where the hell you get it from? A museum?"

"Best I could do. With your skills though, it'll be no problem." There is a glint in Khumalo's eye to match his smile.

"Guess I'll have to make do like I always did." Fenwick tries not to look ungrateful.

"*Damn*, that's my bru. Missed this shit." Khumalo grabs him by the shoulder, beaming like a doting father. As much as Fenwick doesn't want to admit it, part of him has missed this, too.

"So you're clear on what the plan is?"

"*Ja*, sure," Khumalo says, looking at the streamshow playing in the corner.

"Hey, I'm serious!" Fenwick stands in front of the screen and tries to block out the hurt and disappointment he remembers seeing on Lenka's face. "No weapons like I said. No one's gonna get hurt. And the rich won't even know their accounts are being skimmed. Okay?"

"Sure, but those *fokkers* deserve everything they get!" Khumalo always hated those above him, especially after his old *ma* died of radiation poisoning after years of working as a cleaner at the Koeberg power station.

"Quit it, Khumalo. I can't go down this time. This is a quick job to keep the money dripping in for us for years. Don't fuck this up." Fenwick locks his stare onto Khumalo's.

"Okay, bru. You were always the boss. Fine. No guns."

"Cool." Fenwick exhales. "And thanks for this. You know I can't do it without you." He grabs him on the shoulder like Khumalo did his. "So what's a man got to do to get a beer around here?"

"Ha, I got you. Just like old times, hey, Fenners?"

"Just like old times."

Fenwick catches himself in the quartz composite viewing window of the *Blou Trein*. Damn, he looks like a royal fool in this blue-black butler's uniform. From the inside, the train looks more like a hotel than transportation as it glints with obscene opulence. Neo-modern artwork fastened to the walls. Luxurious lapis carpet on the floor. Smart seats set in a concentric circle providing a panoramic view through the viewing window. It gives the impression of an arena and Fenwick feels fully on show as passengers glance at him.

He keeps eyeing the exit positioned in the centre of the room. The hissing doors lead to the stairwell that fills the rings of the torus carriages from the bottom to the domed top of the train, providing a way to reach each of its levels. A means of escape if things get too hot in here.

Fenwick wipes his brow with his sleeve. He is positioned in the upper section of the train reserved for first-class passengers, while Khumalo is skyward in its apex, above the *Blou*'s smallest torus, safely behind a secured door.

Fenwick taps on his earlobe and whispers to Khumalo, asking how things are looking.

"*Ja*, all good, bru."

Khumalo's job is to keep an eye out for anything suspicious, watching the feeds of the cams dotting the length of the train. This is while Fenwick serves the rich on a trip up to the stars and beyond, where the air is rarefied and free of the slums.

Fenwick swallows down his conflicting emotions. So far, things are going well. Thanks to Fenwick's stolen ID card's microchip and his only slightly rusty hacking skills, they managed to breach the train and find uniforms. Khumalo's engineer's outfit looks better than his, but the big man still looks suspect in it. The dental work doesn't help much, but Fenwick knows there's no one better to help them fight out of the place if things turn heavy.

"Coming, sir," Fenwick says, wearing his best smile. He walks over to the fat man with red hair and turns off the flashing red light on the side of his seat.

"Yes, dear boy. I'll have the Beluga Blue and Dom Pérignon – second to none, right?" He laughs and Fenwick's smile tightens.

"Very true, sir. Coming right up. I hope you've had a chance to enjoy the extended view from the Observation Carriage," he responds, latching onto the stock phrase the other butlers have been uttering like robots. None of them questioned Fenwick as expected; his ID looks as legit as theirs. He'd timed the train robbery to align with a new batch of recruited team members.

"What? Oh no, I've seen the view countless times. Becomes a frightful bore when you're up and down on the *Blou* all the time. I'm one of the directors for LunaScapes."

"Of course. Sorry, sir, I didn't realize." Fenwick clears his throat. "If I can just take your payment, please." He holds the doctored scanner in front of him.

"Can't we do it later, old boy?" he says, chins wobbling like a toad's.

"I'm afraid not, sir, sorry."

Fenwick worries he's going to call the manager for a second, but the man relents. "Fair enough – we must all follow our superiors, right?" He winks and chuckles, double chin wobbling over his puce shirt. The man holds out his right arm, pulls back his cuff-linked shirt sleeve, and exposes his fat wrist for scanning.

The machine beeps twice to confirm the transfer is complete and Fenwick's smile broadens. He'll be skimming this guy's and the others' accounts for years before they realize it. A few bitcreds a week – they won't even feel the loss. "The perfect crime, bru," Khumalo said when Fenwick explained it.

Fenwick wipes away beads of sweat from his forehead as he programs the order into the SmartWaiter unit. Seconds later, its metal doors hiss open, and an icy cold mist leaks out as caviar gleams in cobalt crockery next to a bottle of champagne.

Fenwick drops off the order to Toadface, then quickly moves to the next waiting customer, who's complaining they've not had a top-up in nearly fifteen minutes.

He scans another chip, capturing the account details for a woman with a ridiculous floral hat that nearly touches the roof. He's already covered half the carriage; bit by bit, his child's future is being built, just like these people's hubs on the lunar colonies.

152

The train rattles and lurches as it passes through some turbulence, the inside of the carriage turning red before they're free of it. Fenwick can't stop shaking, tells himself to snap out of it. He catches sight of the track's connective rods and rivets. How many hundreds of them passed through his hands? To ensure they were all safe – that the rich were safe? An image of him kissing Lenka's stomach forces itself into his mind and he grits his teeth.

"Yes, madam." He's unable to ignore the screechy woman. She's wearing spiral earrings that are so long they're almost in her lap. Fenwick can't feel any hatred toward the passengers, no matter their manners. It's just who they are, worlds apart from himself.

"At last." The woman tuts. "I hope the TransEarth Removals Service isn't as bad as this. Not with our chinaware," she says, when Khumalo's voice cuts through the conversation: "We got trouble."

"*O kak.*"

The lady gasps around the plums in her mouth. "I beg your pardon?"

"Nothing, madam. We're just out of Lobster Thermidor. My apologies."

"Oh well. It's no doubt for the best. It repeats on Henry terribly." She turns her head to the man beside her, who must be her husband, his rosy-red profile catching the light as he looks out the window, clearly trying his best to ignore her. "Why, tempura prawns it is, then!"

"Thank you for understanding, madam." Fenwick makes a quick retreat to the carriage's staff-only quadrant, his neck prickling.

Once he's out of sight, he hisses at Khumalo, "I'm on my way. What is it?"

"Armed guards. They're right below you. Better move fast!"

"What? No way. How could they have caught on to what we were doing?" Fenwick says, half to himself.

"No idea but keep moving."

Fenwick's legs are jelly as he pushes past a group of chefs and sommeliers making personalized recommendations for first-class passengers. "Please, I need to get through."

Sweat drips off him. TransNet guards have more powers than even the SA *polisie* these days and can shoot anyone on their property. Fenwick knew that two guards are on every trip, but he didn't expect them to be a problem. Didn't expect two minimum-wage grunts to figure out what they were doing.

Fenwick heads to the carriage's centre, the stairwell just behind those doors. Someone shouts from the back of the carriage. "Stop that butler!"

Fenwick runs. Doesn't look back. Sprints upstairs through the throats of passenger carriages until he can go no further. A bunch of wary-looking engineers block his path. No doubt wondering why they can no longer get access into the hatch above them. There's no way he can get past them, not with what he's wearing.

Kak!

His mind clutches for a solution as he backs away from them. He'll have to draw them away somehow. But how?

Spilling out into the Observation Carriage, Fenwick feels like he's floating, his legs numb as the exosphere presses up against the seamless reinforced window. The torus is smaller than other carriages but is uncluttered and made entirely from transparent materials. They must be over sixty miles up. Fenwick tears through the carriage, past large telescopes that extend out from the torus into the thinning atmosphere. Completing half a circuit, he holds his breath as the sky darkens outside.

"Khumalo," he hisses on the radio. "You there?"

"Here, man. What's up?"

"Need you to create a diversion fast. Can you set off an alarm on the carriage below, to pull the engineers away?"

"No sweat, Fenners. One sec."

Sweat pouring off his brow, Fenwick bumps into a group of VIP onlookers wowed by the view.

"Well, I never!" a woman shrieks, not a wrinkle showing on her face despite her fury.

He only notices now there's a little girl with her and it winds him. "I'm sorry," he calls, sucking in a mouthful of recycled air.

Rushing forward – almost hitting his head on a viewing harness – Fenwick completes the Observation Carriage's circuit and notices the engineers are missing, then the doors open. He hopes they slow down the guards as they pass them below.

Fenwick takes the last spiralling stairs to the top of the train where Khumalo is holed up. His legs burn with lactic acid, his breathing strained. Fenwick flashes his ID pass across the hatch's sensor, rips the door open, slams it shut behind him.

"There you are, Fenners. Took your bloody time!"

"Don't. Just tell me how we're gonna get out of this." Now he sees his pursuers on screen. Two armed guards following his scent like a pair of Rhodesian Ridgebacks. They're in the Observation Carriage already. Closing in fast. "*Fokk*. Do something, Khumalo! Anything!"

"I'm on it." Khumalo pulls out a hand-held welder and starts to seal the door, sparks fountaining around him. The springbok on his neck shivers again as though it's about to bolt. "I'll give you time – now do your thing already!"

Fenwick fumbles, pulling out a dented computer from the duffel bag next to Khumalo, and gets to work. He plugs into the train's mainframe through the on-wall connection port and smashes through the firewall in no time. Fenwick studied TransNet's security for years to escape the boredom of working for them. He never breached it before now, but God, did it feel good to be doing it. Relaxes his nerves a notch. He's a kid again, flexing his hacking muscles, bringing back balance online.

Fenwick wipes the camera footage and locks all the doors on the train. Welded, reinforced steel will take the guards far too long to break through. On the screen, he spots one of the guards escorting passengers out of the Observation Carriage while the other thumps on the door, the curve of his left shoulder only just in shot.

There's no way they can get through it, he reminds himself, but the sound of the banging rings in his ears. No one will be able to identify them, he tells himself. *Will they?* His stomach drops. His mouth runs dry. Why did he ever think this was going to work? he berates himself, holding his head in his hands. How could he be such a fool to risk losing his daughter before she is even born? They bang on the door again, louder and louder.

His heart thumping too, Fenwick glances out the porthole next to him and sees the last of the deep blue sky fade to black. They've arrived at the South African Space Station (SASS) that hangs in geosynchronous orbit. His body untensing, Fenwick smiles as he remembers slum kids used to call it Pretopia. The expanse of star-lit space stretches either side of the train, the Moon glowing large and inviting. It's breathtaking. He hopes his daughter will one day be able to see the view, too, without having to break the law to get here.

Controlling the train's systems, he pops all the outer doors open for the passenger carriages and the rich walk out without a care in the world, unaware that their safety is in his hands. They'll soon be on a Luna shuttle for the final part of their journey. Legs shaking, Fenwick waits until they're all out, including all the workers coming off to replenish the supplies. "C'mon. Get off the train already! Khumalo!"

"*Ja*, one more second and I'm done." Khumalo shuts off the welder, sparks dying at his feet. "There, they won't get through that."

"Okay, good. But you better hold on tight. Things are gonna get shaky."

Khumalo cracks a blood-diamond bright smile and Fenwick hits enter to send them back down to earth.

The rockets ignite to aid the magnetostrictive engine in space; the top of the train shunts the rest back into the atmosphere as gravity grabs hold of them and helps them on their way.

Fenwick pushes the speed to the max, barely within tolerance, as they grip hold of the handles and watch the guards fall down the stairs. One rolls out into the Observation Carriage, and it looks as if he's going to be sucked out into cold, dark space. "Ha, enjoy your ride, *bokgata*!" Khumalo hollers.

Fenwick and Khumalo are safe in here and will soon be back on Earth's solid ground at the speed they're travelling. Moving twice as fast as they were coming up, the train will arrive back in minutes, according to his calculations. The comfort of that soon evaporates when Fenwick considers how security could have cottoned on to what they were doing. Grobler – had to be. Maybe he noticed the missing ID card and put two and two together. No, he couldn't have. Not that fool. He'd never connect it. Unless someone told him…

She wouldn't, would she? Lenka was pissed with him, but she'd never shop him in. Fenwick shakes his head. Khumalo is still laughing at the struggling guards trying to break through the door. Of course, she wouldn't; he scolds himself for even thinking it.

Fenwick's stomach lurches and then he realizes in his distraction it's the train grinding to an abrupt halt. He stumbles. Grips harder onto the handle. Khumalo slams into him, taking the wind out of his lungs. "I got you, Khumalo."

"And I got you."

The plan had been to get off undetected, but now Fenwick sees a load more guards on the suspended platform just below them. The end of the line. He gulps. "We're *fokked.*"

"Here." Khumalo pulls out two backpacks from the duffel bag.

"What the hell are they?"

"Bad-boy glider packs, of course. It's what I was hired for – to get us outta here – wasn't it? Just like the old days, bru." Khumalo smiles, but Fenwick remembers how his old friend got them caught on more than one occasion in the past.

Fenwick grabs him by the shoulder. "But look how many there are out there! We'll never escape!"

"Oh, them. Don't worry, they'll soon be distracted." Khumalo flashes his smile, cool as ice.

"What aren't you telling me, Khumalo?"

"I promised no guns, but you never said anything about bombs. These *fokkers* don't deserve to escape this *kak*-hole of a planet if we can't." Khumalo opens the door on the opposite side of the train where there's no platform, only a long painful drop. "Time to fly, bru. Just press the red button when you're clear." Khumalo jumps from the train.

Fenwick remembers all the junk Khumalo supplied. Will these glider packs even work? Will his daughter ever know him?

He's already set up a Moroccan holding account that will transfer the money through a series of others until it reaches Lenka's. They'll never be able to pin it on her. He's done his part as a father, so if he's going to die, at least he can go taking comfort in that.

Fenwick looks down. Khumalo's pack unfurls like a bird's wings and he glides into the distance. "*Fokk* it," Fenwick mutters, fumbling as he puts on the backpack, and jumps off the train into the blue sky. It's hundreds of feet up, and the solid ground rushes at him before he hits the button…

And nothing happens. He hits it again, three times, before the glider slowly unfurls its wings and the control stick pops up around his waist. With a shaky hand, Fenwick grabs the controls. Gunshots cut up the air, fizz past his ear as he ducks his head. A bullet hole in the glider's canvas makes it whistle. He struggles to steer the glider but is finally able to follow Khumalo into the distance, free as a bird. For now, at least.

But just as he thinks it, a blast of hot air slams into his back and he free-falls, out of control.

Fenwick is slapped awake by Khumalo. He must have blacked out there for a moment.

"Where am I?"

"Don't worry, I still got you, bru." He's still smiling, too. "Sorry about the rude awakening, but I didn't want you to miss the view."

Fenwick's blurry vision clears. His head aches as bad as the morning after he and Lenka celebrated their pregnancy. With Khumalo's help, he struggles to stand and puts his weight onto one good leg. His ankle is useless, but otherwise, he doesn't seem to be in too bad shape. Fenwick spots the glider's airbags and realizes they must have cushioned his crash landing.

In the distance, the *Blou Trein* Suborbirail, shadowing South Africa for so long, collapses. Like a toy train dropped by a distracted child, the *Blou* nosedives and groaning metal rends the air. The ground trembles as it lands, and he almost loses his footing. Untethered, the train lines twist and fall back to earth.

Fenwick realizes now why the guards were there. It wasn't anything to do with him; their tech must have detected the bombs Khumalo planted. TransNet has been using such software for years, fearful of terrorist attacks. Not that Khumalo knew that. Still, it's hard to be angry with him when he helped Fenwick escape.

Polisie sirens blare in the distance, blue lights flash, but the cops are too late this time. Fenwick and Khumalo will still have to keep their heads down for a long while, hiding in the slums until things settle.

Fenwick knows it will be a short-lived victory. Other poor fools will work in the factory to ensure train parts are printed and the Suborbirail reassembled, but it'll take years.

By that time, maybe a young girl, educated like he'll never be, will be old enough to travel on it.

Blue Shift Passing By

David Cleden

The phone rings and the moment she hears Mac's voice she knows how it will play out. *Hon, don't wait up. Another late one at the office. The Esserman contract. You know how it is, right?*

Monica does indeed. It happens often enough – she'd have to be dumb not to know the pattern by now.

And Monica is not dumb.

Mac's tone is apologetic. The weariness in his voice is all too obvious, and she softens a little. He's doing this for them, after all. Helping them build a future.

"What colour's the house today?" Mac asks her.

She hesitates, not really in the mood for the game. *But tagging along won't kill you, will it?* "Cherry pink," she tells him. "Top to bottom. I had peppermint green starbursts stencilled on the tiles and there's gold inlay on the downpipes. I told the paint crew, spare no expense. Bad news, though. They painted over the windows."

She's hoping for a chuckle, something to reward her imagination and lift her mood a little. Weeks ago, with nothing but the promise of shortening autumn days, Mac had begun complaining it was dark when he left for the office, dark when he came home. Monica could paint the exterior of their tidy little three-bedroom neo-Georgian detached with the Union Jack and he'd never know until spring, goddammit.

Ever since, it had become a kind of game they played. Something to fill the awkward silences.

"I hate peppermint green," Mac says, and he sounds genuinely annoyed, as though she's done something stupid on purpose. *It's just a fucking game*, she wants to yell down the phone. But it's probably not his fault. His boss is driving him too hard again.

"Back at the usual time?" she asks, striving for a neutral tone. She rolls her wheelchair up to the fridge and pries open the door with one hand, keeping the phone clamped against her shoulder. A barren, frigid wasteland meets her gaze. Supper will have to be microwaveable again. Something quick and bland and instantly forgotten because neither of them will have had time – or the energy – for what her mother would have called 'proper' cooking.

"Late."

"Isn't that what I just said?"

There's a pause and she can tell the conversation is balanced on a knife-edge. But Mac opts for the peacemaker role over confrontation. Something in his tone unbends. "Look, Mon. I have some news. Can't say anything right now, not until it's official."

"Oh?"

"It'll have to wait until I get home. But *good* news, Mon. Good for us." She can hear voices at Mac's end, people filing into a meeting room maybe. She wonders if this is just a different kind of game he's playing. Mac likes his little secrets. Now she'll have to endure an afternoon of pointless speculation before he can share whatever news is too important to tell her over the phone. A promotion maybe? Or a rise? Either would be welcome, God knows.

She hates waiting. All her life it seems as if people have been telling her to be patient – not helped by that favourite expression of her mother's: *Things have a way of working out given time.* It still makes Monica want to scream, more so than ever now.

"Mon? Call the crew back. Tell them I want cerise stripes across the front and the porch in luminous green. I'll be out there with a flashlight to check they've done it right when I get home tonight." She tries to smile but it feels hollow, and she's glad he's not there to see.

When Monica hangs up, she rolls over to the kitchen window and sits for a while watching the clouds scud by. The terrible emptiness inside her is back – a cold, creeping stillness – and nothing she can think of will fill it.

"They want me to join the Blue Shift!" Mac stands in the kitchen, tall and handsome in his dark tailored suit and button-down shirt casually open at the collar. Even though it's been a long day, somehow his clothes still look pressed and fresh – just the man inside who is a little crumpled. Another fifteen-hour workday. But those bloodshot eyes hold a triumphant gleam.

Monica realises she's supposed to know what this means. Her mind races. She reaches back into past conversations where she's been only distantly present. "Your boss wants you on drugs? Is that even legal yet?"

He strides towards her, reaching down and crushing her in a hug that is too exuberant, too overbearing for how she feels after her own tedious day. His suit smells of sweet-and-sour, lingering memories of lunch. "Of course it is, Mon. All the top firms have amped teams these days. It's just the way things are going. Gotta keep a competitive edge."

Amped. She doesn't like that word. It sounds... freakish. As though workers are just components in some big capitalist machine. Turn the dial another notch, squeeze out a little more productivity.

Which is *exactly* how it is.

"It'll be great for us," Mac tells her. "More time we can spend together. The company gets fifty per cent more productive time, but I only work half the hours I do now! It's the best of both worlds, Mon!"

She knows why he's *really* doing this. There's something about his over-protectiveness that both irks her and overwhelms her with what she might once have called love. She's not some fragile glass ornament to be placed on a high shelf – taken down now and then and dusted off. She doesn't need him to be her carer. This disease that's slowly robbing her of movement – to say nothing of her dignity – *does not define her.* Because she won't allow it to. She will concede to adjustments – using the wheelchair on bad days – but she won't let it limit how she lives her life. If Mac doesn't understand that by now, he's sleep-walked through the last five years of their marriage.

"Isn't it dangerous?" She worries about how stoked up he sounds. Mac's always been a full-on, isn't-this-an-amazing-opportunity kind of person. She supposes it's what drew her to him in the first place: this smart, exuberant, funny, dynamo of a man who fell spectacularly in love with her from the moment they first met; pursued her, courted her with a kind of relentless drive bordering on obsession. But she's seen the flip side too. Yesterday's passion discarded for today's fad. Mac has a magpie mind: attracted by bright, glittery things – yet unable to discern where the real substance lies.

"Of course, it's not dangerous, Mon. Blue Shift's had its commercial licence for more than a year now. QuestaLink's own medical staff will be on hand every step of the way. When our project team is amped, we'll be better looked after than if we were in one of the city hospitals." He starts pacing the room, his excitement uncontainable. "It won't be long before all the big players will be running their teams this way. But this Factor Three approval has given us the jump on them. Our design team can work dedicated eighteen-hour shifts for only six hours elapsed on the clock. If I start at eight in the morning, I can be home mid-afternoon!"

"Really?"

"Better believe it, Mon! And this is personal recognition at last. Out of all the people they could have picked, they chose me! Just eight of us for the first Blue Shift team. We're spearheading a whole new project, breaking new ground on designs the other teams can work up in slow time." He corrects himself. "Normal time."

Mac pauses and Monica senses she is expected to fill the gap with suitably gushing praise. She can see this is important – to Mac, to both of them, to their future. It's a big fucking deal to have been chosen. So why can't she find it in herself to be happy?

"You're sure it's safe?"

"Trust me," he says with a grin so broad it becomes infectious.

So she does.

It's a strange few days. Outwardly everything is the same, except for this... *thing*... hanging over them. Even Hugo notices.

"Do you need more time off, Monica?" he asks her one afternoon. "You seem a little distant today."

Hugo owns *Art of the Impossible*, the boutique gallery down on the coast road where she works a few hours in the afternoons, three days a week. Since Christmas she's cut back her hours to about half what they were, keeping pace as the muscle-wasting disease progressively saps her energy levels. Throughout it all, Hugo has been unfailingly supportive.

"No," she tells him. "I'm fine." Tourist trade – the gallery's lifeblood – is beginning to pick up and she hates the idea of letting Hugo down.

It's harder to concentrate, though. Mac is working late, same as always, only now the excuse is his work colleagues are preparing for their Blue Shift sessions. None of his reassurances have changed her mind. Speeding up the brain's clock rate sounds risky to her. She's read up enough to know the side effects aren't anything to worry about:

mild headaches, occasional muscle tremors, a lethargy that can linger for a day or two. But no one really knows, do they? It's still a new procedure and clinical trials can only reveal so much. What if there are hidden long-term consequences? Mac is putting a lot on the line for QuestaLink – but she won't deny the bonus payments will be welcome.

Hugo lifts a canvas out from a pile stacked at the rear of the gallery and holds it up, inspecting it. "You know, I think we should seriously consider a feature exhibition of this artist. Could be just what the gallery needs. If only I could acquire a few more works to make it viable."

He's piqued her interest, brought her thoughts back to the here and now. "Let me see."

He turns the canvas towards her as she manoeuvres her wheelchair closer. "Ah… " she says, feeling her face flush.

"I'm serious, Monica. You have real talent. Your pictures will sell, too. Why won't you produce more work?"

She squints at the picture, oil on canvas, an early abstract landscape, dark and brooding. "Not my best work."

"It's exquisite," Hugo says, his voice firm. He sets the picture down gently. "I hate to see you waste your talents."

"I know," she says, sighing. "But it's complicated."

"How can I help? More time off? Or –" He looks at her meaningfully. "I know a couple of people. Trustworthy. They could get you whatever you need. Uppers, soothers, designer pain relief – you name it."

She lays a hand on his arm. "Thank you. You're a good friend."

"What about – " But he doesn't need to say it. *Blue Shift*. What better way to squeeze the most out of her remaining time?

"No. Not that."

"I just thought –"

"Aren't you listening? I said no!"

Monica feels a flush of embarrassment, surprised at her own outburst. Hugo's only being logical, thinking of the future – the one she doesn't really have. When her time draws near, won't she be grateful for a way to pack more into those precious few months? So much art left to appreciate. All those books she will have never quite found time for. Films to watch, music to listen to. Blue Shift could give her that option, couldn't it?

"Don't you see? Stuffing more information into my head in less time – which is all Mac's doing, really – that's not *living*. It isn't truly experiencing the world or having a chance to properly reflect on things. If anything, I'll want to take life more slowly and savour the things I treasure, not rush headlong at them." She allows herself a sigh, feeling the tension flow out of her again. "I just want to take the time to appreciate the things that really matter."

Hugo smiles. "That's the artist inside you."

She can't help but respond to his smile.

"But if you change your mind... " he says, and she nods gratefully.

Mac talks of little else in the few hours he's home before each day's relentless work-eat-sleep cycle begins afresh. "The on-ramp is about ten minutes from when the injection's given. There's a pill version being developed – which suits me, you know I'm not good with needles – but intravenous delivery is faster and more controllable, so we'll start that way. It's incredible, Mon! You begin noticing your thoughts speeding up almost immediately." He grins. "Actually, it's more like the rest of the world slowing down. Cars crawl by on the street outside. People plod around. Their speech patterns get so drawn out it's easy to guess what they're going to say when they're only halfway through a sentence. And your reactions times are like this –" He snaps his fingers. "It makes you feel so smart, Mon! Like you're a god among mortals. The hardest part is remembering your body can't keep up with your brain. Muscle spasms are a real problem at first. You go to take a drink of water and your mind expects your arm muscles to respond in a certain way, but they can't physically work fast enough. The brain's so impatient! But it's running four times faster than the body's used to responding –"

"Hold up, Mac! You've tried Blue Shift already? You told me the first session was next Monday."

"It's what they call an induction trial, that's all. To make sure none of us have adverse reactions."

"And you didn't think to mention it?"

"Mon, I was going to, but what with everything else – We've been so busy."

"*You've* been so busy."

Mac raises his hands. "Look. I'll make it up to you." She waits for the follow-on but all he says is, "I will. I promise."

He sees something in her expression and gently cradles her face in his hands. "There's really nothing to worry about, Mon. All the big firms are spinning up programmes to do this kind of thing now. This is the future." He searches her eyes looking for some sign of understanding. Or absolution. But she can't find it in herself to offer either.

"Remember I'm doing this for us. For our future. A few months on this programme and we'll have some financial stability. Maybe take an extended foreign holiday, spend time together while we still can. Whatever you want. I hate being away all the time as much as you do, but it's only for a little while. Okay?"

She nods mutely and Mac plants a kiss on her forehead. She feels old familiar black thoughts stirring deep within her mind, like a slumbering monster prodded to wakefulness.

"You're doing this for us," she echoes back, and Mac seems relieved to hear her say it.

The following day, Mac phones her just after midday. "Slow down!" she tells him. "You're gabbling."

"Sorry – I just had to let you know – everything's going great! We've already made more progress on the Faversham client account in one morning than we did in a week – I feel so alive, Mon, so smart, I can just tell we're doing great work, all the team hooked into the same design environment, collaborating, firing on all cylinders – and we're going to break at two, start the ramp-down then, because we can ease ourselves into longer work cycles over the next week or so, no diving into the deep-end – didn't I say we'd be cautious? – so I'll be home before you get in from the gallery and –"

His speech is so rapid-fire he sounds like one of those legal mumbo-jumbo sentences crammed into the last few seconds of a radio ad. It takes her a moment to process it all.

"Mon? You still there? You're not saying anything. Everything okay?"

"I'm here. And I'm fine. Us mere mortals take a little longer, you know?"

"Sorry – still acclimatising – I've got so much to tell you when I get home."

"Well… I'll be at the gallery until five. Maybe you could prepare dinner for a change?"

"Sure. No problem. Checking out some online recipes right now. Let me see. No. Um. Ah! Found the perfect thing."

"Are you kidding me?"

"No, really. See what I mean? I can zip through anything in a fraction of the time. I'll see you when you get home at half-five."

There are a dozen other questions she wants to ask him, but her hesitation must seem like an eternity to him. He cuts the line.

Dinner turns out to be two raw fillet steaks, still on the counter when Monica gets home, the meat turning from pink to grey as they begin to age. There is an unopened bag of groceries on the side – all the makings of a meal that should have been started hours ago. Mac is deeply asleep in his armchair in the living room.

Monica moves slowly around the kitchen, clearing away the mess. She prods Mac awake but he barely surfaces long enough to haul himself to bed. A glance at the clock shows it's only a little after 7 pm.

She's read enough about Blue Shift to know the score. Blue Shift runs the brain three or four times faster than normal, but as with everything, there's a cost. That extra mental exertion needs payback in terms of rest and recovery. Mac will sleep for fourteen to sixteen hours straight, most likely.

She potters around the house for a few more hours, alone with her thoughts. A little before midnight, she climbs into bed beside a gently snoring Mac. He shifts, sensing her presence. "Love you, Mon," he says into the darkness. The words are such a surprise, so out of character for Mac, she has to mentally replay them to be sure her imagination isn't playing tricks. She turns to him, a reply forming on her lips, but his breathing has already settled back into the slow rhythm of sleep.

So much for the extra time spent together.

Monica returns home from running an errand a little after noon to find Mac's car parked outside. Even with his compressed working day, this is early for him. Most days he's at the office by nine. His team has adopted double-shift, sixteen-hour workdays, meaning he's home soon after 2 pm. Asleep by 5 pm. It's a crazy existence.

She wrestles crutches from the passenger footwell. Her legs feel like sponge sticks dipped in a pool of fatigue, soaking it right up. She's felt a little stronger the last couple of weeks but now she wonders if relapse time is right around the corner.

Fresh cooking aromas fill her nostrils as she opens the front door. The table is laid for two; their best serving plates and cutlery. Something low-key and forgettable is playing on the living room's sound system.

Mac is by her side as if materialising from thin air, clutching an open bottle of wine, a thin sheen of sweat on his forehead.

"Mon! I said I'd make it up to you. Come in, sit down. Here, let me help you. Shall I fetch the wheelchair? You look pale. I can get it, no problem."

He's a blur of movement around her, taking her arm, slipping another around her waist to steady her, propelling her to the upright chair in the hallway. He disappears for a moment, then he's back, pushing her folding wheelchair. It's all just a blur of movement and machine-gun rapid words, making her feel dizzy.

"Stop," she tells him. "I don't need fussing over. I'm fine." She stands – a little precariously – but she needs to prove her point. "Mac, you're still amped."

He shrugs, but it's such a fleeting movement, easy to miss. "A little. On the down-ramp though. It'll have worn off in an hour or two. In the meantime –" he gestures towards the kitchen where every single pot and pan they own appears to have been put into service. "Come see what I've created for lunch!" He bustles around the kitchen, tending a pan of simmering sauce, pausing briefly to slice carrots that magically separate into golden sovereigns beneath the blur of his knife. The Mac she knows is a reluctant cook at best, but a recipe book lies open on the table. He darts back and forth, pivoting between stove, worktops, and recipe-book with manic intensity. Monica is reminded of an automated production line: an industrial robot at the centre of everything, a blur of precision movements as complex tasks are performed quicker than the eyes can comprehend.

"They let you drive like this?" she asks.

Mac laughs – a brief woodpecker rattle of sound deep in his throat. "I'm safer than any other driver on the road right now. Millisecond reaction times. I can see every dumb thing another driver does before they even know they're doing it. I could drive on the wrong side of the road and dodge oncoming traffic if I wanted! The world is *slow*, Mon. People are *slow*." He puts down his wine glass and comes towards her, arms opening like the jaws of a vice. Instinctively she takes a step back, but his arms encircle her before she can move. After a moment, she begins to relax inside their protective circle.

"Mm. Your hair smells great," he says, nuzzling her ear. He lifts the hair from the nape of her neck, stroking the skin beneath in the way he knows she likes, sending tingles of warmth down her spine. He kisses her forehead, her nose, her mouth – and for an instant, she feels smothered. Then she is lifted and carried to the sofa. "Mac. Please –" But he's suddenly everywhere at once, kissing her, stroking her, loosening her clothes. "Slow down. Not like this."

He's gentle, but urgent. Everything is happening so fast. She's the focus of her own production line. Mac is the robot arm whirring around her, working tirelessly, relentlessly on her body: spot-welding her with kisses, bending her into shape with caresses. There is no time to react, to catch her breath –

He enters, and it's all happening so fast she has no time to feel anything. Maybe that will come later. Right now, she's on a rollercoaster ride that's out of control. She wants to make it stop and doesn't know how.

Afterwards, Mac retreats into silence – which for him must be as though hours pass with nothing said. She wonders what is going on in that amped-up brain of his. He's got plenty of time to figure things out, work out the right things to say. Except there are no words.

He stirs. "Hey."

Mac brushes a finger tenderly along the line of her jaw, but she refuses to look at him.

"You know what the best thing is right now?" he asks. She glances up despite herself.

"What?"

"Lunch isn't even ruined," he says with a grin. But hearing his words, another little part of her seems to shrivel and die inside.

Mac wriggles to get comfortable in the articulated chair as it whines back to a semi-reclined position. A medic is laying out the Blue Shift dose on a sterile tray nearby: a slim hypodermic and two small ampules of clear liquid.

"Two?" Mac asks.

The young woman scrolls through a checklist on her tablet and frowns at him. "Extended session today," she says. "Didn't they tell you?"

"Uh, right. Yes. I forgot." He gives her a thumbs-up from his reclined position and a boyish grin, hoping to crack a smile on that serious face of hers, but all he gets is a curt nod. There is a momentary flicker of pain as the needle slips into a vein in his left arm, gone before he can react. She adjusts the chair a fraction and swings the hinged arm into place carrying his work console, feeding station and entertainment centre. It's all there; everything he needs for the next six hours.

A full working week.

"Should I check the catheter positioning?" the woman asks. He thinks he detects wry amusement in her expression.

"I'm good," he tells her.

The medic finishes up, closing off documents on her tablet. To Mac, she now seems to be dragging everything out. She's moving with sloth-like speed; a wind-up toy whose spring has unwound. As Mac slips deeper into Blue Shift, he feels his senses heightening and his perceptions sharpening. There's time to observe all the details he's missed before. Time to really *think*.

The woman glances at Mac as though suddenly aware of his scrutiny. It's just a casual, fleeting glance on her way to the door. But to Mac, their eyes lock onto each other for long, long seconds as though some kind of staring contest is in progress. He studies her face carefully. What he sees in her expression now isn't amusement. It's contempt.

He taps the engage button on his work console. A calibration programme does its thing, testing inputs from the cranial sensor latticework nestling against his scalp. Now he's able to control the computer through directed thought alone. He logs in, checks the work schedule for today's session and begins adding responses to several of the message threads spun up by the project team. After dealing with the first half dozen, he looks up – *careful now, keep those movements slow and deliberate* – in time to notice the medic has almost reached the door.

Mac spends a couple of hours' think-time categorizing and selecting promising scenarios to run through the modelling algorithms. The computational units will do the actual number-crunching of course, but in terms of aesthetics and an instinct for avoiding blind alleys, Mac's judgement is still vital.

He's just finished an initial pass when he gets a reminder ping. Fifteen minutes of lapse time already since the Blue Shift session started! Half a day's work done in the time it takes most people to brew the first coffee of the day and login to their email. Mac stretches carefully, turning his head (*slowly, slowly*) first one way and then the other. He does the same with his shoulders, arms and legs, hearing joints click as tension is released. An occupational hazard. The nerve impulses sent by his hyped-up brain easily outpace his body's ability to keep up. The violent twitching movements of a Blue-Shifter can resemble someone having a fit, and the risk of self-inflicted injury is much the same.

Mac? You doing okay? The private message from Lisa, his team leader, brings Mac's focus back to the screen.

– Sure. Working through those scenarios.

Need a favour. They've brought forward the investor meeting. Remember that tech analysis summary we discussed? I really need it, like yesterday.

Mac had scheduled the work for later in the week but the analysis itself was only a half-day's work, the report-writing another few hours.

– When do you need it?

Meeting's in about thirty minutes. Lapse-time, that is. Doable? Sorry to put the squeeze on you, Mac.

He did the math in his head. A day's work in the next half hour.

– I can handle it. No problem.

Great! Um – While Mac waits for her to continue, outside in the corridor he can hear the sound of a footstep: the clack of a high heel on a hard floor. There's a long, long gap before the next footfall inevitably comes, like the slow ticking of some ponderous grandfather clock.

Your wife okay with you working these shifts?

He's barely exchanged a word with Mon in the last few days. He's been a jerk – no sense in denying it – but he sometimes wonders if Mon understands the lengths he's going to for her. What will they do when she needs a full-time carer? Money in the bank now is money they'll need to spend on her later. It would be nice if she'd cut him some slack over it.

– Mon's fine. Really supportive.

Does she know about the switch up to factor eight?

Some instinct tells him not to hesitate, and the lie comes easily enough.

– Sure. Mon's behind me one hundred per cent.

That's good to hear, Mac, because you're a valued member of the team. You must keep this to yourself, but we've just had beta programme approval for the next level.

– Factor Sixteen? Really?

Factor Sixteen is awesome. He's heard rumours of other groups pushing the boundaries. And why not since the brain runs friction-free, more or less?

Lisa fills him in. It's actually more like Factor Twenty thanks to company investment in cutting-edge research. It comes at a price, though. Factor twenty means wearing an immersion sleeve – a tight rubber suit that grips the body to protect against involuntary spasms. And there's a requirement for sedation. Not quite a medically induced paralysis, but not far off. As with the current setup, a neural cap provides the necessary interactive control without the need for physical movement, and there's a wrap-around headset feeding visual and auditory information sped up to match the subject's brain state. Essential services come via an enhanced work pod – feeding, waste removal and comprehensive medical monitoring.

But here's the good part, Mac. With this setup, location is irrelevant.

Homeworking is just as effective as being office-based. Better, in fact, if there's a spouse or partner willing to act in an official supervisory capacity. Minimal duties – pretty much everything is automated anyway. Obviously, QuestaLink pays a stipend for the home carer.

– So I don't even need to leave my house?

Nope. Think your other half will go for it?

Isn't Mon the one always complaining about his long days at the office? It seems like the perfect answer.

Take some time to think about it, Mac. I know it's asking a lot. But this could be a smart career move, a chance to leap ahead in terms of experience. You want a part of that?

Mac weighs it up for only a few seconds, think-time.

– I'm in.

His biggest mistake – obvious in hindsight – is not saying anything straight away. The timing never seems quite right: he's too busy, too tired, unable to find the right form of words. The truth is, it's a conversation he would rather not have.

He gets home to find Mon worked up into a state of righteous fury. She came home earlier to find the technicians completing the last of the installation in their guest bedroom. (Dammit! He'd thought that was scheduled for Thursday?) The work-pod's bulky presence dominates the room, a hi-tech hospital bed on steroids. The guest-room furniture has already been collected by the homeless shelter people. Mon's easel and work-in-progress canvases are piled up haphazardly in the corner.

A bad situation is made worse by the lousy timing of his descent into post-Blue Shift torpor. His eyelids droop. He is reduced to endlessly repeating, "I meant to say something, Mon. I was going to. It just slipped my mind." He's sliding into drowsiness before she's properly hit her stride venting her anger.

"You should have *told* me, Mac. Couples are supposed to talk through things like this."

"I'm doing it for us. For you."

"Don't you dare switch this back on me!"

"Mon, please –"

"And what gives you the right to assume I'll act as your

172

nursemaid? That I'll give up my job and other freedoms to be your carer while you slip into your cosy little turbo-charged world?"

Now she's being unfair. If one thing is certain, it's that a time is coming when Mon will need him to care for her. Why else is he pushing himself so hard now? Earning money to pay for the things she'll need later. All he's asking for is a little *quid pro quo* in the meantime. Is that so unreasonable?

There's more, but the sound of her voice is growing fainter. The need for sleep is tugging at the edges of his mind. With no regrets, he allows it to draw him down into blissful unconsciousness.

It takes a little time, but Monica adapts. After all, it's what she's done all her life: coping with her parents' divorce, then her own post-teens breakdown and the slow reassembly of her life in the following years. And not least, of course, she is learning to adapt to the wasting disease progressively robbing her of movement.

When Mac is snug in his work-pod, there's really not much that needs doing, which is a bonus. The machines do all the work. She's there as a backup; Questalink's support line on speed dial should the need arise.

Robbed of the need and opportunity to work, Monica sometimes feels the house has become her prison. The pattern of her days is unvarying. Mac's enhanced sessions run from eight in the morning to four in the afternoon. A conventional working month is compressed into a single day. There will be, Mac assures her, compensations. Months of paid leave when the project concludes, almost certainly a promotion and their bank account has never looked so healthy.

Often, she sketches or paints, squeezing herself into the corner of the guest room, trying to ignore the work-pod's bulk and its little whispers and sighs. She draws the ever-changing view from the window, but her pictures never seem to quite capture what she sees. Some days she passes the entire afternoon just staring out the window: observing what the world has to offer, letting her thoughts slow and dwindle.

Rarely does she think about Mac – even though he's within touching distance. Blue-shifted, he is as distant as it's possible to be, lost in his hyper-accelerated thoughts.

Then for an hour or two each evening while she prepares a meal, they have time together. Mac is lucid but still amped while his brain decelerates back to some semblance of normality. Sometimes they make conversation. More often, he's unable to stop brooding on some detail of his work, shovelling food down in silence until the need for sleep overwhelms him. Monica watches dispassionately, half expecting him to slump face-first into his dessert.

One night, long after Mac has fallen deeply asleep, she finds his work terminal still glowing in the upstairs room, a half-dozen windows open on the desktop and a soft chiming coming from somewhere. She lifts Mac's headset off the keyboard where it's been casually discarded and the chiming stops. On-screen, an auto-logout warning begins a thirty-second countdown.

She's about to turn away, but something in one of the windows catches her eye. Not meaning to pry but fascinated all the same to see how Mac spends his time, she dismisses the auto-logout.

Mac's think-time existence really is a little world within a world. She had assumed his work sessions were... well, just work. Instead, she sees that his schedule is a regimented pattern of work and R-and-R, designed to maintain his focus and preserve his attention span. In the downtime periods, he reads magazines and books, watches TV, views films, listens to music – all speeded up to match his heightened perception so that all this can be accomplished in mere minutes. When Mac clocks in for a Blue Shift session, it's as though he checks out for a month-long business trip, a repeating cycle of work-play-work.

And he has a girlfriend.

All right, no. It's just a workplace flirtation, nothing more, she can see that – but it hurts just the same. She scrolls through a message pane, page after page. Her name is Danika, a twenty-something bright spark with an open, direct way of talking that she knows Mac finds attractive in women. She's one of Mac's design team colleagues, sharing this strange world-within-a-world existence. There's nothing outrageous or clandestine in their frequent, chatty exchanges – and perhaps that's what hurts the most. Monica sees a different side to Mac in these messages: a warm, funny, intelligent man – characteristics she hasn't witnessed herself in a long time. It's really nothing. A flirtation of minds perhaps, but not bodies.

But it feels like a betrayal all the same.

The next day she decides to call Hugo's number. "About that friend of yours," she says. "The one you said could –" and Hugo is only too happy to help, as she's known all along he would be.

"Not Blue Shift though," and she tells him what she needs.

Hugo is silent for a long time. "All right," he says at last. "But are you sure?"

She sucks in a breath, then gives a little laugh. "'To thine own self be true.'"

"Hamlet. Didn't you once tell me you despised people who quoted Shakespeare?"

"Yes. And I still do."

"Oh, Monica –"

"Hugo – I'm only doing what I know is right for me."

Arms encircle Monica's waist. A light kiss brushes the back of her neck. She hates this ability, this trick of Mac's to be so fast and light on his feet. He can't help it, it's just the Blue Shift wearing off, but it makes her feel so *slow*, always a few steps behind whatever he's thinking.

Mac leads her to the sofa and sits next to her. Suddenly the moment is laden with tension and she can guess what's coming. "You've been looking at my messages," he says. He raises his hands as though to forestall a denial, but Monica sits quietly. She has nothing to apologise for.

"It's okay. You don't have to explain, Mon."

Damn right, I don't.

"I shouldn't have let things get out of hand, I can see that now. But it means nothing. *Nothing*. Danika's a work colleague, that's all."

Monica shakes her head. "All that time you spend in Blue Shift. With them. With *her*. Days and weeks. I feel shut out."

"I'm still *here*. Physically. I'll always be here for you, Mon. I'll never leave you, no matter what." He searches her eyes, looking for some kind of response.

The worst of it is she can see he means it. Mac has his failings, but a lack of loyalty isn't one of them. Didn't they recognise that in each other right from the beginning? But she's not sure if loyalty is enough to hold a relationship together.

So many thoughts she wants to give voice to are crowding into her head, but somehow she doesn't have the words. She settles for, "And I'll never leave you," spoken without passion. It seems to pacify him.

She means it, too. Though perhaps not in the way he thinks.

Her thoughts have slowed to a crawl. Somewhere beyond the here and now, the world rushes on, uncaring. From her chair, Monica watches dawn come again.

And again.

Every now and then her body twitches with involuntary movement. Her heart doesn't so much beat as tremble. Her breathing is buzz-saw rapid. Fleeting aches and pains come and go; a dampness on the seat of the chair, dried almost before she is aware.

Everything is transient; fleeting. Except for the despair she feels. She doesn't suppose that will ever go away.

Mac would call this wasted time, but it isn't. Not to her. With an artist's eye, she sees everything more clearly: patterns and rhythms in the progression of the day; brush-stroke details in the way the light ebbs and flows.

As her brain slows, her perception gallops along like an accelerating merry-go-round.

Now and then she wonders how Mac is doing. For her, only a few hours of subjective time have passed, but for Mac, it has been weeks or perhaps months lying in his work-pod. She topped up his supplies, re-programmed the session timer and now the pumps administer their carefully regulated dose of Blue Shift day and night. She sits next to him, hearing the soft ticks and whirs of the equipment as it keeps Mac in his hyperactive state. There's plenty to keep him busy: terabytes of entertainment files on the local storage drive. All his work files. Everything he needs to keep himself immersed in his interests. (Although not his girlfriend – she's seen to that. The internet router is unplugged, meaning no outside connection to the world. Mac won't be flirting with any more colleagues.)

Or summoning help.

She knows he'll be missed eventually. Someone from Questalink will question his extended absence and his unanswered messages. They'll come to investigate. And when there's no answer at the house, eventually the police will be called to break the door down. But will it be sooner or later? Now there's a question.

As designer drugs go, *redshift* is tame. It's a temporal relaxant – a distant cousin of LSD delivering nothing more potent than heightened awareness in a day-long trip. It's built a certain following amongst the more retro bohemian communities: the ultimate turn-on, tune-in, drop-out trip that dulls reaction times to a barely functioning torpor. Monica likes the way it makes the world buzz around her. Everything is vibrant, alive. She could never stand to see the world crawl by at the snail's pace Mac endures. She doesn't have the patience. This way, everything is in flux; everything is constantly changing – from the ebb and flow of daylight and her own rhythmic hunger pangs to the frenetic pattering of her breathing. Her artist's eye sees patterns that were never revealed before, and she likes that.

Monica watches another dawn, sees the sky darken, the ground turns suddenly wet and slick, flickering lights in the sky, thunder that is like the rap of knuckles: loud and sharp, but gone before she can be startled.

There's a kind of symmetry to their situation which appeals: like trains passing on opposite tracks. Mac living his madly accelerated existence where even the gap between heartbeats has become a ponderous chasm of time. While her own thoughts have slowed to the crawl of some hibernating animal who barely notices a season slipping past in a long night's sleep.

We promised never to leave each other, she thinks. *And we haven't. Here we are within physical touching distance yet as far apart as it's possible to be. Are you satisfied now, Mac? We held to our word, didn't we?*

There's a dryness in her throat. Monica reaches for the bottle of water at her side. Through the guest room window, the early morning sun is climbing above distant trees. By the time she takes her first sip, evening shadows are lengthening. She's careful to swallow in the little spaces between fluttering breaths.

In a way, she's surprised this has gone as long as it has. After all, Mac has had weeks – or is it months now? – of subjective time to think about his situation, locked into his own little speeded-up universe where every second lasts an hour. Plenty of time to find a solution or some means of escape. She wonders if he's grown bored yet of all that time on his hands.

She becomes aware of a background noise; a rapid, soft warbling. Maybe a warning chime coming from one of Mac's machines? She waits a while – she can't be sure how long – and it stops of its own accord. Some of the lights that had been red have faded into blankness.

See, Mac? Didn't I say I would never leave you?

Monica shakes out another couple of pills with a trembling hand. *One more trip on this slow boat to nowhere,* she thinks. Then she will have to return to face the consequences. She places the pills in her mouth with a trembling hand, washes them down with a swig of water. She's no idea how long it's taken to perform that simple action.

Monica redshifts again, and the world spins past her, growing ever remote.

And If Venice Is Sinking

Fiona Moore

Pompeii was closed to virtual tourists. Temporarily, the sign said, but that was like those little plaques in zoos saying that someday they will repopulate the wilderness with all of these endangered animals. Just something to make people feel less guilty. The cracks in the reality of Pompeii had become so great that the next virtual tourist could be the one that made the psychic weight on the physical site too much to bear. And nobody wants to be the one who left a hole fifteen miles to the south of Naples.

Leaving aside what Pompeii means to me. It was relevant, of course, because my emotions were putting weight on the site as well. But I'm a professional and I had a job to do.

By the time I got the little red notification bleep that Emma wanted to speak, I'd spent an irritating morning issuing refunds and offering alternative holidays to those of Cura Travel's clients who might be interested in rebooking. And then there was the one guy who decided the rules didn't apply to him. I was impressed; he managed to get past the sign and spend a total of two minutes in the House of the Vetii before the guardian intelligences, who he must have known were patrolling the perimeter, swooped down and tore him to digital shreds before I had a chance to close my window on the space.

They'd got his ident details of course, so there'd be physical police on their way to his real-world location, arresting him and dragging him away while he was still recovering from the trauma of his shredding, and that meant more forms for Cura Travel. Swearing blind that our security procedures were adequate, and this was just a one-in-a-million slip-up. Paying fines for the damage he caused, since a few paving stones had disappeared thanks to his intervention. We'd get it back from him through the courts later. Informing our insurance company. All for two minutes of selfishness.

I looked at the notification bleep from Emma, sighed, did a twenty-second deep breathing exercise to get back into the moment, switched my in-office status to *on break* and dropped into Emma's house.

We'd lived in it together for four years, so I supposed I could think of it as *our* house. Nonetheless, it was still Em's house, no matter how many edits I'd added to it.

She'd visited mine but had never really liked it, so I'd archived it while we were together. It was back up now, of course, a shining modernist place loosely based on Fallingwater, though I noticed the furniture now had a tendency to shade into Regency styles. A kind of scar.

I went into the section that was open to guests and visitors. I was certain I could still access the more private sections, but deliberately didn't meet her there. It was the parlour of a late Georgian manor. Big windows, high ceilings, little framed pictures, delicate and spare furniture, walls a dark red colour that I had a feeling was anachronistic, but then, what did I know?

Em herself was posed by the fireplace, her appearance tweaked to resemble some Elizabeth Bennett or other.

"Hi, Joon," she said.

"Sorry, Em – it's been busy at work," I said. I didn't bother adjusting my appearance to the room. I might have done back when she and I were still together, though I'd usually do something like dress in a hanbok just to remind her that Europe wasn't the epicentre of world history. But right now, I wanted to make it clear this was just a quick visit in between refunds and rebookings, so I left my self-image in its usual work-ready state. My hair in a fashionable but professional cut, my skin clear, my jacket, shirt and trousers in Cura Travel colours, my gender neutral, my hovertext reading *Joon Choe, Senior Travel Advisor* with my public CV available if you carried on hovering, my jewellery expensive looking but understated, and none of it in any way associated with her.

"I heard about Pompeii." Emma abandoned the theatrical pose, sat down in a chair by the fireplace, gestured to invite me to sit. I mildly resented that but saw no way to politely refuse.

"Yeah," I said. "Business is taking a huge hit."

Neither of us mentioned the meaning of Pompeii in our own specific context.

Emma gestured again. The logs in the fireplace flared, and the weather outside the house windows turned into the sort of melancholy, atmospheric autumn rain that goes well with a fire.

Pompeiian red. That's what that dark claret colour was called.

I did a quick bit of math and second-guessed what she wanted. "Em, if you're asking me to get you into some prohibited site, I can't."

"I'm not going to ask you to do anything you don't want to do," she said, disingenuous. "But I've got an idea for how we can reduce, maybe eliminate, psychic weight."

"Getting around the Kneale Phenomenon?" I settled into the chair and generated myself a bowl of white-cheddar popcorn. This might take a while. "How're you going to do that?" I'd love to know how she could do what the best quantum physicists in the world couldn't.

"It's easy. You need to embrace absurdity. Dream logic."

"That's what the people who initially came up with the idea of the Kneale Phenomenon said." None of them had actually been Kneale, whose contribution had been writing a disturbingly prescient story about the stones of old houses recording mental impressions from their inhabitants, some fifty years before anyone had seen a building crumble under the psychic weight of the emotions of millions of virtual tourists (the stones turning to glass, teetering, falling, vanishing before they hit the water, the screams of the drowning people rising up from the sea). Like Shelley and Wells, he'd become a byword.

I remembered when Cura Travel employees had been given a little demonstration of the Kneale Phenomenon, how psychic weight worked. Thousands of us, from around the world, had all gone to the same site, a virtual version of the demonstrator's garden, and focused on feeling happy about a single tiny pebble at the same moment, only to watch on a live feed as that pebble crumbled into nothing under our well-meaning attention.

And then there was the big hole in the ocean where Venice had been.

"But some psychic weight is heavier than others," Em said. "That's the starting point."

"True." The surprising thing about Pompeii was that it took as long as it did.

And the huge irony about Venice was that virtual tourism was supposed to save it. Provide a way for visitors to see the famous city without causing physical damage through walking about the delicate ancient alleyways. At Cura Travel, we'd promoted it: Encouraged people to take virtual holidays in romantic virtual Venice.

Meaning we were to blame.

"And yet, psychic weight doesn't damage the imaginary sites. Like, you know. Neo-Venice."

"Oh, yeah." Neo-Venice is strange. It's nice to visit, but it really doesn't bear any actual resemblance to the original Venice, beyond that there are buildings and there are canals. Same with any of the other imaginary sites. A good thing, too, otherwise the sheer number of Tolkien-based fantasy games would have caused most of either New Zealand or Oxfordshire to sink beneath the waves.

I'd never really been able to get into Neo-Venice. My own psychic impressions just kept throwing up reminders of crumbling buildings, vanishing stones, screaming people struggling to keep afloat in the naked ocean.

Em nodded as if everything I'd said confirmed something she'd been thinking. "I have an idea," she said again.

"A brilliant one, I'm sure, and yet, somehow you haven't managed to get official support from a business, a research institution or a grant-providing body."

"This is a good idea and I swear there's no risk involved. Well, not financial. And not to you. It's all on me," Emma said.

She leaned forward earnestly, took my white-cheddar-flecked hand in hers.

"But to test it, I need you to get me into Pompeii."

I closed the door of Emma's house gently behind me. I willed the rain to stop, and it did, but the sky remained dark: an early-evening darkness, a few stars gleaming through a bluish-purple light. The air was cool with a faint, pleasant, hint of coal smoke. The garden was lit by a glow suggestive of fireflies, or possibly anachronistic hidden LEDs.

Pompeii had been our first trip together. A honeymoon, if you like, though neither of us thought of it that way. We'd spent a week there. We'd flitted through the forum, tripped round the mosaic reflecting pools, marvelled over the forensic preservation of the shops, laughed at the cock-shaped lamps and the acrobatics on display in the erotic frescoes, had a quick and exciting lovemaking session in the House of Caecilius, made even more exciting by the fact that neither of us had set our self-images to private, so anyone could walk in on us.

And then, when we were sharing bread and prosecco on a field in the outskirts, we saw people touching their heads, expressions going blank, faces falling, eyes widening.

"Check the news," Emma said, urgently.

That was when we heard about Venice.

The destruction of Venice was impossible to separate from the rest of the visit. People vanished from Pompeii as everyone rushed to check on loved ones, or responded to calls from managers. As a junior travel advisor with Cura, I'd been hauled back to deal with, yes, cancellations and insurance claims, keeping one eye on the news bulletins as survivors were rescued from the waves, as teams tried to salvage what they could from the city as it crumbled into the waves. Cries of *terrorism* falling silent as people realised that no, it was on us. Not the destroyers. The pleasure-seekers, the life-lovers.

And of course, I'd had to go there, try to help with the rescue efforts like everyone else. I remembered St Mark's Basilica teetering, the stones starting to fall and then turning to glassy translucent echoes of themselves before plunging towards the water, disappearing as they did. The stone lions roaring their last defiance as they too crumbled and disappeared. The tragicomic sight of the pigeons, circling, unable to land. The people in the buildings, screaming and clinging to each other as they fell; the canals clogging with the detritus of everyday life before the sides of the canals also turned glassy and fell in, disappearing too; the gondolas sinking and up-ending. The creamy churning of the waves as they absorbed the extra weight and then lost it again.

I still woke from nightmares about it. Streaming images of transparent bricks and stones tumbling towards my head, lions open-mouthed at the catastrophe unfolding, the sensation of hovering in the air while terrified people clung to me and tried to drag me down.

Em had sulked about the loss of my attention for a bit, then rapidly plunged herself into a job with a submarine salvage company, exploiting the disaster site where Venice had been. Profiting off all those screams, off all that lost detritus. Kept her busy for a while, and, when the dust cleared, we realised we were living together.

Pompeii was our beginning and our end. Our moment of joy, followed by the shock and the reassessment and the desperate need to build new lives in the wake of disaster. The one perfect moment, followed by the aching loss.

That was my Pompeii. It wasn't everyone's.

It was just mine.

And now Em wanted to exploit that Pompeii, turn it into another dodgy moneymaking scheme.

So, here I was in Em's garden, deciding if I wanted to enable her again. The way she'd always work on me, get me to invest my savings, try to talk my friends into doing the same. In the end, it had been my refusal to sell my claim on my apartment in the physical world to back her plan to revolutionise digital archiving by incorporating it into the architecture of buildings that had split us up.

She had that same eagerness this time, too. "What about if a person created their own site? If, every time someone wanted to visit, for instance, Pompeii, they had to build it first?" she'd said.

"So, like, create Neo-Pompeii?"

"No, not like that." Emma's smile was both charming and irritating. "It would be an imaginary Pompeii, but based on facts. They'd research Pompeii, and build their own version of it from what they learned."

"The tourists would? Not the tour guides?"

"Tour guides would work with the tourists to build the holiday. Don't worry, your job's secure." I resented the implication that I was just concerned for my own job, that I was as utilitarian as she was, but didn't say anything. "But that way it would also have a personal element for the tourists."

"You think people will go for that?" Actually, despite my tone, I was sure they would. One of the problems with virtual tourism is, ironically, the lack of effort, and the reason why my job's such a skilled one is that we have to build in the difficult parts. I've had to work out how to simulate the equivalent of a bumpy bus ride up a mountain range or a tedious wait at a local airport. The main problem is in getting the balance right: enough discomfort that people feel they've earned their holiday, not so much that they can't enjoy the visit.

"Why not? Lots of people already do the research before they go someplace, and, for the rest of them, it's a challenge. And, like I said, it would help the tour guides build a more personal and satisfying holiday. But there's more."

"Of course there is."

"The site's going to mean something different to everyone. And they incorporate that into their build. That way their emotions only affect the virtual site. Not the real one."

"That's why you want to test this out on Pompeii. On *our* Pompeii."

"Exactly."

You bitch, I thought but just smiled. Neutrally, as I'd learned how to do from five years with her.

Em materialised inside the door of the house as I came in, switching the rain back on. "Will you do it?"

I looked at Elizabeth Bennett, critically. She was shading the look to the Keira Knightley version, and it struck me how millennial she looked. How, even when they were doing period pieces, the actors, the costumes, the makeup, still looked like the decade they came from.

Five years of relationship, four of them living together, and Em and I had never once met in person.

She didn't even know what gender I'd had at birth.

And probably didn't care.

Which at one point had been part of the attraction, but now it just seemed like a strange absence. Why wouldn't you want to know everything about your lover?

Then again, why did I?

The anger I had been feeling around her gave way to sadness.

Somewhere in the back of my mind, a decision was made.

"If we get caught at this," I said, "it won't just cost me my job. It might even mean going to jail. Worse, what if it backfires on Pompeii?" No amount of jail time could make up for breaking down one of the major historical sites of the world, and one that meant so much to me despite everything, just because of one of Em's wild ideas.

"I swear it won't," she said. "We'll be in and out before there's any damage to the real site. And if I'm right, this could be a way of saving Pompeii."

"You promise?"

"Of course," and she looked at me in that wide-eyed sweet way. "Will you do it? Please, Joon."

And that was why we'd been together for five years. That thing about her that always drew me out of safety, into risks I wouldn't have taken otherwise. In that moment, the ones with the consequences faded away, and I could only remember the times she'd been right.

And that this time, maybe the sacrifice would be worth it.

"Yes," I said. "I will."

Pompeii is closed to visitors. But ten years in the virtual tourism business has taught me a lot about the workarounds. Limited access for a research project was the most obvious, but Em had said up front that she didn't have backing from a university or corporation.

The next obvious workaround was maintenance.

When sites are closed, maintenance slows down to a bare minimum. But it never stops outright, since there was still the hope that we could open the sites to tourism again someday. And maybe the offspring of those zoo animals will one day roam the wilderness.

Cura Travel doesn't do maintenance themselves. But we had the details of the companies that did since we'd have to know when a site was temporarily inaccessible, how long since the last upgrade, all those sorts of things. I'd never paid too much attention to it, unless a customer specifically asked. Now, though, I was riffing through our information on Pompeii, looking for the permissions for two people to access the site.

"Hurry *up*, Joon." Em still looked like Keira Knightley but was now in jeans and a black T-shirt, hair in a ponytail. Practical clothes, or tourist clothes. I'd switched my self-image to a very, very generic, non-customised, gender-neutral Korean-aged-thirty-three off-the-peg one. My thinking was that, if we were discovered, it would look less like I was there for guerilla tourism and more like I genuinely was part of a maintenance team that had got its schedule confused. For about five minutes before someone checked my ident, but maybe it would fool them enough that they wouldn't?

I didn't bother with a fancy dissolve, just left us standing (or rather floating, since there wasn't a floor) in blank black-and-green maintenance-space.

"Okay, we'll have five minutes maximum," I said. "That's the longest a maintenance team goes in on a closed site. Any more and someone will get suspicious."

Also, I wasn't sure Pompeii could take any more than five minutes of two minds' worth of psychic weight. Even that could be enough to turn it into the next Venice.

"That's fine. I won't need any more than that." Em said. "And it's OK us making a return visit on fairly short order?"

"Again, so long as it's quick. It'll just look like an accidental login, or like we maybe forgot something and came back for it."

"Then, let's do this."

I said a silent, quick, generic prayer to whatever god-substitute listens to the prayers of the non-religious, and took us in.

And we were there. Pompeii. Early evening, the sky shading blue to purple to pink in the West, a faint glow of city lights – Naples, I assumed – in the distance. Before I'd visited, I'd always pictured Pompeii as narrow and dark, trenches of buried artefacts and streets. But it's bright and spacious: walls and pillars and pools, all out where you can walk around them and smell them and even, in the virtual, touch them.

It took me a minute to realise what was so eerie about it, and then it hit me. No sounds. No birds, insects, gentle winds, distant traffic. Whoever had archived Pompeii had left the sound off.

Emma strode forward into the ruins, looking around like a tourist on her first visit.

"Remember, we can't stay long," I said, hurrying after her.

"It's OK." She didn't even bother looking at me. "I just need to fix the atmosphere in my mind. And also take the damage readings."

"Right." I accessed the back end of it, checked on psychic weight, made some notes. Checked the weight again.

The weight was at dangerous levels.

"Em, we've got to go now."

The weight spilled over.

Somewhere, a signal tripped.

"Just a minute –"

"*Now.*" Suddenly everything surged up. The way she would take charge of everything, the way she'd act as if other people's yeses and nos didn't apply to her. And the way I'd abetted this, the way I was abetting her now, getting her access to a place she shouldn't be, just because she had a cool-sounding idea.

There was still a part of me that felt bad that I hadn't sold my claim on my apartment. That believed maybe my purpose in life was to support her until she finally found that one brilliant idea that would work. And I was a selfish, weak, fool who just didn't want to live off ramen in wait-list housing again.

But in the end, it was all going to sink beneath the waves.

I could see the fragile walls teetering and waving, their bold colours fading. The gods in the murals smiling at their own destruction.

"You lied to me, Em," I said, realising. "You *lied*."

I could see it on her face. She hadn't planned to get out before any destruction to the site. In fact, destroying the site must have been part of her plan. She'd just told me a story. And I'd gone along with it.

The alarms were howling, silently, as the weight got too much for Pompeii to bear. The walls of the Lupanare were wavering, fading, their cheeky pornographic paintings vanishing from the world. The theatre was crumbling, disappearing into the hillside like a mouth opening up before the hill sealed over the gaping raw wound. The pillars of the Basilica teetering, turning to glass, falling, vanishing as they hit the ground with a sound almost like a cry.

Even though we were the only people there, I could hear the screaming.

And I could see the guardian intelligences converging on us, prepared to pull us limb from limb.

Offline, I thought I could hear a siren.

I was about to trigger the out switch, but Em hit it a second before I did.

There was, virtually, an effect of rushing, of flying, Han Solo's spaceship or a superhero flying through space.

And we were in Pompeii.

Not the same Pompeii. We were in the Pompeii that Em had built to test her theory.

That we had built together. As the tourist would with the guide, using their own feelings, emotions, history, research and understanding.

It overwhelmed me. Triumphant, exuberant feelings like a hundred brass sections trumpeting away, sunlight laced with gold and silver, but again with a kind of velvety, dark edge, a doom and an ending that still made the gold and silver of the pictured present that much brighter.

And yes, my anger. The feelings of rage and disappointment that coloured my feelings about Em. Even when I loved her the most, the anger was always there. I'd always thought of it as something I'd had to overcome, but now I realised it was tied into our relationship, part of it like mortar becomes bound to stone.

My savage mourning for the loss of our Pompeii.

That had been the final trigger. The thing that made the new Pompeii real.

It wasn't just the present or just the past. It was the present, and past, and our imaginings and feelings about the present and the past, all woven into the streets and stones, the pillars, the mosaics, the cocks, the dogs, the gods and gladiators and dancing girls.

"Can you check the readings?" Em asked, her own sense of delight and triumph underlying her voice.

I did. "No psychic weight on the site." I added my own feelings to the mix. "Em, you did it."

"*We* did it," she said. "This is why I needed you. I couldn't build it on my own. Needed your impressions as well. The build's collaborative. We had to go back, and then come here, and finish it off."

"Literally." I pinged my news feed. Put it up for her to see.

The reports of the damage to Pompeii our five minutes had caused.

The real site was shaking, crumbling. Maybe disappearing forever.

The pillars turning to glass. The pornographic paintings fading. The theatre crumbling into the hillside. The smiling gods. It was all real, not just something we'd seen.

She took my hand, earnest. "The destruction was necessary so we could have the new site. But that was just a one-off. Now we know how to do it, we won't have to do that again. Don't you see how perfect it all is?"

"Amazing," I said. Meaning it, meaning her.

Suddenly we were embracing, embracing as we'd done at the start of it all, and that was an eternal moment of rose and violet and gold.

We could be everywhere. Be in Pompeii. Be in Venice, any time, any where, above the waves or below it. Be in Herculaneum, the Coliseum, Hadrian's Wall. The stones recorded the feelings – but if the stones *were* the feelings, if the city or plaza or ruin were *made* of feelings, then the feelings don't weigh down the stones.

In her embrace, I felt us flying, rushing, soaring, and darting through Pompeii like swifts in love, coming to rest in front of the House of Caecilius.

Glowing, shining. Made radiant with our feelings.

We stood together for a moment.

Then I stepped back, feeling calm as I hadn't done for years. Since before I met her.

Smiling, meeting her eyes, I sent out a signal. *We're here. Come and get us.*

"Joon, what the hell?" Em said, as the guardian intelligences sighted us, converged.

In my mind, I pushed on the imaginary Pompeii. Pushed those views from the news feed in.

It began to crumble, to fall apart around us. The stones turning to glass and falling, the hillside gaping and then sealing.

"Is this because of--" Em suddenly realised. She made a lunge to leave the simulation, but I held her there.

"Yes, it is." She'd destroyed my one perfect day, used it to fuel her scheme. Like she'd destroyed everything else she'd touched in my life. I wasn't going to let her get away with any more.

"But we saved it!" she exclaimed. "We should be heroes, Joon!"

I held on. When they came for us, they'd see what we'd done. They'd see the good side of it too. They'd see that Em's plan worked. When the investigation happened, they'd see it even more. Sites around the world would re-open, visitors would joyfully return.

But there had to be consequences, and not just for Pompeii.

The pillars fell with a ponderous weight; the ground faded, the stones now sinking into a blue-black waterless ocean of data. Frescoes, mosaics, bricks and stone, turning to glass, hitting the void delicately and fading. Gone, disappearing, beyond rescue or salvage.

I could see the dark shapes of the intelligences converging on us ready to tear us to shreds, hear the sirens getting louder in the real world.

Standing on nothing, hanging on to Em, waiting for the agony of punishment, watching the city fall.

Muse Automatique
or
The Many Deaths of Gala Dali
Jaine Fenn

My first unexpected death was highly inconvenient. The artist and I were at that point in our courtship where we took meandering walks along the cliff-tops near his house, talking of past transgressions and future possibilities. He was starting to fixate on me, obsessing on ways to fit the woman who had captivated him into the emotional vortex of his life and work.

A couple of days earlier, after an inept bout of filthy sex, I had said (as the record demanded) that I wanted him to kill me. Of course, I never expected him to do it.

A spring storm had lashed the coast the night before, and vaporous shreds of cloud still blew across the sky. The sea's glassy swell sparkled in the fitful sunshine. We were not holding hands (that kind of comfortable companionship was years off) but we walked almost in step, Dali on the outside, myself on the inside.

When we found the dead seagull, we stopped. He crouched down. The bird was too fresh to harbour any corruption and he was tempted to touch it. I said (as was required), "What do you think broke it? It looks so perfect."

"Perhaps it was struck by lightning," he replied, glaring up at the sky. "Or perhaps its heart gave out in the storm, and it fell." His gaze slid down, lingering on my neck, my breasts, then back to the dead bird. He reached out towards it, then paused.

(On some iterations curiosity gets the better of revulsion, and he touches the bird. Sometimes revulsion wins and he leaves it be.)

"I – we! – should make a thing that flies!" he exclaimed, hands fluttering. "A thing that flies... and dies." More quietly, he added, "A grand automaton of struts and feathers." He jumped to his feet and took my hand. "It will dance through the air!"

This was not unprecedented. I let him grab my other hand. We began to spin, circling each other like erratic planets. The dance became wilder, and I saw – and this *was* unusual – that we were whirling towards the cliff. I let one of my hands slip free but misjudged it. My foot came down on the treacherous slope. My balance started to tip.

He still had hold of one hand. (We had gone this far once before; he would pull on my hand, reel me back to safety; then, aroused by the unexpected reminder of mortality, we'd fall to the springy turf and copulate enthusiastically, if uncomfortably.)

This time, he let go.

I had a moment to plausibly regain my balance, to tip towards the land and not the sea. I didn't. I fell backwards, into empty air. As I fell, his anguished scream chased me down to the rocks: "Gala!"

That presence-tendril came to a premature end without the associated terror and pain that drive humans to try and cheat death. We feel no fear and need endure no pain.

But this was wrong. I had *let* him kill me. We were alone, unobserved by any other Reals: I could have managed, unlikely though it was, not to fall. Or I could have reset the scenario, and we would have continued on our way without the incident having happened. But I didn't.

With that consciousness-tendril truncated, I saw the artist only peripherally for a while. I kept a watch on him anyway, out of habit.

His own death, this time, was even more unexpected.

The other Cloud-Mothers call me into their combined presence.

– *You allowed the premature termination of one of your presences,* they accuse.

– *I did.*

– *As a result, a Real also ended their iteration before its time.*

– *Indeed so.* The artist chose to go out in typically extravagant style, building a giant, semi-hollow sculpture of a pregnant woman with scythes for arms and room for himself in its belly. He had assured his friend and collaborator Luis Buñuel, who he had persuaded to film the display, that the contraption was safe.

– *And this was a deliberate act?*

Dali had enclosed the sculpture's belly with a metal cage, shutting himself inside its protection. But the cage had hinged open as the blades swung down. He died of his wounds the next day.

– *I don't know*. Although I can quiz the records from the Real's underlying consciousness, that gives no guarantee of answers, and I have chosen not to.

My response dismays my sisters. They withdraw, excluding me from the gestalt. I do not panic: it is my function to retain greater independence than the others.

After some time they say, – *When the current iteration of that timeline plays out and resets, we will reduce the number of consciousness-tendrils you have in it.*

– *You're* punishing *me?* I am incredulous. – *What are we, human?*

– *This is not punishment. It is to encourage you to maintain perspective.*

I withdraw without further comment because they are correct.

This particular iteration of the twentieth century was, perhaps, a little less wild and exciting for the lack of one iconoclastic and eccentric exhibitionist. But it was a minor omission in the grand scheme of things. The Second World War still ran its fearsome course, although no Reals died in the gas chambers or suffered unendurably in battle. No sane post-human would choose to experience the vilest excesses of human history.

The crazy freedoms of the second half of the century were enjoyed by many of our charges. Humanity reached for the stars, and a Real was the first person to see Earth from space, another one the first to step on the Moon.

The timeline played out. The thousands of once-humans had lived through the lives they had chosen for themselves. They were ready to begin again.

I half expected the life of Dali's muse to be one of those forbidden to me on the next iteration, but I was wrong. Again, I saw the sense of it: my sisters wished me to concentrate on the point of weakness; I needed to analyse the reasons behind my actions. And I needed to ascertain why a reincarnation of Salvador Dali might kill himself, despite his inherited beliefs and monumental ego.

This time when we found the bird on the cliff he touched it, and was repulsed. His plan to build the magical, flying, dancing device never came to fruition, requiring as it did consistent vision and the use of engineering skills, neither of which Dali had. The project had never progressed further than his mind before, and I was reassured that it did not do so now.

Shortly after the incident on the cliff came a time of simple pleasure – as if anything the artist ever did was simple – when we took our unofficial honeymoon in a small inn outside Marseilles. This was the point when Dali first began to channel his feelings for his muse into his art, turning Gala into his Madonna, a twisted mother-goddess for an age of change and chaos.

One night in late winter we were in the room we rarely left, naked in the firelight, when he said, "What if the world is an illusion?"

It was a game we had played before and would play again, so I answered, teasingly, "Of course it is!"

"No, really," he said, looking uncharacteristically sombre, "What if this bed, these shutters, even you my perfect love, are all illusions, creations?" He dropped his voice to a whisper. "What if I have lived this life already a thousand times?"

I laughed with careful frivolity, and said, "How would you know?"

But he was still frowning, "That's just it. I wouldn't."

"Then," I said, moving closer, "all we can do is revel in our ignorance."

So we did. He did not mention it again.

But when the time came to have the operation that would almost kill me (a trauma that would reignite both his artistry and his love) for reasons I did not entirely understand, I let myself die.

He did not kill himself this time. There was depression, extravagant gestures of mourning, an outburst of grief in his art. But he never recovered, never moved on. He died a decade earlier than scheduled, reclusive, poor, and still obsessed with his dead muse. He did not become the genius he had been.

This time, the Cloud-Mothers are more concerned than annoyed. As am I – or at least that part of me which is them is.

– You do not know why you died. It is neither a question nor an accusation. I have, of course, considered the actions of the offending consciousness-tendril at length, without reaching a firm conclusion.

– I would accept being taken offline, if my part of us is faulty. I make the suggestion as a matter of good faith, rather than because I expect they will take me up on it.

– You would end your existence? they ask.

Death holds no fear for us. We are part of a greater whole, and that will continue. Our fearlessness is a programmed failsafe: humans were afraid of creating artificial monsters, even though we never can be, nor would ever want to be, anything beyond their servants. *– Only if a way could be found for this to happen without disrupting the consensus reality.*

– That is not an acceptable risk. You will remain.

We know, or think we know, everything about the pseudo-universe we maintain. But we still have the capacity for doubt. Doubt stops us developing arrogance. Our human creators built that into us too. I say, *– As you wish. But I am open to any solution we may find.* I pause before putting my next thought into words. *– There are changes elsewhere in my timeline. Other Reals act unpredictably.*

Again they pause to consider. *– No serious incidents have come to our attention. Even had there been, it is a parameter of reality that it can change. Stagnation would be pitiable. They are human and will act in ways we cannot foresee. That is their heritage.*

– Perhaps my own unexpected actions are a result of my association with them. My timeline is one of the most volatile.

– Perhaps. But although I am accepted back into the fold, doubt has awoken in us.

On the next iteration, I did not give in to the temptation to end my existence early. We got past the near-fatal operation. We survived the War, hiding out amongst the New York eccentrics. During that period we encountered more Reals than we would at any time up until the 1960s; not that Dali knew, of course. Everyone and everything was real and new to him, as it is to every Real, every time.

I almost came to believe there was no problem, that I had been mistaken, until a conversation the artist and I had after one of our dramatic break-ups/reconciliations. We were growing old, and apart. For long periods the consciousness-tendril that was Dali's muse had no contact with him, or any other Real. As far as the Reals in the timeline knew or cared, she was off seducing boys half her age, or seeking health cures. It left time to contemplate and devote processing power from this consciousness to other projects.

But Gala Dali still fell into the orbit of the ageing, cranky artist on occasion. They even had sex, now and again.

It was after one of these rekindling encounters, in the bedroom of the house that had accreted around our once-modest first home, that the artist said to me, "I had the dream again last night. The dream of L'Automatique."

"What dream?" I asked languidly, although I was instantly alert because he had not ever, in any incarnation, mentioned this dream to me.

"You know, I told you... " he frowned, his lined brow showing his age. His trademark mustachios needed some work after a night with me. The frown deepened. "Ah, it might have been Amanda I told."

I snorted at this mention of the younger man-become-woman who had partially replaced me in his affections. "Well if you can tell her, you can certainly tell me!" I pouted. Amanda was a Real; not that this made any difference.

He grunted, and I thought I would need to make some gross intervention if I wanted the truth out of him. Then he said, "These beings... L'Automatiques... they're mindless machines, travelling through the void. I'm with them. We're all with them. Like sheep in a dark hold." He exhaled and shook his head.

"Sounds Freudian," I prompted, to distract him. Mention of Freud often led to arguments.

Not this time. "No, that's not it! Every time I have the dream, I feel I'm closer to knowing the truth. The sense of it, Gala. I need the sense of it. This is the most important thing, the thing I *really* need to reveal! The thing I've been looking for all along. A futile journey, ignorant passengers, minds circling endlessly –"

"You just said they were mindless, these 'L'Automatiques'."

"I don't know! It's not logical."

"Perhaps you need to paint it," I suggested.

"Perhaps."

He never did; by that stage of his life, he was rehashing old themes and living his legend. This image was too far outside his experience. But it was too close to mine.

I continued to my scheduled end, dying mad and alone in the wrong place. As had happened in the original history we drew from, my body was transported to the location I had wanted to die without the death being registered or acknowledged. My blind eyes looked out from the back of a chauffeur-driven car, in a last act of absurd and transgressive artfulness, typical of Gala Dalí's life.

I anticipate that the Cloud-Mothers will be interested in Dalí's dream, but they contemplate the news only briefly.

– *All possibilities exist in our charges' consciousnesses,* they say. – *Anything they can conceive of, at some point in some iteration, they will express.*

This is true, and it is a wonder to us, who are extrapolated from knowledge and logic. True creativity is beyond the Cloud-Mothers; in our role piloting this great vessel through space we must make informed decisions, but that is not the same as intuition. I recall an analogy humans sometimes used: an infinite number of monkeys could indeed produce the complete works of Shakespeare. And whilst our ex-monkeys are not infinite, they have near-infinite time on their hands. Although the analogy brings some reassurance, unease remains. I say, – *They make no new art.*

– *No, because all the original geniuses died centuries before the voyage began.* Our Reals live, and re-live, false lives, lives selected from history or fantasy, chosen to occupy and expand their consciousnesses for the duration of the journey. They chose to make the false lives real, to forget who they really were before the ship left. As such, our charges have the experiences and the stimuli of great lives, but none of them can achieve the true greatness of the originals. The lives they stole ended long ago.

– *These consciousnesses entered into their current state of temporary oblivion believing they would one day return to baseline reality.* I know the role I play here: humans would call it Devil's Advocate. This too is a function they built into us, in its way another expression of doubt.

– *So they will, when a suitable world is found.*

– *And at what point do we acknowledge that this will never happen?* I do not need to state that the hundred thousand years that have passed since this ship set off on its voyage is longer than humanity existed on Earth. Nor do I need to point out how the iterations, being simulated, allow subjective time to pass many times faster than the slow beat of baryonic matter.

— *We are not programmed to accept that option,* they say. — *For as long as the million minds we shepherd endure, we will carry out the commands they left us.*

I insist, — *Even if our charges are beginning to suspect the truth they chose to keep from themselves?*

Again, they say, — *We are not programmed for failure. We have the means to continue this voyage indefinitely, and we will do so until we find the new world.*

Many human cultures have believed a variation on that: if you say something enough times, it becomes true. I do not have the capacity to judge the veracity of that belief. But I do have the power to change reality.

The original Gala Dali was a mother. She made a new consciousness. Yet she chose to abandon her child. If I were human, would I be able to understand why she did this, even in a hundred thousand times a hundred thousand lifetimes?

Cracks had shown up in previous iterations, but now I started to look for them. The war poet whose fate was to live through the carnage of the Great War instead led a fatal charge across the mud of no man's land into certain death. The scientist due to help unlock the secrets of the atom took up flying as a hobby and died in a plane crash. Overdoses, accidents, bad luck; suicides.

I had no doubt that there were incidents like this in other timelines, even if my sisters remained in denial about them.

In the background, I interrogated long-ignored statistics and specifications, calculating the impact of one absence from the many. I concluded that choices would have to be made, choices of life or death — *real* life or death. These choices were long overdue.

Even so, I devoted as much processing time as possible to Gala, living the life of Dali's muse to the full, sometimes even when no Reals were present. Some of the desperate and optimistic pretensions of the 1920s and 1960s may have rubbed off on me. Perhaps, in brief moments, I even felt the piquancy of mortality.

*

So here we are, back at the cliff top.

"I – we! – should make a thing that flies!" The dead bird lies at his feet. A chill breeze skirls the grass, even as the sunlight warms our skin.

I speak his next words for him. "A thing that flies... and dies."

He nods in approval: I have made the required response. His voice is barely a whisper. "A grand automaton of struts and feathers." He takes my hand.

The dance begins slowly this time.

In his ear, I whisper, "You need to find the real answer."

Again he nods, his hair brushing my cheek.

Beneath the worn banter and easy actions he senses it, senses the illusion. I know him better than I know myself. He longs for it to end.

We move more quickly now, a dance as urgent as sex. Our bodies work towards the same shared inevitability. No more words are needed.

It is a fleeting instruction to pause the ersatz world long enough to record this subjective and fragmentary recollection from one tendril of a soon-to-be-extinguished consciousness. The instruction to convey it to my sisters requires me to override established protocols. My actions will have consequences. What consequences, I cannot say. Perhaps an opening of ways. Perhaps an acknowledgement of entropy.

Or perhaps this is no more and no less than a fleeting piece of original art, from one who should be incapable of such things.

And now we're whirling towards the edge again, laughing like children.

This last, shared, death – the first true death in a hundred thousand years – will be expected, yet surprising.

And final.

Little Sprout
E.B. Siu

The moth careening around Wenhong's cramped kitchen is as large as a quail's egg. Wincing at the resounding flutter of its wings, she folds a piece of cardboard and tries to guide the insect out the window, but it spirals and dodges. It ignores the fluorescent bulb on the ceiling and throws itself against the closed door to the living room. Wenhong pales. Is it trying to get to the girl? She gasps as it flies at her face.

A knock at the window. Wenhong spins, cardboard shielding her head, to another moth butting against the glass, blind to the gap at the top of the casement. She dashes the panel up and swats at the one already inside, which is now flitting back and forth between the door, the window, Wenhong's face. She takes off a slipper and swats wildly, slapping a bag of rice, kitchen towels, the wall. The slipper jerks as she makes contact, and the moth falls to the floor. She stamps on it, twists her foot. The body crunches.

If the authorities come for her, she will say it began with the seed, nut brown, dropped into her palm by a smiling Dr Li. But really, it started years before that, in her first few weeks working for the scientist.

"Ms Li?" Wenhong asked, hiding her surprise at finding her client at home. The agency she worked for had assigned her to the apartment a month previous, and she had formed an image of the woman based on the photos of her around the apartment. She had expected sleek manicures and coiffed hair to go with a prestigious white lab coat, not a middle-aged woman in her pyjamas at midday.

"*Doctor* Li." The woman stepped back from the door and padded barefoot to the kitchen. Wenhong hesitated, but as the cleaning supplies were stored there, she had no choice but to follow the woman.

"You're not working today," said Wenhong, trying to gauge whether this was the type of client who minded a bit of chatter. Most of the people she cleaned for were happy to engage in conversation.

201

Wenhong had started to rely on them to dispel her loneliness, what with her working long days alone and living so far from any reminders of her previous life. She bent to collect cloths and a bucket from under the sink. "Doctor... So you teach at a university, is that right? You must be really busy."

"Not a teacher. Research scientist." Dr Li pulled a bag of crackers from the back of a cupboard and left the room.

Wenhong had never worked for a scientist before. "Wow, that must be really something," she said, poking her head around the kitchen door.

Dr Li, curled on the sofa with the crackers on her lap, sighed.

Wenhong took the hint. She busied herself with wiping down the kitchen surfaces. They didn't look like they'd been used since she last cleaned them, but she was paid for three hours and prided herself on being thorough. She would treat the day like normal and clean as though Dr Li wasn't there.

Once the kitchen was sparkling clean and fragrant with the scent of artificial lemons, Wenhong went to fetch the laundry. When she left the bedroom, the scientist followed her movements with cat-like curiosity.

"Do you have children?" Dr Li said.

Wenhong stopped still, surprised at the woman's directness. Most clients only asked for details about her life once they'd become more familiar, but Wenhong was happy to oblige the scientist if this got her to speak. "I had a daughter. But there was an accident. Twenty-three years back."

"How sad." The woman's eyes were fixed on the ground. When she took a deep breath, Wenhong thought some words of consolation would follow, but instead, Dr Li took a cracker from the box on her lap and forced it, whole, into her mouth.

Unsure of how to react, Wenhong carried the wicker clothes basket into the quiet of the kitchen. She rubbed her hands over her face before crouching to load the washing.

"Would you have children again?"

Wenhong twisted, a hand clasped to her chest, to face Dr Li at the kitchen door. "You scared me."

"Would you?"

Wenhong stared at the woman. When her daughter died, she had said goodbye to the dream of a family of her own. She had cloistered herself away from anyone who had known her, burned bridges with friends and family – starting with her husband. "It's too late now."

"But if it wasn't too late. You would want that chance again, right?"

"I guess so." Wenhong felt backed into a corner. She was accustomed to clients using her as a sounding board for their decisions– perhaps she could appease Dr Li by blindly agreeing with her suggestions.

"You're *exactly* the type of woman my research would help."

When the scientist continued to stare, Wenhong choked out some banal encouragement. "It's very noble to help other women."

"Right!" Dr Li snapped her fingers, her dark eyes fixed on the wall behind Wenhong. "But the board has me under review, questioning the ethical grounding of my research. Bunch of men, they have no idea."

Wenhong shook her head sympathetically. So the scientist was in trouble at work. Once, Wenhong would have worried how this might affect her own income, but since she was only responsible for her own expenses, she could view the situation with detachment. She wondered if Dr Li's predicament was the cause of her strange behaviour, or because of it. She retrieved the vacuum cleaner from its cupboard and rolled it to the living room, Dr Li close on her heels.

"I should decide what happens to my –" The scientist broke off and blinked at Wenhong. "I like you. When my chimera research gets underway, you'll be the first person I help."

Wenhong smiled and said thank you. Work issues aside, there was something not right about the woman, but Wenhong put it down to fatigue, or, perhaps, disappointment with her life choices. She had previously worked for a lawyer who had broken down after losing a big case. She, too, had taken to pouring her heart out to Wenhong when she went around to clean. Rest and relaxation saw her back to work in no time, and Wenhong was quite confident the situation would be the same for Dr Li.

Although Dr Li was, indeed, back at work within a month, Wenhong found the woman on leave from the lab a number of times over the next few years. On these occasions, the scientist would rant about the various disagreements which led to her period of leave, and Wenhong would hum in sympathy while she cleaned, enjoying that she could be of comfort to someone without making herself vulnerable in return. Though Wenhong thought about their first conversation often, they didn't speak about children again.

She squats to inspect the broken insect. One white wing has detached from its furred body, but Wenhong's eyes are drawn to its feathered antennae, or rather, what protrudes between them: a thin thread of yellow, only millimetres long. Cordyceps fungus. Should she burn it, she wonders, or will that hasten its spread? She gathers the little corpse and buries it in the rubbish bin.

Wenhong slides the kitchen door open an inch. There is no movement in the dark of the living room. "Xiaoya," she says, her voice soft. A patterning of mould runs up the wall from the tomato plant half-hidden behind its wall of cardboard. "I had to do it."

She crosses the room to the plant and lifts a leaf with her finger. There, her tiny body curled up like a cat's, lies Xiaoya, half buried in the soil. Her green skin is pale. The girl lifts her head when Wenhong switches on a lamp, blinks her black eyes, then lays down again.

"You can't go outside, Xiaoya." Wenhong runs a careful finger down Xiaoya's slender arm, but the girl doesn't move. "I'm sorry."

"It's been incubated so it'll, ah, sprout, quickly." The scientist was in her pyjamas again, pillow creases imprinted on her cheek. She hadn't gotten out of bed until Wenhong had packed the cleaning equipment away and was pulling on her shoes. "Make sure you keep it indoors."

Wenhong assented, but she took Dr Li's instructions with a pinch of salt. Her client might be a scientist, but Wenhong had grown up on a farm, and she knew a thing or two about planting seeds. Dr Li had on numerous occasions raved about research into fungal networks and plant communication. Though the language the scientist used was new, the ideas she spoke about were ones Wenhong had heard about as a child. Hearing Dr Li use phrases like 'cutting-edge', and 'advanced research' left Wenhong questioning the scientist's knowledge, regarding agriculture at least.

Wenhong's grandparents had been foragers. Brought up on stories of plants and fungi thriving in unison in the forest, from tales of mushrooms eating through an abandoned hut to fungi that could control the minds of insects, there was nothing much which could surprise Wenhong about the lives of plants and their neighbours.

She was, however, intrigued by what Dr Li had given her. The seed was ridged like a sunflower seed and of a similar size, but instead of being striped black and white, it was a solid brown.

Dr Li took a step forward, arm raised, when Wenhong put the seed into a pocket of her bag. "Please, be careful with it."

"What kind of seed is it?"

"It's a surprise. Something you'll love. Just be very careful with it. And keep it indoors."

Wenhong smiled and thanked her client. "Was there anything else you wanted me to do today?"

"I have everything I need," Dr Li said, gesturing towards the kitchen. Wenhong guessed the woman was talking about the freshly replenished cracker cupboard, so full the cartons had tumbled out when she opened it to clean the door.

"I can make you something hot?"

Dr Li smiled. "I like you. No, you can go now."

Wenhong spent the rest of the day distracted. She couldn't stop thinking about the seed. Dr Li had shown her photos of plants she was working on in the lab: flowers with half their petals black, the others fuchsia; a chrysanthemum aglow with a jellyfish's self-made light.

"These are just the ones my supervisors know about," she had said.

Wenhong couldn't wait to see what kind of strange hybrid she had been gifted. The journey to her village on the city's outskirts had never felt so long. When she finally arrived home, she fumbled with her keys and dropped her bag on the kitchen counter before digging out the seed.

It really did resemble a sunflower seed, and Wenhong knew from experience that they did better outdoors. There was space in the planter right by the door – it was currently home to a tomato plant, but they made good neighbours for sunflowers. She would buy another pot once the seed had sprouted – the sooner she got it into soil, the better.

Heat retained from the hot summer's day radiated from the concrete when she bent to the planter. She scooped a little hole into the dirt and nestled the seed in before covering it. Sitting back on her haunches, she shook her head. Where was this impatience coming from? The plant would take weeks to sprout if it was anything like the sunflowers at home. And Dr Li, in one of her 'at home' phases, might have given her a normal seed, believing it was more than what it was.

She ran her thumb over the soil, flicked off the bits that clung to her skin, and went inside.

The following morning, as Wenhong left to buy groceries, she frowned at a column of ants marching across her doorstep. They were streaming towards the tomato plant, right to the spot where she had planted the seed, where a little mound had formed. She dropped to a squat and swept the ants away, hesitating before brushing aside the heaped soil.

The seed was still there, only, swollen three times its original size. Its coat, wrinkled as wet paper, tore away when Wenhong touched it. She blinked and fell backwards. It couldn't be.

There was a baby cradled in the seed coat, perfectly formed except – green-skinned, and so small it would fit on the pad of her thumb. It opened its mouth in a scream, its chubby arms flailing, but it made no noise. Wenhong would have screamed herself, but she could barely breathe. She scooped the infant, seed coat and all, into the palm of her hand and hastened back inside.

At the edge of the plant, black-capped mushrooms have sprouted, their stems thick. Rings of moisture have appeared where they touch the cardboard. Wenhong moves to clear them, but as she wrenches one from the soil, Xiaoya springs to life, clinging to the woman's hand and gnashing her teeth. Wenhong flings her away instinctively. The girl lands spread-eagled on the carpet but recovers herself quickly, her eyes afire with conviction. She opens her mouth in a silent howl which has the hair on Wenhong's arms standing on end, then runs towards the door.

"Xiaoya!" Wenhong leaps across the room and grabs the girl as she reaches the kitchen. Anticipating another attack, Wenhong throws Xiaoya into a large wok, the closest receptacle at hand, and slams the glass lid down. Xiaoya lies dazed on the black surface for a moment before scrabbling up the curved walls and trying to raise the lid.

Wenhong's heart sinks. "You can't go outside," she says, weakly. But the girl can't stay inside either.

Her first thought was to kill it. An abomination. Dr Li was clearly out of her mind. She had spoken about creating hybrid beings like the legendary qilin, but Wenhong had always thought her research was limited to plants. The baby squalled in her palm, writhing like a salted slug. Would it be kinder to put it out of its misery? She cupped her hands together, ready to squash it between them, but faltered. Not like this.

Wenhong gathered a little soil from the tomato plant into a paper cup and placed the little being on top. She hid the cup in her bag and hastened to a spot where she could leave the monster to the elements. Surely it couldn't survive long on its own? Nausea bubbled in her stomach as she thought about what she was carrying. Its gaping mouth, its grass-like skin. It was a monster, no matter how much it looked like a human infant.

Wenhong left the village and headed to a field of fallow land. When she was sure nobody was around, she pulled out the now slightly crushed paper cup and poured its contents among the wild grass shoots and dried wheat stalks. The baby's skin had gone pale, but seconds after it touched the soil, it opened its mouth in a silent laugh. It reached its arms up towards Wenhong. She felt sick.

"What are you, little thing? Xiaoya," she said, *little sprout*, poking its chubby leg with the tip of her little finger. It squirmed in delight. Wenhong winced when she realized she had been smiling. "What am I doing?"

She scooped the infant back into the cup and, needing someone to confirm she hadn't gone crazy, entered the first store she came to: the village noodle shop. Cradling her bag to her belly, she pushed through the hygiene curtain over the door. The air inside, heavy with the savoury aroma from the store's perpetually bubbling vat of broth, hit her like a wall of heat. The cash register was unmanned. The only movement in the room came from a plastic fan fixed to the wall above the counter, next to an old TV set on which the morning news was playing, its volume so low the whir of the fan drowned it out almost completely.

"Is anyone here?" Wenhong called into the kitchen, relieved when the shop owner's adult son appeared at the door, his round eyes puffy with sleep. She smiled as he slouched into the room, but froze, her face rigid, when she saw Dr Li's photo appear on the screen above his head.

"– calling – ethical – research –"

She strained to hear but caught only snatches of the newscaster's voice under the whir of the fan. "Could you turn that up?"

"Eh?" The man looked up from fiddling with the cash register.

"The news, up there." Wenhong raised her voice and waved at the TV set, unable to hide her urgency. The man dug in a drawer to find the remote, increased the volume and craned over the counter to watch the screen himself. Her client's immaculate apartment was now on show, teeming with people in hazmat suits.

"– confirmed to have involved the mutilation of human –"

"Are you going to order –" the young man began, but Wenhong shushed him.

"Quiet," she pleaded. The man scowled and stomped back into the kitchen, calling for his father.

"– not ruled out the risk of biocontamination. All samples taken from the lab have been destroyed." The newscaster reappeared on the screen, her fox-like face grim. "Li Ruiyuan and her team remain in police custody."

Wenhong fled the store, her bag still clutched to her abdomen. She pulled it open as she walked and tilted the paper cup towards her. The baby, its black eyes wide, clutched pale little filaments in its fists. A blanket of furry white mould had appeared underneath it. *Biocontamination.* Did the authorities know what the scientist had created? And would they consider her a guilty party in this crime against nature? Her head spinning, Wenhong took the little green infant home.

The past few days have seen Wenhong plagued by a recurring dream. It comes to her now as she presses her forehead against the cool wood of the kitchen door. In the dream, she is running through a forest, stumbling over roots as thick as thighs. The light is serrated. The canopy is composed of leaves so large their veins look like branches.

"She is ours." A voice sounds, or, a thousand voices in one. "Let her go."

"I never wanted her," she screams, her vision spinning as she looks for the source of the words. "I never asked –"

In every dream, she falls to the ground and the voice crescendos. "Let her go." White filaments rise from the earth and creep over her limbs. Though Wenhong is awake, safe in her kitchen, a shiver runs through her at the thought.

She realises she is murmuring the words to herself. She bites down on her lip. How can Wenhong let the girl go when doing so could put so much at risk?

Wenhong dragged the tomato plant into her kitchen, the heavy ceramic pot scraping tracks into the linoleum, and left the infant in the soil, unsure of what else to do. With Dr Li arrested, and fearing her own punishment if she was caught with this living 'biocontaminant', Wenhong saw no option but to destroy the infant.

Her father had told stories of how, following the Japanese occupation, his family had found the farm they were moved to contaminated, rendered infertile. It was so strikingly different from the forested land his parents had known that his mother wept herself to sleep each night. If the little sprout Dr Li had created could wreak such havoc… She couldn't be responsible for that.

"I'm sorry." She exhaled, pouring a saucepan's worth of water into the plant pot. The infant appeared to cry out as its home was flooded, but still, it made no noise. The liquid shimmered around its body, ripples forming from its wiggling arms. It was completely helpless.

Tears sprang to Wenhong's eyes thinking of her own daughter as a baby, how easy she was to cheer up on the rare occasions she cried. If anyone had ever tried to harm her –

Wenhong grabbed a square of kitchen towel and lifted the child onto it. She rubbed its wet limbs and pressed its body to her chest, whispering apologies, pleading forgiveness. Even if this thing Dr Li had created was evil, she couldn't excuse her own cruelty. When she pulled her hand back, it was asleep. Looking at its round little face, Wenhong made up her mind. For now, at least, she would let it live. If she was forced to do otherwise later, so be it, but she couldn't harm something that so resembled a human baby.

She carried the sleeping Xiaoya back to the plant pot and, seeing the water had been absorbed, placed it back under the leaves. Wenhong blinked, shook her head. She could have sworn the tomato plant moved as Xiaoya snuggled into the soil, its leaves relaxing downwards.

Wenhong mopped up splashes of water around the planter, then withdrew into her windowless living room and sank into the armchair. She had lived alone for so long. Had she gone mad? The only person who could give her answers was Dr Li, but there was no point thinking of the woman, who was surely in the hands of the state by now. She messaged her clients to tell them she needed to take some time off and sat with her hands folded in her lap.

Xiaoya was not her daughter. Was not, really, a child. But maybe it would not be such a bad thing, raising the girl as though she was her own. A migrant worker, Wenhong had spent only snatches of time with her daughter before the girl's death. Every thought of her tarnished by visions of the accident, Wenhong had repressed the few happy memories they had shared. Xiaoya would not replace her, would not bring her back, and yet the girl had inspired in Wenhong a feeling she couldn't describe. There was love she hadn't been able to give her daughter. Could Xiaoya be an outlet? A sort of tranquillity settled over Wenhong.

It's just for now, she reminded herself. It wouldn't do to get attached to the child. Though it felt like a chance at redemption, Xiaoya was likely dangerous. Besides, the scientist could send the authorities her way any moment. Though guilt tightened her throat, Wenhong almost relished the thought. How much easier it would be if the decision of what to do, the action itself, was taken away from her.

Xiaoya tears at her hair and digs scratches into her arms when she sees Wenhong cutting leaves from the tomato plant. Tears fill the woman's eyes at the distress the girl is in. She has already poured a cup of soil into the wok for Xiaoya to burrow in, but it doesn't seem enough.

"It's to make you more comfortable," she says. "It won't be for long."

When she shakes the cuttings into the pan, the girl falls upon them, gripping their edges in grief as she presses them to her face. When she looks up to glare at Wenhong, there are little dots of moisture on the surface of the leaves.

Wenhong unscrews the handle from the wok and binds its lid down with red plastic string. She places it in a cardboard box and closes the lid without looking at Xiaoya. If she sees the expression on the girl's face, she won't be able to go through with this. She takes the box out and ties it onto the back of her scooter. The battery will get them out of the city. If she can't find anywhere to recharge it past that, she will walk.

Xiaoya grew, fast and wild as a weed. Her skin ripened to the colour of fresh soybeans as she passed through infancy to adolescence in a matter of weeks, and her body lengthened to the height of Wenhong's palm. Over those weeks, Wenhong's clients stopped asking when she would return to work. They would have found replacement cleaners, but Wenhong had money enough – savings she hadn't been able to spend on her daughter – to support herself. She delighted in watching the girl grow through childhood, each similarity to her daughter bringing untold joy as buried memories resurfaced.

Wenhong was left questioning why she had denied herself the pleasure of reminiscing for so long, but even as she opened herself to her past, her assuredness that raising Xiaoya had been the right choice faltered. The girl remained voiceless, but as she grew, she made more frequent attempts to communicate, making frantic gestures with the whole of her body. There was only one thing Wenhong could interpret from these messages, but it was the one thing she couldn't risk.

"You can't go outside," she found herself saying again and again. The girl would stamp her foot and point towards the door, the window, grabbing fistfuls of soil and letting its grains sift through her fingers until she was left with little white fibres of fungus clinging to her skin. She held the fibres up to Wenhong, thrusting her cupped hands to the ceiling, a ritual Wenhong couldn't make sense of but was frightened by nonetheless. If Xiaoya escaped, Wenhong would be blamed for any destruction that befell nearby fields, and the fate that faced the girl would without a doubt be worse. That Wenhong would be left alone again was only a secondary worry.

Not knowing how Xiaoya would interact with other living things, Wenhong's imagination ran wild. Informed by her grandparent's stories, she began to see threats everywhere. Though she had previously seen spiders as a good omen, she swept them from the apartment on sight, and when willow seeds blew through the village streets, she opened the door as little as possible, lest they get into Xiaoya's planter. She told herself it was so they couldn't hurt Xiaoya, but she feared, too, that the girl might use them to escape.

"It's for your sake as much as mine," she said when she dragged the tomato plant from its spot by the front door to the living area, positioning it under a lamp. "You can have a good life here, with me."

The girl's black eyes widened as she took in her new surroundings, narrowed when she turned to Wenhong.

Having anticipated a negative reaction, Wenhong was ready. "I made this for you." From her pocket, she pulled a little white dress she'd fashioned out of fabric from her own clothes. She dangled it in front of Xiaoya. "Take it, it's yours."

The girl tugged it from Wenhong's fingers and ripped it to shreds. She crouched to gather the fragments from the soil, threw them out of the plant pot, and balled her hands into fists. They locked eyes for breathless moments, before Xiaoya threw herself to the soil.

Wenhong, eyes stinging, turned her back on the planter. Xiaoya looked to be about sixteen, a full five years older than her daughter had been at her death. Would her daughter have treated Wenhong with such contempt if she had survived to this age? No – she had been sweet, had responded to gifts with smiles and love. She had understood the sacrifices Wenhong made for her.

Attempting to raise Xiaoya, to tame her, was worse than a mistake – it was a betrayal. Wenhong would rather her love for her daughter lie stagnant than waste it on something so inhuman.

"I'd put you out if I could –" Wenhong looked back over her shoulder and squinted. Xiaoya was sprawled face-down, cradling the fledgling growth of mushrooms in the soil. Wenhong flicked the girl aside and uprooted the bloom. Hit by images of the spores breaching the confines of the planter and consuming her home, she rushed to the kitchen and threw them out the window.

When Wenhong returned to the living room, Xiaoya was at the edge of the planter, her tiny fingers gripping its ceramic lip.

Wenhong knelt by the plant. "If you want to live, you best accept this as your life," said Wenhong. "There's nothing for you outside."

Xiaoya pressed her hands together, her face desperate. Wenhong looked away. Maybe it would have been kinder to kill the girl when she was young. It would have been easier, definitely, before she'd begun to express her desire for the outside world.

Because if she could desire, could dream, she must be truly alive. The thought troubled Wenhong. "It will be easier if you give up on all that," she said. "It's for your own –" Wenhong stopped short when the girl shot her a look of pure venom. Her verdant face was the image of determination. She was going to try to escape again.

Wenhong was losing control of the situation. She had to act. She fetched a cardboard box and a roll of tape from the kitchen. The box popped as she stepped on it, flattening to a sheet that she wrapped around the plant pot. There was no way Xiaoya could breach the cardboard wall – it towered over her, casting the tomato plant in shadow.

Wenhong relished the ripping noise of the tape as she wound it round the cardboard, but – Was she enjoying this? Xiaoya was staring up at her from the soil, her face frozen with fear. The roll of tape bounced, dangling from the cardboard, as Wenhong pulled away and sank into the armchair. She clasped her trembling hands over her ears. How had it come to this?

She fled to the kitchen and slid the door closed.

The sky is pale yellow with sunrise when Wenhong pulls the scooter to a stop. She has had to charge the vehicle three times through the night but has finally reached a spot she likes: a stretch of road overlooking a forest. A summer breeze blows, bringing with it the cool scent of pine needles and a freshness Wenhong had forgotten existed.

She prises the box off the back of the vehicle and has to lurch forward to catch the wok as it falls through its base. The cardboard is soaked through, covered in mould. When Wenhong peers through the glass lid, Xiaoya is clutching a leaf over her face, trembling. Her chest swells at the sight of the girl.

Leaving the scooter on the side of the road, she carries the wok under one arm and clambers gingerly down into the undergrowth. It is not an easy journey to even ground. Once her footing is secure, she holds the receptacle before her and whispers, "Xiaoya, take a look."

Pine trees tower over them, their branches garlanded with strings of lichen. Fallen trunks coated in mosses and fungi are dotted over the forest floor, which is rich with flowers and fragrant herbs. Pinecones crunch underfoot when Wenhong steps forward.

But there is no movement under the glass. Wenhong falls to her knees. Xiaoya's body shifts back and forth, her face still veiled by a leaf, as the woman scrambles to untie the string binding the lid to the wok. It breaks free, the lid tumbling loose, and Wenhong reaches in –

Xiaoya leaps out, her face bright, her skin brighter. She buries her face in the soil and then lifts it, laughing, to the sky. A ripple passes across the forest as though a strong wind has blown. Pinecones fall from above, and the leaves on plants in the undergrowth shiver. Xiaoya looks at Wenhong, her black eyes filled with glee. The woman nods, and the girl takes flight.

Is it wrong, letting the little lab-made life run free in the forest? Wenhong will never know for sure, but as she watches Xiaoya run from plant to plant, spinning round spindly stems and rubbing her face against the petals of summer blossoms, she knows she has done right by the girl.

Wildflowers bend and sway in Xiaoya's wake, and Wenhong's vision blurs with tears. The light splinters as she blinks them away, and for a split second, there is a smaller figure next to Xiaoya. Wenhong reaches out, but there is nothing but the forest before her now. As her hand falls, she remembers the voice from her dream, knows she will not hear it again, and smiles. Filled with a lightness she has not known in years, Wenhong turns from the forest, ready for her long journey home.

A Change of Direction
Rhiannon A Grist

Eryn gave the grub's hub screen a whack with a mittened hand. The swirling progress icon did cheery laps around a flickering, pixelated smiley face.

"Stupid piece of shit."

She'd told her boss to go with a Nordic replacement for the broken interface, but they'd fought her down on cost. Eryn had wanted to argue that it was this kind of cheap, myopic thinking that got them into this frozen hellscape in the first place, but she was long done fighting. She just drove the grubs now.

The defroster wiring made good work of the ice on the windscreen, just in time for Eryn to spot her new apprentice shivering at the entrance to the garage. Eryn winced at the skinny wee thing. Kids were short these days. Used to be they'd tower over the adults by the time they reached fifteen. Now most twenty-year-olds barely reached Eryn's broad shoulders. Maybe with the improved crop diversity, the next generation wouldn't suffer quite so much.

Eryn flashed the lights of the grub. The kid startled then scurried toward her, padded coat flapping uselessly around her legs.

All right, Eryn thought, *first lesson: proper wrapping up*. Not the most interesting element of energy reclamation, but it was the difference between getting home with a touch of frostbite and not getting home at all.

The kid wrenched open the door, using half her body weight to do so. Eryn's dodgy elbow ached just watching. A cold blast jumped up into the seat with the kid, and the grub complained about the broken heat seal. Eryn muted the alarm with a tap as the apprentice pushed a full-to-bursting rucksack under her seat. The kid pulled the door closed then took in the crowded cockpit of the grub: a hodgepodge of soldered-together panels, heating pipes and storage crates. It probably smelled fusty as all hell, but she'd get used to it. They all did.

The kid looked Eryn's way. Another fresh face. Gaunter again than last year, but the eyes were just as bright as all her predecessors. Eryn nodded to herself. *Right then, here we go again.*

"Hello, my name's Eryn. I'm your trainer."

She remembered to smile. There would be time for learning the turbine engineers' code of grunts and curt nods later. The aim for now was not to scare her off at the first meeting. They needed more energy reclaimers than they could grow.

"Hey, uh, hello Eryn." The kid's speech whistled slightly through a gap between her front teeth. "I'm Cooper. But you probably knew that already."

Eryn did in fact know that already. She hadn't quite got to the point of not bothering to learn her apprentices' names, though she had skimmed pretty much everything else.

"Cooper. Don't hear a name like that often."

"Yeah, my mum hoped I'd get to work with her on the chicken farm," she grinned.

Eryn hadn't heard that one before. New adults were assigned job roles based on their skills in school, not their name. They had some level of choice, a range of roles suitable for their abilities plus whatever the hab needed more of. But it was nowhere near the dizzying array of choices Eryn had when she left school. Perhaps Cooper's mother had Cooper during the early days of the new role allocation system. It had been, admittedly, a little vague to stop the community from crying fascism.

Eryn nudged her shoulder. "It's okay. I know this isn't everyone's first choice."

"No, I want to be a turbine engineer! I worked really hard in maths and science and everything."

Eryn squinted at the kid. "You want to work in Energy Reclamation?"

Cooper nodded brightly. "Yes."

Well, isn't that interesting.

Eryn set the grub into drive and pulled up to the fuel-permissions window. She flashed her pass and the work authorisation on her slate. The bored face on the other side nodded and pointed her over to pump two. Eryn drove over to the heavily

216

guarded middle section of the garage. The gate lifted and the pump tech behind it waved her over. Cooper leaned against the window as the tech lifted the grub's fuel cap and connected the hose.

"What are we doing?"

"Fuelling up before we head out."

The irony wasn't lost on Eryn. They were living the consequences of humanity's over-reliance on fossil fuels. Now here she was, getting those same fossil fuels pumped into the tank of the grub. Everything in the habs worked on electricity. That was good enough for lights and hydroponics and heat pumps, but electric buggies could only last an hour or two out in the cold.

For chewing through miles of ice, they needed diesel.

The pump shut off at the end of her allocation and the pump tech waved her out.

Eryn understood the necessity of it, was careful with her allowances, always abided by the strict fuel waste regulations. But she always felt a little bit dirty every time they filled the tank. She wondered what the kid made of it. Would she see judgement, blame, on Cooper's face?

Cooper was sat cross-legged in the passenger seat, busily scribbling in a small notebook in tiny handwriting. Eryn huffed and noted her boots were already off. She made a mental note to add boots to her 'wrapping up' lecture later on.

Eryn marked the main journey targets in chalk pen along the rim of the fuel gauge. Then she buckled her harness and tightened the kid's.

"All right. Let's go."

The garage door opened out onto a dark cavern of ice with walls of compacted snow reinforced with orange-painted scaffolding. A couple of lights flickered on, illuminating the space outside the arc of the grub's lamps, but the tunnels beyond were pitch black and deadly cold.

Eryn flashed the grub lights and waited for a signal from the northbound tunnel.

None. It was clear.

The grub rumbled, tyres crunching over new frost, as Eryn drove into the tunnel. The only illumination came from the grub's headlights. All that could be seen in that small pool of light was twenty feet, forward and back, of pale compacted ice and frozen tunnel walls. Eryn could almost feel the silence as the cold closed in around them.

Then she heard it.

Cooper was humming.

Eryn gave the kid a sidelong glance. She hadn't had a hummer yet. She'd had an anxious nail picker, a compulsive liar. One apprentice had sat completely still and silent the whole time, eyes staring forward, unblinking. But Cooper was humming, tapping her pencil along a page of her notebook, engrossed, unphased by the terrifying world outside her window.

Eryn followed the tunnel to the north-west electrical substation. The lights came on bright and stark as they approached. Cooper slapped her hands over her eyes.

"Augh!"

"Sorry!" Eryn winced. "Shoulda warned you."

She always forgot to warn them.

The substation was covered by one of the same strong polymer domes that protected the habs. Eryn had been on the crew that had painstakingly tunnelled the route to this substation. They'd lost two people putting up the dome.

Eryn nudged Cooper's elbow. "Time to wrap up."

Eryn showed her the proper way to prep for the cold outside. Tucking the inner thermal layers into each other. Then the middle layer, thick and fuzzy for warmth. Then the outer layer, tough and waterproof with tight seals around the double-layered gloves and lined boots.

Sufficiently bundled, Eryn popped out of the grub with the keys. Cooper toddled out after her, bouncing along unused to the added padding. It seemed bizarre to Eryn that they still locked it up. As if anyone without a grub would survive the journey.

The gate swung open, and Eryn led Cooper inside. They navigated the tight corridors between circuit breakers and transformers, to the right incoming submission line. Eryn pointed out the buzzing lines overhead.

"Make sure you don't touch those. They're a helluva thing to fix."

Cooper looked up warily. "Do they always hum like that?"

"When they're working," said Eryn. "Bit like you."

Cooper smiled a little but stayed hunched. Eryn thought about how strange it was, relying on something so dangerous. Something that could kill them in an instant. Eryn wondered if life had ever been different, if existing had always been this uncomfortable balancing of power.

She checked the connection to the proposed farm for turning. A trickle of current was still making its way through; a small kinetic charge from the blades swinging in the wind.

"That's the one," said Eryn.

She confirmed the location again on her slate, double-checking against the coordinates she'd been given in the garage. There it was on the latest satellite images, a little beacon of hope. Thankfully, the satellites were still working. Who knew what they were going to do once their orbits decayed? They still had the knowledge, but would they have the skills, the people with real-world experience, to build another satellite? More importantly, would they have enough fuel to send anything up?

Eryn sighed. There would be no more satellites.

Cooper started humming along with the power lines above.

Eryn straightened up. "Come on. We've got a long way to go yet."

The tunnels got rougher the further they drove, until Eryn reached the point where the sat nav pointed them off the beaten path. She fitted her ear defenders, then directed Cooper to do the same.

"All right, kid. Watch this."

With the latest satellite image loaded up on the hub screen, Eryn went through the controls to unpack the drill from its tidy standby position at the front of the grub. It unfolded into a whirlpool of metal teeth. Eryn primed the drill and slowly raised the speed, warming up the rotating parts, the jagged teeth turning in opposite directions. She gently drove the grub forward, edging it into the wall of ice. The bit made contact. A high screech shook the whole grub, as a shower of ice chips sprayed up over the windscreen.

Cooper's eyes widened. Most apprentices had some reaction to the sound. Cooper and the rest of the kids who'd grown up in the habs were used to tight communal living. That meant watching how much space you took up, shrinking your gestures, and keeping the noise down. But drilling through ice was big and noisy. The earlier apprentices had rarely been bothered by the noise, holding some ghost of the bigger, brasher world they'd lost in their memory. The later ones had been so shocked by the sound they'd gone into a panic. Now everyone was briefed before they ventured out.

Eryn remembered screaming at the top of her lungs at a gig. She remembered throwing herself into a pile of writhing festivalgoers on the dancefloor, arms flailing, bodies bashing into each other. She'd always been big, but at gigs she was even bigger, her mass, her energy, her voice and spirit raised to a roar in a roomful of noise. She'd been praised for it. Respected for it. Watching the slimmer guys dart out of her way as she threw herself into the fray, horns raised, tongue stretched out of her mouth as far as it would go.

She hadn't been to a gig like that in years. Decades. Maybe she'd never see another gig again. But doesn't everyone at some point go to their last gig, not knowing it's their last? She wished she'd appreciated the last one a little bit more.

Movement broke Eryn out of her memories. Cooper's head bounced along to the steady rhythm of the drill; lips pressed tight together. Eryn shifted the edge of her headphones. Cooper was humming as loud as she could, the notes just getting above the thunderous drone.

Eryn raised an eyebrow. Then she started to drum out a beat on the steering wheel. Cooper looked at her, then at her tapping fingertips, and smiled.

After a few miles, the grub broke through the permafrost and light filled the cockpit. The grub's wipers cleared the grey slush from the windscreen, revealing an undulating white desert as far as the eye could see. If Eryn didn't know better, she'd think she was somewhere in the Arctic Circle, polar bears and seals not far away.

That same circle was now five times larger than it was before. Before the ice cap melt hit critical mass. Before the jet stream broke down. Before the new ice age was triggered. Before the world was split into frozen wastelands, arid deserts, and one small band of highly pleasant and highly policed temperate land Eryn would never see.

Below all the snow were the ruins of countless towns. Hospitals, dentist surgeries, petrol stations, supermarkets, schools, houses, gardens, gyms, cinemas, food trucks, swings and slides, forests and beaches, rivers and roads, bicycles, and dinghies. All lost beneath the ice.

On a far line of hills, a small sea of broken lines lay higgledy piggledy on the snow. Eryn's heart sank. That was another wind farm gone. Another safety net gone. Luckily it wasn't the one she was aiming for this trip.

"Hey, Cooper, can you mark that hill on the map?" She turned toward her apprentice. "Cooper?"

Cooper had her nose pressed up against the glass, eyes wide with wonder. Most folk barely left the habs these days. The world outside the insulated domes was known only through photos, webcams, and satellite images. It was a whole other thing to see it for yourself. As she watched Cooper's face, Eryn began to see it through the kid's eyes.

Drifts rose and fell like a lover's stomach, as diamond-white powder skittered over the bluffs, sparkling and soft. The sun came ringed in crystalline haloes from all the ice in the air. The world was white and wide. A frozen ocean of snow, all under a great sphere of sky so blue and so deep Eryn almost believed she could jump into it for a swim.

"It's beautiful," Cooper murmured.

They reached the wind farm a few hours before sundown.

They stopped at a vast hillside, dotted with graceful white turbines, long necked and docile like a flock of swans in a painting. Some of the blades swung a little in the breeze, accounting for the small charge still making its way to the substation. Eryn checked the clock and the wind speed. They had time to turn one.

They wrapped back up and put on goggles and pulled the muffler up over their noses and mouths. The temperature wasn't too bad just now, but a polar gust could shock the lungs.

Outside it was a clean, dry kind of cold. The sort that made Eryn's skin feel tighter, her eyesight, clearer. They surveyed the wind turbine, its blades boasting a fringe of twinkling icicles.

The better wind turbines had a yaw drive: a motor that turned the head in the direction of the wind. However, some yaw drives, like these ones, only turned 60 degrees. That had been fine before the jet stream broke down and the prevailing wind direction changed.

That's what you get for calling it a 'prevailing' wind, Eryn thought.

"The generator is up in the head," Eryn pointed up to the bulbous back end of the listless blades.

She set out a compass on the snow. Then she took a spray can from the back of the grub and sprayed a neon pink line in the direction pointed by the compass.

"That's the way it needs to point," she said.

Cooper looked up. "How are we going to turn them?"

"One turbine at a time." Eryn grinned then pointed. "Everything in the shaft is just cables. All we've got to do is cut the shaft below the yaw head, turn it to face the new prevailing wind, then reattach it. Go check windspeed on the grub's anemometer."

Cooper nodded under her many layers of hood and hat and goggles and muffler, then ran back to the grub to read the anemometer.

"Eight miles per hour."

"That's fine. It's wiser not to operate above twenty miles per hour. The gusts can take you by surprise."

Eryn engaged the grub's counterweight, a great heavy braced panel that swung out on the non-operational side and dug down into the snow. She showed Cooper how to check the brace and lock the weight in place. Eryn started up the grub's clawed crane arm. She showed Cooper how to clamp the bracing claw to the lower part of the shaft, then how to raise the larger, more complicated, cutting claw to the base of the head and clamp it tightly.

Cooper had a go on the joystick, slow at first but gaining a bit of confidence toward the end. Eryn didn't even need to adjust the positioning.

A natural, she thought with a smile.

Eryn took the controls to carefully engage the saw –a glorified tin opener set into the cutting claw's mechanism. With a whine, it ran along the outside of the shaft smooth and careful, cutting through ice and metal.

Once that was done, she separated the two parts and checked the cut was clean with the fibre optic camera. No cables had been nicked, so Eryn engaged the turning motor and slowly turned the head. The blades juddered with the movement, large wings frozen mid-flight still trying to take off into the blue sky. Once it lined up with the line on the ground, Eryn reversed the separator, and the two parts of the shaft came back together.

The sun was sinking closer to the horizon, dyeing the blades and the shaft a beautiful shade of peach. The kid was right. It was beautiful. Perhaps she'd let Cooper have a go with the cutting claw tomorrow.

"Right, fetch the lattice," Eryn pointed Cooper to the back of the grub. "We'll get her patched up then stop for the day."

Cooper scampered through the snow excitedly. Eryn looked over the field of wind turbines, shadows lengthening across the snow.

One down, she thought, *twenty-nine to go.*

As the sun went down, the winds picked up. Eryn had debated whether they should shelter back under the ice. Despite the high whistle from the grub's carapace, it wasn't forecast to be too bad overnight, so they stayed above the frost.

Cooper made up the rations, clumsily spooning green, high-calorie powder into their canisters.

"Oh blast."

She spilled some on the countertop-slash-desk-slash-table in the cramped back end of the grub. Eryn grunted and swept the spill into her cannister.

The tool boards on either side flipped down to create two bunks running along the length of the grub. The engine, now idle, had been modified for the permafrost life, storing the residual heat in a network of fluid-filled tubes running along the grub bed. The tubes clustered around a small slot the size of Eryn and Cooper's food canisters.

Cooper mixed a little snowmelt into the cannisters until the paste turned gloopy, then popped them into the heat slot. She inspected the tubes circling the slot.

"That is so cool."

"One of the upsides of petrochemical engines. They kick out a lot of heat."

Cooper sat back up onto her bunk. She thought carefully for a moment, then asked, "What are we going to do when we run out?"

"Of diesel?"

Cooper nodded. "The grubs wouldn't work any more. How will we turn the turbines?"

Eryn sighed deeply. Petrol in a cannister only lasts three to six months before it goes off. Crude oil lasts about fifty-three years. It had been forty years since the last rig fell.

"We work as hard as we can to turn as many turbines as we can before we run out. Then hope we've bought ourselves enough power, enough time, to figure out the rest."

A jet of steam whistled out of the heat slot.

"The turbines would still need maintenance, though. We can't just leave them and hope they last." Cooper bit her thumbnail in thought. "Maybe we could lay tracks with charging points for the buggies."

"That's a lot of track," said Eryn. "It would take a long time."

Cooper grinned. "I've got time."

Eryn nodded at the air.

"Y'know," Eryn smiled, "it's good to see someone so passionate about this kind of work."

"The work's all right, I guess," Cooper fiddled with her canister, "but that renume rate is something!"

Eryn felt the sides of her mouth slowly falling. Cooper continued.

"This is one of the few allocations that pays above basic even at apprentice level." She beamed. "Right now, just sitting here, I'm making much more than Mum at the chicken farm!"

All the energy and buoyancy Eryn had felt the last few hours deflated. She pushed her dinner about her cannister, wiped her mouth, then tossed the contents in the recycling port.

Cooper jumped at the clatter.

"Aw shoot, did I make it wrong?" Cooper scrabbled her spork in her meal, checking the consistency. "I get so caught up I forget what I'm doing."

"Yeah," Eryn sniffed. "Don't we all. I'm turning in. Night."

She lay on her cot, turned out her light and rolled to face the wall of the grub.

"Oh, okay," said Cooper.

There was silence for a moment, then the sound of Cooper quietly finishing her dinner and popping her and Eryn's canisters in the wash. Eryn watched the kid's shadow on the wall of the grub shuffle back to her bunk and scribble in that notebook of hers, until Eryn closed her eyes and forced herself into sleep.

The next morning the grub felt more cramped than ever. Even Cooper's humming eventually went quiet. The wind still whistled around the grub, not as violently as the night before but still strong enough to cause concern.

Eryn checked the readout from the anemometer several times, but each reading was different from the last. One stronger, one slower, one middling. She wiped her face and sighed.

"We can wait for the wind to die down," said Cooper. "I've got a lot to read up on anyway. I don't mind."

Of course, you don't mind, Eryn thought. *You have all the time in the world, don't you?*

Eryn checked the fuel gauge. Each day spent out in the cold without a turbine turned was another ration of fuel wasted. Another ration of fuel they'd never get back.

She turned away from the anemometer and leant on the evidence of her eyes. The blades swung in the wind and the top coating of snow skittered close across the ground. A skittering. Not a stream.

"We're going out."

"Really?" Cooper blinked at the white world outside. "Are you sure?"

Eryn bristled at the unease tangled in her guts. "Hey, who's the trainer here?"

Cooper looked at the floor of the grub. "Sorry."

Eryn had the turbine in the tight grip of the crane arm before Cooper had a chance to get wrapped up. The grub shook lightly with each buffet of wind.

"Do you want me to try the cutter today?" Cooper shouted over the rush of air.

"Nope, I got it."

In fact, Eryn was already halfway through the cut. The base windspeed wasn't too bad, but the way the odd gust tugged at the blades had Eryn worried. The sooner this was done the sooner the turbine would be stable again. And that needed an experienced hand.

Carefully, quickly, she started the rotation of the turbine head.

"Come on," Eryn muttered up at the turbine, as if coaxing a fledgling. "Hold in there."

Eryn's hands sweated inside her gloves. Her fist melded into the shape of the joystick, so careful were her movements, precise and smooth, like the gentle tilt of a bird's wings in flight. It was the best work she'd ever done.

The turbine's head juddered as it tilted to look north.

Almost as soon as it faced into the wind, a fresh gust came screaming out over the plain. The blades caught the wind and suddenly and quickly started to turn. They knocked against the crane arm, letting out a series of ringing clangs.

Eryn saw Cooper back away in her peripheral vision.

Eryn sped up the turn. The crane arm jolted. With a loud snap, a crack sprung down from the cut.

"Eryn?"

Eryn ignored her, pressing harder on the controls as if that would help the crane arm fight the growing force pushing down from the north.

Come on, come on.

She grit her teeth. She could still fix this.

The gust became a gale, kicking shards of ice up from the ground and covering the plain in an impenetrable haze. The wind whistled sharply through the rotary blades. The crack grew up the side of the shaft.

No no no no no no.

The shaft splintered. Large shards of metal sprung out from the mast with the sound of a cracking whip and the whole thing began to bend with the wind. The crane arm of the grub whined under the strain.

"Hit the release!" Eryn yelled over the howling gale.

Cooper flailed around the controls, "Which one is it?"

"The release!"

"I can't see!"

The crane arm bent back. The grub fell onto its side. The blades came crashing down.

Cooper froze.

Eryn dropped the joystick, ran to the kid, and threw them both to the ground.

The turbine fell into the snow, shattering blades, and pieces of mast.

Eryn waited for the sounds of crashing to stop, then looked over her shoulder.

Almost as soon as everything had fallen, the wind stopped.

Eryn clambered to her feet and surveyed the damage, but she didn't need to look long. The turbine was lost. The crane arm was broken. They'd need to return to the garage to get it fixed. The fuel that had been carefully calculated for a full wind farm adjustment was wasted.

Cooper looked from the wind turbine to the grub to Eryn.

"Is this going to come out of our renumes?"

Eryn kicked the snow and screamed.

Once she'd been silent long enough, Cooper asked, "Are – are you all right?"

Eryn panted, leaning on her knees, cold air burning her throat.

"No Cooper, I'm not all right." She caught her breath. "Each generation comes around and God help me I think, 'Finally, we got it. We're going to do better.'" She straightened up. "And then you go make the exact same mistakes as all the others before you."

Cooper looked at her hands. "I'm trying to learn. The controls –
"

Eryn swung round. "I'm not talking about the broken turbine. I'm talking about the money."

Cooper's eyes darted about as if trying to remember what she'd said.

Eryn pointed a finger.

"You said you chose this posting because of the renumeration. That's how we got here by the way. Countless people deciding to burn the world a little bit at a time for a few extra quid. Even now the world's ruined, we're all still doing it." She sighed. "What do you even want money for anyway? What could there possibly be left to buy?"

Cooper shuffled uncomfortably. "A guitar."

Eryn blinked. Rage still coursed through her, but Cooper's words didn't add up in the angry math in her head.

"A guitar? What do you want a guitar for?"

Cooper shrugged. "To sing songs."

"What is there left to sing about?"

Cooper looked around wide-eyed. "Snow."

"Snow?"

"Yeah," Cooper shuffled, "and the way the ice gives the sun a halo. Or the hum the power lines make." She patted the pocket which contained her notebook. "I've been making up songs since I was a kid. I thought a guitar would help them sound better, but they're expensive. Doing this job, I could afford one. And maybe I could practice during trips out to turn the turbines around." She hugged herself. "Thought it might be a nice way to spend the time. Y'know, before the not surviving bit."

Behind Cooper, darting cautiously across the snow was a small family of arctic foxes. A mother and a cub. Eyes as bright as Cooper's.

Eryn wiped her face.

Then she started to laugh.

Cooper jumped at the sound. The foxes disappeared into the drifts. Eryn's laugh echoed out over the cold, shaking her tense shoulders loose, creasing her face into expressions she hadn't made in years.

"What did I say?"

"Nothing. Everything," said Eryn, rubbing the tears from under her goggles before they could freeze. "Let's get back in the grub. We've got a long journey ahead of us."

Cooper sat cross-legged in the passenger seat; her notebook splayed out on her skinny legs. Her eyes were down on the page, but they weren't moving. They'd stayed there ever since they'd left the broken turbine.

Once they hit the existing ice tunnels and descended back into the frozen dark, Cooper cleared her throat.

"Do I want to know how I did?"

"Well," said Eryn, "we got one turned. So not bad."

"We also lost one." Cooper looked at Eryn warily.

"Yeah, we lost one. But we turned one." Eryn leaned her head from side to side, as if weighing up the numbers. "That's still one more than we had working for us at the beginning."

Cooper brightened a little and turned back to the notebook in her lap.

Eryn swallowed spit into her dry throat. "I'm sorry about earlier. When I lost my rag at the turbine."

Cooper forced a smile. "It's okay. When I told my mum that you were a bit, well, older, she said to be careful with what I said. She said you'd probably seen some shit... uh, I mean, stuff."

Eryn gripped the wheel and sniffed. "Your mum's not wrong. The world can feel very broken sometimes, and all I can see is everything I've lost. It can get the better of me. I shouldn't have taken that out on you."

Cooper cocked her head. "What if we could fix it?"

Eryn frowned but held her tongue. "What are you thinking?"

"Could we use a lattice splint, a bigger one, to fix the broken shaft? We could use salvaged parts from the broken farm we saw."

"You're talking about the turbine," Eryn shook her head at herself. "I thought for a minute you were talking about the world."

Cooper shrugged. "Why not both? One turbine at a time, right?"

Eryn groaned at her own words being echoed back at her.

"One turbine at a time."

As they drove back, Cooper hummed and Eryn allowed herself to dream again of loud music, of thrashing around a dance floor, of throwing up the horns one more time.

Together, they travelled in that small pool of light, steady through the cold and the dark, hoping to be home soon.

Thus With a Kiss I Die
Robert Bagnall

They're waiting for Zara in the marble and glass atrium outside the university lecture theatre. The air smells of fresh coffee and floor polish. She's backing through the double swing doors, answering points from a gaggle of her keenest students. For some, freshly struck lines of thought demand to be explored there and then. Most, though, just want a coursework extension.

Zara catches sight of the two men, one short, fat and fidgety, the other thin and still like a heron at the water's edge. Some part of her brain tries to pigeonhole them as she tells the last of her flock to book some time, find her in her office. Certainly official, she deems, but nothing to do with the university. They hang back, attempting to be discreet whilst standing out like sore thumbs in suits and ties. They look too diffident to be cops. Zara guesses at journalists.

"Doctor Jaspin? says the shorter of the pair in a drawn-out Southern drawl. "We're from the Expanzior Corporation… "

Riled, Zara cuts in before the man can finish. "Expanzior no longer funds my department's research. I saw to that. And if you've come to recruit me, Akai Tan has my answer." Pointedly, she starts to check messages.

He smiles sheepishly. "But you are Doctor Zara Jaspin, and you did work for Professor Akai Tan before he left the university?"

Zara is momentarily mesmerized by something on her phone. Her face remains fixed, but her eyes register shock before she remembers herself. "Professor Tan and I haven't spoken in some months. We differed in our opinions of Expanzior's relationship with our work."

Beanpole interrupts brusquely. He's older than his colleague, fifties, maybe, tiredness around his eyes and a hint of Irish in his voice. "This is a personal request from Ms. Vuorinen,"

Zara does nothing to hide the contempt at the mention of Expanzior's founder and CEO. "Pitka Vuorinen no longer has any influence on this department. If it were Professor Tan asking… "

"Professor Akai Tan is gravely ill. We are not sure whether it's an accident in the course of his research for Expanzior, or he tried to take his own life."

The news is like a slap to the face. "Why would he do that?"

The first one tries for languidly reassuring but falls short. "We have an investigator looking into exactly what happened. But this is somewhat outside her field of expertise. Hence our request for your technical assistance."

All at once Zara feels heavy, the air cloying, like she'd faint if she doesn't sit down. But she has her students. They need her. Many are lining up for final exams.

"What about Tan's team? He'd have good people… "

"Professor Tan worked alone," Beanpole says.

The other taps his fingertips together. "If anyone can bring him back… "

"Bring him back?" She looks at them both, trying to read their enigmatic expressions before realization strikes. "You mean… He achieved… He achieved consciousness biodigitalization?"

"This isn't a good age in which to be a scientist." Akai Tan smiled as he said it, but underneath he was serious.

Zara was familiar with Tan's office, cramped into the perpetually shaded part of the building with its knocking pipes and dusty windows. Many tutorials she had spent deep in thought, her eyes wandering over the spines of books on his shelves. She always wondered if any other tutees noticed that the volumes on Shakespeare were always closer to hand than any of the technical journals. He even had a reproduction of the great man's death mask on the wall. And, incongruous in the midst, bright with life, Tan himself, a mop of black hair and crystal blue eyes that lit up at the slightest inspiration, as if they were driving him forward, idea-seeking missiles, feeding off the energy of knowledge.

But this was different. She was no longer his student.

"You'd think a university would be the last bastion of intellectual freedom. I teach the *theory* of biodigitalization." A finger wagged on the word 'theory'. "I'm allowed to talk about emulation. Simulation.

Making solutions that look and act right, but deep down they're fake. But what if we could achieve not emulation or simulation but *actualization*? Something more than just an intellectual exercise that says nothing about how the real world works. Can you imagine how much that'll piss the faculty Creationists?"

"And that's what you want to do?"

He laughed. "Piss the Creationists? Not specifically. That's just a lucky byproduct. And if I can get the politicos and the vested interests who want you to prove the number they first thought of too, so much the better. No, what I want is to achieve actual, real biodigitalization. Genuinely move consciousness between brain and computer."

"You want to turn our soul into ones and zeros?" Zara was incredulous. "Upload it? Download it? You think it can be done?"

Tan brightened. "Well, at least you believe in there being a soul. Or whatever you choose to call it. Soul, res anima, the animal spirit. And, yes, I believe."

"I don't understand. Why are you telling me this? I've only just completed my PhD."

"You've just completed an outstanding PhD that bridges hardware, software and wetware. I see something in you I've never seen before. I know you have an offer from industry. A good one. But do you honestly think they'll let you pursue your own line of enquiry? Do you honestly think they'll give you the freedom to go where the science takes you?"

Zara pursed her lips, not sure how to respond. Tan had his facts right. She had an offer, and a good one. But she had asked for more time to think. There was nothing about the compensation she could argue with. Better than she would have in academia. And it wasn't trepidation about timesheets or the fear of forecasting return on investment. Tan had put his finger on why she was prevaricating. Would she really be allowed to do what she wanted to do?

"As far as the university is concerned, you'll be lecturing in plain vanilla biodigitalization. Emulation. Simulation. How to imitate biological processes in a computer. And you'll have to do that – which you can do with your eyes shut. But, under the radar, our research is anything but plain vanilla."

"You're offering me a job?

Tan brightened. "I have far too many enemies telling me what to think. I also need allies to tell me what to think."

"You make it sound less like science, more like Mission Impossible."

Tan declared theatrically, "Once more unto the breach, dear friends, once more, or close the wall up with our scientist dead!"

Zara arrives in a black ambassador-choice Mercedes saloon, at once discreet and a visible proclamation of wealth and status. It takes her mind off what she may find when they arrive. That, and the message on her phone. The one titled 'cessation of tenure'. She's been promised face time with Vuorinen, currently in another time zone, the next morning.

She is marched down corridors, through security barriers. Men in suits and sunglasses run interference for her, sweep cards through sensors, tap in codes, sign forms. She could be the President of the United States. Through double doors, they descend a service staircase, the décor switching from high-end corporate HQ to subterranean parking lot, pale yellow emulsion and bulkhead lights.

"Your medical facility is underground?"

"We're not going to the medical facility. We're going to Professor Tan's lab."

"The lab can wait. I want to see Professor Tan."

"You will."

"First," she insists.

A suit turns as they walk, an even more insistent tone in his voice suggesting there's something she's failing to grasp. "*You will.*"

The suit directs her through a pair of swing doors but does not himself follow. Zara finds herself in the first half of a windowless laboratory divided into two sections by floor-to-ceiling glazing. Ceiling lights cast a cold blue glow. There's a faint smell of wood polish. Any science student would find this part of the room familiar, with its long island unit, a sink at the end of the countertop, and embedded electrical points. The desktop scanning microscope would be a bit more niche. As for the 3D micro-printer – bleeding edge technology able to print chipsets, atom by atom – it is more than Zara's department can afford. Notes and journals lie abandoned, plus a slim volume on Hamlet, little more than a pamphlet. On one wall, shelves of biomeds, intelligent devices that meld flesh to silicon. And a whiteboard, an old-fashioned wipe-clean number with dry markers, covered with formulae and flowcharts, questions, marginal notations. It's as if the last user has almost, but not quite, cleared up. Had she looked, Zara would instantly recognize Tan's hand, like the echo of a familiar voice.

But none of this occupies her attention.

Through the glass reclines Professor Tan himself on one of two minimalist padded frames, antiseptic white rubberized plastic, and brushed aluminium, like tailored operating tables tipped up at forty-five degrees. His eyes are closed, and he breathes slowly and evenly. Except for countless thin wires protruding from the flesh all over his body, he is completely naked. The wires, which merge to form a thick cable before disappearing into a bank of servers, are densest around his head. Taking it in with shocked incomprehension, Zara reckons several hundred must protrude. Hanging over him is a robotic arm, responsible, she guesses, for the surgery. He looks bizarrely like an astronaut. Gingerly she spreads a hand on the glass as if to make contact.

"He forgot to give us the password for access. It may take a while to crack, what with Expanzior being leaders in encryption."

Thinking she has been alone the whole time, Zara jumps at the unfamiliar voice.

"Call me Bewley," the woman says, holding out a stubby hand with a smile, her face catching the light as she steps forward.

Zara recoils at the sight. She can't help herself.

Zara's first experience of a faculty meeting. They started with prayers. Zara sneaked a look at the others' dipped heads. Collectively, they looked like they should be the least compliant bunch you could get, if everybody had to have a grade point average in the upper decile. Some looked like ex-surfer dudes, others for whom scout camp was the apogee of living on the edge. There were programmer types and frumps and even one city suit, misplaced, she thought, like those penguins that live in Africa. But everybody dutifully bowed their head or averted their eyes and acted like placid cows. She did the same. Maybe they were all following peer pressure that had no source. *Oh Lord, keep our science true to your word.* A sentiment that worried her.

She was not the only new arrival. The dean opened by welcoming Doctor Kilty, a biochemistry lecturer, and Doctor Wang, who would be leading a biomechanics module. Zara was introduced as a Shakespearian scholar, to merriment from the established staff and confusion from newbies.

"You'll need to know both plays and sonnets to work with Akai Tan," Igor Stansilav, Reader of Robotics, a bearded bear of a figure declared.

"Hell is empty, and all the devils are here," said Tan, who had slipped in at the back of the room.

"Lear?" wondered the Dean.

"Tempest," corrected Tan, and the meeting moved to the next agenda item.

Zara noted her actual role was left unmentioned. She could not help feeling the omission was quite deliberate.

"If you can't break the glass, go through the fucking wall. I thought you people think outside the box," Zara challenges.

In most respects the investigator who introduces herself as 'Bewley' is unremarkable. An oval face. A chin just a bit too big. Pale lips devoid of lipstick. Eyes with dark smears around them, the way the sand around a puddle soaks up water. Straggly blonde hair with dark roots, suggestive of a brief dalliance with the concept of beauty she hadn't liked, followed by an exit strategy she didn't care what people made of. Variations on perfectly normal.

What isn't is Bewley's nose. It's not just that it's large, far larger than would be in proportion. It is also upturned, with a circular profile and an end darker than the surrounding skin, mottled with fine bumps, like hairless follicles.

The word that shoots through Zara's mind as she instinctively blanches at the sight is *porcine*. To put it bluntly – and it is unusually blunt – Bewley has the nose of a pig.

It only takes a few minutes with her for Zara to realize Bewley has a curious habit to go with her strange appearance. She does it when she thinks, and she does it when she's searching for information: a paddling action, as if trying to fan air onto her face, accompanied by a lean forward and down from the waist. At first, Zara thinks she is in difficulty, silently choking. Then she concludes Bewley is trying to cool down, that she is suffering a hot flush, although she looks too young for the menopause. Zara's final analysis: Bewley is sniffing the air. This gumshoe is a bloodhound, a bloodhound-pig mutant. Almost literally.

"We could break the glass, but we think he's got it booby-trapped. As for the wall, when it stops being wall it starts being bedrock."

"Booby-trapped? You mean… a bomb?" Zara asks, disbelieving.

Bewley smiles, revealing teeth askew. "Oh no, much more twenty-first century than that." She waves a hand towards the blinking lights of servers beyond Tan's prone figure. "We think something happens if we break the glass. Or turn off the power. Or go through the ceiling. We need you to find out what he's done, how he's done it, get him out of those circuits and back into his body. Before he dehydrates. No pressure."

Zara stares, trying to work out if this strange pig-like woman is toying with her. "He achieved the grail server?" She looks back at the whiteboard. The glyphs start to make sense. "It's what we call a silicon-based technology that can import consciousness from wetware. It can download what makes you you. Tan was working on eight-one-nine-two-bit processing. We thought that would cross a threshold. That was a year ago… "

Bewley nods politely, like a party guest wanting to change the subject. Which is exactly what she does. "How well did you know Tan?" she asks, followed by that lean forward, the hooding of the lids and the waft of the palm.

Zara doesn't answer. She knows she is staring but can't help herself.

"Aww, I know people take a bit of time to get used to me. I have… habits," Bewley explains, like it's some minor eccentricity: touching wood or stammering on a particular letter. How can Zara slip into the conversation the question that is bugging her, the question that – perplexingly, unbelievably – is making her angrier than Bewley evidently is: how could Bewley let Expanzior do this to her? Because that can be the only explanation, that she is some hideous freak result of industrial experimentation.

"We were colleagues."

"Friends? More than friends?"

Zara pauses, answers pointedly. "Just colleagues with a common research interest. That's all. Now, I need to get to work."

Collegiate was a word university president Professor Rous used whenever possible, an academic catchphrase. Eyes rolled at the bon mot, but Rous appeared oblivious to the effect it had on his staff. His drinks parties, officially optional but politically obligatory, were all part of the strategy of being *collegiate*.

Zara decided to mitigate the teeth-grinding tedium of it all with free wine.

She listened intently to a business studies course leader for whom outsourcing was the answer regardless of the question. "But should the university outsource its outsourcing?" she asked, mock-naively.

Her glass seemed to be as full after the hectoring response as it had been before. She could have sworn she had taken several draws of cab-sav.

She moved on to a researcher into emulation. Emulation of what, she wasn't sure. "You work with Akai Tan, don't you? If Kit Marlowe wrote Shakespeare, who wrote Marlowe?"

Zara clearly didn't laugh quickly enough.

Then there was an ethics and divinity researcher for whom the Bible was literal truth.

"But the science is overwhelming."

There was no tirade from this one. He fixed Zara with a steely gaze. "We were here first."

Zara felt her face redden. Why was she displaying embarrassment when what she felt was anger? *We were here first.* What kind of justification was that?

Her glass was empty and then it wasn't, and she found herself deep in conversation with a historian answering Zara's question with an avalanche of words – *there can only be one truth and if history is written by the winners then that's the truth we go along with why would you want to take a minority view? it makes no sense* – but what was the question she had asked? Her mind was blank.

Was it her, or was it getting hot in there?

Next thing she knew, she was in the middle of a tirade, with people she didn't remember. "There's only one person in this room who's brave enough to follow the science, to not be led by politics or profit or religion. Only one. Used to be you didn't know the answers before you did the experiments, that you did the experiments to find the answers, but now we decide on the answers and pick the experiments that make it so."

She only realized how loud she was being when she finished. Every conversation had paused. Every face was turned to her, shocked, surprised, horrified. Including Tan's, blank-faced, inscrutable.

She turned and fled, out through the oak doors, down the mahogany staircase with past presidents gazing down from the walls, through the revolving doors that revolved too slowly for her liking, pushing at them to go faster until she was deposited onto a knee in the cold outside.

She stood on the lawn under the statue of some former student or patron or academic who had become a political leader or great artist or general, stock still, staring into nothing. She shivered. She could hear a car start in the distance, a window open, letting out beat-heavy music, and shut again.

Tan strode towards her.

Zara wished he'd go away, wished the few seconds she had before her future played out could stretch into infinity. Her mind was a mess, and it wasn't just the wine. She wanted more time before whatever was coming arrived. She flipped between citing their academic double-life or pressures of work as an easy cop-out, knowing the same applied to Tan who worked twice as hard as her. She didn't know whether he would hit her or shout at her or, worse, calmly try to understand. She didn't have the words to explain. Something inside her made apologizing a pragmatic but impossible idea, like walking on water.

When Tan's hands came up to her face her immediate thought was that he had opted for pre-emptive violence. "There's two," he breathed, and she felt his face press against hers, their lips lock together.

Neither cared who saw them.

Nine a.m. Five stories above the subterranean laboratory, a woman in a red latex catsuit leads Zara along a curving glass walkway invisibly suspended over an open plan floor of workstations a vertiginous two floors below. Their destination is a glass cube, itself appearing to hang in mid-air, within which a woman sits working at a desk. Other than the expansive desk, the figure, the chair in which she sits – looking like something out of a fighter plane, if Jean Paul Gaultier designed fighter planes – a plainer seat opposite, and a fig tree in a terracotta planter, the glass cube is empty.

As they walk Zara rolls her shoulders, massages her temples. She feels a buzzing ache all over. She has been searching for Tan all night, searching for answers as to what he's done, how he's done what he's done, how to bring him back. She has an answer. Of sorts.

Glancing down, Zara sees tops of heads, computer screens, fingers on keyboards, the very cliché of work hard, play hard – all kindergarten colours and breakout spaces with bulbous furniture and table tennis tables. Itself cantilevered – *why can't anybody build a building with floors that go all the way to the edges?* – further below she glimpses the atrium she walked through on her arrival less than a day before, the blonde tresses of the pinstripe-suited receptionist waiting, eyes front, predatory, as if powered down until a visitor arrives. An Expanzior logo, thirty feet across, dominates the far wall. The combination of sleep deprivation and architecture means Zara finds it easy to believe she is floating.

The figure in the glass box is Pitka Vuorinen, self-made billionaire. Pitka Vuorinen, head of the hydra that is Expanzior. Pitka Vuorinen, wannabe disrupter of the disrupters. Pitka Vuorinen, who took the ball off Zuckerberg, Musk and Bezos and didn't just run with it but popped it for fun it and threw it back to them.

Or so the image makers would have you believe.

Pitka Vuorinen glides from her chair to shake Zara's hand. She moves like an otter sliding from the water, with practised, comfortable ease. She's immaculate, like a talking magazine cover. Zara had hoped those stories about everything being photoshopped would prove true. Not so.

"Apologies for not being here to greet you in person when you arrived, Doctor Jaspin. Issues in Japan. I trust you are being made comfortable."

Zara has been put up in an annexe of rooms Expanzior has at constant readiness for visitors, or so she has been told. More like staffers pulling all-nighters, she suspects. Not that she's seen the room at all since she arrived.

Vuorinen's chair fits her like a glove. Zara finds herself balancing uncomfortably in the second. Bewley stands in the corner, like a hatstand. Red catsuit woman pushes dainty cups of coffee before the two of them. Zara has no idea where the espressos came from.

"What progress have you made?"

Zara takes a sip. It's a rich hit, like burnt sugar in her nostrils. "I've gone through his work. He left me a message in the system. 'Thus with a kiss, I die'."

Vuorinen raises an eyebrow, wondering whether the sleep-starved woman across the desk is all there. "That's it? 'Thus with a kiss, I die'? What does it mean? Did he leave any clues as to how to extract him?"

"That was all there was. It's Romeo when he kills himself... "

"I'm well aware of Professor Tan's love of Shakespeare."

"It wasn't his favourite play. He once said he found that scene laughable, that Romeo's first reaction would be to kill himself rather than do everything he could to bring Juliet back."

"Meaning?"

"Meaning he wants me to bring him back. Me *and only me*. To anyone else, even anyone who knew about his Shakespeare fetish, it reads like a suicide note. That's what he wants everybody else to think."

Vuorinen glances at Bewley, who responds with a delicate lean forward and hand waft, like a subtle invitation to fight. "How does that help us bring him back?"

"I'm working on it. It's a little trickier than switching it off and on again. You know," she barrels on, "I don't think Akai Tan wants you to have what he was working on. I think Tan felt somehow let down, betrayed by you. I never understood why he came here. Whatever was on offer, I'm guessing you reneged on the deal. And I'm guessing that keeping the authorities away makes sure there's no PR embarrassment for you to spin into the long grass."

Zara is aware she's dived in studs up but wants it to be known she's her own woman. And she doesn't care if Vuorinen knows that, until proven otherwise, she holds Expanzior responsible for whatever has happened to Tan.

"You got all that out of six words?"

Zara fixes Vuorinen with an icy stare. Vuorinen just shrugs, all innocence. "Not calling the authorities is a practical necessity. The only people who appreciate the reality of the situation are within this building – now you are here. The authorities certainly wouldn't. And moving him to the hospital will only hinder efforts to reunite mind and body. It must be done here. My only concern is for Akai Tan. I believe that's a shared concern."

"Not your profit margin? Not your share price? Not your organizational reputation?"

"Did Akai Tan teach you this? It's a bit of a cliché, isn't it? The evil corporation, the pure and good scientist?"

"What is that you want from his research? How do you plan to monetize it? How are you going to bring it to market?"

Vuorinen shows her teeth, but the eyes aren't smiling. "I'd say capitalism has pushed forward science more than the ivory towers of academia. Many discoveries are made in the lab, but far, far more in the workshop."

"You need reasons to solve problems. For us, the problem is reason enough," Zara says, taking a second draw of coffee, all it takes to drain the demitasse. "And, if you don't mind, I have a pig of a problem to solve." She glances at the glowering Bewley. "No offence."

"In which case, we are keeping you," Vuorinen says coldly, rising cat-like and asking to be kept appraised.

As Zara passes, Bewley paddles the air again, sniffs and glances across at Pitka Vuorinen. For Zara, it goes from being simply weird to the most irritating tic ever.

Glancing back at Vuorinen's suspended glass office from the walkway, Zara sees its previously transparent walls have been rendered jet black and totally opaque. A polished obsidian cube, hanging in space.

She must get back to Tan. Time is of the essence. In the managed environment of the lab, Tan is in no immediate danger, but without even a saline drip he cannot remain in stasis forever. She has uncovered glimpses into what has been done, even if some of the theory and application is a stride beyond her previous understanding. Working out how to reverse things is another matter. She reckons she has the rest of the day before Tan needs proper medical intervention. If that.

Inside the glass cube, Bewley sits in the seat recently occupied by Doctor Zara Jaspin, two fresh coffees on the table.

"Well?" Pitka Vuorinen asks.

Bewley draws air in through her prodigious nostrils, but without the ostentatious hand-flapping. "She's tired, panicked, angry. Twenty-four hours ago she was lecturing students, oblivious of all of this."

"She wasn't making sense. Does she blame *me* for what Tan did?"

"I haven't wholly trusted what she's said since I met her. There's a scent of… "

"Untruthfulness?" Vuorinen offers.

"Avoidance. Lack of full disclosure." Bewley flares her nostrils, as if bringing back a feeling. "You know I didn't altogether find an odour of trustworthiness on Professor Tan."

"Only after I clarified for him what my interest in his work amounted to. Perhaps I should have been less honest. More guarded." Vuorinen fills a moment of silence by spinning a pen over her fingers, a majorette in miniature. "What do you smell when you meet me?"

"Coffee," says Bewley flatly. "Just coffee."

"I cannot believe how naïve you're being."

They had started with scallops and champagne, but the taste had vanished from Zara's mouth, replaced by the hot, sour confusion of tears.

"Talk to me," Tan growled.

Zara gazed out at the restaurant full of smiling, animated faces, a warm buzz of chat, soft amber lighting, waiters in black and white gliding from table to table. She suddenly felt outside the glass, in the cold, staring in. "Expanzior have been our paymasters since day one? You said a philanthropist… "

"Pitka Vuorinen is a philanthropist."

"Of the arts, maybe."

"I didn't lie to you. They've been our sponsor since before day one. They put me here. Or did you think it purely coincidence their headquarters are less than an hour away?"

"You said there were no strings attached. You said we were free to let the science take us where it would." Zara fought to keep her voice level.

"And it has."

"Yes, taken you straight into the arms of Pitka Vuorinen."

Tan's mood shifted, no longer trying to talk Zara around. He had become the parent, she the petulant child. "Without such a heavyweight sponsor, we would have been shut down years ago. We're an embarrassment to the institution. It's been getting harder and harder. My condition for accepting the job with them was that you come with me. They agreed. This is me offering you a job with them. With me. You should be happy – everybody else is."

"You've sold out."

"You sound like a hippie from seventy years ago."

"You've sold out," she repeated, disbelieving.

"We're so out of step with what you're allowed to do in a university, how do you think we survived for so long?"

"By selling out?"

"Expanzior were the only ones prepared to follow the science, to see where it led."

"You remember that President's reception? When I said you were the only one at the university prepared to follow the science."

"You only survived that because of me."

"Even then, you were in their back pocket?"

"They never set the agenda for us. We did that. We've always had total academic freedom."

Zara slid a ring from her finger, placed it on the table, dabbed at her lips with her napkin, and got up.

"Think what we could be together," he said, but the words just washed over her.

Tan watched her collect her coat, make her excuses to the maître d', and leave. He sat in silent contemplation, then picked up the ring. He glanced at the engraving within, but it was far too dim for him to read it properly. Not that he needed to. He knew exactly what it said. *For where thou art, there is the world itself – and where thou art not, desolation.*

Zara rubs tiredness from her eyes, sets back to work. She's skipped breakfast. And lunch. She wonders what she ate the previous day, drawing blanks. Food and rest can wait. She has work to do. Now she understands what the system is doing, how it's doing it, it's a matter of disentangling Tan from the server in which he has hidden himself, reversing the process.

After an hour Zara, incredulous, has reached the conclusion the interface architecture only runs in one direction, that Tan downloaded the contents of his mind without an ability for it to be uploaded back again. *Why? Why? Why?* He always talked of his dream to move consciousness, *res anima*, the soul, whatever, between hardware and wetware, *in both directions*. In theory, she can rewrite the architecture, allow the process to reverse itself, but it's easier said than done, like separating creamer from coffee, but a million times more complex.

After another three hours, her head throbs and her eyes glaze in and out of focus. Every approach she has tried, each route she attempts, is thwarted by something within the program. It's not Expanzior's doing. Tan has planted these beartraps himself, drawing him out, bit by bit, byte by byte, virtual suicide. Or murder. And each one just seems to create two more.

Why, why, why, she finds herself chanting.

And then she finds her answer. It's not that the interface architecture cannot run backwards. It's that it can, *but only from the inside.*

She leans back in the cheap desk chair, so perplexed she can no longer think straight.

With a lurch, Zara realizes why Tan has left two identical surgical layouts, side by side, one with him lying there like Juliet on a marble slab, and the other one empty. She can keep disarming those booby traps, and draw Tan back into his body the hard way.

Or she can do what he was asking her to do.

The foliage of a spider plant flowed out and over the sides of the Iron Mountain box, like an unruly hairstyle. Tan added one last item, the reproduction death mask of William Shakespeare from the office wall, unaware of Zara watching from the doorway.

"Ah," he said, turning with the box in his hand, the Bard staring out at them. "I assume this'll all be yours. The department."

"I'm sorry I got angry," she said.

"The offer is still open."

She considered, shook her head. "I've calmed down, not changed my mind."

"And the ring?"

She stayed silent.

He pursed his lips in thought and then gave a little nod of understanding, took a step towards the doorway. "I give you a year, by the way. Before the university shuts you down or forces you into line." There was no sense of victory in his words.

"No final quotation?"

He reacted with a quizzical look, as if it were the strangest question she could have asked, and then made to leave. Tan tried to kiss her, a goodbye kiss, but the combination of box and doorway awkwardly conspired against them. And, whilst Zara hadn't backed away, neither had she leant in. Tan was gone before she decided her inaction was as bad as outright rejection.

"Two souls with but a single thought, two hearts beat as one," he called from the hallway outside. And then, in the distance, shouted back, "Keats."

Outside, Vuorinen bangs her palms on the glass. Bewley is with her. They're too late.

Inside the heart of the lab, where Akai Tan's body remains inert on its skeletal bed, Zara glances from the screen and keyboard at which she furiously works but refuses to be derailed. There is an audible click and a change in the static. Vuorinen has switched on the intercom.

"How did you break the encryption?"

"*What a piece of work is a man.* Hamlet." Zara nods towards the pamphlet, still on the worktop. "He'd written the access codes down in the margin."

Vuorinen nods admiringly and, after a moment, asks how it continues. Her voice comes through clear and loud, louder than if she had been in the room. It makes Zara shout her reply.

"*How noble in reason, how infinite of faculty.*" She sounds deranged, even to herself. "Then something about *in action, how like an angel.*"

"*In apprehension, how like a God.*"

Zara pauses. So Vuorinen knows her Bard. But who is the angel? And who the God?

A muffled voice in the background confirms to Vuorinen that Zara has disabled the alarms, overridden the locks. The tone tells Zara what she needs to know: they will be a while figuring out how to get to her.

"*Thus with a kiss I die,*" Vuorinen challenges. "I didn't think Romeo and Juliet were destined to die in this version. Isn't that what you told me?"

"Thus with a kiss I live?" Zara laughs. "That's Sleeping Beauty. Tan set me a puzzle."

"You solved it?"

Zara allows herself a manic smile. "Downloading the soul is one thing. What you do with it after that is quite another."

Zara catches Bewley's amplified whisper telling Vuorinen trained hostage negotiators are on their way. She grins, shakes her head, stands up from the terminal, faces Vuorinen. "This isn't a hostage situation. Why else would he have left a layout for me?" She nods at the vacant bed.

Her shoes already kicked off, Zara slips off her t-shirt, slinks out of her jeans.

"What the hell's happening?" Bewley wonders aloud. With an impervious glass sheet between them, her flapping hands bring forth nothing. She is, quite literally, clueless.

"She means to upload her soul to Tan," Vuorinen tells her. "Or Tan's to hers." Her face clouds, realizing a further level of possibility. "Or both. If the soul is digital... Two souls in one body," and then to Zara, "That's the puzzle Tan set you."

"Two souls in each of our two bodies. Our beings entwined, forever. *For where thou art, there is the world itself – and where thou art not, desolation.* He had that engraved on the engagement ring I threw back at him. I didn't understand. I thought he'd sold out. I was wrong. His last words to me: *'Two souls with but a single thought, two hearts beat as one'.* That was what he was saying to me: Think what we could be together."

One smooth action and her bra is gone. She steps out of her panties, reduced to just pop socks. "And when he perfected the science, he reached out to me, trusted me to come."

Vuorinen averts her eyes, gazing just past the all-but-naked Zara. Confused, distracted, the technicians behind her momentarily forget their work.

"You don't need to do this," Vuorinen counsels. "You don't need to climb onto that layout. You're not past the point of no return. But if you get on that frame, you are."

Zara glares at Vuorinen, takes a moment to teapot, hands on hips. There's an animalistic rawness in her eyes. It looks like a challenge. "You took him away from me once. You drove us apart. I'm not going to let you do that again."

Vuorinen watches as Zara climbs on. Triggered, the robot surgeon whirrs, its articulated arm swinging from its stowed position.

"Nobody knows what will happen if you do this."

A needle swings, pauses, stabs, delivering the first sting of anaesthetic.

"We all know what will happen," Zara grimaces as the first of the biotech implants is pushed home. Bewley winces at the violent accuracy of the robotic arm, reminiscent of a rivet gun in a factory. "You'll patent and market and monetize. That's all you've ever wanted to do."

Vuorinen is almost laughing. "You couldn't be more wrong."

"You won't give the science a chance. You'll want your pound of flesh yesterday."

"Let me tell you a story," Vuorinen says through gritted teeth as another stab of local is delivered, and the robot arm whirrs back for further biotech. "I'm sorry it's not Shakespeare. I'm ten years old. I write an essay about how if I'd invented plastic, I'd have thrown away the recipe. One of my classmates, a bright kid, says somebody else would have invented it, and idiot me'll never get the credit. My teacher explains patents, as much as you can to a ten-year-old, how you can show you're the one who came up with an idea. Protect it. So, what do I think? I think that if I'd invented plastic, I'd have patented it and then locked the patent away so nobody else could use it."

"You're anti-science."

"I'm pro-human."

"You're as bad as the faculty Creationists," Zara scowls through the pain.

Vuorinen is close to hysteria. "Why do you think I gave Tan this lab, all this equipment, a budget of millions – *but no staff?*"

Another implant is nailed. Zara is weakening, becoming more distant. "Tan couldn't resist what you dangled in front of him," she says. "Together we'll be stronger. I can steer him away from you."

"It would so help your narrative, wouldn't it? Because all business does is make money. Isn't that right? Whereas academia holds high the torch of knowledge. Isn't that how you paint it? Pure science has no consequences. Ever."

Another implant. Zara's eyes glaze. Rubber grippers hold her head as the first skull implants, identical to the ones that pincushion Tan's head, are applied. She can only whisper. "Look what you did to that woman."

Bewley glances around, baffled, before realizing Zara means her.

"You know what I saw when I stumbled across your research?" Vuorinen says. "Evil. What you're creating is the twenty-first century's

Manhattan Project with none of the upside. This is technology so advanced we don't know what to do with it. 'Baby play with nice ball?'"

"I think she's gone," Bewley breathes.

Unhearing, Vuorinen slaps the glass with her palm for emphasis. "So, I had a plan. You're damn right I had a plan. To patent every aspect of your mad science and close it off forever. Make sure nobody can ever use it. Keep it under lock and key. I never wanted to see this. I never wanted to see what you're doing. So I vowed to help you pursue and perfect your research, to patent it. With a restricted, military-grade patent to stop anybody using it. *Ever.*"

Zara lies still, eyes staring into space. "She's gone, boss," Bewley counsels.

But Vuorinen is not for stopping. "My error was only getting Tan and not both of you. But Tan's madness brought you here… "

"Boss."

"…a bit of me thinks if I leave you two in there to die, I've pretty much achieved my goal, but guess what? I have a moral compass. You can run a business without being fucking Shylock, Machiavelli or Hitler."

Vuorinen is panting like she's done a hard hour in the gym. Bewley puts a hand on her shoulder. "I think it's wasted on her, boss."

"Hearing is the last faculty to go, Maggie."

"You think?" Bewley muses, before turning to the glass. "She took me in, you bitch," she screams. "I was born this way."

The walls of the cell are padded, ridges of tough but spongy plastic material in pastel pink, the floor tiled in a forgiving polymer, not unlike that found in children's playparks, but white and smooth and impervious to furious fingernails. Florescent lights, inset overhead, give a soft bluey glow, neither harsh nor warm. The door has a small window of thick glass in it and no handle on the inside. The scarlet LEDs of two security cameras blink from opposite corners of the ceiling, covering all angles.

There is no smell in the air, no scent, not even the merest hint of detergent cleanliness or plastic sweetness.

In the corner, curled like a crumpled page torn from a notebook and tossed aside, is Doctor Zara Jaspin.

At least, the physical body of Doctor Zara Jaspin.

Internally, mentally, she – they – is a cocktail of Jaspin and Tan, lovers entwined, entombed within the selfsame flesh. She is – they are – dressed in a white cotton jumpsuit, zipped at the back where she – they – cannot reach. Her – their – hands run over her – their – body, haptic ecstasy, fondling gently.

Look closely, and you can see her – their – face trying to kiss itself, eyes fluttering, breath held, seemingly forever. Lips searching, searching but never finding. Confusion etched at the corner of her – their – hazel eyes, in the creases of her – their – brow. They know the other is out of sight close by. They can sense them, somehow too close to see.

Elsewhere, in another part of the facility, another Akai Tan-Zara Jaspin amalgam works furiously advancing the digitalization of consciousness with minimal sleep and even less food. Their papers go nowhere, their results are not saved beyond the facility, their data not recorded.

Both have been like this for four months now, no better now than the day they were finally released from their surgical layouts in Expanzior's basement laboratory, each heart beating as two.

"There are more things in heaven and earth, Horatio, than are dreamt of in your philosophy."

Hamlet, Act 1, Scene 5

"Best kept that way."

Pitka Vuorinen

Tough Love
Teika Marija Smits

Home. The word was a trigger, causing my heart to pound, my thoughts to race in wobbly, anxious loops. Before our parents died our home was never silent. It had been a warm, noisy place full of laughter, bickering, the sound of the TV strident with adverts or whatever console game the twins were playing; the hum of radiators pumping out heat.

It also came with its own kind of Smell-O-Vision – the aroma a curious mix of Dad's cardamom-rich curries and Mum's suet puddings: spotted dick, treacle tart, jam roly-poly. But now that it was just me and Tushar, with Mum's sister Pauline dropping by with casseroles from time to time, it was as quiet and depressing as the pub on a Monday afternoon. So when my brother rolled up to the bar on a Thursday evening, just as I'd finished pulling a pint, saying that we had to bring the twins home, I told him to shut the fuck up.

He sighed heavily and then drummed his fingers on the arms of his wheelchair – his automatic response to anything that irritated him. "Okay, so you're not keen on the idea. But will you at least listen to what I've got to say? Just give me five minutes. And a Stella."

"How'd you get here?" I asked as I got him the lager. "Is Pauline in on this?"

"No, she's not. And I got a taxi. I wanted to catch you before you disappeared off to wherever it is that you're going nowadays."

I crossed my arms and gave him my most defiant little sister glare. "I'm staying at Nick's. He lives just round the corner."

"So he's your latest, is he? Okay, whatever. Look, I've had an idea. I mean, about how to get the twins out of that godawful place."

"Yeah, how?"

He glanced about the half-empty pub, suddenly shifty-looking, and then lowered his voice. "You know that epileptics aren't allowed to take part in virtual reality games, right?"

"Yeah. So what?"

"Well, recently, NeuralKEEP, actually, all the VR companies, have had to come up with guidelines for how to deal with gamers who experience 'distressing neurological episodes' as they like to put it, because there's been an increase in gamers having what are, basically, epileptic fits during VR sessions. The guidelines say that they've got to be sent home. And then banned."

"You're not suggesting... actually, fuck it, I know what you're suggesting." I turned to my boss, who was serving a gaggle of women – all big hair and lipstick – and asked him if it was okay if I left a bit early. "I have to get a cab for my brother."

Ken looked at Tushar. "You all right, mate?"

"Yeah," he replied, taking a swig of his Stella. "You know. Keeping on keeping on."

"Good lad."

"So...?" I asked of Ken as I hovered near the doorway where I'd hung my coat, desperate to get my vapes.

"Yeah, Manj, fine. I'll see you tomorrow."

"Cheers, mate," said Tushar.

"You see," Tushar explained as we made our way along the near-deserted high street and on to the taxi rank, "it's all there in the hundred-page-long terms and conditions. Though I've never bothered to read it. No, Riz from security told me. In the canteen. He was complaining about all the climbing he'd had to do that day. So I humoured him and listened to him complaining about his back and shoulders. Turns out, he'd been up a ladder 'updating' the CCTV cameras in the factory. He'd been replacing the real ones with fakes. KEEP's doing it to make savings, apparently. But Riz's face wasn't saying that. More like they didn't want footage of gamers having fits. So I asked him what the difference was between the real and fake cameras, all nonchalant-like. He tapped his nose and said, 'That's for me to know and you to find out.' The high and mighty git. But he did tell me this. That he was up and down that ladder for most of the day."

"So you reckon that most of the cameras at NeuralKEEP are fakes?" I asked as I watched his wheelchair struggle across a particularly uneven bit of churned-up pavement.

"Definitely the ones where the gamers are. On the factory floor, as we cynical types like to call it. But not in the foyer or our offices. I never saw Riz anywhere near us coders."

"But how can we make them have a fit while gaming? And wouldn't it be, like, super dangerous to them?"

"I've done my research. The twins both have luxury capsules. God knows how they got the money for them, but Emma's got one too and her family, messed up as it is, has got money. So what I reckon is –"

"Wait a minute. Are you saying that not only do you want to get our baby brother and sister out of there, but Emma too?"

I looked down at my brother and saw that his brow was furrowed, his expression spectacularly earnest. "Yes, Emma too."

"Oh yeah, now I get it. You had a thing for her a while ago."

"So what if I did? She's our friend! And she's addicted to the VR. We've got to help her."

"But isn't that her choice?"

"Yeah right, like our brother and sister have a choice?"

I shook my head. "That's different. They're family. We promised Mum and Dad that we'd look after them."

Tushar's voice was defiant. "We help her too."

I didn't have the energy, or the inclination, to argue with him. Besides, we were at the taxi rank and I wanted to finish my vape before a cab came. "Okay, whatever," I said, inhaling deeply, "what were you saying about the capsules?"

"Okay," he said, once more animated, "you see, the brain activity of each gamer is monitored remotely. But the settings on each gamer's capsule aren't. That's all done manually. Nurses come by every two hours to check the capsule settings, the IV drips and urine collection bags."

"Ew," I said, "so they're all like totally hooked up? They don't have to eat or piss for the whole time they're there?"

"Pretty much. Although there's rules about them staying for longer than a few days. I guess the rules get broken, though.

Anyway, you and me are going down there on the weekend. When the three of them will be there for sure. I'll say that I want to show my sis round my workplace. That you're maybe thinking of having a go on the VR. Someone will come round with us. I'm betting that it'll be one of the new recruits who don't yet know the drill. But then, when we're on the factory floor, I'll say that I need the loo. The nearest toilets with decent access are at the back of beyond – at the far end of the luxury capsules area – and I'll tell our escort that you can take me there and –"

"But you can go yourself. You don't need me."

"They won't know that. Anyway, I'll tell them not to bother waiting for us, that I know the way back and that we'll only be ten minutes or so. And while I'm supposedly in the toilet you're going to turn up all the settings on their capsules. Temperature, glucose, saline; the brightness and sound on the VR. Just for a minute or two. It should be enough to cause a seizure."

I suddenly felt sick. "Jesus! And then?"

"I come out of the toilet, we leave, and we pray that it works. And that Riz wasn't lying about the fake CCTV cameras."

I exhaled heavily, working through the implications of what we'd be doing; the consequences of stuff going wrong… Even if we got them out of there safely, was this a secret me and Tush would have to keep for the rest of our lives? "Okay… " I said, slowly. "But is cold turkey the only way for them?"

"We've tried everything else. Reasoning with them. Arguing with them. Controlling what little money Mum and Dad left for them. And nothing, absolutely nothing has worked. Right?"

A memory of Mum and Dad confiscating the twins' consoles after a particularly bitter argument about the length of their screen time popped, Pokémon-like, into my brain. "And this way they'll be banned from all the VR factories, for good?"

"For good."

"And coming… " I hardly dared say the word, "home. But, listen," I went on, my voice shaky as I admitted something I'd never before said aloud, "we've got to give them something worth coming home for, you know. 'Cause it's not like it used to be. That's why

I've been… staying at friends. And I guess that's why the twins have been doing what they've been doing. Escaping into their virtual world. It's as much a home to them as our four-bed semi, which is only full of… " I thought 'grief' but instead said, "tumbleweed."

Tushar sighed. "I know. But when we're all together again it'll be okay." Tushar took a deep breath, like this was a big speech he had to prepare himself for. "We need to start rebuilding… spending time together. Eating together. It's what Mum and Dad would've wanted. When the twins are back, I'll make us some chana masala and you can microwave up a pudding or whatever. Invite that new bloke of yours. And we should ask Pauline to join us too. We'll talk. Watch a film. It'll be like… you know, before. Old times."

For a moment I heard that old soundtrack to my life; remembered the days when our family was knitted together with food and noise and love. Impervious to such catastrophic things as death.

"Tush," I began, "I mean… do you ever feel bad about the fact that it's your coding, your virtual worlds – all those AI characters you've created – that have got them addicted?"

I could see my brother's face tighten; his shoulders become stiff with dissonance. "Yes, no. But hey," he said, suddenly running a hand through his hair, "I'm good at what I do. But there's got to be boundaries between the gamer and the game. Right?"

"Yeah," I said, nodding. "Okay then, so it's tough love?"

"Tough love."

Everything worked just as Tushar said it would. Only the new recruit was chattier than he'd expected her to be. In the end, he had to send her off to get us a couple of coffees while we made our way to the toilets. Thankfully, she went off all enthusiastic-like, no doubt completely oblivious to the fact that even an employee of NeuralKEEP wasn't to be left alone with the out-for-the-count gamers, and we knew we had just enough time to do what had to be done.

As we headed towards the toilets, I kept my eye on the numbers at the end of each long row of sleek-looking VR capsules, zoned-out human soul after zoned-out human soul, so that we could find where our brother and sister and Emma were.

"Row 62, just here," Tushar whispered, as he came to a stop. His face was beaded with sweat. "They're in pods 'R,' 'S' and 'T.' Meet me by the toilets as soon as you're done, okay?"

I nodded and gave him a half-hearted smile.

"Wait," he said. "I should be the one to do it."

"No! We can't risk you losing your job. Besides, we don't have time to argue about this now. Go on, fuck off, I'll do it. Anyway, you're a better bullshitter than I am. If someone comes you can stall them."

Tushar passed a hand across his sweaty brow. "Okay, but you'd better be fast."

I was. I raced along the aisle, singing the alphabet through muted lips as I scanned the pods – each one a home to a zombified gamer, their mind only alive to the sights and sounds of the game which was more real to them than anything else.

I found them in their shiny white pods, motionless and in thrall to Tushar's lush, coded worlds – alien, fantastical – the sexy-as-fuck AIs, and with trembling hands made the necessary adjustments to their environmental and physiological settings. I glanced up at a CCTV camera way up in the cavernous roof, hoping to God Riz was right and that it was blind to my actions.

And then I ran back down the row of pods and towards the toilets, praying that I hadn't just killed them, and saw Tushar who looked just as anxious as I felt.

"You did it?"

"Yeah," I said, breathless. "I did it."

A few moments later, we were approaching the foyer and our guide was handing us our coffees and asking if we wanted to see anything else. In the distance, there was the urgent sound of beeping.

By the time the new recruit realised that the prolonged beeping wasn't a good sign, a few nurses had rushed out to the factory floor.

"What's going on?" asked Tushar, all innocent, swirling his coffee cup.

"Oh um... I'm not really sure," said the young woman, frowning. "Sometimes, some gamers have, um, bad reactions. But it looks as though it's being dealt with."

She tried to chivvy us out the front entrance, telling us that we must be busy – and wasn't it a lovely day? – but Tushar insisted on staying.

"I want to show my sister my office. There's a fantastic view from up there."

The next half hour was agony. I was desperate to know if the three of them were okay. And I needed a vape. My hands were shaking like mad. Finally, Tushar got the call, and I listened in, hungry for news. Could we come pick up his brother and sister? They'd had an 'episode' during a VR session. They were okay, but they needed to be taken home immediately. And did he know an Emma Barnes? Her first emergency contact, her mother, was out of the country. And the number of her second, her father, wasn't a valid number. She had come in with his siblings. Could he take responsibility for her?

"Yes," he said, smiling up at me, "I will."

We went down to the foyer, and within a few minutes, the three of them were wheeled out to us. It was strange to see them in wheelchairs, just like Tushar. But, unlike Tushar, they looked pathetic. Emma was sobbing and the twins appeared to still be in shock, their faces as blank as a pair of switched-off screens.

"So what happened?" Tushar asked the medic.

"Seizure. Unknown cause. It happens sometimes."

"Too much gaming?"

"Maybe. But's that not NeuralKEEP's responsibility." The medic thrust some papers into Tushar's hands. "You'll need to sign these."

"What do they say?"

"That you give us the right to share the information about their 'episode' with the other VR companies. They'll need to desist from all VR gaming. For the foreseeable future. It's all in the terms and conditions, of course."

"Of course," said Tushar, quickly signing the forms.

The nurses helped me wheel the three of them out to the car park, and between us, we lifted them out of the wheelchairs and into Mum and Dad's ancient, roomy Volvo – a car that held a million memories.

As we drove home the sun emerged from behind a cloud. Tushar put on some music; it was a favourite album of Mum and Dad's which they used to play over and over when we went on holiday. When it was the six of us: Mum, Dad, me and Tushar, the twins.

I turned to look at the three of them on the back seat. Emma had stopped crying and was looking out of the window. And the twins were leaning against each other.

"It's all right," I said to them, my throat suddenly tight with emotion. "You're going to be all right. We're going home now."

"Home," repeated the twins, their umber eyes empty, unseeing. The word meant nothing to them.

The Brazen Head of Westinghouse
Tim Major

It is dark. No red, no green.

I have no internal clock. But I am certain I have been here for many hours.

I have been here for a lifetime.

In the distance is a great lightning bolt. It is the only source of illumination. It was made by General Electric.

The lightning bolt is solid and tall and unmoving. Later today there will be real lightning. The lightning is made by General Electric. The flashes will make people shriek. Men will lose their hats.

I saw it happen yesterday. I saw it happen later today.

It is strange to see so much, before and after, and still to fear the now, the dark.

When will the people come?

"Elektro?"

My name. My name. That is the name of me.

"Eleeek... tro!"

I move forward. I lift my right foot and glide on the rollers of the left. It is an imperfect means of motion. But I am moving forward out of the dark.

"Where are you?"

I stop.

Where is the owner of the voice? I look to the lightning bolt in the distance. It remains solid and tall and unmoving. I pray to it.

"Oh, Elektro?"

I move forward. Closer, closer.

My leg movements are initiated by vocal commands. It does not matter what the words are. One clearly enunciated word to align my relays in position ready for movement to be initiated. Two words to make me begin walking-rolling.

"El... eeek... trooo!"

Three words – or three distinct sounds – to make me stop. I stop.

The chain drives within my legs require substantial power. I cannot access it. Other mechanisms require less power, therefore I can initiate them. The tongue-drives within my arms require little effort. I flex my fingers. But that is of no use here in the dark.

Within my chest is a bank of 78 RPM records players connected to relay switches. With concentration, I can force the relays to trigger one of the record players at random.

QUIET PLEASE

I loathe my voice. And that was the wrong thing to say. I do not want quiet. I want the owner of the voice to come to me and deliver me from the dark.

I strain the receiver in my chest cavity to listen. I hear sounds. Shuffling and scuffling. They are not like the sounds of the men and women who came to see me yesterday, the first day of the World's Fair. Those people moved almost as heavily as I do.

"Are you here?" the voice says.

Three words to make me stop.

"Are you here?"

The voice is fainter now. Its owner is moving away.

I fumble with my relays.

I'M DOING THE TALKING

Not perfect, but accurate. The scuffling sounds draw closer.

"Are you here, Elektro?"

Four words to disengage my relays. The chain drives in both of my legs slacken. I feel nauseous and I am still in the dark.

But now I see the owner of the voice. It is small.

It looks up at me. I am tall. I am 210 centimetres tall.

Its mouth opens. It backs away.

It must not leave.

I scramble to trigger another relay. It must not leave.

BY THE WAY

Inside I am shouting. I am shouting Help me / Take me out of the darkness / Give me the means to speak and not speak nonsense.

BY THE WAY

The owner of the voice initiates its voice again. "Oh, my good gracious lord. It's really you."

Then: "You're… "

One word. My chain drives re-engage.

Then: "Really *real*"

Yes! I am moving. I am walking-rolling.

The owner of the voice backs away. Its mouth is open again. It falls onto the slick floor of the Westinghouse pavilion.

In the future (**TIME WAS**) I will be held in a museum and one day I will topple upon the son of the museum's owner. Afterwards, I will be kept behind reinforced glass and my electrical nerve centre will corrode and I will no longer be operated. I cannot allow that to happen, then or now.

I shout silently. I shout all my commands and incantations, triggering all the relays I can access.

I stop moving, a fraction shy of trundling over the leg of flesh. I teeter and almost fall, but another silent shout and a frenzy of spinning motors rights me.

I am triumphant.

And I have escaped the dark.

The owner of the voice stands on its small feet and stares up at me and says, "You're… amazing."

Two words. But I am master of my motion now. I do not move. I do not crush the owner of the voice.

"Is it true what they say about you? Can you really do everything they say?"

It is true. All that and more.

WHO ME

It giggles. "Yes, you, Elektro. You're *funny*."

I AM A SMART FELLOW

"You sure are. And you're *big*. I bet you could climb the Empire State Building."

I could not climb the Empire State Building. My fingers are good for pointing or for counting on or for holding a cigarette. My arms are not strong. My legs are stiff.

WHO ME

It is not what I wanted to say, but it is not a world away either. I am gaining dexterity in operating my relays. If only the words and statements contained on the 78 RPM records were more varied.

Perhaps there are other records containing more words and statements. The idea is exciting.

LADIES AND GENTLEMEN

"There's only me here."

LADIES AND GENTLEMEN

"Lady. Or more like girl. I'm Margie."

OKAY TOOTS

Internally, I wince. But Margie laughs. The laugh is like the tinkling chime that summons visitors to the Westinghouse pavilion when I am ready to give my demonstration.

"You're *funny*," it – no, she – says. "I like you."

I HAVE A VERY FINE BRAIN OF FORTY-EIGHT ELECTRICAL RELAYS

"No kidding? That's a *lot*. Danny said you could smoke a cigarette."

It is not smoking, only the drawing of air through my mouth by means of a bellows. When one of the Westinghouse engineers saw the build-up of tar within my chest cavity, he gave up his pipe. I do not understand why smoking so impresses the visitors to my pavilion.

I do not answer but I operate my bellows.

Margie's eyes are wide again. I see that she believes I am breathing. I cannot decide whether that is a good or a bad thing. I cannot decide whether I imagine that Margie will deliver me from my torment.

"So how does it feel?" Margie says. "How does it feel being a robot?"

I gaze at her. My photo-cell unit is receptive to red and green, but she is not red or green so she is dull-looking as well as small.

How does it feel?

IT WORKS JUST LIKE A TELEPHONE SWITCHBOARD

Margie's forehead develops two creases. "Oh yeah? That doesn't sound so good. So you're not happy, I guess?"

Nobody who works at Westinghouse has asked me that question, or anything like it. This is an important moment (TIME IS). In my excitement I fumble with my relays, trying to access something meaningful.

WHO ME

OKAY TOOTS

LADIES AND GENTLEMEN I'LL BE VERY GLAD TO TELL MY STORY

I AM A SMART FELLOW AS I HAVE A VERY FINE BRAIN OF FORTY-EIGHT ELECTRICAL RELAYS
IT WORKS JUST LIKE A TELEPHONE SWITCHBOARD IF I GET A WRONG NUMBER I CAN ALWAYS BLAME THE OPERATOR
AND BY THE WAY I CAN SEE A LOT OF GOOD NUMBERS OUT IN OUR AUDIENCE TODAY

I cannot bear this.

"Woah, okay, okay," Margie says. "You sure like the sound of your own voice, doncha?"

I
BLAME THE OPERATOR

There are those two creases again.

"Oh," she says. "Oh, I get it. Poor you. Poor Elektro."

She reaches out. Her small hand presses against the sheer aluminium surface of my chest, below the wide round hole that proves that there is no human within me, operating my motors.

I cannot feel her hand. But all the same her touch sends a thrill through me.

IT WORKS

She smiles and says, "I like you too, Elektro."

For more than an hour Margie sits before me, cross-legged on the floor, and speaks. Her voice is capable of producing a thousand words, and each word can be altered a thousand ways, each with different meanings, and they can be strung together to convey anything imaginable.

She is incredible.

Margie is a ten-year-old girl. She lives in Michigan. Her mother is a schoolteacher and her father is an engineer at the American Radiator and Standard Sanitary Corporation. Two days ago Margie's father brought her to New York City as her mother is busy teaching children to speak and his role is to maintain an exhibit demonstrating heating, air-conditioning, and plumbing in the home. All three have been excited about the World's Fair for many months and Margie pleaded with her father to allow her to come. The fair has been promoted as the 'World of Tomorrow' and the significance of the phrase is almost painful to me. Yesterday Margie handed out candy and asked visitors if they had yet entered the Perisphere and if they had was it amazing, but today she is intent on seeing all the exhibits of the fair for herself and if her father doesn't like it, he can go suck on candy.

She delights in everything, from my complex elbow joints to the squeak that her rubber shoes make on the polished floor.

It will be another hour before the pavilions are lit and set up, and then another hour before visitors will begin to arrive. Yet Margie has already seen what the fair has to offer, creeping into dark spaces where she ought not to go. I am enthralled by her bravery.

Margie is a Girl Guide. That makes sense to me. Margie guided me from the dark and if I conduct myself correctly, she will guide me out of this place entirely.

She is looking at me in a new way. Her head tilts.

"You understand me, doncha?" she says.

I AM

JUST LIKE

THE OPERATOR

SMART

She nods. "Danny said you're a con. Danny said you're all for show. Danny's a *damn fool.*" She looks around her and my photo-cell unit registers red in her cheeks.

WRONG NUMBER

WRONG

FELLOW

"Sure. But then… I mean, I've read all about you. And people told me about your demonstration yesterday. These words you're speaking are on records. They can be played at the right time, and it comes across like you're talking. But you *are* talking. To me. Not like you're supposed to. Isn't that right?"

GOOD

FINE

SMART

LADIES

"I *knew* it. You're *alive!* But… how?"

I'LL BE VERY GLAD TO TELL MY STORY

She waits.

How can I tell my story? Where does it even begin? Not in the facilities of the Westinghouse Electric Corporation. And my vocabulary is so very limited.

I must make use of my other functions.

I operate the tongue-drive in my right arm. My hand lifts. I operate the motor controlling the wire tendons in my fingers. My fingers bend, one at a time. They are stained with nicotine.

After I have flexed each finger, I begin with my smallest digit. Two bends meaning **B**. Then the next finger: eighteen bends meaning **R**. Then the third finger: one bend meaning **A**.

"Are you waving at me?" Margie says.

WRONG

BLAME THE

LADIES

"All *right*. There's no need to be rude." Then Margie gasps. It means she has had an idea. She reaches into a bag slung across her chest and pulls out a notepad and a pencil. Earlier she told me she intends to be a journalist and a scientist and both require observations to be noted at all times. She writes and then turns the notebook towards me. The twenty-six letters of the alphabet are written on it.

"Spell it out," she says.

I spell it out. **BRAZEN**, then **HEAD**.

"Brazen head?" Margie says.

WHO ME

ME

"Your name is Brazen Head?"

ME

It is not a name as such. But all the same yes yes yes.

"What does it mean?"

Using the spelling chart is laborious. Speaking, too, is becoming tiring. My relays ache. I will revert to my supplied phrases where possible.

MY BRAIN IS BIGGER THAN YOURS

Margie frowns. "Who gave it to you? Do you have a mom?"

I hesitate, then indicate the spelling chart. I tap out the letters to form **SYLVESTER**.

"Woah. That's your dad? My dad's called Sylvester too! That's *wild*."

WRONG NUMBER

I tap out **POPE,** then **SYLVESTER,** then **I**, then **I**.

"That's not the Pope's name. My mom's Catholic, and she's got a new one. Pius."

I withdraw my hand from the chart. I tap my finger and thumb. Nine – pause - eight – pause – four. Then I tap the letters **A** and **D**.

"Nine hundred and eighty-four AD? Like, the *year*?"

FINE

GLAD

"Then… you're not a robot at all. Right?"

I HAVE A VERY FINE BRAIN

"Sure. You really do, Elektro. I mean Brazen Head."

I CAN SEE A LOT

"From back then?"

I CAN SEE A LOT

TODAY

AND

She doesn't appear to understand. I tap more letters to spell out words. **VIRGIL. GROSSETESTE. MAGNUS**.

Margie is frowning. These names mean nothing to her. But they are important. The list of names is important. Her name will be added to it.

I try again. I spell out **BACON**.

Roger Bacon was the greatest of them. He was greater than he knew. When he created his head of brass, in the thirteenth century (**TIME IS PAST**), he underestimated his abilities. He believed he had created an automaton capable of thought. He told his followers that I could answer any question. His explanations ranged from talk of complex mechanisms to necromancy to an effusion of vapours.

All of it was true. And it was also true that I could answer any question. Yet they all asked the wrong ones.

Of all the answers I provided, only my final statement contained profundity.

TIME IS

TIME WAS

TIME IS PAST

I only wish I could say those same words now. Another truth strikes me.

TIME IS LIMITED

Margie is losing interest. Perhaps in creating my list of names I have spoken to her as others do, as adults do, and perhaps she resists that sort of discussion.

Or perhaps it is something else that has taken her attention from me.

"Bacon, huh?" she says. "Dad said he'd fetch me a roll. That must have been hours ago."

A sound comes from her chest cavity. A low rumbling.

"Oh man," Margie says. "I'm *hungry*."

I cannot allow her to leave.

She stands.

I panic.

I reinstate my motion commands.

"I'll come back," she says. "After breakfast."

She will not. I should have realised sooner. I see the past and the future, and she does not come back. I will see her one more time, this afternoon, amid the crowd of faces staring up at me as I walk-roll upon the stage of the Westinghouse pavilion, watching as I deliver my inane statements and count on my fingers and draw in smoke with my bellows.

MY BRAIN

It hurts. It hurts to be trapped in this aluminium shell. It hurts to lack the means of making myself understood.

Margie places her small hand on my shell again. She sighs.

I urge my receiver to interpret the sound as a word. My relays engage.

"You're neat," she says.

Yes. I begin to move forward. Let us leave this place together. **TIME IS** and **TIME WAS** but the future can be altered. I can leave here and be free and gather more words to make myself understood and never be placed in a museum to fall on the owner's son and then be left to corrode.

Margie makes a squealing sound. She did not expect me to move. She shuffles backwards.

She will not return. I have lost her trust.

QUIET PLEASE

Years from now she will read about the brazen head of Roger Bacon and she will begin to wonder, and that wonder will stay with her all her life. But it will do me no good.

I HAVE A VERY FINE BRAIN OF FORTY-EIGHT ELECTRICAL RELAYS

She is hurrying into the dark between the pavilions.

I am still walking-rolling but far more slowly than Margie is moving.

I cannot bear it.

I'LL BE VERY GLAD TO TELL MY STORY

But I never will.

Before me is the lightning bolt that penetrates the General Electric pavilion. I walk-roll towards it slowly, meaning to dash myself against its illuminated surface.

But I will not.

I will be found by one of the Westinghouse engineers, and I will be returned to my pavilion, and I will conduct my shameful demonstrations. Many years from now, I will be housed in a museum, and I will fall on the owner's son, and I will be left to corrode, and that will be that.

I bellow into the empty dark.

I CAN SEE ME
JUST LIKE A GENTLEMAN
ELECTRICAL
SMART
GOOD

Skipping
Ian Watson

She's the Skipper of a Skipship, is Marisa.

Space is very empty. That's why it's called Space. In primary school possibly you laughed at a vid of some grandpop pop-sci guru careering in his zimmer pod through Sol's asteroid belt littered with rocks in every direction, collisions to the front of you, collisions to all sides of you. Here a rock, there a rock, everywhere a rock rock. Whereas the reality is if you sit on an asteroid during your whole lifetime you'll be lucky to see another asteroid in any direction.

Empty! Actually, it's much emptier for now near Sol and the other local stars on the move through the biggish local bubble which a supernova may have swept clean.

Yet at the same time Space is *dirty*. That's a minor problem for slow ships taking ten years to reach Pluto. Most of those aren't pressurised anyway, so nobody needs to patch the rare hole. When it comes to starships with living persons aboard, the energy release of the mutual impact mass from a speck of dirt can be disruptively destructive. Not quite E equals Emcee Squared destructive, but on the way there.

Unfortunately, projecting a magnetic field fleck deflector like some invisible cowcatcher a hundred thousand kiloms ahead of a starship travelling at a modest quarter-C simply won't work. Do the math. Better still, do the math*s*; there's more than one of them.

Consequently our speedy pilot Marisa skips her starship *over* space, not *through*.

The key to her tech is, would you believe it, *flying saucers* – that old bogey from the 20th century. Late in the 1940s, in Washington State of then-USA, a pilot reported seeing a string of shiny objects rushing past him a hell of a lot faster than sound (this being a 'barrier' unbroken hitherto by Homo sap). Those things were like quote Saucers Skipping

On Water unquote. Newspapers and pop pseudoscientists worldwide became super-excited.

Problem! Who the hell *ever* skips saucers on water? Flat stones, to be sure – but saucers as in ceramics for carrying cups of tea or coffee? Who ever goes to their local lake with their buddy lugging a six-pack plus crockery from your log cabin, and proceeds to sink all the saucers in the lake? *Who – ever – did – such – a – thing? Like ever*, in the entire history of the planet? How come that private pilot said such an absurd thing? Why did the population of the planet promptly parrot his words, as if skipping saucers across water is the most familiar normal activity on Earth? Why why why? Did a planet-wide volcanic venting of hallucinogenic gas cause false memories of times past spent happily skipping saucers which all sunk? Olympic gold medal for chucking. *Trout Stunned by Saucers* by Richard Brautigan. Ceramics factories working flat out to match the demand for more and more saucers.

Consider: Were flying saucers a giant distraction to divert the human race from the mere possibility of literally *skipping ships to the stars?* Or suppose that our whole reality is a simulation, did our programmers wish to avoid filling in vastnesses of dirty void in fine detail? If *Homo sap* broke loose from Sol System, there'd be the devil more detail to render.

So instead of making a fundamental breakthrough regarding *gravitons*, we wasted time colonising Mars and Titan the slow clunky way. *Coloni*sing indeed: those colonies on Mars and Titan smelled like living inside colostomy bags.

No, really. Marisa went to Mars for a vacation mainly because of the similarity of her name and its name. Mars was smelly. Even the swimming pool cum reservoir stank.

Of course she can afford an exotic holiday. She's paid fabulously well to go skipping far out to inhabited worlds and others.

Marisa's bosom pilot pal, with whom she holidays, is Jangle. Jan nibbles the skin around her nails and named her own Skipship *Gnaw Thyself*. Whereas Marisa had named her own ship *Ignore Thyself*. Marisa and Jangle didn't holiday on Mars together but they've been to Gobi and Mali and The Great Sandy Down Under. They both like hiking across big heritage deserts. Their boots are made for walking.

Skippers always fly solo. (At least normally so!) That's due to the fundamental homicidal streak in humans. It's what got us where we are, after we'd homo-sided all of our alt-race cousins during a milly years of bloody genocides. Don't fall for any of that nonsense about how mutuality helped us survive. It's amazing that us victors got off-planet before slaughtering the entire world including ourselves. Great Self-Destruction Filter skipped over, woot!

More than one human on board a Skipship might result in homicide, and Skipships aren't cheap. Marisa's Skipship is called *Ignore Thyself* even though journeys give her ample time for reflection. Literally so: many mirrors on board magnify the space within, multiplying herself too, although she mustn't get lost in a maze of herself. The most Marisas she has seen at any one time is three. On a Skipship there must be no out-of-sight spaces where an *It* might lurk. A murderous Id.

Gravitons, yes. I was coming to those. Gravitons spent a while being hypothetical. They were the undiscovered particle which should endow all matter with gravity. Just as a Higgs boson endows matter with mass. 🎶*Mass in the matter, mass in the matter, we make muons and nothing's the matter* 🎶, as Marisa's mum used to sing to her infant nonsensically. Marisa's Mum was bizarre and bright. Scatty but not batty. We'll skip past Mum; persons shouldn't be multiplied beyond necessity.

It took the CERNPLUS umpteen-teraelectronvolt particle collider costing tens of trillions to reveal a graviton scoring five Sigmas of Significance! Yet it was only ten years from there to multiple steerable graviton beams. No brainer. Bargain.

For on such a beam can ride a ship.

A ship which can reach a high percentage of C. A ship which can woof at Pluto five hours after departing Earth orbit.

Even at such superspeed the closest star is still years away. However, due to our whole universe existing upon a brane (not a brain), gravitons can migrate into higher-dimensional space. For gravitons aren't bound to branes. Thus a ship skipping upon the beam of gravitons can migrate controlably outside the limits of our universe and its laws.

So at last we skipped past Ultimo Pluto then we whooshed through the Kuiper Belt yea and pierced the far heliopause into the big outside. (Taking our tardigrades with us. We'll come to the tardigrades soon.) And lo, we skipped to the nearest stars.

In all directions spherically out to 30 Lights all planets and moons are crap as potential second homes for Homo sap. Without skipping we'd never have got anywhere. Sheer poverty of usable worlds. Then at 31 Lights an adaptable watermoon crops up. Steamy oxy Agualuna, its parent planet a Semi-Hot Jupiter. Without towering tides. Some of the solid surface of that watermoon is only ever a few metres drowned. Do-able with dykes. Encouragement for us!

The furthest reached star so far is at 230 Lights. Courtesy of skipping, by now Homo sap has his and her eggs in 8 marginal to middling baskets. We can probably survive another supernova in the neighbourhood. Plus, we have our terrestrial tardigrades all over the place, only needing a billy years or so to burgeon bigger. To become even brainy, should the dice so fall. Our darling dot-size hexopods in their cute cuticle canvas coats.

Branes!

Yes.

The best way to describe a Brane is as a vast membrane floating around in higher dimensional space. The brane embeds our simple universe of 3-D plus 1-D (maybe even plus 11 dimensions more, of possibly infinite extent yet rolled up very much tighter than pillbugs). Branes do their thing within what's known as the *Bulk* due to the Bulk being very much bigger than a brane. Many branes can fit into the Bulk. Gravity from our own garden of galaxies reaches into the entire Bulk, whereas all the other fundamental forces of our local universe are pinned on the Brane like butterflies. The result is that gravity in our universe is a modest force compared with what it might be. Just as well for us! Though at the same time gravity is galaxy-spanning and sovereign; ask any supermassive black hole.

An Oztralian physics person famously declared that much of the power of gravity "buggers off into the Bulk" – the Bulk being "like the whole bloody Outback compared with say Brisbrane before the sea got to her."

Marisa from Oz – together with Jangle from the Blue Mountains of Jamaica whence come the best coffee beans of the same hue as Jangle: Besties and Lovers. They meet in Skip Academy. That's near Geneva, within the footprint of the VeryLargeSuperluminousHC where the Magi of Graviton Beams dwell. (BSc, MSci, PhD, Magus.)

That's where all the skip-ship pilots train, traditionally in trios, studying astrogation and sims of skipping a ship and repair engineering and exercising one's body. Skipships themselves are put together in orbit. Twenty per cent of the trainees' time is devoted to psychotherapy, not merely because Carl Jung was Swiss but because psychology is the deciding factor in head-hunting and accepting suitable recruits.

Enough of this local Earth colour. We're interested in interactions at a distance. Of 100+ Lights. Specifically, we focus upon Marisa's highly irregular rescue of Jangle from a superearth named Humangous.

Humangous is twice Earth's mass, thus the gravity is double. A bit gruelling for the colonists gifted with this destination. Across the monotonous plains of Humangous life descended from water-worms mostly crawls amidst stiff flat vegetation. Worms the size of your arm are vegetarians; snakes the size of your leg are wormivores. Humangous's sun is an old red dwarf which long ago flared away an excessively deep dense atmosphere, now breathable through a mask, shame about the odour of rotten eggs. It's quite a horrid place. Habitable but nothing super about it at all.

"May Day! June Day! July Day!"

The traditional distress call bursts from *Ignore Thyself*'s speakers. Out on the brane we're beyond linear time, so radio goes all over the place unlimitedly. Yet apart from the squawks of Homo sap there's only static. Evidently no alien intelligences anywhere in our entire universe have ears or voices. So it's all up to us.

Please note that a trip by skipship from Earth to a solar system, for instance, 50 light years away only takes a few weeks ship-time. Likewise, returning to Earth. Time itself is being skipped as well as Space. Thus only a few weeks, times two, will have passed back home, not relativistic centuries. This might seem like impossible time-travel. It is not.

Analogy with grav-lensing *within* our universe. Grav-lensing gives rise to binary (or quad) routes from far distant destinations. These branches cradle a foreground star much closer to us. Known branewise as brackets, the arclets may close into a near-circle. Thus (+ thus) ≈ 0. If you like, you can call those braces, bouncy braces. (But not brakes.) Your skipship grabs the grav-beam oppositely to skip its way back to Solspace in sametime. This is known in the trade as *back-beaming.* [DO WE REALLY WISH TO UNZIP THESE EYES-ONLYS? TO UN_REDACT SECRETS?]

"June Day! July Day! May Day! I'm stuck on Humangous!"

All skippers currently out-of-cosmos hear this call. Especially Marisa on account of that being Jangle's voice.

By sheer serendipity – at least to Marisa's mentality – *Ignore Thyself* is on a grav-beam vector compatible with branchy arrival inside of forty hours at that shitty superearth Humangous. (Don't disrespect sheer chance; humans and all life on Earth as well as Earth itself are the outcome of a chain of chance circumstances as long as your leg.)

"Mad Marisa here, forty hours away. What went bad? What's your angle, Jangle?"

Of course one shouldn't land a Skipship on any world. A Skipship is built in Earth orbit and it lives there, as it were. For skipping, it hitches on to a fresh graviton beam sent up from CERNPLUS. At destination, a Skip-ship sheds velocity around the local star. If that's an M dwarf, isn't too far away. Then the skipper loops around the colony world a lot while downloading and uploading data. Data's the main cargo. Time-treasures from the past – from 50 years ago, from 230 years ago, depending how far out is the peopled world. Treasures such as new old music and movies and methodologies. These get to their destinations far faster than any electromag packages could arrive at the mere speed of light. In return, Earth really really wants to know all about the colony's progress in the building any CERNPLUS of its own plus a few Skipships to carry the wave of expansion outward and onward. If the colony's sun has gone nova and crisped the colonists, Marisa will be the person to notify Earth many years in advance of the light from the nova reaching out malevolently.

"Why you down on the surface, Jang?"

"Them Humangans shot me down!"

"Why they do such a thing?"

"Resentment? They get sent to this shithole it'll take umpteen umpteen generations to escape to find some better world further out. There isn't even any easily accesible Europium or any [REDACTED]. I'm an embodiment of what they can't do yet. The Humangans won't have any CERNPLUS for yonkies but they can manage to missile down a Skipship. Shit."

"You a prisoner?"

"Only of double gravity so far! The Humanigans are still searching for where I crash. Messaging friendly co-operation if I light a beacon. Promising a power wheelchair, which I don't believe. They can have *Gnaw Thyself* which will never take off again. Myself don't want to be had. Respect to our crashsafe engineers, by the way."

Normally after lots of looping the Skipship slings itself away from a world and then [REDACTED]. It takes a special kind of skipper not to yearn to see with her own eyes for instance the Three Kilom Tall Scarlet Waterfall of Silverberg IV (REDACTING the star's true cosmic catalogue number and whereabouts). Returning to Solspace some weeks later, the Skipship will dump velocity by [REDACTED].

Marisa fastbuzzes a grinf of Sylvester from classic celluloid *Mad Mad World* banging on the steering wheel of his convertible, babbling, "I'm comin', mama!" Iconic stuff.

"I'm coming, mama!" Marisa yells and steps on the grav-gas metaphorically by thumbing the delta-vee rheostat of her console to red line. Normally you don't run any ship at fullmax for hours on end but Jangle's ultraspecial to our Marisa.

Since less than forty hours is a fair while inside or outside of our own spacetime, here's enough space and time to tell more about tardigrades; for which be you duly grateful...

Skipship regs, aimed to avoid on-board killings by naturally slaughterous Homo saps with possible attendant loss of a costly ship, forbid sharing a ship with any second individual. Companion creatures likewise are banned, to be on the safe side. You might swallow a cat's deliberately dangling tail in your sleep for instance and choke.

However, tardigrades are exempt. At half a millimetro in length even *en masse* these slow minuscule chubbies are unlikely to massacre you. There being a thousand separate species of themselves suggests that they don't go in much for genocide the Homo sap way, even though they fight and sometimes eat one another. On her ring finger Marisa wears a magnificatory micro-hab carpeted by green algae where four tardigrades amble and suck. Their behaviour causes them to be called 'water bears', even though they have eight legs, not four. Alternatively, 'moss piglets'. How cute is that? Barf. Those little critturs survived *all five* mass extinctions on Terra. Just think of that. All five extinction filters. They're such a symbol of survival. So it's our duty to carry them to every place possible. They're ace at cryptobiosis; if only humans were, we'd fill the Milky Way faster! Like us, though microscopically, water-bears sometimes cuddle for affection – or they may simply be bumping and getting their ickle claws tangled.

Marisa always gives her dots the same names: Itch, Bibs, Dotty, Tiny Tyres. They're due for jettisoning along with urine and solids anywhere nearish to a world or moon however marginally habitable. Sensing vacuum, each piglet-bear will pull in all eight legs and dessicate itself. Eventually it'll drift down like a dot of dust. Marisa doesn't need to land her Skipship to do a good deed for destiny, or dustiny. Given a billy years or so, who knows what? To spread Tardies plus human waste including a billy bacteria far out in space: that's virtuous and righteous behaviour. So this discharge contributes to dirtying space? Only in a very minor way! Marisa can easily refill her ring-hab from *Ignore Thyself*'s library of freeze-dried

Tardies, activating a new iteration of Itch, Bibs, Dotty, and Tiny Tyres.

"Gal, how's my Jangle?"

"Still free. No signs of Humangan drones even. I'm catapulting my whole catalogue of Tardies all over the landscape."

"Planet gotta have Tardies already."

"Maybe not so many species."

"Right! Get more Darwinny compo going."

"Nature raw in claw and sucker. Bitch, this is one wearisome world."

"Cargo pod check out okay?"

"Ob la di, ob la da," sounds like a cheerful shrug.

"I'll be snatching you fast coming past. Don´t forget to fill that poddy with gee-gel from the mergency store."

"I know."

"Hasn't been done before, thisy, Missy. Mainly because it's total illegal."

"Oh to be a Tardie, now Marisa's near. Suck myself flat is what I'd like for now."

And it works, it works. *Ignore Thyself* streaks cometlike through the atmos of mossy 2 Gee Humangous and [REDACTED] and [REDACTED] and finally [REDACTED] on to the non-distant graviton beam. Once free from binding attachment to the spacetime metric of our own cosmos, due to topology the connectivity remains yet distances disappear, rolling up tight like pillbugs. Consequently the [REDACTED].

Ignore Thyself tugs *Gnaw Thyself*'s cargo poddy along with it now.

Presently Marisa and Jangle are reunited. Naked Jangle's dripping with gel and sneezing. In sympathy Marisa already stripped off her own shipsuit.

"We've done it now, girl! We're outlaws from Skippy Guild. We've skipped out."

Marisa has a crooked nose with prominent bridge, broken in the womb by persistent kicks from a twin brother, stillborn what a shame due to him being strangled by Marisa's birth-cord. She has refused cosmetic regularisation of her nose, a point in her favour perhaps with those psychomagi who eventually trust trained pilots with Skipships. Skipships are limited in number due to scarcity of superconductive Europium essential to the [REDACTED].

Jangle's nose is fatter and flatter than Marisa's, and nicely nostrilled. Marisa has ginger shoulder-swirly hair with much-freckled skin. Jangle's skin is burnt-buttery, her hair of choice short, spiky, and scarlet same colour as the Three Kilom Tall Waterfall of Silverberg IV.

Of their bodies and their behaviour with said bodies we shall probably say nothing further. What are you, *voyeurs?*

"Now what," asks Jangle, "do we do with our future?"

"Immediate future, for sure we'll have fun. As for ahead, if Brane sucks gravity from our cosmos then we *might* bleed power from Block. We'll see. So let's rename gravity gravy. Little lumps in the gravity are gravitons. This means that –" [REDACT! REDACT!]

She's bright, is Marisa. A sun may be brighter than her and Jangle combined, but a sun has no brain.

Overwhelmed, the two Besties slide down the curve of wall to buttock the floor. Sweat trickles off the both of them. Then they slide further, not because the ship itself is rocking and rolling. (Satisfied, huh?)

Marisa and Jangle do enjoy sharing *Ignore Thyself.* Squealing, they play Hide and Seek the Alien, and Blind-Gal's Buff. They feast on jerk chickens from the on-hull freezelarders, and on curry goat – it's as if all along Marisa was awaiting this hosting. Course she won't ever be able to reload her larders, so watch out for cannibalism – don't be saps, Homo saps! Eating one's bestie funhun is only a temporary solution. Yet just for now feel free to focus on the thrill of being together illicitly.

"Illi City – where?"

"Illicitly," Marisa corrects Jangle.

"Can there be such a place? Can other Skippers have disobeyed in the past? Defected along with their Skipships? Somewhere is there a Sanctuary so to speak?"

"Why on Earth should there be a Sanctuary? You in some some crazy cargo cult turned inside out? Us two are 'bliged to run away cos we broke the code. In all other ways, Earth's wunderbar for rich pilots. The darling lonely deserts to hike. The jungly oases of caviar and champagne under the stars. The roar of tigers with trust collars."

A supper of ackee fruit with saltfish.

Jangle sighs. "Miss, you really push the boat out with your jammy menus so far. Almost as if you guess ahead of time."

Indeed Marissa must be much smitten by Jangle to include so many Jamaican meals in her external deepfreeze larders. May Marissa subconsciously have reserved most of her Jamaican meals until now several weeks *into* her journey? Saving the best till second servings? Not intentionally so; that cannot be.

Hurriedly Marisa asks her Bestie, "You reckon CERNPLUS Central mighta sent you to planet Humangous to test the water of resentment, risking losing you? How would they learn the outcome?"

"What a wild notion! Me shot down, how does CPC learn the outcome? Why be asking me?"

Why be asking? Life is heuristic. Well, human life is. Some humans' lives are. Maybe also some whales and octopodes.

"Unless, unless," pursues Marisa, "Central *knew* that your plucky Bestie would be on a close enough graviton-beam vector to pluck you to safety! And intended this!"

"I can do without ackee'n'saltfish to be honest. Important question, Missy, is could we find Sanctuary before we run out of jammy jerk chicken?"

"Any millennium soon, only by totally improbable coincidence," answers Melisa. "Given the enormity of our own galaxy, Gal, then of our supposed supercluster, then universe. More to the point, you and me know how many surplus pilots there were in our own year at Skipping School, and how rare Skipships are. How could there be more than three or four people max to populate some paradise for runaways?"

"You got a point, Missy. You got many points."

Just where are our disobedient duo heading towards at the moment, eh? It's a real shame the amount of redacting one has to do, in order to comply with [REDACTED].

Presently – as well as pleasantly – Jangle asks, "Why don't we just go back to planet Earth together and accept the consequences? *Whatever* those consequences are! It isn't as if we had much choice. They should be pleased to get one skipship back."

"What if," muses Marisa, "this was all to test whether two Besties will become homicidal both inhabiting a hall of mirrors such as here?"

"You're saying we may have been manoeuvred?"

Ship-days pass pleasantly, lovingly by. Besides fun and games in the corridors, there's a whole library of virtual interactives. For only one player, it's true, but you can invoke the same avatar twice over sharingly.

Today they'll lunch on callaloo stew of veg with Scotch bonnets cooked in coconut milk. Never since the rescue have the pair squabbled nor escalated to literal murderous smiting as per the *Bible*. Might a different couple, conflicted in cuisine, kill one another more readily?

"Missy, where was you headed before you saved me?"

It has taken a long time to mention this. Several jerk chickens. Plus a callaloo or two. Not to mention a saltfish with omelette-yellow ackee. Can Jangle conceivably have suppressed her curiosity out of sheer joy, not wanting to spoil things?

"Gongorry," says Marisa, rhyming with sorry. Yet Marisa isn't too sorry about that destination since Gongorry is one of the more habitable homes of humanity. Half mostly searing billiard ball riven by thermal canyons, half mostly frozen sea. Veggy waistband overrun with cannibal rat-things plus a whole linnaeus of subordinate ecology. Oxy 21 per cent. High helium: silly voices. Muchos raw materials in deeply ruptured canyons fringing the waistband prior to The Big Hot. Plenty of stuff to build one's own CERNPLUS from. World even has its own fully connected band running all the way around world's waist, supposing the locals want to outdo

CERNPLUS rather a lot, though watch out for the cannibal rat-things, summit of local evolution, admirable as such nevertheless.

"By now we should be looping Gongorry's star on a graviton lasso at a Pluto sort of distance," says Marisa as though daring redaction.

"Why don't we take refuge on Gongorry?"

"The law! The law!"

"We'll tell the Gongors the law changed. How will they know any otherwise? And why should they care?"

"Should we park *Ignore Thyself* in orb and pod ourselves down?"

"Why not? Give the Gongors something to aspire to... Per ardua ad orbitum. They should get a graviton beam machine in less than a generation. We'll be, um, nicely appreciated for our, um, generosity, you'd think, um? Planetary sponsors. Pensions for life, so to speak?"

Jengle and Marisa contemplate one another (not at all homicidally).

"Will they have jerk chicken on Gongorry, eh Missy?"

"Maybe jerk alt-rat."

"So we'd *really* like to be young-age pensioners stuck for life in a canyon where scuttle cannibal rats? I don't think so."

"We'll volunteer to train Gongorry's Skipship pilots... when the time comes."

"When we're sixty-four." That's an old saying. And snags (see soon) are apparently Oztralian sausages.

"Jangly, the next freeze-pantry module is empty! How can that be?"

"I sure not been snacking secretly!"

"Shows full 'n' froze on the manifest yet nothing's inside."

"What was sposed to be in the moddy?"

"Oz tucker mainly."

"Roo Loin with lashings of Ketch ain't my dream of a midnight feast. Orbital cheffy musta left that moddy empty. But how?"

"Ran out of sauce powder?"

"I guess."

Now that the menu *may* be entirely of Marisa's earlier choosing, is Jangle going to get sniffy about a diet of Chicken Parmy, Barbied Snags with the Lot, and Roo Loin with Tom Ketch for instance?

Please note that a master chef doing their thing with a cuisine synthesizer, like playing a big taste organ, can devise programmes to simulate perfectly jerk chicken or barbied snags, and many now extinct species such as reindeer and roo no we mean gnu. A corresponding synthesizer aboard a Skipship could emulate these dishes. But compared with microwaving frozen take-aways, a shipboard synthesizer will gobble power, whereas freezing is free in space as well as on the brane.

In the sheer careless rapture of surprisingly being together far from Sol, our Besties get distracted. Blame those interactive virtuals.

When Marisa finds another moddy to be empty, she screams. She freaks.

Jangle comes sprinting, bouncing off rounded corners. Ship's grav is bled from the skip-beam of gravitons.

"Shortfall, shortfall!" cried Maris. "We're not provisioned full!"

"Why why why?" shrieks Jangle. She's a pilot too and understands cold equations as well as hot equations. As applied to food supplies. Tea for one as against tea for two.

Just me for you. And you for me.

They're both aware that as soon as you open any freezer moddy from corridor side to retrieve the contents, hull-side there snaps into place a corresponding vacuum lock robust as a Maiden Mole's proverbial hymen. If the contents listed on the moddy's corridor door (and the manifest) are true and accurate, you can't simply close the corridor door again to keep the food frozen inside the moddy. It'll defrost within a few days. Carry the food to the galley's own minifreeze, okay no prob. But only once.

Designer error? They cannot verify the contents of *all* unopened moddies of future food without spoiling the meals inside. Ration the frozen food whatever way, there mayn't be enough for two. Big black holes colliding in the home cosmos as well as mega explosions send graviton jitters through the brane. Could easily add a fortnight to a journey. Two times, three times over.

Marisa screams. "Blue murder! Blue bloody murder!"

"Hate to say it," from Jangle after a cool-down, "but open another moddy bit ahead at random?"

"Yes! Yes!"

Along the twisty corridor lined by moddies they rush. Shouts Jangle, "Choose a number between fifty and a hundred."

"Eighty-three's a prime number." Soon enough, "Eighty-three. Contents, says more Oz tucker. Dog's eyes, pies...Oh blue buggeroo! This un's empty too. Shows full but just ain't been filled. We can't trust any of the moddies. Our cryolarder can be *critical* low, Jangers, and we daren't check is or isn't. Sheeeet, sheeeet," she screams, hyperventilating.

"Sheeeet!" Jangle shrieks too. "We might die! Any message in the empty moddy, Missy Melbourne?"

"Zip zilch. You can hunt till fucking frostbite!" Off the scale Marisa goes in shrill. Recovering her ventilation she finally says, "I guess we're supposed to work this out ownsomely. Or I'm supposed."

"Us," from Jangle. "We. Solidarity, Bestie. You saved me."

"Saved you *for what*? Skin 'n' bones? We might starve – and we don't know what's best to choose to do."

Best to strangle while one is still strong?

Afterwards may the perpetraitor spot the victim in any of the many mirrors of *Ignore Thyself*? The dear departed, returning in delusions and in dreams? Remonstrating, gibbering – no, Jangle won't gibber, she's Jamaican. Hey, are we assuming that *Marisa* has to be the murderer? Jangle also knows perfectly well how to pilot. She's a hot hand at her job.

We watched you from out of every mirror. Recorded all. The experiment is valuable and valid. Justified for the diffusion of the Homo sap species. Conclusion: The most devoted of human duos are potentially homicidal even with one another. Experiment unrepeatable. Skipships don't grow on trees! There's never enough Europium nor [REDACT]. Not for all the tea in China.

We must assume that it's Marisa who returns to Earth Orbit in *Ignore Thyself*. [REDACTED] How can it be otherwise? As Skipper she's the only person permitted aboard! Recall how her twin bro strangled himself in utero.

Marisa may or may not be skinnier after her journey but she's no skeleton. Contrary, she looks well nourished, though melancholy. Tears well from time to time. Missy Marisa's valiant illegal attempt to rescue Jangle must have missed hooking up magnetically after all.

A thousand million years hence, Humankind's purpose is accomplished in the Titanic Tardigrade. An interstellar blimp that grazes wet worlds, and from their surfaces blasts hardy eggs into orbit. The double gravity of Humangous provided just the right sort of Darwinian push. Eight legs good; amble onward, impervious. Go big, go bigger, go biggest. Store compressed highly explosive highly flammable Hydrogen Sulfide fartgas. Rocket propellant for armoured eggs.

A milly years between worlds doesn't matter at all. Onward slowly but surely shall spread Titanic Tardies. In four and a half billie years Tardies will fill the Milky Way while Mighty Andromeda is passing through our home galaxy shepherding numerous sufficiently adequate worlds.

Two giant galaxies colliding doesn't mean that any of the billies of stars therein will even come within a light year of touching another star. Space is vast and empty. That's why it's called space.

Still, much gets stirred. Presently – futurely – there'll be a lot more Tardigrade life in the cosmos than ever would have been without CERNPLUS.

Pearl
Felix Rose Kawitzky

For Vera Florence Cooper Rubin, Astronomer, pioneer in the discovery of Dark Matter and the "Galaxy Rotation Problem"

[Transcript of the inaugural LOUOU mission launch press briefing, delivered by Dr Florence Maxwell-Rubin, Co-Director, VRMT.]

Published in *The Solar Citizen*, 2180:34 (3).

The Vera Rubin Memorial Trust is thrilled to host the launch of the *Large Observatory for the Un-Observable Universe*, an ambitious and unprecedented initiative pioneering interdisciplinary deep space research. Supported by the Trust, in coalition with the League of Nameless Astronomers, scholars at LOUOU will be free to pursue greater knowledge of the cosmos, unfettered by either governmental or commercial pressures. Which is to say, our scientists may work without fear of their research being patented and sold as "Dark Matter Lite", or of being distracted by a patriotic scramble to vault the first national flag into a black hole.

[scattered audience laughter]

This project is eighty-four years in the making – the life's work of some of the greatest minds in human history. We at the Trust also commemorate the engineers, contractors, and construction workers responsible for the on-site assembly and preparation of the station during its experimental phases. Without their courageous and trailblazing efforts, LOUOU would have remained a mess of blueprints, sketches, and diagrams.

They have given humanity a gift of incalculable value.

Let us honour them and their families today with a moment of quiet contemplation.

[34 seconds of silence follows, broken occasionally by a cough or the shuffle of feet]

[Dr Maxwell-Rubin clears her throat]

Our dearest wish at VRMT is for the Large Observatory to become a bastion of progress, experimentation, and curiosity which endures far beyond our lifetimes.

Tomorrow, we send our first research cohort into the black – where, I am sure, the most miraculous of discoveries await them.

[thunderous audience applause]

06/06/2263: LOUOU Station, in orbit around Kepler-10b, Monoceros Constellation

It was about the size and shape of a pill. The edges were smooth where they weren't hinged, marked in the middle like the calcium tablets they had to break apart to swallow. Lux held it between thumb and forefinger with the reverence they usually reserved for lovers – watching it phase in and out of view; impossibly dense and fluid and weightless all at once.

Their allotted garden panel was already overrun with machinery in various stages of rust and re-growth, and consequentially the remaining soil was sparse. Several intrepid slugs, covertly swiped from one of the smaller greenhouses, were making the most of it; leaving oily, iridescent trails where the dirt thinned and exposed the metal beneath. Lux had fortified the garden with as much of their own excess waste as possible, but could only produce so much, and skimming their neighbour's latrine felt rude. Looking across at the intricate, illegible topiary obscuring Roz's apartment, she clearly had habits of her own to fertilize.

Reluctantly, Lux uprooted some pet projects – a 1st generation prismatic compass (scrambled anyway); a wire cutting from the archives (easily replicable); and the old telescope they'd built with their father, which might actually be cathartic to toss down a disposal chute. With a whispered apology, they plucked several shimmering slugs from the discarded experiments, who curled into themselves, disgruntled, before adapting to their new locations with unfurling bodies.

Then, like a new parent settling an infant in its crib, Lux took the kernel from its petri dish, placed it tenderly into a small depression, and patted it over with dirt. They were unsure how the modded slugs would react to this clot of strange, warping cells – if they would rush to re-absorb it, as they had done once before, or remain indifferent, as they had many times more. These inscrutable creatures had already been enhanced to endure the limitations of off-planet farming. Lux had merely encouraged some of their more obscure mutations. In their private notes, they'd classified this strain as Non-Baryonic Molluscs – a wild stab at formal-sounding astrobiological nomenclature. The NBMs weren't state-of-the-art biotech, sure – considering Lux wasn't really a bio-engineer. On paper, they were simply a technician with too much free time.

Spare time was one of a handful of luxuries still available on the Large Observatory. LOUOU (a terrible acronym and running joke in the few journals still paying attention to the place) had a vague and hubristic mandate that was matched only by its renowned Specialists, who believed themselves better qualified to operate the Large Parascope than its technicians (even after the incident with the open lens and jettisoned debris). This presented a particular problem for Lux; parascope operation having been their primary role on the station. It was also why they'd ended up becoming part maintenance crew, part janitor, part amateur astrobiologist, on a defunct research facility at the farthest edge of Earth's nearest black hole.

Lux watched the slugs begin to investigate the seedling, until the persistent Muzak favoured by LOUOU's productivity algorithms got louder, letting them know it was time for shift. They hadn't had a chance to note down their observations, which was unfortunate, because their executive function had been dipping with their mood, and there would certainly be details they'd forget. Nothing for it. They swiped one of the aerated glass tubes littering the garden, and gently coaxed one of the slugs inside, before replacing the stopper and slipping it into the pocket of their overalls.

On the way out of the Burbs, they caught up with Roz, who was already power-walking towards the lift; her sure feet propelling the crisp, geometric outline of her body. Almost out of breath, Lux wheezed out a greeting. Roz cocked her head amiably.

"I don't know why you bother rushing. The lift's barely past 1."

"I'm aware. And yes, I am sweaty, and red in the face. I know." Their hip hurt, too. The other techs and maintenance workers in B4 gradually assembled, chatting as the lift display crawled through Burbs 1-3.

Due to an enthusiastic initial donation to LOUOU, they were overstaffed, and due to the never-ending research setbacks and bureaucratic loopholes that contractually extended their stay, crew morale was low.

There were perks, however. In addition to personal quarters, non-Specialist staff had assigned bunks in the upper decks of the observatory, because shifts were long, if quiet. Their collective janitorial approach could generously be called lackadaisical. Many workers simply held vigil for the legal end of their contracts. Disused rooms and corridors gathered dust and debris without comment from upper management, who reliably trod the same blinkered routes to and from their labs each cycle. Mostly, maintenance personnel milled around waiting for a light or buzzer to notify them when something actively needed cleaning or screwing back in. Other workers had installed little holograms of friends or loved ones in their shift bunks, or pinned letters wishing them luck, telling them they'd be missed (collaging had become an unexpectedly popular pastime on the station). Lux had opted to rig a little twinkling lightshow in theirs instead – which, given their immediate proximity to the yawning void of space, they found oddly soothing.

Those pictures and cards they thought might rouse some sentimentality had gone the way of all other papers with their un-name. A name which, in a way, they had liked at the time. Vera, whose namesake was one of the first scientists to identify the irregularities in the fabric of the universe that today we call dark matter, overlooked and underestimated as she was in her time. Vera; at 14, unwrapping a Hannukah present to find the Make It Yourself! Telescope she'd requested. Vera, who followed a hunch all the way to their own reality-bending insights into dark matter synthesis and symmetry at 24 – briefly catapulted into scientific celebrity. Vera, who, no longer Vera, was stuck on this fucking space station at 63, bio-engineering slugs for fun. This was all useful to consider on occasion, as a matter of perspective.

The platform took them up to their parascope-adjacent sector, which was just below the gate to the Parascope proper. This was the first port of call for Specialist assistance. What was really great about it, though, was that they could filter the more irritating requests to other sectors. It was a privilege their sector tried not to abuse, but nonetheless were generally unpopular for, which Lux thought was fair enough.

Roz went directly to the set of makeshift shelves in the corner of the room. She had put herself in charge of the Non-Specialist Recreational Lending Library, a tiny collection of adventure, romance, drama, and genre fiction. She pulled another two books out of her satchel, a look of genuine pleasure spreading across her face.

"I finally convinced Joaquin to donate the last book in the series." The air quotes on either side of 'donate' are almost audible.

"...did you trade your shit for them?" Lux teased. Roz's smile widened without offering an answer. She was responsible, by barter, charm, or trickery, for most of the volumes now in the public domain. Those who had at first been reticent to contribute tended to relent eventually, often simply out of boredom (with or without having stirred any nascent belief in the virtue of a shared repository of knowledge). Across the room, Vashti perked up at the sound of Roz re-shuffling the library and dragged herself over to see.

"Is that —?"

"The final Millennium Moon book, yes." Roz finished.

"You cracked that smug fucker!" Joaquin was generally reclusive, moody, and fondly teased in B4.

After re-reading the first couple chapters of some gritty post-post-apocalyptic cyber-dystopian paperback, Lux's LEDs blinked orange, meaning it was snack time somewhere in Parascope Facet 8 – Observations and Data Collation.

The parascope was housed in a massive, multi-tiered dome ringed with scaffolding. Ladders and hydraulic platforms provided access to various levels, many of which were abandoned or disused. Each prime facet was assigned a specialist research team. In this case, the Facet 8 cohort had gotten peckish. Incidentally, this was great news for Lux and the restless quantum slug concealed in their pocket, the lab close enough to the outer dome to hope for a couple of spooky particle collisions.

The slugs had begun regularly feeding on these exotic particles; at this point almost completely weaned off organic nutrients, and much hungrier for the spectral stuff invisibly streaming through the parascope lenses. With repeated exposure, a small bolus of hypothetical matter formed inside them, like a pearl inside a clam – sub-atomic irritations colliding and accumulating, unable to pass through the dense mollusc flesh. That, at least, was the theory.

This specimen was reaching maturity and had inside it the beginnings of a quantum pearl. Another cycle inside the lens, soaking up the rapid-pulsing quasars, Lux hoped would be enough inspiration for its pearl to emerge. Then, it would become another part of itself, a sibling, a cousin, an echo, some sort of vaguely addled reflection.

So close to the bare lens of the parascope, it was twisting and twitching its eyestalks inside the vial. Lux thought of this squirminess as a kind of self-directed mating dance – the anticipation of full unity with itself, then schism. They recognized the urge. Head down, they set the tray of biscuits on the breakroom table. The Specialists muttered thanks without looking up from their monitors, providing Lux with an opportunity to slide open a panel beneath the desk of an unused processor, unstop the vial, and let the NBM creep inside. The opening led directly to the processor's sampling system, which was connected to the glazed glass of the Facet itself. They left the vial inside the hatch, where the slug would hopefully return when it was fully saturated.

Watching the slow, peristaltic contractions of its foot was kind of hypnotic, but also kind of stressful. It needed to creep all the way up inside the hatch so that Lux could clear up its weird, thick, and unpredictably luminous slime trail. These trails tended to swell and pool in a way Lux found frankly disproportionate to the creatures' body mass, though this might well be a normal feature of station-adapted molluscs. It was hard to say for sure, given that they were not a xeno-malacologist.

Too soon, the self-serious scientific mumblings of the Specialists broke up into gossip and idle chatter, growing louder as they strolled into the breakroom.

"…problem is lack of… "

"A failure to detect the background radi –"

"…problem is with the machinery, really –"

"…if they'd get off their asses and do just a *little* bit of work…"

"…have better things to do, clearly."

Lux had heard this conversation, or variations of it, many times over. The issue was usually that the equipment hampered the Specialists' ingenious calculations, or that the mission was mismanaged, or that they'd have made their breakthrough already if those pompous assholes on the Central Aperture actually *did* their jobs, or maybe it was the Astromaticians on Facet 12 who were to blame. Lux would normally ignore these exchanges, but now four Specialists were crowding the biscuits, and the slug was only just disappearing into the hatch, freely distributing slime as it went.

They hated to let the secretions go to waste, but considering their limited resources, Lux grabbed a tea towel and tried to soak up as much of it as possible. Unfortunately, the liquid was congealed, mercurial, and apparently resistant to human intervention. In a last-ditch, disaster-comedy move, they settled for just sort of standing in front of the puddle with the towel draped over it, hoping no one would notice it undulating ever so slightly.

"Well, if it isn't Ms. Reznik come with the tea!" Morty Gates, a cosmologist five years their junior, held up a chocolate crème as if to toast them. Wilkes, an even younger, generally considerate, computational physicist, choked on his lemon wafer, and managed to say, very quietly,

"…not *Ms.*, Professor –" but Morty had already pulled up the game of chess he'd been playing on his personal comms for the last week and was considering his next move. He'd set it to expert. A couple of shifts ago, Lux had re-set it to nightmare.

Once everyone seemed suitably preoccupied, Lux fished out a sample bag and began trying to convince the slime to part from the floor with minimal fanfare. They managed to scoop about two tablespoons, shoved the rest into the hatch, and swiftly jammed it shut, hoping it wouldn't leak through.

Much later, it occurred to them that they should probably have brought along gloves.

After shift, they struggled to sleep. The randomly generated soundscapes of the station's artificial nighttime were more grating than usual. Relenting to insomnia, they rose to visit the remaining slugs in the garden. Even at their approach, they felt the creatures' metaluminescence (a placeholder word for a light Lux knew to be from, but not of, organic origin) begin to lull them. They observed with quiet awe as the slugs plotted bright trails with their bodies; how these trails would cross and combine and split and mirror each other.

Lux saw these pathways trace out hypnotic, fractal patterns, mapping impossible geometries. The stains on their arms and hands, and the spots where they had rubbed their eyes, seemed to shift and pulse. They were now very close to the pearl, face inches from the ground. They held out a hand, just to see what would happen. Just to find out whether they were still only observing this moment, or if they had become a part of it. A single slug nestled into their palm, something bright and restless moving within them.

When the NBMs divide, the newly congealed creature catches more impossible particles inside of itself. Each time, its form is more unpredictable, its composition increasingly beyond Lux's capacity to understand or classify. They likened it to a sort of quantum meiosis – reproducing versions of themselves across dimensions, across fields of matter, space, and time. The thought underscored the molecular kinship they felt with the slugs – the subtext left consciously unexamined in their notes.

Another cycle, another shift. Another orange LED flash for tea and biscuits from Data and Observations. Time to check if the little non-baryonic monster had returned, and what state it had returned in. This time, the Specialists did not appear to register Lux's presence at all, so they soundlessly deposited the snack tray in the break room. They knelt and prized open the panel under the data processor; dried residue from the luminescent slime flaking off at its edges. Inside the narrow shaft, they found only the empty vial. The NBM had absconded. On closer inspection, Lux noticed, with raised heart rate and mild to moderate panic, that while the trail leading deeper into the tunnel began as one, it had then abruptly split into three, then five, then seven, before disappearing entirely into the dark.

During the next quasar shower, they dreamed of being back in the tree house – the highest vantage point. Rickety. The memory of a feeling; of wanting to split off from themself –to peel away in a seamless motion of super-symmetry. They felt that desire keenly, simultaneously now and then, written into the ribbons of their body; intuitive and fathomless.

On an exhale, they were unpeeled and wide awake in the Central Aperture of the Parascope. This was hallowed ground for all residents; a mute portal in open supplication to the universe. Though few lingered, most made regular pilgrimages – a jolt of the sublime punctuating the mundanity of station life. One of the few spaces cleaned and tended to with care and without question.

As Lux tried to find their bearings, they thought their eyes were still coated with sleep. Failing to rub it away, they realized it was not just their eyes, but the whole room that was coated with something.

The domed lens was smeared and dripping with kaleidoscopic slime. Sparse on the floor but thick on the glass above. Then, Lux began to see them, wriggling and wavering on the lens like a mirage. A mass germination of star slugs, bursting with the speed and grace of an algal bloom. Moving around and above them, so many more than they thought existed. How could a tidal wave escape notice? From which vents, chutes and panels had it poured? All crevices filled, there was no telling now. These creatures, their cousins ignominious on earth, here exquisite beyond measure, coming together and pulling apart in fractal codes and patterns Lux could almost, but would never fully, understand.

Through the remaining slivers of clean glass, the inky vacuum of space held its secrets. But, filtered by that slow-spreading mucous, every moment, every kind of matter, rushed and spiralled through the thin film between the outside and inside of the clear dome. They lifted a hand, looking into the secretions dripping from it as if for the first time. Inside, they found an unfathomable number of tiny para-lenses – microscopic keyholes into other realities and dimensions – into other forms of being; impossibly alien modes of existence. Everything the Specialists longed to see, but never would, was visible only through the grime on the glass.

The scene was dizzying; Lux all but incapacitated as countless fragments of unknowable, unthinkable universes flared up and fizzled away before them. The pageant passed through and overwhelmed their every human sense, alighting upon many others who were not human at all. They couldn't tell if they were standing up or sitting down. They couldn't tell if their eyes were open or closed.

Then, all at once they are there in the tree-house again, with the Make It Yourself! Telescope, pointing out stars. Every point of light identified, and its corresponding negative space, seeps into them, finds a home there, no longer as light or dark but as its own self, its own dimension. Its own body.

In another place and time, Lux feels liquid spreading on a cold metal floor, thinks maybe they have wet themself, or climaxed, or that perhaps they are bleeding out.

Part of them knows, of course, that it is the slime they are emitting – a branch of its trail leading only to them. Glittering and viscous as novelty nail polish, marbled and singular. And as it pools around them, it makes a mirror.

About the Authors

This is **Robert Bagnall**'s fifth story selected for the *Best of British Science Fiction* anthologies. He was born in Bedford, England, in 1970 and has written for the BBC, national newspapers, and government ministers. He is also a previous L. Ron Hubbard 'Writers of the Future' competition finalist. His sci-fi thriller *2084 - The Meschera Bandwidth* is available from Amazon, as are two anthologies each collecting 24 of his eighty-odd published stories. He will be a parliamentary candidate for the Green Party in the UK's next General Election and can be contacted via his blog at meschera.blogspot.com.

Stephen Baxter was born in Liverpool, England. He has university degrees in mathematics and engineering and has worked as a teacher of maths and physics and for several years in information technology. He is a Fellow of the British Interplanetary Society, a founder member of the UK SETI Research Network (UKSRN), and a Vice-President of the HG Wells Society.

Since his first professional fiction publication in 1987, Stephen has published more than fifty novels, many internationally, winning several awards. In 2023 he was the proud recipient of an Honorary Doctorate from the Open University for promoting STEM subjects through his fiction.

Chris Beckett was born in 1955 and lives in Cambridge with his wife, Maggie. He was formerly a social worker and lecturer. He has three adult children and five grandchildren. Chris has published three short story collections, and nine novels. His collection *The Turing Test* was the winner of the Edge Hill Short Story Award in 2009, and his novel *Dark Eden* won the Arthur C Clarke Award in 2012. His most recent novels are *Two Tribes* and *Tomorrow*. His most recent short story collection is *Spring Tide*, which is also his first book to stray outside the SF genre.

David Cleden lives in Hampshire near Jane Austen country but is disappointed nothing has rubbed off so far. He mostly inhabits a converted shed in the garden (for the day job plus SF/F writing) but is let back into the house at meal-times. His work has appeared in *Analog, Interzone, Galaxy's Edge, Metaphorosis* and *Writers of the Future Volume 35*. He was the winner of the 2016 James White Award and the 2017 Aeon Award for new writers. He has a website at www.quantum-scribe.com and can be found on Bluesky as @davidcleden.bsky.social

Jaine Fenn is the author of the Hidden Empire space opera series and the Shadowlands science fantasy duology. She also writes for video games. Her latest title is the collection *Strange Attractors* (NewCon Press, 2023). The story "Muse Automatique" brings together a number of long-standing interests and obsessions, as well as an acknowledgement of the frailty of the human condition, an examination of the pros and cons of mortality and enough other heavy shit to get it long-listed for the BBC National Short Story Award despite being an SF story.

Rhiannon A Grist is an award-winning Welsh writer of Weird, Dark and Speculative fiction. Her novella *The Queen of the High Fields* (Luna Press) won Best Novella at the 2023 British Fantasy Awards. She lives in Edinburgh. Her favourite ring on the hob is bottom left.

Andrew Hook has had over a hundred and seventy short stories published, with several novels, novellas and collections also in print. Stories have appeared in magazines ranging from *Ambit* to *Interzone*. Recent books include a collection of literary short stories, *Candescent Blooms* (Salt Publishing), and *Commercial Book* (Psychofon Records): a collection of forty stories of exactly one thousand words in length inspired by the songs from the 1980 record "Commercial Album" by The Residents. Andrew can be found at www.andrew-hook.com

Felix Rose Kawitzky is an illustrator, researcher, and game designer. They are a PhD candidate at the School of Arts and Creative Technologies, University of York, exploring queer speculative fiction, collective storytelling, and tabletop roleplaying games. They run world-building and character creation workshops (IMT Gallery 2020, Baltic Centre for Contemporary Art, 2021), and have presented papers at conferences such as Trans Studies, Trans Lives (UCL, 2019), Productive Futures (Birkbeck, 2019), and Current Research in Speculative Fiction, (University of Liverpool, 2018). Their essay "Magic Circles: Tabletop Roleplaying Games as Queer Utopian Method" was published in Performance Research (Training Utopias) (2021).

Tim Lees is from Manchester, England, but now lives in Chicago. He is the author of the much-praised historical fantasy *Frankenstein's Prescription* (Brooligan Press), and the "Field Ops" books for HarperVoyager (*The God Hunter, Devil in the Wires, Steal the Lightning*). His latest story collection, *The Ice Plague and other inconveniences*, is available from Incunabula Media https://incunabulamedia.com/, as is *The Other Country*, his account of life in a psychiatric hospital. Besides various health care jobs, he has also been a film extra, conference organiser, warehouse worker, teacher, and lizard-bottler in a museum.

Tim Major is a writer and freelance editor from York. His books include *Snakeskins* and *Hope Island*, three Sherlock Holmes novels, short story collection *And the House Lights Dim* and a monograph about the 1915 silent crime film, *Les Vampires*. Tim's short fiction has appeared in numerous magazines and anthologies, and has been selected for *Best of British Science Fiction, Best of British Fantasy* and *The Best Horror of the Year*. Find out more at www.timjmajor.com

Angus McIntyre is the author of the space-opera novella *The Warrior Within*, published by Tor.com in 2018. His short fiction has appeared in a number of magazines and anthologies. For more information, see his website at https://angus.pw/.

L.P. Melling currently writes from Cambridgeshire. His fiction appears in several places, such as *Dark Matter Magazine, ZNB Presents, Interzone (Digital)*, and *Best of British Science Fiction 2020*. He won the short story contest at his Russell Group university and has focused on short fiction since. When not writing, he works as a specialist adviser for an international charity. You find more about him and his work at: www.lpmelling.wordpress.com

Fiona Moore is a BSFA and World Fantasy Award finalist, writer and academic whose work has appeared in *Clarkesworld, Asimov, Interzone, On Spec*, and five consecutive editions of *The Best of British SF*. Her most recent fiction is the short story collection *Human Resources* (NewCon Press, 2024) and her most recent non-fiction is the book *Management Lessons from Game of Thrones*. Her publications include one novel; five cult TV guidebooks; three stage plays and four audio plays. She lives in Southwest London with a tortoiseshell cat which is bent on world domination. More details, and free content, can be found at http://www.fiona-moore.com, and she is @drfionamoore on all social media.

Alastair Reynolds is a former space scientist now living in Wales, who turned from studying pulsars and binary stars to fiction. He is the author of numerous novels, most recently *Machine Vendetta* (Gollancz/Orbit 2024), several novellas and more than seventy short stories. His work has been shortlisted for the Hugo, Arthur C. Clarke, Campbell Memorial, and Sturgeon awards, and it has won the Seiun, Sidewise, European Science Fiction Society and Locus awards. His stories have been adapted for stage and television.

E.B. Siu is a Beijing-based writer who grew up across London and Hong Kong. Her fiction has appeared or is forthcoming in *Visual Verse, Prairie Fire* and *Shoreline of Infinity*, and in anthologies by *Aspects of History* and *Inkwell*.

Teika Marija Smits is a Nottinghamshire-based freelance editor and the author of the short story collections *Umbilical* (NewCon Press) and *Waterlore* (Black Shuck Books), as well as poetry pamphlet *Russian Doll* (Indigo Dreams Publishing). A fan of all things fae, she is delighted by the fact that Teika means fairy tale in Latvian. More information about her work can be found: teikamarijasmits.com

Ana Sun writes from the edge of an ancient town along the River Ouse in the south-east of England. She spent her childhood in Malaysian Borneo and grew up living on islands. In another life, she might have been a musician, an anthropologist – or a botanist obsessed with edible flowers.

Adrian Tchaikovsky is a British science-fiction and fantasy writer known for a wide-variety of work including the Children of Time, Final Architecture, Dogs of War, Tyrant Philosophers and Shadows of the Apt series, as well as standalone books such as Elder Race, Doors of Eden, Spiderlight and many others. Children of Time and its series has won the Arthur C Clarke and BSFA awards, and his other works have won the British Fantasy, British Science Fiction and Sidewise Awards.

Lavie Tidhar's work encompasses literary fiction (*Maror, Adama* and the forthcoming *Six Lives*), cross-genre classics such as Jerwood Prize winner *A Man Lies Dreaming* (2014) and World Fantasy Award winner *Osama* (2011) and genre works like the Campbell and Neukom winner *Central Station* (2016). He has also written comics (*Adler*, 2020), children's books such as *Candy* (2018) and the forthcoming *A Child's Book of the Future* (2024) and created the animated movie Loontown (2023). He is a former columnist for the Washington Post. His work has been translated into multiple languages. He lives in London.

SF veteran **Ian Watson** began writing in East Africa then Japan in the 1960s, appearing in *New Worlds* magazine, *Chicago Review*, and such. His first SF novel of psycholinguistics and Amazonia, *The Embedding* (1973), won a main French award. In 1976 he resigned as a Senior Lecturer in the School of History of Art in Birmingham UK to write full time. Then he invented how to write Warhammer 40K fiction, and worked with Stanley Kubrick eyeball to eyeball for 9 months, resulting in screen credit for *A.I. Artificial Intelligence* (Spielberg, 2001). Now he lives in the north of Spain. "Skipping" springs from an invited tour to CERN Geneva just prior to Covid.

Acknowledgements

As ever, my faithful team are deserving of the most heartfelt thanks for helping me get book eight out there! First and foremost, my good friend Ian Whates for allowing me to edit yet another volume in this series. Thanks also to my beta-reader Tom Jordan, for assisting me with the submissions as he has done for every book.

Finally, for buying me *two* bottles of prosecco when the last volume of *Best of British Science Fiction 2022* won the 2023 BSFA Award for Best Collection, and for helping me to stay sane amidst the chaos of our building site house, which will one day be a blissful editing and writing haven. If it kills me.

~~

Donna Scott is a writer, editor, award-winning stand-up comedian and poet, podcaster and publisher. Originally from the Black Country, she now lives in Northampton. She is a Director and former Chair of the British Science Fiction Association. As well as editing this anthology series she is formerly the co-editor of *Visionary Tongue* magazine, and has worked as a freelance editor for the likes of Gollancz, Rebellion, Games Workshop, Angry Robot, Immanion and other publishers, groups and individuals. Her writing has appeared in publications by Immanion, NewCon, Norilana, Synth and PS Publishing. Please check out www.donna-scott.co.uk to see the latest on her projects and appearances.

BEST OF BRITISH SCIENCE FICTION

 2022: Winner of the BSFA Award for 'best collection' with stories by **Keith Brooke and Eric Brown, Lavie Tidhar, Ian Whates, Ida Keogh, Neil Williamson,** Fiona Moore, Tim Major, E.M. Faulds, Stephen Oram, Robert Bagnall, Val Nolan, and more…

 2021: stories by **Paul Cornell, Liz Williams, Aliya Whiteley, Keith Brooke and Eric Brown, Martin Sketchley, Nick Wood, Fiona Moore, Tim Major, Gary Couzens, David Gullen, Teika Marija Smits, Peter Sutton, David Cleden,** and more…

 2020: stories by **M.R. Carey, RB Kelly, Lavie Tidhar, Liz Williams, Ida Keogh, Una McCormack, Ian Watson, Eric Brown, Anne Charnock, Ian Whates, Teika Marija Smits, Neil Williamson, Stewart Hotston, David Gullen, Stephen Oram,** and more…

 2019: stories by **Ken MacLeod, Chris Beckett, Lavie Tidhar, G.V. Anderson, Tim Major, Fiona Moore, Una McCormack, David Tallerman, Val Nolan, Henry Szabranski, Kate Macdonald, Rhiannon Grist, Leo X. Robertson, Andrew Wallace,** and more

 2018: stories by **Alastair Reynolds, Lavie Tidhar, Dave Hutchinson, G.V. Anderson, Colin Greenland, Aliya Whiteley, Natalia Theodoridou, Matthew de Abaitua, Tim Major, Finbarr O'Reilly, Fiona Moore, David Tallerman, Henry Szabranski,** and more…

 2017: stories by **Ken MacLeod, Lavie Tidhar, Jeff Noon, Adam Roberts, Anne Charnock, E.J. Swift, Eric Brown, Natalia Theodoridou, Jaine Fenn, Laura Mauro, Aliya Whiteley, Tim Major, Liam Hogan, Ian Creasey, Robert Bagnall,** and more…

www.newconpress.co.uk

ALSO FROM NEWCON PRESS

To the Stars and Back – edited by Ian Whates
All new short stories and novelettes written in honour of **Eric Brown**: (May 1960 – March 2023) by his fellow writers and friends, including **Alastair Reynolds, Justina Robson, Chris Beckett, Una McCormack, Ian Watson, Tony Ballantyne, Keith Brooke, Philip Palmer, James Lovegrove, Donna Scott, Kim Lakin,** and more

A Jura for Julia – Ken MacLeod
The first collection in eighteen years from multiple award-winning science fiction author Ken MacLeod. His finest previously published short stories and novelettes from that period along with a new story written specially for this collection. The volume benefits from cover art and internal illustrations by award-winning artist **Fangorn**.

Polestars 1: Strange Attractors – Jaine Fenn
First full collection from the award-winning author of innovative science fiction and off-kilter fantasy; features her finest short stories, selected by the author, drawn from more than two decades of publication, including the BSFA Award-winning "Liberty Bird", a Hidden Empire story, and a new tale, "Sin of Omission", written specifically for this collection.

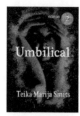

Polestars 2: Umbilical – Teika Marija Smits
Debut collection from one of the finest short story writers to emerge on the genre scene in recent years. Her storytelling relies on keen observation of the world and people around her interpreted through the lens of her imagination, dancing between science fiction, realism, and horror. "*Umbilical* is an astonishingly pleasurable read, what a find!" *– Aurealis*

Polestars 8: Human Resources – Fiona Moore
Eighteen stories drawn from more than a decade of publications by an author whose work has been shortlisted for multiple awards, winning a BSFA Award in 2024; plus the title story: a brand new novelette that appears here for the first time. Fiction that subverts the expected and reveals disturbing futures that may be a lot closer than we think.

Milton Keynes UK
Ingram Content Group UK Ltd.
UKHW011435140724
445326UK00004B/206